BIRTHRIGHT

A Novel

ANDREW COBURN

S I M O N   &   S C H U S T E R

Simon & Schuster
Rockefeller Center
1230 Avenue of the Americas
New York, NY 10020

Simon & Schuster and colophon
are registered trademarks of Simon & Schuster Inc.

Designed by Jeanette Olender
Manufactured in the United States of America

1   3   5   7   9   10   8   6   4   2

Library of Congress Cataloging-in-Publication Data
Coburn, Andrew.
Birthright: a novel / Andrew Coburn.
p. cm.
1. Lindbergh, Charles A. (Charles Augustus), 1902–1974—Fiction.
2. Lindbergh, Anne Morrow, 1906–   —Fiction. I. Title.
PS3553.023B57   1997
813'.54—dc21   97-11723   CIP
ISBN 0-684-81529-X

ACKNOWLEDGMENTS

Michael Korda and Chuck Adams for seeing

this story through its fragile time.

For my wife Bernadine and our four daughters;

my sister, Julie; my old friend and mentor,

Ignatius Piscitello; my first line of defense,

Cathy Timmons; my agent, Nikki Smith . . . and

in memory of my mother.

AUTHOR'S NOTE

Charles and Anne Lindbergh remain larger than

life. When Charles took wing across the Atlantic he

became mythic. When he married Anne Morrow,

they became figures in an American dream. When

their firstborn was stolen, the tragedy was classical

Greek. Fate put them at risk, and the gods did

them in for no obvious rhyme or reason.

Birthright is an attempt at rhyme, not reason.

BIRTHRIGHT

PART I

Another Life

"GOD INVENTED DUST TO PROVE THE PAST."

— ROBERT SOUTHWARK

CHAPTER ONE

IN THE HEAT OF THE IDLING AUTOMOBILE, A MINIATURE rubber fan whirring to keep the windshield from fogging, Shell transferred flannel and wool from warm flesh to cold. Two babies, nearly identical in age, were in his care. Both were blond. Both were boys. Quickly he wrapped the live one in a soft blanket and gave each a loving look, as if the dead child were the chrysalis from which the other had emerged.

He left one warm and snug on the seat and carried the other half under his jacket into the dank drizzle of the night. Entering the roadside woods with a shovel in his other hand, he stumbled through bramble and blindly chose a site. After kissing his child good-bye, he told himself he was not Joseph Shellenbach but a pirate burying treasure. The grave, rudimentary, resembled a meager compost heap. Standing over it, he murmured a prayer that came from his depths. He had seen Catholics make the sign of the cross and, standing tall, did likewise.

He slid the shovel into the back of the car. The car was a Chevrolet sedan, a box on wheels, the engine tuned for high performance. The headlamps heaved gleams of light through the refracting drizzle. Listening to the swish and thump of the wipers, he drove at cautious speeds, for the road was narrow and at times curved eccentrically. Tension lessened when he reached the highway, the power of the automobile gearing for speed. He glanced down at the bundle beside him.

"David," he whispered. "You're David."

David slept, woke, fussed, and slept again. The drizzle was constant all the way to Newark.

||| ≡ |||

They killed time in the booth of a diner, where hot meals were slop-served by a big-armed waitress who smelled of her work and had a good word for everyone. For Helen, she showed concern. "Don't you like it, dear?"

Helen had ordered a slice of apple pie and taken only a bite. Her hands encircled a chipped mug of coffee. "It's fine," she said. "Thank you."

"More coffee?"

"No, thanks."

The man sitting across from her stifled a cough. After a few moments he said, with a slight accent, "Don't draw attention to yourself."

She seemed surprised. "Is that what I'm doing?"

"Maybe you can't help it."

She had a pale oval face that bespoke loneliness and melancholy eyes the green of seawater. Her bobbed hair was a natural sunny blond. "Maybe we shouldn't have come here."

"Give me the pie," he said. "I'll eat it."

When she made no movement, he edged the plate toward him, furtively. He never seemed to do things cleanly but at an angle, as if wile were always necessary. His hair was carefully combed to conceal thinning, and his face was drawn tight, as if his mind were always made up. His name was Rudy Farber.

"You should've gone with him," Helen said suddenly.

"We did it his way, not mine." Farber started to cough and broke it off. "What's your complaint?"

Looking over his shoulder, she could see into the next booth, where an elderly man was slurping soup as if recuperating from something dreadful, the soup vital to recovery. Turning her head, she stared at the hunched shoulders of men sitting at the counter, men who got their haircuts at home. "I wish I were as cold-blooded as you."

He finished the pie and maneuvered the plate back in her direction. His squint lines ran deep. "You are. You just don't know it."

For a moment her face burned. No one knew her, least of all him, though Shell came the closest. Shell kept her on course, helped her up hills, and loved her without judgments or jealousies. Her deepest wish was that they would grow old together, wear each other's looks, and speak each other's thoughts. Farber lit a cigarette, a Camel.

"You shouldn't smoke," she said.

"*Es freut mich.*"

"What?"

"It pleases me."

The waitress gusted by, then breezed back. "You ate it after all. Good for you, dear." She spoke as if Helen were a girl of ten instead of a woman of twenty-six. She left a check and whisked away plates. They kept their coffee. Helen looked at her watch.

"Plenty of time," Farber said.

She trusted neither her watch nor his words and at times was unsure of her own name. Only with the breath of Shell's love in her ear did she feel wholly herself. She felt they shared a darkness in which they were the only light.

"You're a lucky woman," Farber said in a neutral tone, and drew a slow look. "He'd do anything for you."

She was growing impatient. "I'd rather wait there than here."

Farber sighed. "Suit yourself."

She opened her handbag, which held too much. It tilted to one side. He glimpsed an object in it that surprised him.

"Who you gonna stab?"

The knife was from a rack in her kitchen. She rummaged past it for money. "You pay the check," she said, "I'll leave the tip."

"Let's make it the other way around."

Stepping out of the diner, she relished the assault of cold wet air on her face. Farber fought it and, shivering, hurried her to his car, a well-kept Franklin he polished on weekends. He knew exactly where they were going, she didn't. He drove along ill-lit streets to the ragged edge of the city and turned left into the shadows of a dead-end street. The street folded up fast against an abandoned industrial building, a casualty of the times. Wrenching the wheel, he turned the car around and parked it facing out.

"Your idea," he said. "Now we have to wait."

"What if a policeman comes?"

"Then we hug and kiss."

The thought repelled her, physically. She lowered her window for air, which was too much for him.

"Close it," he said. The sound of his cough was like the bark of a fox.

"How sick are you?"

"Who says I am?"

She didn't like breathing his air. Quiet for a long while, she finally said, "Why are you doing this, Rudy?"

"Not hard to figure out," he said. "I'm doing it for the money. Shell's doing it for you."

||| ≡ |||

Shell turned on the little overhead light so that Helen could see the child. She stared at the sleeping face, and Shell stared at her, her reaction vital to him. "I won't wake him," she whispered, and lightly rearranged the blanket. "Is it David? Really David?"

"You tell me," he murmured, touching her arm. He felt her stiffen.

"No, I want to hear it from you."

"Yes, our son."

Her face was larger than it was a moment ago. "I love him."

"I can see that," Shell said softly, and reached for something beneath the seat. "I'll be right back."

A fine rain nicked his face as he hurried from his car to Farber's. He rapped hard on the glass, and Farber lowered the window enough for Shell to stuff a small baggy garment through the opening. All he could see of Farber's face were his teeth when he spoke.

"No hitches?"

"The ladder broke on my way down. I almost fell."

18

"But you didn't," Farber said. "The kid OK?"

"He slept most of the way."

"Did you leave the note?"

Shell nodded. Events replayed at high speed in his head. The scariest wasn't the cracking of the ladder but the struggle to disengage the child from the crib blanket pinned to the mattress, the child all the while staring at him with docile curiosity.

"It's your ballgame now, Rudy. I'm out of it."

Farber smiled. "Why ain't I surprised?"

"I don't want anything from this except the kid."

"I'm not arguing. It'll mean more money for me." Farber cranked the window down a little lower. "Mind telling me something? What's Helen doing with a butcher knife?"

"She's afraid of the dark."

"For a while there I thought she was planning to do me in. Thought I saw it in her eyes."

"You saw wrong."

"Wouldn't have made a damn bit of difference to me, you know that."

Shell stepped back when Farber started up the Franklin, the sound a drumroll. The sudden glare of headlamps gave the thin rain substance and the night another dimension. Moments later Farber was gone. Shell returned to the warmth of his car, to Helen.

"Look, he's awake," she said. She was holding the child in her lap and smiling broadly. "He needs a change."

||| ≡ |||

At the Lindberghs' manorial home near the remote village of Hopewell, a mountain to the north and wasteland to the south, a dark wet wind rattled shutters and hacked at windows. It was ten o'clock. Charles Lindbergh, ensconced in a leather chair in the library, scanned a magazine article about himself and was not pleased. Private and aloof, an authentic hero since his solo flight across the Atlantic, he resented obtrusions into his personal life and despised journalists for transforming him into a curiosity.

In the kitchen the housekeeper prepared a mug of hot lemonade for her mistress. Anne Lindbergh, pregnant with her second child, was upstairs readying herself for bath and bed. A mirror reflected dark sensitive eyes in an asymmetrical face pixie from one angle and vulnerable from another. The large bathroom connected the master bedroom to the nursery.

A few minutes after ten the young nursemaid, proud of her position with the family, entered the nursery for a final check on Charles Lindbergh Jr. Light from the corridor guided her into the dark. A window was open, and she quietly closed it. Bending over, she plugged in the electric heater to take away the chill in the room. Then she looked into the crib.

Seconds later she rapped on the door of the master bedroom and opened it. "Do you have the baby, Mrs. Lindbergh?"

Anne Lindbergh, holding her robe together, emerged from the bathroom. "No," she said, surprise turning rapidly into confusion.

"Then the colonel must have him."

Anne Lindbergh did not speak for a moment. Then she said, "Of course, who else?"

CHAPTER TWO

SHELL WAS BORN IN A BRONX NEIGHBORHOOD ISLANDED
in a sea of Italians, Poles, Jews, and the ubiquitous Irish. He was the
sole child of German immigrants who struggled to put bread on the
table in their third-floor flat. His father brought home money until he
lost half his hand at the paper factory and started drinking. His mother
worked at the button factory and on weekends plucked chickens and
skinned hares for Mulheim the butcher.

Rudy Farber was nearly seven when the family arrived at Ellis Island
and settled in the same dense neighborhood where Shell lived. Rudy
had an elder sister and two younger ones. Before he was eight, his father died of double pneumonia. His mother, who had hidden strength,
was a plain little thing who proved herself pertinent with her clothes
off. The money she made with men supported the family. Mulheim,
her most frequent visitor, in time made himself her only one. He was
said to be in love with her.

Shell and Rudy became unlikely friends at school, where the visiting
nurse suggested that nits found in Shell's hair came from Rudy's. The
teacher, pieties engrained in her manner, liked Shell, who was quiet
and introspective, and disliked Rudy, who was too thin-skinned to

hold his temper and too refractory to admit a wrong. Another mark against him was his struggle with English.

Rudy was the scrapper, the fighter. He wrestled to the ground a Jewish kid who called him a *schlock* and went toe to toe with an Irish tough who'd laughed at his English. Shell was of an opposing temperament. He preferred when possible to sidestep provocations, though he stood with Rudy if the need arose.

They stole rides on the trolley and on the rear of grocery wagons. Rudy, who had the quicker hand, snitched lead soldiers from the five-and-ten and illustrated magazines from the kiosk. In Crotona Park they came upon a man lying serenely on grass in sight of spring flowers. They knew he was dead and not asleep because his eyes and mouth were open. Rudy went through the man's clothes and held up six dollars, which he shared with Shell. Rudy bought a two-tier box of chocolates for his mother. It was her birthday. Shell bought a baseball glove.

They played in pickup games in the lot behind Mulheim's shop, and occasionally Mulheim came out in his bloody apron to watch. The ball, which had lost its skin, was swathed in black tape and resembled a glob of iron. Playing shortstop, Rudy fielded grounders with his bare hands until the day Mulheim called him aside and gave him a brand-new glove like one worn by Honus Wagner. Without a word, Rudy socked his fist into it and trotted back toward his position.

"Don't you say thank you?" Mulheim shouted.

"*Leck mich am Arsch,*" Rudy said over his shoulder.

Later Shell asked why he hated Mulheim, and Rudy said, "You know why. I gotta say it?"

Strict with her daughters, Rudy's mother had little control over him. He came and went as he pleased and brought home poor report cards. "You have to be responsible, *verantwortlich,*" she said. "You're the man of the family." His look was cynical, without pity. "I know what you're thinking," she said, "but it's how I put clothes on your back." Rudy's flush was the closest he came to an apology.

When America entered the war against the Kaiser, Shell's mother lost her job at the button factory, which had become a military supplier. She was a Hun, a potential saboteur. But jobs had become plentiful, and she was soon working in a bottling plant. Shell followed the war's progress in the newspapers, kept a scrapbook, and pinned battle maps on his bedroom wall. He told Rudy he wished he were old enough to join the army.

Rudy said, "Which one?"

They were fourteen when they got their first piece of ass. The donor was Gretchen Krause, effusive and gushy, her adolescent body an upheaval. For Shell, who kept slipping out, it was vaudeville and finally a comic achievement. For Rudy it was a somber experience, all of it suspect. For Gretchen, who had done it before, it was a means of holding on to people.

"Who loves me the most?" she asked.

Sheltering his genitals with one hand over the other, Rudy said, "Shell does."

The next year the three of them were orphans. The Spanish flu ravaged the Bronx and expunged Gretchen's parents. It took Shell's mother and, indirectly, his father, who couldn't handle the loss and found a home in the Harlem River. Rudy's mother and his youngest sister had the larger funerals. Mulheim made sure of it.

Before leaving to live with an aunt in Queens, Gretchen held Shell in her arms. Sex was no longer comic but precious to him. It was warmth under the covers, flesh hugging flesh. "Love me," he beseeched.

"I do," she whispered. "You and Rudy."

III ≡ III

Shell stayed in school, Rudy did not.

Mrs. Zuber, the widow in the flat below, took Shell in, a move that somewhat cushioned his grief. She was a seamstress with a foot-treadled Singer that was the fulcrum of her life. Feeding satin to a needle, she said, "Not a boy, are you. Almost a man."

Rudy went out on his own the day he was sent home from school for misbehaving. He found his elder sister Elsa in her slip and Mulheim with his pants off. He understood Elsa's reasons but could not live with them.

For Mrs. Zuber, Shell was company. She was in her late thirties but on certain days looked older, even haggard. The early death of her husband had been bearable but not the loss of her daughter to diphtheria. Work had kept her whole. Creative, she made bridal gowns and Sunday dresses from her own patterns. Nimble and quick, she altered hems and turned frayed collars while customers waited. Busy times she worked into the night. Slow times she collapsed on a horsehair sofa and made faces in her sleep.

Weekends and after school Shell pumped gasoline at a filling station and gave most of his wages to Mrs. Zuber for room and board. His bed was in her daughter's room. She seldom mentioned her daughter, too painful. Memories of her husband were another matter, her recall precise, the details frank. She said his feet were fat, the nails always in need of a clip. When seating himself, his belly had stunted his legs. Drunk, he had slobbered affection, forcing her to endure his touch like a toothache. Shell blushed, a reaction he soon got over.

He bathed in a galvanized tub in front of the kitchen stove, and Mrs. Zuber soaped his neck and back. Handing him the soap, she told him not to forget to wash his *ding*. When he rose to dry himself, she warned against gathering places frequented by women of mixed nationalities and questionable health. Alluding to Gretchen Krause, she said, "I know you're not an innocent."

"I miss her," Shell said. "I think about her a lot."

"You and how many others? Best you worry about schoolwork."

Rudy Farber received no such guidance. He got a room in a boardinghouse in the Yorkville section and knew the loneliness of four walls. He shared a bathroom with two prostitutes and shaved with the razor they used for their legs and underarms. On moonless nights he crept out on the fire-escape landing that ran from his window to theirs and discovered that their true love was for each other. They accused him of *Schaulust,* the sexual pleasure of looking.

He earned money unloading grocery crates in Bathgate and cleaning spittoons in a speakeasy. Later he ran errands for a shylock, shilled for the banker of a crap game, and chalked odds on a blackboard in a gambling parlor. A nickel bought him a hot dog bedded in sauerkraut, and five dollars clothed him in a secondhand suit and crowned him with a slightly soiled fedora. He was, he felt, on the way to better things.

His dream was to work for a bootlegger named Beckel, who had the look of a *Brillenschlange,* a hooded cobra, drove a big Packard with a fancy spare wheel and studded mudguards, and did business at a back table in Hoffmeyer's Chophouse. Rudy came through the door with his fedora tilted low and a cigarette dangling from his mouth. Beckel and a woman with a mouth red like a radish were gnawing and nibbling from a platter of spareribs. After listening to Rudy for ten seconds, Beckel said, "What makes you think I can use you?"

"I got balls."

"If you didn't you'd have tits. That's the way the world's cut. You don't look big on brains, kid."

"I ain't dumb."

The woman's smudged lipstick made her mouth seem torn, but her words came out smooth. "Give the kid a break, Becky."

"A chance is all I want," Rudy said quickly.

Beckel licked his finger, narrowed his gaze, and said to the woman, "What d'you see in him I don't?"

"Nothing," she said, "but so what?"

Beckel's smile was sawtooth. "Don't make me regret it, kid."

While Rudy was realizing his dream, Shell was living in one of Mrs. Zuber's making. He was her pet, her boy, her dead daughter's big brother. When he entered his last year of high school she began measuring him for a graduation suit, three-piece, light wool, wearable through the seasons. She fussed with it more than she did with a wedding dress and subjected him to many fittings, which made him wonder whether the suit was worth it, especially when deep in the night he heard her catching up on her regular work. When she finally finished the suit she made him put it on in front of her and pose in the triple mirror.

"I look like John Barrymore," he joked.

"And I look like Mary Pickford," she scoffed, but she was pleased and gave him a little spank.

She was in the audience, tears in her eyes, when he graduated in the upper half of his class. After the ceremony he came to her in cap and gown and gave her his diploma for safekeeping. She was wearing a dress she'd made for the occasion, with lots of lace and flounces. He told her she looked great, and she said, "I'm all dressed up, but put a bucket in my hand I'll look like a cleaning lady."

In the evening he attended a graduation party with an Irish girl from Arthur Avenue who had quivery breasts under a film of imitation silk. Mrs. Zuber was waiting up when he got home with hooch on his breath, lipstick on his collar, and a cigarette burn on the lapel of his suit jacket. She turned her head and said nothing.

A week later she asked about his plans. He had none. He was working full-time at the filling station and seeing the Irish girl in the evening. "You could go to City College, free tuition," Mrs. Zuber said, and laid out the accumulation of his board money on the kitchen table. She had socked it all away for him. "Enough to buy books and other things. And you could still live here."

He didn't know what to say and said nothing.

One night he found the flat dark. No little light burned in the kitchen for him, no soup on the stove for him to heat up. Mrs. Zuber's sewing room was dark. Her bedroom door was wide open, the room awash in moonlight. Out of the covers lay one of her legs, naked and forlorn. He couldn't tell whether she was awake, asleep, or dead. Her voice startled him.

"Come in, Shell."

He was frightened without fully knowing the reason. Light and shadow tattered her face. Her hair, out of its bun, was outspread on the pillow.

"Are you planning to leave me? Is that what you've got in mind?"

Creeping toward the bed, he assured her he had nothing in mind. Standing over her, he felt a heavy obligation and meant her no harm, though lately he seemed always to cause her some.

"If you get that Irish girl in trouble," she said, "it'll be all over for you. No future." When he didn't respond, she patted the mattress. "Take off your shoes and lie down beside me. Talk to me, Shell."

From outside came the passing hoot of an automobile horn and the shout of a drunk. Shell dropped a sturdy shoe, a cleat on the heel. A sudden shift of the covers left Mrs. Zuber momentarily exposed. Her white angular body seemed in hibernation, wintering toward an uncertain spring. When he settled beside her, she spoke in his ear.

"You don't need that kind of girl, not at this time of your life."

He shut his eyes when her fingers worked at the buttons of his trousers, buttons she had sewed on. The moonlight was ebbing, and in the murk she looked undimensional. A succubus with streaming hair. She used her hand on him as if shaking dice, her world as much as his at stake.

"You understand why I'm doing this, don't you?"

He nodded, without a thought in his head.

Later he tiptoed to his own room and slept soundly, without movement. In the chill of morning he woke abruptly, in a dank sweat, as if he'd slept through a killing.

||| ≡ |||

Rudy Farber worked under the cover of darkness. He and others unloaded high-grade whiskey trucked down from Canada, without incident, for the police had been paid off and conveniently stayed away. The only threat came from competitors, particularly an Irishman named Moynahan, who was said to be crazy. Rudy carried a small revolver inside his belt, but it was unloaded. Beckel wanted no shooting.

When hijackings became common along the whiskey run, Beckel changed tactics. He rented speedboats to rendezvous in the night with cargo ships anchored off Long Island's shoreline, ragged with inlets and secluded coves. Rudy, who wanted more action and more money, begged Beckel to let him man one of the speedboats.

"You got balls, I still don't know if you got brains," Beckel said. "This business I don't carry insurance. You make a mistake, you pay the price."

In the murk of an overcast night Rudy sped into international waters to the blinking light of a waiting ship, where men in watch caps overloaded his boat. For the first time he felt fear. He couldn't swim. On the twelve-mile trip back, confused by conflicting shore lights, he became disoriented and chose the wrong cove. As soon as he set foot on the dock two men in overcoats lumbered toward him. One aimed a flashlight at him and said, "Who the fuck are you?"

"I work for Beckel," he said fast.

"Yeah, well this ain't Beckel's spot, you dumb shit."

Too late he realized they were Moynahan's people. The butt of a pistol struck him square on the head, dropping him, concussing him. A kick broke a rib, maybe two. A big hand snatched the toylike revolver from his belt, and a second later he heard a click in his face, then the grunt of a laugh. He lapsed into unconsciousness and didn't come to until the sun was breaking over the waters. They had taken the crates of whiskey and set the speedboat adrift.

A doctor stitched his head wound, taped his rib cage, and told him to stay off his feet for a few days. Beckel awaited him in Hoffmeyer's Chophouse. His head bandaged and his body hurting, Rudy approached the table like a war casualty. He stood still and knew enough to offer no excuses. Beckel regarded him with hooded eyes.

"You cost me a lot of money, kid. How you gonna pay me back?"

Rudy's head throbbed. It hurt him to think, to breathe. "I'll work for nothin', " he said.

"That would take years." Beckel's tongue came out of his mouth as if to lick a stamp. "How's your sister?"

The question set him back. "Which one?"

"One uses her ass as legal tender. Maybe we can work something out."

Rudy wanted to cry and was afraid he might. "Don't do this to me, Mr. Beckel."

"You did it to yourself, kid."

Rudy put a hand to his chest and then to his stomach. His legs were wobbly. "I don't feel so good."

Beckel swallowed beer from a stein. "You got another choice, kid, but it ain't a good one. You can run, hope I don't find you."

That evening, taking only a few small items, a toothbrush and the like, Rudy ran.

III ≡ III

Shell worked extra hours at the filling station and mailed a late application to City College. Mrs. Zuber changed the curtains in his bedroom and at night left the door open to hers. For his birthday she bought him a book satchel, along with a necktie and a stickpin to go with it. Once a week they went to the moving pictures. She was a fan of Wallace Reid, Valentino, and the Gish sisters. Shell liked westerns, and she pretended to.

Every other week they went to a social club to listen to popular music, most of it Irving Berlin. On such occasions she blackened her lashes, rouged her cheeks, and wore a loose-fitting dress. She was good on the dance floor, her body in full stir. He was clumsy. "Don't look at your feet," she coached, "just go with the music." A single look told others that much was going on between them, which she ignored and he tried to, covering his discomfort with a wooden expression.

One evening in the kitchen, watching her rub a sliced lemon on her elbows, he said, "People are talking about us."

She was silent for a moment and then glanced up sharply. "Doesn't bother me. Does it you, Shell?"

He shrugged. He was seated at the table with one of her magazines, *Motion Pictures,* Clara Bow on the cover.

"If it does, say so," she said.

He swore it didn't and watched her raise a hand as if to shadow a thought. Her face, utterly still, looked abandoned. The smell of lemon was strong.

"Do you think me a fool?"

He wished his mother was still alive and Gretchen Krause still in his life. He wondered what Rudy Farber was doing. "No," he said.

"I'm alive again, Shell. For a long time I was dead."

His expression turned apologetic. "Mrs. Zuber, I—"

"For God's sake, call me Petra."

That night in her bedroom they spoke to each other's nakedness. She was irreproachably white, he was ruddy. Both were bony. Snug inside her, he asked himself what more he could want. Later when he made a move to return to his room she gripped his arm.

"Don't go."

In September, wearing a V-neck sweater she had bought for him, he entered City College and in one of his classes met a young woman who told him she had spent many years in the larval stage and was now a butterfly. Her name was Helen.

III ≡ III

Rudy Farber fled to Newark and got a room in the YMCA. For nearly a year he worked in the scorched air and hellish world of a foundry, where he dunked slabs of metal into vats of hissing chemicals, the spill from which could sear flesh to the bone. Some of the workers proudly exhibited their deformities. Those long on the job resembled the living dead. Rudy was fired when he let himself get run-down and fainted near a bucket of acid waste, which made him a danger to himself and others.

The director at the YMCA told him he couldn't live there permanently and gave him two weeks to clear out. He got a room near the waterfront and a job bundling papers at the *Evening News*, where he lost his first week's pay in a poker game, his best hand a monkey flush, good for nothing. He thought of going to night school for his diploma but didn't, which killed his chances with a strapping Italian girl who clerked at the paper and wanted a fellow with prospects. She caught him ogling her and said that lustful thoughts would disfigure his face.

In his room he ate beans from the can, sardines as an occasional treat, and drew cockroaches. In bed he dreamed of his mother, the sister who had died with her, and the baseball glove Mulheim had given him. He even dreamed of his father, though memories of him were faint. Beckel appeared once, in a nightmare.

He went to the moving pictures often, alone. He had no chums except the weekly ones with whom he played poker. And there were no women in his life except occasional prostitutes, who had reservations about his health. His shadowy eyes and his pallor made him look nocturnal, daylight unnatural to him. Otherwise they liked him because he caused no trouble and sought no extraordinary services.

He bundled papers at the *Evening News* for four years. He was there when the Italian girl showed off a diamond ring and announced she was getting married. And he was there for the extra press run when Charles Lindbergh soloed thirty-six hundred miles over open sea from Long Island to Paris. In the same edition, page four, was an item about the gangland killing of a Bronx bootlegger.

Rudy gave his notice the next day. His exile was over.

III ≡ III

Her name was Helen Dodd. Her diary documented venial sins, none she felt would interest God. It was time she committed one that did. Shell hoped it would be with him, but she chose someone else and then a couple of others. She chose him for conversation because he listened to every word and never took his eyes off her. In the ice-cream parlor near the college, where she relished banana royals and never gained an ounce, she said, "I don't believe in too many morals, do you? I mean, they get in the way of so much."

Everything about her caught his imagination. She was an intense version of Gretchen Krause. She was blonder than Gretchen, built closer to the bone, and carried a faint degree of unreality. He suspected something was wrong with her, but he was already in love with her. As if to confirm his suspicion, she said, "I've been in a couple of nuthouses. How about yourself?"

He thought she was joking, but she was merely exaggerating.

She had attended summer camps for adolescents with emotional problems. She had grown up, she said, on Staten Island in a house that had belonged to her grandmother. Shell pictured white clapboards, red trim, and window boxes of geraniums. She came, she said, from a family of narcissists. Her mother had no tolerance for conversations in which she wasn't the central character. Her father wore a hair net to bed and fancied himself a ladies' man. Her brother timed a camera to take countless pictures of himself, his left profile the prettier one.

"Who's this woman you live with?" she asked. "She a relative?"

He didn't want to lie, but he didn't want to tell the truth either. "She's like an aunt," he said.

Their sophomore year he made sure they shared more classes. Tuesdays and Thursdays, the free hour between English literature and sociology, they studied together in the library. From behind her hand she whispered she was sick of the upperclassmen she'd been seeing, all without substance, some with moronic tendencies. "I need someone like you, Shell."

In a coffee shop after their last class she laid down rules. If angry with her, he must not raise his voice, and he must be sensitive to her moods and she to his. She warned against jealousy, which, she said, would deaden her the way frost nips the soul from a flower. Lastly, she felt she should ration her favors, for otherwise he would tire of her.

"Never," he said, and reached across the table for her hand. The cigarette in her mouth kept him from kissing her.

She roomed ten minutes away from the college and allowed him to visit her on Fridays. On his first visit she made him promise not to grunt. The walls were thin. Tender talk and prolonged foreplay were postulates. Anyone who wanted to get right to it, she said, was banished, no second chances, for she believed beginning moves revealed everything. On the bed it was she who guided his hand into her underpants. Having idealized her, he expected to graze baby's hair, but it was a woman's tussock thrilling his palm and a woman's intimate odor drawing him down. Much later, raw and panting, he lay with an arm over his eyes.

"You've had practice." She rolled against him. "You must tell me all your secrets."

Toward the end of the school year he accompanied her on the ferry to Staten Island to meet her parents. The house, not what he'd expected, was a gothic Victorian in varying states of disrepair. The front lawn was mowed, the back wild with weeds. Helen's parents were on the porch. Mrs. Dodd stood half in shadow, where a hanging impatiens in full bloom looked like a headdress for a garden goddess, presumably her. Her girlish figure allowed her to dress young, and her goldfish-orange dress made sure she wasn't ignored.

"This is my new beau," Helen said.

"Your *new* beau?" Mrs. Dodd's bright sticky voice seemed to cling to her lips. "I didn't know you had any old ones, dear."

Mr. Dodd, whose silver-wet hair was wonderfully waved, shook

Shell's hand and told him to sit. The flimsy rocker Shell chose seemed overly aware of him. He sniffed a fragrance, which was Mrs. Dodd. Mr. Dodd said, "German, are you?"

"I was born here."

Mrs. Dodd said to Helen, "Don't get yourself pregnant."

Her mother, Helen had told him, was foremost in correcting her and penciling critical comments on the margin of her life. Her brother, three years her senior, the favored sibling, was trying to make his mark in Hollywood.

"Any skeletons in your closet?" Mr. Dodd asked Shell.

"His father drowned himself," Helen said.

"Good God!" Mrs. Dodd said. "I suspect you two will make a sweet pair. Anything else?"

Helen smiled. "He lives with a woman he says is his aunt."

He started to explain, but Mrs. Dodd shushed him with a look. "At least you're interesting," she said, staring at him. Helen, he noticed, had her aquamarine eyes.

Helen showed him through the house while her mother made a light lunch. The furniture was from her grandmother's day, old hulks overfilling rooms of modest size. Sepia photographs of relatives no longer living adorned the parlor walls. An oil portrait of Helen's mother at a tender age dominated the sitting room. Helen in the lead, they shuffled up narrow stairs. Her childhood bedroom, small and shadowy, held a powerful quiet. Poised in the doorway, she seemed to wish for a sound.

"Houses are like people, Shell. Some sad, some happy. This is an unhappy house."

In the dining room, the table covered with aged lace, Shell sipped from a frail teacup he feared would shatter in his face. The sandwich he ate was crustless. Mrs. Dodd, her silver hair spun afresh, kept him at the margin of her vision, as if that were his assigned place, her daughter the victim of a careless choice. Framing the sentence with cold concern, she said, "I hope you two don't plan to marry."

"Eventually," Helen said, though the possibility had not been discussed.

"Husbands seldom turn out as they're supposed to," Mrs. Dodd said.

Before leaving, Shell let Mr. Dodd guide him into the kitchen. Standing near the sink, where a dead housefly floated in dishwater, Mr. Dodd said, "Be good to my little girl. She's breakable."

||| ≡ |||

He felt fingertips through the back of his shirt and turned. Mrs. Zuber's eyes arrowed in on him. "Isn't it about time you told me about her?" she said. "I don't even know her name."

"Helen," he said reluctantly.

She grabbed the front of his shirt and clenched a wad of it. "Am I not enough?"

"Petra, please."

"What happens when she breaks your heart?"

"She won't."

"How naive you are. My fault for spoiling you." She released his shirt and tried to brush away the wrinkles. It was a shirt she had ironed. "I should meet her."

"Yes," he said with foreboding.

"Alone," she said. "We won't need you."

Helen came the following Sunday afternoon while Shell was working at the filling station. Mrs. Zuber served coffee and cakes in the front room and stared into Helen's eyes, which seemed as green as they were blue. Seating herself, Mrs. Zuber said, "You're very pretty."

Helen bit into a cupcake that had an apple flavor. "This is delicious."

"What has he told you about me?"

Helen smiled, woman-to-woman. "I don't think he left anything out."

Mrs. Zuber's eyes never shifted from her. "Then you know I taught him everything."

"And I thank you. He's very good."

The strain began to tell on Mrs. Zuber. She tasted her coffee to moisten her mouth. "What kind of woman are you?"

"Special," Helen said. "I always have been."

"I want his happiness. I want to make sure he marries right."

"He's not your son. He's not even your nephew."

Mrs. Zuber felt herself coloring, losing not simply a skirmish but the whole battle. Rising, coffee cup trembling in her hand, she wanted winds to lift her off her feet and take her away, out the window, across the sea. "I love him," she said. "Does that matter to you?"

"No," Helen said.

||| ≡ |||

From her bed Mrs. Zuber heard him when he came home from the filling station and from wherever else he might have been. She had left soup for him and some of the leftover cakes. She heard him draw a bowl from the cupboard, a spoon from the drawer. He was tiptoeing about, his shoes off. Every sound magnified itself in her ear. Later she heard him laying out books, rustling papers, and sharpening pencils with a knife.

He studied late into the night at the kitchen table, final exams, graduation a month away. It was after two when he put the books aside and peered into the murk of her bedroom. Her eyes were closed, her cheek pressed to the pillow, but she was not asleep. Fear and anger assaulted her. Squatting in her life, he had eaten from her table, enjoyed her favors, and taken seven years from her life. He was still young, she was old.

He edged toward the bed to give her a goodnight kiss. It was what he'd been doing lately instead of joining her under the covers. Without moving her head, she said, "All these years I've saved my daughter's baby teeth. I suppose they'll be thrown away when I die."

"Please don't talk that way." He bent down and kissed her cheek. "You'll always have a home here, Shell, no matter what."

He started to say something, but the words slithered away. Two women in his life, two forces, each a truth. When he straightened to leave, she reached for his hand.

"Stay."

||| ≡ |||

He and Helen married the month they graduated. A justice of the peace performed the ceremony. Strangers stood up for them. Helen phoned the news to her mother, who said she could have done better and hung up. Mrs. Zuber accepted the inevitable with a slightly desperate smile and offered the newlyweds room and board.

"That's sweet of you," Helen said, "but I don't think it would work."

Helen had money Shell hadn't known about, a small annuity from her grandmother, which helped set them up in a tiny flat on East Eighty-seventh. The bedroom window overlooked a barricaded construction site teeming with dust and smoke from busy trucks and cranes and muscled workers. In the morning when Helen appeared in the window large Irish faces peered up at her.

Shell got a reporter's job with the Bronx *Home News,* but the money wasn't much and fellow workers resented his college degree. "Good for wiping your ass on," the police reporter told him. He collected lists of wedding guests and funeral mourners for publication, wrote up club notes, interviewed couples celebrating anniversaries, and occasionally covered a fire. Once a month he telephoned Mrs. Zuber, but conversation was difficult. His brain stood still.

Mrs. Zuber said, "Remember when I used to wash your back?"

Helen considered teaching kindergarten or doing social work, but her interviews went badly. Her attention wandered, her voice receded, and her manner hinted of disconnection. She did not really want a job, for she had the sort of husband she had dreamed of. Shell kissed her awake in the morning, brushed his fingers down her back under the warm covers, and soon was off to work, leaving her with the whole delicious day for herself. Her greatest pleasure was her morning bath. Her body wrapped in hot water, she stirred suds to her chin and made her world a womb, all dreams possible. Sunny afternoons in the park she read library books thumbed soft by past readers, here and there a passage underscored or checked or starred, which made her feel like a traveler coming upon signposts left by adventurers. Gloomy afternoons she warded off melancholy by going to the motion pictures. Bedtime she pretended Shell was John Barrymore.

Shell was good to her. He brought home groceries, made the evening meal, and did the dishes. In winter he always got into bed first to warm

36

it for her, and in summer placed the fan where the breeze would favor her. Twice she thought she was pregnant, but the alarms were false.

Shell gained favor at the paper and received slight raises and better assignments. Busier now, he lost touch with Mrs. Zuber and suffered guilt but not enough to make him pick up the telephone. Finally, after more than a year, she phoned him at his desk.

"I don't know what you look like anymore," she said in a voice he first failed to recognize. "Come see me. Please."

He went the next afternoon and experienced heartache. She looked old and tired and wore glasses low on her nose. When he kissed her cheek he felt her tremble and heard her whisper "*Schatzi.*" A small mongrel puppy scampered about, pages of the *Home News* spread out for it to pee on.

"I need the company," she said.

A radio was playing, more company. A voice reported crowds in Paris cheering Lindbergh, but her ear was tuned only to Shell's voice. Her gaze drew him in.

"I'm so proud of you," she said.

He sat at his familiar place at the table, and she served coffee and strudel and told him about goings-on in the neighborhood, her voice slow as if to stretch out the telling. No, she'd heard nothing of Rudy Farber or of Gretchen Krause. What was there to hear? Two no-accounts. At times she spoke dreamily, her mind ten years in the past, and placed dead people alive and well in the present. She let out a lively fart that didn't embarrass her at all, as if for that moment she'd thought she was alone. The puppy tried to jump onto her lap, but she shooed it away. Sitting erect, she asked Shell to scratch her back.

"Down a little," she said. "Ah, yes. Right there. Good. Thank you."

An hour passed. Almost imperceptibly, with a deep-seated sigh, she inclined her head. She was tired, but she didn't want him to leave. He was on his feet, his hat in hand, his prized press card wedged in the band. Her eyes soared over her glasses.

"Stay," she said in a stricken voice, and hollowed a fist to show what she might do for him. He pretended not to notice. Bent at the waist, he kissed her cheek and through the skin felt a sorrow he could do little about.

Two days later he sat on a hard chair in the police station with his hands on his knees and his shoulders slumped. A detective with an Irish brogue showed him a note written in a plain hand and told him Mrs. Zuber had slashed the puppy's throat and then her own.

"Note says this is yours," the detective said, and passed him a tiny velvet pouch with a drawstring.

He didn't open it. He knew what was inside.

||| ≡ |||

Rudy Farber returned to Yorkville, to the same boardinghouse from which he'd fled. The two prostitutes were gone, driven out, he was told. Hoffmeyer's Chophouse was no longer in existence. Gangsters had shot out the windows and torched it a month before they dispatched Beckel the bootlegger. Rudy scanned the want ads in the *Home News*. Within the week a building contractor hired him as a carpenter's assistant.

He worked with an immigrant named Richard Hauptmann, who taught him how to saw a board straight and stroke a nail. Hauptmann was close with money but sometimes sprang for a cup of coffee. After reaching America only four years ago, Hauptmann already had a bank account, the passbook kept in his back pocket and molded to the curve of his buttock. A skilled carpenter, he drew a weekly wage of fifty dollars, more than twice what Rudy was paid.

In halting English he said he'd lost two brothers in the war. He himself had been wounded and gassed, western front, where he'd been a machine-gunner, age nineteen. He was sent home to his village in Saxony, no jobs. No jobs anywhere in Germany. Arrested for breaking into houses, he spent four years in prison.

"So you're a gangster," Rudy said with a smile.

"*Nein*," said Hauptmann. "I valk straight, narrow. I a married man. You vant to meet?"

"What?"

"My vife. I show you her."

38

The Hauptmanns lived in the top-floor apartment of a two-story stucco house deep in the Bronx. Anna, two years older than her husband, was pink-cheeked and pleasant. Hauptmann had come to the States as a stowaway with a forged landing pass, and Anna had arrived legally with a command of English. Shortly after they met, they married. She waitressed at a luncheonette, and they lived off her pay while saving most of his. They were saving for an automobile, a child, and a better life.

Introducing Rudy to her, Hauptmann said, "Ve lovebirds. Tell him, *Anni*."

Anna blushed, laughed, and stroked her husband's head. "We get along."

Rudy lit a cigarette.

"Bad habit," Anna said, reappraising him.

"But a good fellow," Hauptmann said, standing close to him. They looked somewhat alike. Each had high cheekbones, deep-set blue eyes, and squint lines, but Hauptmann was stockier and had a healthy head of hair. Rudy's was thinning.

Later Hauptmann took him into the parlor and showed him new furniture, no secondhand stuff. "Lamps ve get in mail from Sears, Roebuck. Curtains too. Rest ve buy at store."

"You got a nice place," Rudy said.

"Two bedrooms, need only one. You like, I rent you one."

Rudy moved in a few days later, the rent cheaper than at the boardinghouse. Anna offered to do his laundry for less than what he paid outside. A meticulous housekeeper, she shook a finger at him when he failed to pick up after himself. He enjoyed the scold, silent and firm. Once, when Hauptmann was out on an errand, he glimpsed her half undressed in her bedroom and angled his head for a better view. Garters on her girdle held up red-brown stockings. Her breasts quivered, celebrating freedom. With a glare, she said, "You like to look?"

"It was an accident," he said.

"Get yourself a woman. Be like Richard and me."

One evening while she was waitressing, he and Hauptmann shared a pitcher of beer at the neighborhood social club. The beer was brewed surreptitiously in the cellar. Irish policemen, always welcome, drank theirs free while eating *Weisswurst*, for which they'd acquired a taste. Sitting with his back to them, Hauptmann said, "I'm lucky man, am I not?"

"You were Irish, you'd be luckier," Rudy said.

The policemen were talking about Lindbergh, who was still much in the news. President Hoover had awarded him the Congressional Medal of Honor, and the Air Corps Reserve had promoted him to colonel. The *Daily News* called him the most famous man in the world. Another paper dubbed him "The Lone Eagle."

"He younger than me," Hauptmann said. "Already rich."

"Get yourself a monoplane and fly the Pacific," Rudy said. "Then you'll be rich too, your picture in all the papers."

"Got to be easier way."

Wiping their mouths, the policemen rose from their table. They were big fellows in dark blue and polished brass, their nightsticks dangling. Watching them leave, Rudy said, "I think of one, I'll let you know."

||| ≡ |||

Many months later he visited his sister Elsa in the old neighborhood. She let him in without a word, led him into the kitchen, served him coffee in a mug, and seated herself opposite him. He was startled by how much she now resembled their mother. She said, "You could've written."

"I didn't have anything to say."

Her gaze moved over him. "You look thin, pale, and you're losing your hair. Don't you take care of yourself?"

His gaze wandered. The kitchen no longer seemed familiar. A refrigerator stood in the place of the old battered icebox. Cupboards had been repainted. He asked about his younger sister.

"She doesn't live here anymore. She has a nice job in Manhattan. Mulheim paid for secretarial school."

"Good way to get rid of her. How are *you* doing?"

"I'm here, you can see."

"Don't you work?"

"I do what Shell's mother did. Pluck chickens, skin rabbits."

"He's got you doing that?" Rudy felt an old rage and glimpsed the ghost of their mother and of the sister who had died.

"I do it because I want to. He's good to me."

"He'll never marry you."

"How can he? He has a wife." Weary of the talk, she shut her eyes and drooped her head back. Rudy reached across the table and undid a button on her blouse. "Don't do that," she said. He loosened another and exposed cleavage.

"That's what he used to do to Ma." Rudy pulled his hand back. "I hate the thought of him touching you."

"Then don't think about it."

"Some things you can't blot from your mind."

Elsa's eyes opened slowly. "Why'd you come back, Rudy?"

"Doesn't make sense, does it?"

"You never did," she said.

||| ≡ |||

There was lots of work for Hauptmann and Rudy, even when the Crash came and soup lines formed and men sold apples on street corners. Their boss, a favorite of the rich, had contracts to build houses on Long Island. Some weeks Hauptmann came home with ninety dollars and put it into his savings. Rudy averaged fifty dollars a week and spent it all. He played craps but was a poor shooter, always going for broke. In poker he remembered none of his losing pots, only the one he raked in with a pair of one-eyed jacks. Every month or so he approached a prostitute and paid more than she asked.

Anna Hauptmann did not like his ways. She suspected he listened at doors, put his ear to the wall at night, and did nasty things with himself in the bathroom. Nor did she like the smell of his cigarette smoke, the sound of his cough, and the sallow look of him. "He's been here too long," she said to her husband. "Time he should go."

Hauptmann gave her a pinched look. "It's money we won't have."

"I don't care. Besides, I think he's consumptive."

Hauptmann waited a week before telling Rudy. Then he did so with color in his face and a twitch in his cheek. "It's Anni, not me. Up to me, you stay."

Rudy smiled. They were in the social club. The pitcher of beer was Hauptmann's treat. Rudy lit a cigarette and said, "You're pussy-whipped, you know that?"

"*Nein, nein*. Anni good woman. Ve talk maybe ve make a baby soon, need nursery." Hauptmann took a large swig of beer. "You, me, ve still vork together. Ve still friends."

Rudy looked away. There were worse things than moving back to the boardinghouse.

"Please," Hauptmann said. "Ve stay friends?"

Rudy shrugged. "Sure. You're the best I got."

III ≡ III

The heat of August agonized Helen. She put on lipstick but no clothes except for stretched underpants and a bra that needed more scope. Pregnant, she had got big fast. Gingerly, cautiously, she traced fingers over her abdomen as if preparing to defuse a bomb. When Shell dropped to one knee to listen for life, she pushed him away.

"Too hot for that."

He rose and drew back. She put a hand to her brow. She had not used a razor and was scrubby under the arm. Her lipstick was crooked, as if a bloodstained finger had applied it.

"What are you staring at?"

Since Mrs. Zuber's death, for which he held himself responsible, he saw sadness in everyone and in everything except Helen's pregnancy. That was a gift from the unknown. Tears stood in his eyes.

"How will I manage when it comes?" she asked. "I won't know what to do."

"We'll learn together," he said.

On the weekend they visited Helen's parents on Staten Island to escape the heat, but it was hot there too. Mrs. Dodd, half in a swoon, wanted to talk only of the past when her beauty and her antics had fascinated everyone. Mr. Dodd, sipping bourbon, was lost in private thought, his eyes bright and blank. His smile was fixed.

"In case nobody's noticed," Helen said, "I'm pregnant."

Mrs. Dodd put on her glasses. "Are you really, dear? I thought you'd just let yourself go."

Mr. Dodd came out of himself and said to Shell, "How'd the Yankees do?"

Helen gave birth to a boy in late winter. Shell got the word at work and ran out to his car, a Chevrolet he'd bought from a man who couldn't afford to keep it. A sleet storm made motoring treacherous. Cars crawled, slipped, and slid. Swerving into the hospital parking lot, Shell dented a fender. Helen was awake, the baby in her arms. The nurse said, "I'll leave you three alone."

Shell kissed his wife and viewed his son. Helen said, "He's not pretty."

"Give him a chance."

"He has no hair."

Shell grinned. "We'll buy him some."

"Look," she said, and likened the baby's private parts to a snail protruding from its armor.

Gently Shell lifted him from the curve of her arm and held him. "I love him."

"I'll learn to," she said.

They named him David after her brother, who was in Hollywood and had changed his name to Dane. Shell brought home books devoted to child care, and Helen read and reread them from a fear that someone would take the child from her if she proved inept. Despite the unpleasant sensation, she learned to nurse. Bathing the baby, she feared he had no center, only gurgling smile and wind, but Shell assured her otherwise. Shell washed diapers, made the supper, and squeezed her hand to certify togetherness. Putting the baby to bed, he said, "He's beginning to look like us."

Helen shook her head and shivered, as if a moment of history had crossed a moment of fiction, each yet to be written. "Look at him closely, Shell. Is he anyone we know?"

III ≡ III

Shell and Rudy met by chance on a Saturday in Bathgate. Shell was returning bottles for the deposit, and Rudy, as in the old days, was loitering near a pyramid of oranges as if to snitch one. Shell had to look twice. Rudy's hair was wet-combed, his chalk scalp shining through, and his once-youthful face had hollowed into a tight discipline of prominent bones.

"Jesus, I almost didn't recognize you," Shell said. "How are you doing?"

Rudy grinned. "I'm alive, but who cares?"

"Not me. I thought you were dead." Shell pinched his arm. "You real or just a rumor? I thought gangsters got you."

They had coffee at a diner. Rudy sprang for pie, blueberry for himself and apple for Shell, ice cream on top. After they brought each other up to date, Rudy ordered more coffee, overused the sugar, and turned his head to cough. After the cough, his voice had only half its normal weight. Shell stared at him.

"I got a question to ask you. You sick?"

"Never felt better," Rudy said, and stirred his coffee. "So you're a college graduate, huh? Big shot."

"Not so big. I lost my job."

"You and how many others? I still got mine. Working in New Jersey now. We're building a house out in the sticks for a rich guy." Rudy restirred his coffee. "So you got a wife, I should've figured that."

"And a son going on two." Shell showed him a snapshot.

"So you got it made. What's she like, your wife?"

"Not like us."

Rudy was silent for a moment. "Remember Gretchen Krause?"

"Sure I do. We were kids."

"Only piece of ass I didn't have to pay for. She gave it from the heart." Nostalgia possessed his smile. "We didn't know what we had, Shell."

"You're wrong," Shell said. "I did."

They finished their coffee. Shell laid down a tip, and Rudy added to it. With a hand on Shell's shoulder, he said, "We gotta stay in touch, you hear?" Outside the diner a wet wind washed against them. Rudy tightened the fit of his fedora and poked Shell with an elbow. "Ask me who the rich guy is in New Jersey."

Shell shrugged.

"Lindbergh," Rudy said.

||| ≡ |||

Helen took an instant dislike to him. The first time Shell brought him home for supper she was coldly polite. She didn't like the way he jabbed at his food and hated the way he looked at her, as if he knew she was having her period and was commiserating. Always she was conscious of his eyes, as if he knew just enough about women, her in particular, to be treacherous. The day she knew he was coming to supper again she went to her closet and swished dresses with a nervous hand. White was defenseless, and blue was accommodating. She chose black, a barrier.

Shell served spaghetti and meatballs. Helen fed David, who was in a high chair. Rudy, wearing his napkin like a bib, watched every movement. Later, while Shell was putting David to bed, she was alone with him. He looked her square in the eye and said, "You're nuts, aintcha?"

She stared back without a blink, without an answer. She had heard his voice in the grooves of her ear but had not allowed it inside her head.

He said, "Maybe what I mean is high-strung."

Shell returned and filled beer glasses from a bottle Rudy had brought, none for Helen. She was going to bed. Her nod to Rudy was cursory, her kiss for Shell perfunctory. Rudy watched her leave, took a slow swallow of beer, and said, "We're living in a scary country, you know that? Everybody's out of work, even you."

"You're not," Shell said.

"I'm not everybody."

From the bed Helen heard him leave. Propping her pillow up behind her, she sat and listened to sounds of Shell cleaning up in the kitchen. Later he stopped in David's room and then finally came into theirs. In the dark, she said, "I don't want him here again."

Shell was loyal. "We grew up together."

She switched on the bedside lamp. "I think he wants to fuck me."

"No," Shell said slowly. "I don't think he really knows how."

45

"I'd kill him if he tried."

Shell sat on the edge of the bed and took her hand. "No need, Helen. I think he's dying."

||| ≡ |||

Rudy Farber had a scheme in which he wanted to call the shots but not actively participate. For that he needed the help of two persons, neither of whom needed to know about the other. One was Richard Hauptmann.

Rudy chose to visit Hauptmann on an evening he knew Anna would be waitressing. Hauptmann was gloomy. Months ago he had quit his job to do special carpentry on his own, a venture not as profitable as expected. Worse, he had dipped deep into his savings to join a friend in buying and selling furs. The business went bust.

"I God-damn fool," Hauptmann said miserably. "I play stock market. I do dumb in that too."

Rudy's look was sympathetic. "Anna know?"

"She don't know nothing. You don't tell."

"She'll find out sometime."

Hauptmann looked up at the ceiling. "Maybe I kill myself, huh?"

"No," Rudy said with a half-smile. "You just got to remember the rich get richer, guys like us eat shit unless we do something about it." He looked directly into Hauptmann's eyes. "You know I've been working in New Jersey."

"*Ja*, I know."

"We finished Lindbergh's house. You know who Lindbergh is?"

"Sure I know. Big fly fella."

"He's an eagle, we're fucking sparrows. We're not even that. We've never been off the ground. Maybe I can change that."

Hauptmann glanced at the kitchen clock. He had to pick Anna up in an hour.

"I got something worked out," Rudy said, "easy money for you and me, drop in the bucket for someone like Lindbergh. You wanna hear what it is?"

"Sure, I listen," Hauptmann said, and Rudy, as if gutted of emotion, laid it out in monotone, with total detachment, his expression fixed. Only the air in the room seemed to have life. When he finished, Hauptmann went into moments of thought and finally said, "Too dangerous."

Rudy reached for his coat. "Think about it."

Two evenings later, in the diner near Bathgate, he laid out the scheme to Shell in the same monotone, with the same detachment, but in a much softer voice. Two policemen were eating beans and franks in a nearby booth. When Rudy finished, Shell said, "Of course you're joking."

"Do I look it?"

"Then you're crazy."

Rudy reached for the check. "Think about it."

III ≡ III

Helen rubbed whiskey on David's gums with the last few drops from a flask. He was teething. He was cranky and whiny and wet. She tried plugging him with a pacifier, but he spat it out. "Go ahead, do what you want," she said. He was loose on the floor, creeping and crawling, rising and falling, her eye on him every second. Earlier she had thought he swallowed something bad, but it was only a bit of paper he coughed up.

Where was Shell? He should've been home by now. She ran her hands furiously through her hair and arched her back. She had to get hold of herself. The radio was on, Morton Downey singing a love song. She told herself it was love that had brought her David, who was more her flesh than Shell's, for she had carried him inside her all those months.

She had plans for him. She would teach him to scan poetry and to catch butterflies with his hands. And she would teach him that what you see in a mirror isn't you.

Her nose told her he needed an urgent change. She swept him up and laid him on the kitchen table. He was crying and stinking. Shell could stomach shitty diapers, she could not.

Springing open a pin, she pricked her thumb and nursed it with her lips while staring down at her child. He had much hair now. "Mine was curlier," she said. "I have pictures to prove it." She had what she felt was a real memory of her grandmother changing her diaper. Her grandmother had died without sound, without company, without telling a soul, behind everyone's back.

She carried David under one arm into the bathroom and tossed his foul diaper into the toilet to soak. She remembered her grandmother telling her that angels tugging on ropes were responsible for ocean tides. Men in sailor hats steered the stars, and men with many matches kept the sun alive. The explanations had been reasonable—and how could a child prove them untrue, especially if they weren't? A part of her still believed.

In the tub was a rubber hose. She fiddled with the nozzle and produced a warm spray gentle enough for a baby's body. David was bawling in the wedge of her arm. Dropping the hose, she lifted him high and flung her face at his screaming one.

"Give me a break!"

Squirming and twisting, he was hot flesh in her hands and a din in her ear. It wasn't fair. Where was Shell?

"What are you doing to me?"

He was strong. Thrashing, he broke her hold, swished free, and plummeted headfirst into the tub.

She heard bone hit tile, but she didn't scream because she didn't believe it. It couldn't have happened. What lay in the tub was one of her childhood dolls. What appeared as blood was spilt nail polish from more than one bottle.

A half-hour later Shell came home. The bathroom door was open, and in the instant, his face freezing, he took it all in. Helen sat on the ledge of the tub with David in her arms, mother and child a sculpture of stillness. Her stained hand covered David's head as if hiding it.

"He won't wake up," she said.

For what seemed an endless moment Shell couldn't move. Nor could he speak. That was not his child. This was not his world. Then he moved. Crouching, he forced Helen's sticky fingers from David's skull.

"He's not dead," she said. "Tell me he's not."

CHAPTER THREE

IN PRIVATE YOUNG ANNE LINDBERGH HAD CRIED CON-
vulsively, but now she was a wraithlike figure of calm. Carrying teacup
and saucer, she drifted to her large bedroom window and looked out at
banks of automobiles. Police cars were parked near the house, and beyond were civilian ones. Local officers kept crowds of reporters and the
curious at bay. When someone sighted her in the window she drew
back as if to avoid a gunshot.

Charles Lindbergh, sleepless and unshaved, spent most of his time
in the three-stall garage, where the state police had set up a command
post. Mrs. Whateley, the housekeeper, provided an urn of coffee and a
platter of sandwiches and received the thanks of Colonel Schwarzkopf,
the commandant, whose tall presence overshadowed everyone but
Lindbergh.

Lowering his voice, Lindbergh said, "You may not be aware that my
wife is expecting our second child."

Schwarzkopf appeared surprised. He had a large face and a small
mustache. "No, sir, I didn't, but don't you worry, we'll get your son
back. I promise."

"I'm prepared to go to any length, and I want to be involved every
step of the way. I want that understood."

"I know what you're going through, sir."

"With all due respect," Lindbergh said, coldly, "I don't believe you do."

A little later he returned to the house. Anne was sitting in the living room with Mrs. Whateley, who heard him coming and quietly excused herself. Anne peered into his face for news and saw none.

"Are you all right?" he asked.

"Yes, but is our son?"

||| ≡ |||

Rudy Farber slowed to a stop on Tremont Avenue and picked Richard Hauptmann up. Hauptmann was nervous. Rudy drove across Third under the El and moments later parked on a side street diminished by failing businesses and uncollected rubbish. He had half-truths and a lie to tell. Before he could speak, Hauptmann said, "It's in all the papers."

"I can read." Rudy cranked his window down for air. "The kid's dead."

Hauptmann, his breath catching, held his head crooked. For a second it seemed it might topple.

"The ladder broke when the guy was coming down. The baby fell. The guy buried it."

Hauptmann cursed, almost inaudibly, in German. Rudy pointed a finger.

"You built the ladder right, it wouldn't have happened. But it doesn't change anything. We go along like it didn't happen."

"I don't want to do this no more."

Rudy smiled, coughed, smiled again. "You want to walk away from the money, leave it for me and the guy?"

Hauptmann straightened his head. "I don't want to burn."

"Nobody's going to burn. Think I'd be sitting here I thought that?"

"Who's this guy drop baby?"

"You don't know him, he don't know you. That's what makes it perfect. You got nothing to worry about." Rudy lit a cigarette, the last from a Camel packet. "Just make sure you do your job right from now on."

"I don't know. I die first 'fore Anni finds out."

"Only way she can is if you tell her."

Hauptmann gazed out at a dusty store window of anonymous furniture. In another store was a naked dummy, a sexless male. With less tension in his voice, Hauptmann said, "What you thinking 'bout now?"

"Maybe we should've asked for more," Rudy said.

III ≡ III

They gave up their flat, sold the furniture, and roped baggage to the roof of the Chevrolet. Shell had withdrawn his savings, a small bulge in his pocket. Seated in the Chevy, Helen held her new child in her arms and rocked him. Shell had cut his curls, which made him look less like his picture in the papers. With a glance at the two of them, Shell started the engine.

"We don't know where we're going," Helen said.

"We'll know when we get there."

They drove north into Connecticut where the March sky distanced itself. Helen sang softly near the child's ear. She pointed out scenery, though much of it was in abeyance, bare trees awaiting leaves, forsythia anticipating bloom. Several times she spoke his new name, but he didn't respond.

"Give him time," Shell said.

"He doesn't look at me."

"Patience," Shell said, and heard her shudder.

"Someone might take him away from me."

"No one will," he promised.

Outside Fairfield he pulled into a secluded rest area for a needed break. Helen disappeared behind a tree, and Shell lay David on a picnic table, changed his diaper, and returned him to a playsuit that had belonged to the original David. Helen reappeared through a haze of sunlight and opened a food hamper. David didn't care for the cooked cereal she tried to feed him, nor for the hard-boiled egg she had mashed up. Shell suggested orange juice. He wanted only milk.

They didn't stop again until they reached Massachusetts, city of New Bedford, where Shell inquired at the local paper whether they could use an experienced reporter with a college degree. The editor peered up over half-moon spectacles and answered with his eyes. On his way out Shell avoided looking at the headline chalked on a blackboard.

He drove at a faster clip. Rain clouds dimmed the day, which was dying before its time. David was crying, wouldn't stop. Shell thought he was carsick, and Helen was sure of it.

They spent the night in an overnight cabin. David slept between them. Helen, fearful she or Shell would roll over him, slept little. Several times Shell woke abruptly, his hand sailing up to touch David and then her.

In the morning he slipped out to gas up the Chevy. A filling station was just up the road, and next to it was a diner. He brought back breakfast in paper containers. David ate a few mouthfuls of scrambled egg and then, ensconced in Helen's lap, drank much milk from a bottle. Breaking into a smile, Helen poked Shell.

"He's looking at me!"

Soon they were back on the road. Skies were sunny, an unblemished blue. Shell cranked down his window to let a breeze blow in. In Brockton they passed timeworn women sitting immobile on stoops as if they were their own portraits and merely needed to be fitted with frames. A man stepping out of a butcher shop looked like Mulheim. Shell considered trying again for a newspaper job but kept going.

He got lost trying to maneuver through Boston. Streets meandered, sirens confused him, and he drove in circles. Three times he glimpsed the gilt dome of the state house. By the time he got back on track Helen was struggling with David, who was crying. He didn't want his bottle. He didn't know what he wanted. A brief stop at a Howard Johnson in Medford helped a little. He ate some ice cream.

They motored north through the quiet downtowns of little communities. A marquee in Stoneham featured a Jean Harlow movie. The same movie was playing in Reading. In North Reading children ran innocent in a schoolyard. David was quiet, but Helen was worried. His brow was hot.

"I think he has a fever."

Shell drove faster.

Midafternoon they found themselves in Haverhill, a small city bisected by the Merrimack River and girded at the core with big brick shoe factories throbbing as if under duress, windows heaved open to let out the din. Seen from the street, the workers resembled inmates tethered to machinery of medieval nomenclature. In Shell's mind the scene was a substation of hell. Helen gripped his arm.

"David can't go any farther," she said.

||| ≡ |||

They settled temporarily in a tiny furnished apartment near the high school and the library and within walking distance of downtown. Shell sought work at the Haverhill *Gazette* and then made the rounds of the shoe shops. Nothing was available. Workers lucky enough to have kept their jobs clung to them. Shell whispered in Helen's face, "Not to worry."

In the library Boston papers drew him to their headlines. The *Herald* speculated that mobsters had Little Lindy. The *Record* chose Gypsies. The *Sunday Advertiser* ran a photograph of Anne Lindbergh, and Shell forced himself to look at it. He figured his fate was a hole in hell, which gave him nothing to lose.

He listened to Walter Winchell on the radio. Citing informed sources, Winchell reported that the kidnappers had sent Charles Lindbergh his son's sleeping suit, assured him his son was safe, and were demanding a ransom. Shell lowered the volume when Helen emerged from the bathroom with David in her arms. She had given him a bath.

"He wants you to kiss him goodnight," she said.

David slept in a crib next to their bed, on Helen's side. Shell lay flat with an ear to Helen's sleep, which was always broken, a series of little deaths. He hoped her dreams were not like his. He dreamed of nooses, chains, cages. A thin sound came from her, and he rose on his elbow.

"What is it, honey?"

"I dreamed they came for him," she said.

||| ≡ |||

Rudy Farber dictated another ransom note, and Richard Hauptmann transcribed it in his rough misspelling hand, at times wetting the point

53

of the pencil to darken the lead. The signature was two overlapping circles, Rudy's private idea of life and death, his own. He read Hauptmann's effort and said, "Good."

Hauptmann lay aside the folded newspaper he had used as a lapboard. He was seated on the edge of the bed in Rudy's room. His voice rose. "No reason they not pay now."

"No reason at all," Rudy said, and sealed the note in an envelope already addressed and stamped. "What are you worried about?"

"Dangerous what I do. Maybe next time you go to cemetery."

The cemetery was Woodlawn in the Bronx, a rolling expanse of skeletal trees and tombstones protected by a high iron fence. There in the dark Hauptmann had spoken with a Lindbergh emissary, a bulky figure in a thick coat to whom he handed over the sleeping suit, proof he held the prize.

"Deal's a deal," Rudy said, and gazed at himself in the dresser mirror. Pomade on his thinning hair made it look thinner. His hair was vanishing, as if it didn't want him anymore. "What's the matter with you?"

"I get scared. Don't you get scared?"

"I got nothing to be scared of. Neither do you."

"Vhat Anni say, she find out ve kill a kid?"

"We didn't kill anybody. It was an accident, and you weren't even there. Neither was I."

"I shoulda build ladder better."

Rudy slipped on a necktie and made a knot in the mirror, then gave a quick glance at his watch. He was meeting someone and didn't want to be late. Reaching for his suit jacket, he said, "What can I tell you?"

"Tell me I von't burn."

"You won't burn."

III ≡ III

They met in a luncheonette in Queens and sat at a corner table, where Rudy couldn't take his eyes off her. Gretchen Krause's adolescent plumpness had hardened into the firm figure of a woman on whom a dress was an event. Her blond hair was darker and cut short, leaving the back of her neck bald. Biting into a bacon sandwich, she said, "What took you so long to look me up?"

"Thought you'd be married."

"I was, for a while." She used a napkin on the corner of her mouth. "And you?"

"No time for women. Life ain't been easy."

"You don't look good, Rudy. What's wrong with you?"

He was drinking Coca-Cola and smoking a cigarette. "I'm fine, a little run-down is all. You look swell."

"Tell me about Shell," she said.

"He's married, has a kid. We don't keep in touch." Agitation brought on a facial tic. "Can I ask you something? Who'd you like best, him or me?"

Her smile was half for him and half for a young couple immersed in each other at the next table. "You were both special, Rudy. You were both good to me."

"I loved you."

"You should've told me."

"I didn't know it at the time." His face was red, as if he'd just screamed. "Something else I wanna ask you. You in the business, Gretchen?"

She gazed again at the couple at the next table. The girl, extremely sweet-looking, had volcanic peaks in her soft sweater. The boy had a hint of Tatar in his features. "How could you tell?"

His expression was fixed. It would have taken a hammer to break it.

"I wouldn't charge *you*," she said.

"That's not why I asked."

"I know that. Maybe you shouldn't have asked."

He brought his face forward. "I'm gonna come into some money pretty soon. I want you to have some of it."

"That's nice of you, Rudy. Why?"

His face showed wear, strain, commitment. "I didn't appreciate you back then. I didn't appreciate my mother either, all she did for me and my sisters. Lotta things I didn't see."

"Where's this money coming from, Rudy? Or shouldn't I ask?"

"From the sky," he said.

"God's gonna give it to you?"

"God ain't never given me nothin'." He turned his head to cough. The cough required a handkerchief, which he didn't have. He made do with a napkin.

"How sick are you, Rudy?"

"I've been better."

The couple were leaving. He watched them slide by, as if they were on slow skates, their world far removed from his. His was closing in on him, his history forewritten and his future a thing of the past. Gretchen regarded him critically.

"You belong in a sanatorium."

"Life's too short for that," he said, and signaled for the check.

Gretchen's eyes reached out to him. "What can I do for you, Rudy?"

"You've already done it," he said.

III ☰ III

A truck was stopped at the roadside. A man in urgent need of a leak hustled into the woods and relieved himself near a collection of leaves and dirt, in which he glimpsed what he thought was the decaying remains of an animal.

The first officers to arrive at the little grave were Hopewell locals and a strapping state trooper. The trooper tenderly raised the child's body from its shallow grave, turned it over, and let out a hard sigh. Shreds of flannel and wool clung to the torso, and bits of blond hair adhered to the mush of the scalp. Some of the face was still intact. The trooper withdrew a snapshot from his breast pocket for comparison.

"Oh, Christ," he murmured. "It's him."

Colonel Schwarzkopf, who arrived a little later, wanted the trooper to be wrong. "It can't be," he said. "Lindbergh's paid the fucking ransom."

"Look for yourself, sir."

Schwarzkopf bagged the remnants of the flannel nightshirt and wool shirt, drove the few miles to the Lindbergh residence, and on the sly showed them to the housekeeper. Mrs. Whateley began to cry.

"Are you sure?" he said. "Look more carefully."

"I don't have to," she said.

Charles Lindbergh was not at home, a relief. Schwarzkopf did not want to face him. Anne Lindbergh was sitting with her mother in the living room, the final rays of the sun striking them. Schwarzkopf stood unseen just outside the archway into the room. Mrs. Whateley was beside him.

"This is the hardest thing I've ever had to do," he whispered.

$$||| \equiv |||$$

The heat of summer was persistently high. Fans whirred in each little room. Shell had installed one even in the bathroom. David, toddling around naked except for rubber pants, suffered a heat rash, to which Shell applied an over-the-counter salve. Often he and Helen took him to Plug Pond, a five-minute drive from the apartment, and let him slosh in the water, Helen holding his hand.

Helen went for weeks without remembering the past. Holding David near a mirror, she said, "I think he looks more like you than me." Then she reconsidered. "No, I can see my father."

Shell went along with the fiction. He said he saw resemblances to both sides of the family. When her memories reemerged, he stayed close to her. At night, David asleep in his crib, he wrapped his arms around her and made love to her with whispers in her ear and promises to keep the world at bay.

On a sweltering day in August he picked up a copy of the Haverhill *Gazette* and read that Anne Lindbergh had given birth to another son. He was sure that what he had taken from her God had decided to replace.

In September he got a job in a shoe factory, Hersh Brothers, where the heave and pitch of machinery, orchestral in fury, vibrated from every direction. Perched on racks like birds were women's shoes in varying degrees of construction, some with their suede flapped out like wings and their heels pointed up like beaks. Black pumps were crows. Spiked sandals were snarled in the wild grasses of their straps. The lasting-room foreman shouted in his ear.

"I'll show you around!"

Cartons stacked high created corridors. Tiny tacks littering the wooden floors leaped into Shell's rubber soles. At sewing machines were women of all ages. Top stitchers and fancy stitchers, the foreman explained, waving to favorites. In another room he pointed out women who were stainers, finishers, cleaners, repairers, dressers, packers. A few gave Shell the eye.

"Watch your step. The owners don't like playtime on the job."

"I got a wife and son," Shell replied.

They entered the din of the lasting room, where Shell saw a man with a gun shoot flames along a shoe from shank to ball, the sparks purple and the stink sharp. Another man, a bed-laster, pressed a pump against his belly and ran it over the mouth of a machine spitting tacks while his torso shook in what seemed a mating motion. Inside the pump was a wooden foot another worker, the last-puller, would wrench free. That was to be Shell's job.

"Twenty-five bucks a week to start," the foreman said. "If you're fast I'll put you on piecework. If you're not I'll fire you."

He went on piecework within the month and was earning thirty-five to forty dollars a week, which pleased Helen in one way and displeased her in another. She had not expected him to become a factory worker. The country was in a depression, he reminded her, and he was lucky to have anything.

He voted for Roosevelt, and she voted for no one. Her only interest was David. She brought home endless picture books from the library and read them to him. Shell bought him books with pop-up pictures, which made him laugh. Helen played music on the radio and danced with him in her arms. Shell gave him a set of alphabet blocks. Watching him play with them, Helen squeezed Shell's arm.

"See, I haven't hurt him, have I?"

*H*ELEN WAS HAPPY. DAVID WAS FOUR AND CALLED HER
Mama. With her help, he could do picture puzzles and chalk his name
on a slate. She framed some of his crayon drawings and pasted the rest
in a scrapbook. Sunday mornings Shell sat him in his lap and read the
funny papers to him. In the afternoon they took him to Plug Pond
and let him romp. Watching him, Shell said, "He's a handsome kid,
isn't he?"

"He's ours," Helen murmured. "He's going to be tall, like you."

"Taller, I think."

"The woman at the library says he has my eyes. Do you think so?"
Shell nodded. "Definitely."

"Am I doing enough for him?"

"You're doing everything."

She slipped an arm around the small of Shell's back. "I've never
thanked you, have I?"

"I did it for us."

"No," she said, "you did it for me."

Each morning she packed Shell a lunch, never failing to include an
apple or an orange. When he returned from work she greeted him with

a kiss and supper on the table. When he crouched, David ran into his arms.

Helen said, "Tell Daddy what we did today."

Sometimes they picnicked in the small park near city hall. Often she took him downtown for ice cream. She bought him a sailor suit in Mitchell's Department Store and another time red overalls. She loved dolling him up and snapping pictures of him with a Brownie that had belonged to her grandmother.

Shell was still at Hersh Brothers but was now a bed-laster and making more money. He and Helen talked of moving to a larger apartment because David had outgrown the crib and slept on a cot beside their bed, where they had quit making love. Helen feared he'd wake up, see them doing it, and be traumatized. Instead, after he was asleep, they tiptoed into the parlor and used the sofa, where his mouth was soon a limpet between her legs. Later, rising up, he entered her lovingly, a slow inch at a time, as if putting his part in a flower.

Helen's good days were free of memories, free of haunting images, free of tears. Shell could always tell when her bad days were coming. She became exuberant, overheated, vivid like a poster, a condition that soon petered into listlessness and melancholy. The vitality boiled out of her, she hung around in a bathrobe and waited for Shell to come home to reassure her that men were not coming up the stairs.

"I don't deserve what I have," she said. "I don't deserve David. I don't deserve you."

He drew her close. "We're a single soul. How can it be otherwise now?"

Shell's bad times came in dreams. In a recurrent one he saw Mrs. Zuber but couldn't see her eyes. Shadows in the sockets ran deep. He told her to put some clothes on. In another recurrent dream Anne Lindbergh held both Davids in her arms and told him to choose.

Helen had her own dreams and believed that people who appeared vividly in them were aware of themselves, knew they were participants in her private dramas, and saw her for what she was.

Shell tried to look to the future. He had started a savings account for David and was depositing five dollars a week. He wanted David to go to Andover or Exeter and then on to Harvard or Yale, though he would bow to Helen's preference for Princeton. Her father had gone there two or three semesters before flunking out.

Shell's spirits stayed level until an unusually warm day in September. Sweat dripping off his nose, he was bed-lasting a rush order of patent-leather pumps when Sarky the foreman said, "Did you hear? They got the son-of-a-bitch."

Without pausing, a shoe vibrating against his gut, Shell said, "What son-of-a-bitch?"

"The guy who killed the Lindbergh baby."

||| ≡ |||

The Lindberghs were living now in Englewood, on the estate of Anne's mother, and barricading themselves against the public and especially the press. When Charles Lindbergh left the grounds reporters dogged him and photographers fired their cameras in his face. An anonymous letter addressed to Anne threatened the life of their new son, whose second birthday had passed.

"Are they going to take him too?" Fear had a perpetual hold on Anne. "Are they going to take everything?"

Lindbergh wore a small pistol, hidden by his jacket, in his waistband. He trusted no one outside the family. "The country's become a jungle," he said. "Unfit to live in."

Anne went to bed that night with the feeling she was lying down forever and would not wake to remember whatever dreams she might have. But she did wake, with a start, from an unsettling dream the memory of which curled back and vanished forever, leaving no threads, only a queer sensation of weariness in her arms, as if she'd been holding a double burden.

After breakfast she went outdoors with a notebook and fountain pen and sat at a wrought-iron table in the midst of her mother's gardens. The September sun lay warm on her slender shoulders. A great herd of starlings rose from distant trees and stampeded the sky. A sadness hovered over the gardens, which had lost most of their bloom. She uncapped the pen, opened the notebook, and wrote in a rapid hand.

Chrysanthemums are the pastework left in place after a thief has stolen the jewels.

"Anne."

Her husband's voice was soft but carried. He was a long shadow on the groomed lawn. As he drew near she recapped the pen and closed the notebook. His face told her he had news, the sort that bore on their loss. He spoke in his quietest voice.

"They got him."

She knew what he meant on the surface of her mind, but she didn't let it sink in. From the distance came the racket of a bird. She often found it impossible to distinguish the caw of a crow from the squawk of a jay. Each sounded outraged.

"He's an immigrant living in the Bronx. Gold certificates were in the ransom money. That's how they finally traced him."

A cloud intruded the sky. One always did. Her gaze fell to the chrysanthemums. A sparrow flitting among them attracted a jay.

"Did you hear me, Anne?"

In the blur of her eyes the jay made off with the sparrow. "Yes," she said.

III ☰ III

"Bet you thought I'd be dead by now, didn't you?" Rudy Farber said with a grin. "I got a woman looks in on me, takes care of me. Makes me drink eggnog."

He still lived in the same rooming house, which had grown shabby. The room seemed smaller, like a cell. He sat propped on the bed in stocking feet, his knees drawn up. Shell occupied the only chair.

"You know why I'm here."

"Sure. You're scared." Rudy held on to his grin. "You don't have to be. Nothing's changed."

"How did they catch him?"

"He wasn't smart how he spent the money."

Shell sat with the rigidity of a mannequin. "What if he breaks?"

"He'll never admit anything. It's not in his interest."

"What'll they do to him?"

"Probably find him guilty and fry his ass. So what? Everybody dies."

"We can't let that happen."

"No? That's up to you."

Shell gazed at the room's only window, which backed on the fire-escape landing. Pigeons lining the rail peered at him. "What are we going to do, Rudy?"

"Nothing. You're gonna live a long life, and I'm gonna live what's left of mine." He reached for a cigarette and lit it with care. "How's the kid?"

"He's OK," Shell said after a hesitation. "He's getting big."

"Helen?"

"She has a few bad days, the rest are good."

"Can't ask for more than that, can you?" Rudy rose from the bed. He was bald now and had a shrunken look. Rummaging in a bureau drawer, he came up with a baseball glove. "Remember this?"

Shell half smiled. "Mulheim gave it to you."

"For the kid, my compliments." He dropped it in Shell's lap. "Be sure to tell him who Honus Wagner was."

||| ☰ |||

Rudy picked Gretchen Krause up in Queens and took her to the movies. The movie was about gangsters, bootleggers, the final years of Prohibition. The lizard eyes of George Raft stirred memories of Beckel, and Raft's cockiness gave him a small look at himself. Gretchen shared her popcorn. When they finished it, they held hands.

After the movie they went back to her flat, a walk-up off Astoria Boulevard. An overstuffed chair in the front room engulfed him. Gretchen offered to make coffee, but he wanted nothing. With half-shut eyes, he said, "Shell was back for a visit. He looks good."

Gretchen frowned. "Why didn't you tell me? I'd have loved to see him."

"He wasn't staying long. He's already back in Massachusetts, with his wife and kid."

"Is he happy?"

"He'd like to be." Rudy sank a little deeper in the chair. "I told him I had someone looking out for me. I didn't say it was you."

63

"Why not?"

"I don't want to share you."

After regarding him with a calm that suggested understanding, she went into the kitchenette and returned with a glass of milk she made him drink. "If you like," she said, "you can stay the night. I'll fix up the sofa."

"You don't mind?"

"I don't mind at all."

His hand reached up. "Why are you doing this for me?"

"Simple. I got no one else."

She took bedding from a closet and made up the sofa while he undressed and waited in his undershirt and running pants. She tucked him in, laid lips to his bare head, and whispered a memory of him in grade school when he had trouble with English and went around with shoes untied and a wad of gum behind his ear.

"I speak good English now," he said.

She straightened. "Want me to leave a light on?"

"That'd be nice."

From his pillow he could see into the shadows of her bedroom. He saw her white bottom when she simultaneously lowered her skirt and underpants, and he scanned the broadness of her back when she dropped her blouse. She glanced out at him.

"You like to look, don't you? You always did."

"I always will."

Before slipping on a nightgown, she said, "Can I do anything for you?"

"I don't want you to catch my cough."

"I think I'm immune. I've been with guys had worse."

He closed his eyes. "Where are they now? Dead?"

"People don't die forever, Rudy. They come back as grass, pretty flowers, bumblebees."

"Who told you that?"

"Shell."

He heard the creak of springs and the sigh of the mattress as she settled in her bed. He imagined her with other men, brutal sex, love

64

husked from the act, and experienced a familiar sickness in his stomach. He said, "Do you remember Mulheim the butcher? His wife died. He's gonna marry my sister. Elsa."

Gretchen was silent for a moment. Then she said, "Yes, I remember him. He was good to your mother."

"Is that what you call it?" He took a breath and let it out slowly. "It was all for nothing."

"What was?"

"The money. I tried to give some to you and the rest to Elsa. She wouldn't take it either. Good thing. All of us might be in a jail cell now."

"Who did you rob, Rudy?"

"The gods," he said.

║ ≡ ║

Extradited from New York to New Jersey, Richard Hauptmann was being tried in the county courthouse in Flemington, twenty miles from Trenton. Dubbed the trial of the century, the proceedings drew some three hundred reporters and caravans of the curious, and turned the little town into a carnival. Hauptmann, sitting square and sullen, proclaimed his innocence. His picture ran daily in papers throughout the country. Walter Winchell in the *Daily Mirror* likened him to a murderous bumpkin. Shell, following the trial in the *Gazette*, prayed he'd be found innocent.

He never mentioned Hauptmann to Helen, who was oblivious of the trial or pretended to be. She was busy buying furniture on time. They had moved into a tall tenement building that backed on the Merrimack, a top-floor flat that gave them a long view of the river. David had his own bedroom, which Helen was decorating.

"The wallpaper of every child's bedroom," she said, "should be patterned. It stirs the imagination. Mine had storybook characters."

Shell was a pretense of strength, Helen a congeries of emotions, eels in a bucket. Shell stood still while she swirled about him until exhaustion stalled her in her tracks. His challenge was gauging her moods and balancing his. He kissed her on the back of the neck and felt her shudder.

"I hate it when you come up behind me like that!"

They watched David shuffling about in Shell's work shoes. "I'm Daddy," he said.

Helen narrowed her eyes and lowered her voice. "You're not perfect, Shell. That Mrs. Zuber, she killed herself over you."

"Don't say that."

"But it's true. And now you're killing yourself over me."

She went up on her toes. Her kiss left a cold mark on his cheek.

The days were short and dark, the nights long. In the privacy of their new bedroom, Helen stretched her legs under the covers and let her feet brush his. In his ear she said, "I wish I had no experience in sex. I wish it were all new again. Pretend it is."

He pretended they were back in college, and she, heaving off the covers, pretended he was someone else, anyone else. Naked, he was un-labeled, generic. He was the salesman from whom she had bought furniture, the policeman who had halted traffic to let her and David cross the street. She timed her orgasms and had several.

Because of her tendency to sprawl, she took a disproportionate share of the bed and slept fitfully, flipping from her back to her stomach. Shell lay awake as if dead, his open eyes gems. His thoughts were of Richard Hauptmann, his prayers for himself and Helen.

||| ☰ |||

The wind had teeth, forcing Anne Lindbergh to tighten the top of her sweater. Leaves raced across the grounds of her mother's estate, and a mammoth pine spun out needles several to a pack. Fluff snatched from the pod of a milkweed fled her spread hand. Low in the sky was a smudge of birds migrating to another world, the distance greater than she cared to imagine.

"Mrs. Lindbergh."

The voice came out of nowhere, with the wind. A khaki jacket and matching trousers gave an old man the appearance of a scoutmaster. It was George the caretaker, whom she'd known since the cradle.

"Mrs. Morrow's worried about you." His eyes resembled old pennies worth perhaps a few dollars to a collector. "She says it's too cold to be walking about."

Her mother tended to convey concerns through others. "Tell her I'm fine."

"She's by the fire, wants you to sit with her."

Anne let the wind grip her hair. She could talk with George, not always possible with her mother. Her mother, like Charles, smothered sorrows in silence. She smiled faintly.

"Why hasn't the pain lessened, George?"

"It will," he murmured. "More time needed."

She valued the answer and cherished the memory of a dollhouse he'd built for her fifth birthday, a labor of love, for he was childless. George, not Nurse, had coaxed a splinter from her finger. The wind gave rhythm to her thoughts.

"How did my boy cross over? Was he given wings or was he carried?"

"Whatever way it was, couldn't have been any trouble."

She accepted his words as if he had a gnostic grab on truth, his mind tipped to the light, hers to the dim. She glimpsed more birds in flight and thought of heaven as Nebraska, where the only scenery is sky.

"Do those there wish they were back here? Does my boy miss me, George?"

"He don't have to. He's got everything he needs."

The wind pushed them toward the gardens, where dead leaves reared up as if alive. Vines dangled naked. In the skeleton of a rosebush a spider that should have packed it in by now clung to life. The web was a harp, the spider fingers. Why couldn't she hear the notes?

"Madness is your mind trying to swallow you up," she said. "I won't let it happen to me."

Several minutes later Anne entered a room of great windows and Chippendale furniture. Flames enhanced the hues of the marble fireplace. Her mother, an aging lady in lavender, gestured from a chair.

"You look all windblown, Anne. Do sit down."

A tea cart stood between their chairs. The heirloom service was silver, authentic Paul Revere. Flames feasted on a good-sized log.

Mrs. Morrow's widowed face was a pretense of serenity, as if it had never undergone moments of gloom or damaging surprises.

"What were you and George going on about?"

"The weather."

The weather was safe. Seen through windows, it had the substance of a motion picture and the sound of a radio report. Her mother hoped for a mild winter, no snow up to the sills. Did Anne want tea?

"I can do it, Mother."

The log crackled and sparked. Flaring, it brightened the air around them and startled Mrs. Morrow, who did not like vivid reality. She preferred it muted. Favored shades were pastels, blissful like lullabies. She looked at her watch.

"Shouldn't Charles be home soon?"

Charles was in Flemington, a determined presence at the courthouse. Anne feared the trial would drag on day after day, week after week, never to end. Her face bared her thoughts and stirred her mother.

"It will be over soon, dear. Then you can be yourself again."

The teapot was heavy, a strain on Anne's slender wrist. Cup and saucer were gold-rimmed. She said, "That self is gone, Mother."

III ≡ III

They sat at a varnished wooden table that looked as if it had come from a library. They weren't supposed to touch, but they did, a quick brushing of fingers. Richard Hauptmann said, "How many teeth he got?"

Tears filled Anna Hauptmann's eyes. She couldn't remember. Their son, Bubi, was born after Hauptmann's arrest.

"You give him kiss for me. You tell him his father honest man, good husband, do no wrong."

"I trust you, Richard. I know you'd never hurt anybody." She wanted to touch him again, but the state trooper standing nearby had his eye on her. "And I know you wouldn't lie."

"I never lie to you, Anni. I never do what they say."

She glanced at the trooper. "You hear what my husband's saying? If you're a good man, you'll pass it on to the judge."

The trooper, a strapping young fellow with a face planed from a shave, merely stared at her. His eyes told her he had no use for her husband.

Hauptmann fidgeted. "You love me, Anni?"

"You're my sweetheart."

"What the lawyer say?"

"You talk to him more than I do, darling. What does he tell you?"

"He says everything OK. I don't believe him. Up to jury now. What you think they do, Anni?"

"I pray," Anna said. "I pray all the time."

The trooper said, "Time's up."

When she stepped out into the cold February air she saw the lawyer, a heavy figure in a bowler, fur-collared overcoat, and spats. He was talking to two policemen. When he was free, she approached him. He placed a gloved hand on her shoulder. "It's been a hard case, Mrs. Hauptmann, but I don't think we have anything to worry about."

That evening, after eleven hours and fourteen minutes of deliberation, the jury found Bruno Richard Hauptmann guilty of murder in the first degree. The sentence was death.

||| ≡ |||

When David entered the first grade Helen took a lover. His name was Weskett, and he was an insurance salesman who came weekly to the flat to collect on policies Shell had taken out on himself. In his three-piece suit Weskett was a volume of heavy tweed. Out of it he was muscular in a way that made his parts seem welded into an overaccomplished whole. On the bed, leaning over her, all mustache and body hair, he gave the impression of a bear ready to hibernate. When he tried to whisper love things in her ear, she said, "I don't want talk. I want this."

Afterward, she didn't let him linger but hurried him back into his suit. He had a smattering of taste, of wit, of charm, not enough of one particular thing to be interesting. Knotting his flowery necktie, he said, "I don't get it. Kid won't be home from school for hours. What's the problem?"

On the floor near a chair was a shaky tower of books, her autumn reading. Biographies, memoirs, a few best-sellers. "I have things to do."

"He's a nice boy. I like him."

"He's not an original."

She often said odd things he let pass. He shrugged and smoothed his hair back. His graying sideburns looked like steel blades. A former athlete, he missed his numbered jersey and cleated shoes. He wanted to tell her about it, but she wasn't interested. He put on his snap-brim hat and squared it. "Same time next week?"

"I don't see why not."

He trudged to the door, opened it slowly, and looked back. "I could love you, Helen. I could do everything for you."

"Somebody already has," she said.

The affair continued into the winter. For Christmas Weskett gave her dangling earrings, which she put into the rubbish after he left. For Valentine's Day he wrote her a suggestive poem in which a woman's anatomy, presumably hers, figured prominently and lovingly. Behind his back she tore his effort into small pieces. She broke off the affair when she caught his cold and gave it to Shell.

"Don't do this to me," Weskett said, but she did.

Shell's cold was a bad one. Helen nursed him with her grandmother's remedy, whiskey laced with the juice of a lemon. The first two nights he slept drunk and dreamless. The third night he dreamed he was climbing a rope ladder whose rungs were letting go, the whole business swaying and soon to unravel.

Helen's dreams were bizarre and she, as Shell did with his, kept them to herself. In the latest a dead man rose and wanted sex with her. She asked what he had died of.

Weskett continued to knock on the door, but he stopped slipping notes under it. In time he was promoted to a salaried position in the Boston office and seldom returned to Haverhill. Helen wrote him off as a figment of her imagination.

III ≡ III

When Rudy Farber felt he was going dark inside he began to rehearse his death by lying still in the night and holding his breath. Waking in the morning was disturbing and disappointing, a blow to his expectations. Hours loomed ahead. He hated the way winter days break late and stiffen early.

Late in the week and early in the evening Gretchen Krause dropped by with soup, which she heated on a hot plate and made him eat. Listening to his cough, she said, "You got any lungs left?"

"I'm breathin', ain't I?"

Gretchen sat on the bed's edge, her legs crossed, her eyes bright. The cut of her hair was different. She kept up with the times, the movie stars. He was seated at a little table with his soup, chicken and vegetable, which he finished off with surprising appetite. Then he got up and fished a shoe box from under the far side of the bed. It was stuffed with money, no gold certificates. Those he had burned.

"What are you doing, Rudy? I told you I don't want your money."

"It's to bury me," he said, pushing a wad of bills into her pocketbook. "Next to my mother."

"You got sisters to do that."

"I got you, that's all."

"When are you planning on croaking?"

"I got a while yet."

She picked up her pocketbook. "Let's get out of here."

They went to the movies, Garbo playing Camille, his choice. Gretchen thought it was a mistake, but Rudy enjoyed it from the start. Shoveling popcorn into his face, he identified with dashing Robert Taylor and not at all with doomed Garbo. At the end Gretchen had tears in her eyes. He had none.

"Can I stay at your place?" he asked.

"Gee, I don't know, Rudy." She looked at her watch. "I have to get up early. Besides, the sofa isn't comfortable for you."

"I don't mind."

"Go home," she said. "Get a good night's sleep."

There was a relatively new resident in the room next to his, a woman no longer young who entertained. With an ear to the wall he determined she was alone. He stepped out from his room with more money from the shoe box, another wad, almost all of it, and knocked on her door. She opened the door and smiled.

"I was wonderin' when you'd get around to it."

The room was a little brighter than his. On one wall was a framed print of potted flowers and on another samplers. A goldfish bowl took prime place on the bureau. He began undoing his shirt.

"First things first," she said, and held out a hand. He took the money from his pocket and gave it to her. Her eyelids fluttered. "Jesus Christ, this all for me?"

Fearing it wasn't, she squirreled it away fast. He was busy with his clothes. Stripped, bare bones, he looked like one of El Greco's contorted saints. His ribs protruded, his hips were blades. His penis, semi-stiff, undecided whether to rise or fall, seemed a quirk of his body.

"Excuse me for saying so," she said, "but you sure you're up to it?"

"Let me worry about it."

She had only a wrap, which she dropped. Her nudity, so much of it, made him squint. She stood near the light switch. "On or off?"

"Don't matter."

She plunged the room into darkness. In bed, burrowed deep, he lay still. Her warmth was exceptional and her hand skilled, but his response was meager. "You just want me to hold you, don't you?" she said, and drew him into the rotundity of her breasts. "How sick are you?"

"I won't die on you," he said.

But he did.

||| ≡ |||

The funeral home was up the street from Mulheim's butcher shop. Mourners were mostly from the neighborhood. There weren't many. Elsa Farber stood beside her husband in the receiving line. She was Mrs. Mulheim now, her wedding band snugly displayed, and looked more like her mother than ever. Extending her hand, she said, "Good of you to come, Shell. How did you know?"

"Gretchen Krause phoned me. Is she here?"

"Somewhere. She arranged everything. I guess Rudy asked her to." Elsa withdrew her hand and leaned toward her husband. "You remember Shell."

Mulheim smiled. "I remember him and Rudy playing ball behind my shop."

Shell nodded and said nothing, loyalty to Rudy.

"You boys were hellions," Elsa said with a soft smile. "Now you're married. Children?"

"A son."

"Rudy should've settled down like you." She gazed toward the casket as her hand sought Mulheim's. "He was a good brother, but he never understood."

Shell had only a faint memory of the surviving younger sister and no memory of her name, but he'd have known her anywhere. Her face, tightly drawn, mimicked Rudy's. She offered her hand.

"He wasn't a good brother," she said. "He abandoned us."

Shell moved into the small gathering and felt a touch on his shoulder that told him who it was. A black dress animated her shape. He had not laid eyes on her in years, but she was still the Gretchen Krause he remembered, though harder in the face and sturdier in her stance. He kissed her cheek.

"I'm glad you made it," she said.

"I'm glad you tracked me down."

"It wasn't hard. Rudy had told me where you were." She sighed with a smile. "My two buddies. Only one left."

For a stunning moment he wanted her in his arms. He wanted Rudy to leap from the casket and join them. He wanted the world to be right again, though he could not truly remember a time when it was.

"You'll be at the funeral?" she asked.

"Yes."

"Where are you staying?"

"I don't know yet."

She stepped close to him. "I have a sofa you can use."

Later he went outside for air. A buxom woman in a red coat was standing on the steps and smoking a cigarette. Turning slowly, she said, "Did you know him well?"

Shell nodded. "We were kids together."

She snapped the cigarette away. Sparks flying, it reached the sidewalk and rolled into the gutter. "I was with him when he died. I didn't even know it happened. Maybe he didn't either."

"I bet he did," Shell said.

||| ☰ |||

The appeals had run out. The delays were over. In his last statement at the penitentiary in Trenton, Richard Hauptmann said, "I die innocent man. My wife know, my son know. Nobody else matter."

Up in Massachusetts, the day before the scheduled execution, Shell drove his aging Chevrolet into the parking lot of the Haverhill police station, squeezed it into a space toward the back, and sat quietly. Desperation lurked inside his calm as he idly watched a woman maneuver a hooded baby carriage through the lot. After an hour he slipped from his car and strode toward the station, which occupied a large corner of city hall. Each step he took seemed irrevocable.

The desk sergeant had a heavy voice. "What can I do for you?"

Images of Helen clasping David cut deep into his vision and for moments blinded him. The sergeant stared.

"You all right?"

His mind raced crazily and came up with a street. "Can you tell me where Highland Avenue is?"

"Who you looking for?"

He thought fast and yanked a name from the air. "McNamara."

The sergeant gave detailed directions while Shell pretended to listen carefully. His thank-you was immediate and his exit swift. The April sky was glassy and made him blink. The woman with the baby buggy stood nearby. There was no baby in it, only returnable soda bottles. Two cents for the small ones, a nickel for the big.

Each step back to his car tortured him.

At a quarter to nine the next night at the penitentiary in Trenton, Richard Hauptmann frantically hawked up words in German others didn't understand and was executed for a crime committed four years, one month, and two days before.

||| ☰ |||

Sometimes Helen didn't get the seasons right. She heard sleigh bells in July and saw snow in the trees. She thought Hoover was still president. Walking with David along a path around Plug Pond, she was certain a bird passing overhead had whistled her name.

David said, "I didn't hear it, Mom."

"Didn't you, baby? You don't have my ears." She gave the sky a pondering glance. "I wonder what birds think of airplanes. Do they wonder why the wings don't flap?"

David pointed. "There's a butterfly!"

"Shh," she said, and the two of them began to stalk it, each in a crouch, their hands at the ready.

"If you catch it, don't kill it," David said. "You did the last time."

In September, David back in school, she had the days to herself again. She walked downtown and had a cup of tea at the lunch counter in Whelan's Drug Store. In the park near city hall she sat slouched on a bench with her knees ajar, no underpants, and electrified an old man seated across from her. From the trees came the frail sounds of early autumn, the start of preparations for sleep or death.

A little later she walked up to the high school and skirted the front of it, where students were milling on the wide stone steps. Some of the boys were horsing around. The girls looked as if their heads were full of love songs. She enjoyed the theater of their innocence and fretted over their blissful ignorance of what lay ahead.

At the library, with a mission in mind, she went into the reading room and pored over old newspapers. Instinctively she seemed to know which one she wanted. She read in one that the Lindberghs had moved to England and in another that Colonel Lindbergh had visited Germany and found much that was good in Hitler. Her hands began to tremble.

A voice said, "Would you like a drink of water?"

Raising her eyes, she saw a woman who reminded her of her grandmother. "In hell, I'm told the water's too hot to drink."

"Who told you that, dear?"

The voice resembled her grandmother's. Her grandmother had sung in the choir at the Episcopal church and died with her eyes rolled back as if from holding a high note too long. She said, "Where's the bathroom?"

The woman guided her to it and produced a key that unlocked the door, which was marked STAFF ONLY. "Right in there, dear."

She took a tentative step and said, "Going to the bathroom is nasty business. God should have devised a better way. And fucking is vulgar. What could God have been thinking of?"

The woman closed the door after her, motioned to an assistant, and said, "We have to get her out of here."

She was late returning home. David was waiting for her, smiling, eating from a bowl of Wheaties. His hair was tousled. "Guess what," he said. "I got an A on my arithmetic paper."

Her gaze fixed on him. "Who are you?" she said. "Are you someone I should know?"

"What's the matter, Mom?"

"I'm going away."

"Where are you going?"

She picked up his arithmetic paper and scanned it as if it were a ticket mailed from hell, ADMIT ONE. "Guess," she said.

When Shell came home from work, David was waiting at the door. He whispered, "Something's wrong with Mom."

Shell found her in their bedroom. She was seated on the bed's edge with a packed suitcase at her feet. Her smile was excessive. "Helen," he said, and the sound of his voice seemed an affront to the stillness of the room. "Helen, look at me."

He placed his face in front of hers, and she looked through him.

Ambulance attendants placed her on a stretcher and carried her down the stairs. Shell followed and rode with them in the ambulance to Hale Hospital, which was on the other side of the city. He spent the night there. David spent it with the family in the flat below theirs.

A few days later Helen was transferred to Danvers State Hospital, some thirty auto miles away. Shell was at the bedside when she came out of the catatonia. Staring at him, she said, "I've lost track of time. Is it yesterday, today, or tomorrow?" Then she went back into it, her smile refreezing.

The doctor assigned to her case said, "These things take time."

"How much time?" Shell pressed.

"I don't want to give you false hope."

"Give me something!"

"I can prescribe a sedative," the doctor said. "I think you need one."

David was waiting in the car, a closed comic book in his lap. Shell slipped in quietly behind the wheel and stared out at sunlight lying in cut-up pieces under an elm.

"When's she coming home, Dad?"

Stretching an arm, Shell drew him close. "It's just you and me now."

CHAPTER FIVE

WILL YOU DANCE WITH ME?"

"That's what I'm here for," Gretchen Krause said with a warm smile that excited him nearly as much as her show of cleavage. She worked evenings at the USO club in Central Park and was known to give affectionate quickies to boys going off to die.

"I like your dress."

"Blue's my color."

They danced to "Somebody Loves Me." He was a soldier without a stripe, a towhead with a celery-stalk neck. His name was Bud, he said, from Evansville, Wyoming. She had never met anyone from Wyoming and wasn't sure it was a real state. Her idea of it was a landscape of scrub, skeletal remains, and harsh realities. Somewhere in her head she heard the whistle of a wind.

"I don't dance good," he said, stepping off her foot.

"Relax," she told him. She didn't ask his age. She knew he was a baby. Sweet boys, all of them.

"I've never been to New York before."

"I didn't think so."

They danced to "Smoke Gets in Your Eyes." She preferred his sort to the grizzled sergeant whose whiskey farts fouled the air of her bedroom, though she liked their uniforms, the insignias and epaulets, the chevrons and hash marks, the tilted caps and shiny boots.

"Easy, Bud." He was on her foot again. She could feel his heart beating and knew his imagination was feeding on her. When the music petered out, she guided him to the sidelines. "Get me a soda, will ya?"

He stumbled into the crowd and returned with two paper cups of Coca-Cola crowned with crushed ice, a straw in each. A dripping hand gave her one. In a trembling voice, he said, "I was wondering . . ."

"Wondering what, Bud?"

His tongue was tied, which pleased her. Words didn't mean anything. In wartime they were of the moment, and no relationship was meant to last.

"I'll think about it," she said, "and let you know."

She danced with a marine who also wanted to take her home, and then with a sailor with the same idea and a sweeter way of expressing it. He had a wonderful rhythm, but it was Bud she left with.

When they climbed the stairs to her walk-up, his legs wobbled as if they might give out. When she unlocked the door, he hesitated before stepping inside. His garrison cap was knotted in his hand.

"I won't bite, Bud."

When she put the lights on, he looked around and told her she had a nice place.

"It's a dump," she said, and led him into the bedroom. Swiftly she shed her dress. She had regained her adolescent huskiness and viewed her body as if she weren't entirely on speaking terms with it. Out of her girdle she was a Maillol nude, more woman than perhaps Bud felt entitled to. He was fumbling with the brass buttons of his jacket and then struggling with the fly on his thick trousers. He let out a yell when the zipper caught the skin of his pecker.

In bed she told him to take his time, but he didn't know how and went at it as if he were on springs, which she didn't enjoy but was used to. A grand sigh at the end was part of her pretense.

"I love you," he whispered.

"Everybody loves me, Bud. I'll add you to the list."

"You're making fun of me."

"No, I'm not." She kissed him. "You're too nice a kid."

After she sent him on his way she made cocoa for herself in the kitchen, where the walls seemed to close in on her. Bundled in a robe, she sat at the table, crossed her legs, and swayed a bare foot. At her elbow was a writing folio. Bud had scribbled his army address on a scrap of paper for her. She wrote to all the boys she brought home, most of them now overseas. She also wrote regularly to Shell. "How's that son of yours?" she always asked, and got back prideful reports. She always signed off with love and added X's for kisses she hoped he remembered.

||| ≡ |||

The woman at the duty desk knew them from past visits and smiled warmly. "She's in the dayroom, Mr. Shellenbach."

Jangling keys, a male attendant found the right one and unlocked a plated door that opened into a corridor painted pale yellow. "I guess you know the way by now," he said.

Shell nodded. "We do."

Helen, who had the dayroom to herself, sat like a planted flower nourished by something other than sun and water. Someone had put a bow in her hair. A newspaper was in her lap, but she wasn't reading it. When Shell bent forward to kiss her on the lips, she puckered her face as if his lips were a lemon. David kissed her cheek and said, "I love you, Mom."

"Do you, dear? All your heart?" Her gaze went to Shell. "How old is he? I've no memory."

"Thirteen."

"You're a handsome boy, David. And tall. He's going to be taller than you, Shell."

Shell knew from newspaper photos that David had Charles Lindbergh's height and Anne Lindbergh's features. And his hair, fair when he was a baby, had darkened, giving him more of Anne Lindbergh's looks. Shell said, "It's all been arranged. He's been accepted at Andover."

"Why not Exeter?"

"Andover's closer."

80

"Of course. You must keep him close to you." She shifted her gaze back to David, admired his looks, and said, "Your father and I would like to talk a few minutes in private. Do you mind, darling?"

David slipped away, closing a large door behind him. Shell stood looking down at her. Her bare legs were candle white. The way she crossed them seemed to mock him. She had good and bad days, and he never knew which to expect.

"I thought you might have given him back by now."

The words squeezed his senses. He drew a chair and sat in it. "How can I do that, Helen? He's a part of me."

"He's not your flesh."

"He is now."

"One day he'll hate you."

"I won't let that happen."

Suddenly she picked up the newspaper and rattled it, as if to shake out the war news. Headlines ran big. "We're not winning, are we?"

"We're starting to."

"Why aren't you in uniform?"

It was a question she'd asked on one of his previous visits. "I'm David's sole support," he said.

"Are you paying for my keep?"

"I contribute."

"I must be a burden. David too. How can you pay for Andover?"

He worked extra hours at Hersh Brothers, where wages had been raised to keep workers, especially skilled ones. Sarky the foreman said he was the best bed-laster in the city. He also worked part-time now at the *Gazette*, a couple of evenings a week covering the municipal meetings.

"You're not a burden."

She put a hand to her head and mauled her hair, displacing the bow. Sitting drawn up, she said, "What do you think God will say to us?"

"He may understand."

"But not forgive. Am I in hell? Tell me the truth."

"No," Shell said. "You're in my heart."

She let the newspaper fall from her lap. "I'm tired, Shell, very tired."

David returned to say good-bye. Her arms went up to him. Once again he leaned down and kissed her cheek, and once again he said, "I love you, Mom."

"I love you too, sweetie," she replied, "but I'm not your mother."

In the failing sunlight they drove back toward Haverhill. Shell's hands were tight on the wheel, and David's were loose in his lap. His head turned to passing greenscape, to an unbroken expanse of field flowers.

"Why did she say she's not my mother?"

"She doesn't think she's worthy," Shell said. "She's apologizing for being sick."

"Poor Mom."

"Yes," Shell said.

||| ≡ |||

David took the call. The woman's voice was peremptory, a bark. It asked for Joseph Shellenbach. Extending the receiver, David said, "For you, Dad."

The caller was Mrs. Dodd. She said, "I suppose that was my grandson."

"Yes," Shell said.

"Isn't it about time I met him?"

"That's always been up to you."

"No, it hasn't. It's been up to Helen. She chose to keep her distance." Mrs. Dodd paused. "And then I saw no point in visiting when she obviously wouldn't know me. Is she still in that stupor?"

"She's been out of it for some time."

"Still confined?"

"Yes."

"You're not to blame, Shell. She was never sound, not even as a child."

"Would you like to talk with David?"

"She and her father are wired the same. He's gone simple on me. That's what I have to put up with."

Shell wished she hadn't called. He wished he were back in the front

82

room listening to Lowell Thomas on the radio. David was working at the kitchen table on a model airplane, a Curtiss P-40, which would join a Spitfire and a Messerschmitt hanging from the ceiling of his bedroom.

"And how are you doing, Shell?"

He began to tell her about his two jobs but soon sensed she wasn't listening. Then he remembered she didn't stay tuned to conversations in which she wasn't the topic.

"I think I should see my grandson," she interjected. "When can you bring him down for a visit?"

Shell chose the first week of July, when the shoe shops closed for the annual vacation. They went by train, then by ferry, on which David recorded sights with a box Brownie. It was his first look at New York, and the Manhattan skyline impressed him. Staten Island did not. The bus ride along a rural road to the Dodds was dreary. Shifting in the cracked leather of the seat, he said, "What's she like?"

"You'll know soon enough," Shell said. "All I ask is you bite your tongue."

The house was in no more disrepair than he remembered, though shrubs and bushes had grown wild. Mrs. Dodd met them on the porch, told them Mr. Dodd was napping, and ushered them in. Her silvery hair had gone white, though she was still slim, still commanding. Her eyes were overly large in a face that high cheekbones gave a hollow elegance. In the parlor she told Shell to sit and David to stay standing.

"I want to look at you, see what I got for a grandson." She peered at him full in the face and then from an angle. "He looks more like you than Helen, but where'd he get that dark hair?"

"My father had dark hair," Shell said.

She edged closer to David. "On the other hand, you look somewhat like my son, your uncle. He's in the movies."

David smiled. "Dad told me."

"But he's not going anywhere," Mrs. Dodd said with a grimace. "His parts keep getting smaller. Last one he didn't have anything to say." Abruptly she focused on the camera David was holding. "Where'd you get that?"

"It's my mother's."

"Not hers to begin with, but you're welcome to it." She looked down at Shell. "We won't talk of Helen. This is to be a pleasant time."

Dinner was at seven-thirty. Mr. Dodd appeared at the table with his hair matted from a sleep still stamped in his face. The alcohol on his breath was from a nip he had sneaked. He stared at David.

"It's your grandson," Mrs. Dodd said.

Reaching across the table, he shook David's hand. Elisions in his memory left him staring at Shell.

"Helen's husband, you damn fool."

Dinner was noodles and rationed hamburg. Oleo margarine in lieu of butter. Radishes from Mr. Dodd's victory garden. Mrs. Dodd, leading the conversation, told of U-boats lurking in the waters off Staten Island and of spies reportedly making it to shore on rubber rafts. Mr. Dodd spoke of Pershing, and Mrs. Dodd rolled her eyes.

"Wrong war, idiot."

She served coffee on the moonlit porch, Royal Crown cola for David, who sat still in a rocker until a neighbor's golden retriever trotted up to the steps. Mrs. Dodd, who had a cat, instantly shooed it away. She didn't like dogs. Dogs licked their balls. Cats were clean. They buried their shit.

Gazing up, Mr. Dodd mulled the stars. "Who put them up there? Who could reach so high?"

Mrs. Dodd gave him a look.

"It was rhetorical," he said with a small spark of anger.

Bedtime, Mrs. Dodd assigned rooms. She gave Shell Helen's and David his uncle's. David undressed near a window open to a stiff breeze. The muslin curtain lurched at him. He avoided the dresser mirror, as if it had been stationed to catch him at something. In his pajamas he tiptoed from the room and looked in on his father.

Shell, caught unawares, was sitting fully dressed on the edge of Helen's girlhood bed. He had one of Helen's dolls in one hand and a small gilt-framed picture of her in another, each of which he swiftly put aside.

David whispered, "Dad, do we have to stay?"

III ≡ III

David slept hard in an unfamiliar bed, dreamed vividly, and woke as if from another life. He thought he was the first one up until he slipped into the high humidity of the bathroom, where Mrs. Dodd had taken a long hot shower. When he was stepping out of his, she barged in and took away his dignity. He groped for a towel, but she stood in the way.

"Stand straight," she ordered. She had her hair in a net, wore a white smock, and stood with the stiff air of a nurse. "I checked your room. I'm glad you're not a bed wetter. Your uncle was."

A cupped hand gave his body token modesty but otherwise left him open for appraisal. Mrs. Dodd tilted her head. Her look was at once offhand and intimate, suggestive more of a doctor than a nurse and little of a grandmother.

"Stay skinny, you'll get by. The public prefers lean men."

Shedding water, his nakedness chilling to him, he waited for her to leave. She didn't.

"The more I look at you, the more I don't see anything of us. You must be all your father's people." She bowed her head for an instant. "Where did you get those big feet?"

He wanted to cry. He wanted to be clothed. He wanted to go home. She tossed him the towel, which he snared with his free hand.

"Cornflakes for breakfast. That suit you?"

The nearly empty box held enough for one bowl. When Shell appeared, she served him Kellogg's All Bran natural laxative cereal, usually reserved for Mr. Dodd, who was sleeping late. Her face a crust of disapproval, Mrs. Dodd eyed what Shell was wearing.

"You were born in this country, weren't you?"

He nodded. "Why do you ask?"

"It's impossible to take seriously a man who wears his shirt collar spread outside his jacket. Coffee?"

"Please."

David excused himself and went outside. Mrs. Dodd poured coffee for Shell and herself. Through the window they watched David pat the golden retriever. Mrs. Dodd liked the look of David's hands. Long and sensitive. "He seems intelligent," she said. "I'm glad he's headed for Andover. Your doing? I wouldn't have expected it of you."

"I'm full of surprises."

Ignoring the remark, she sipped her coffee and made a face. "Someone in the family should make his mark. Might as well be him."

She didn't protest when Shell, concocting a flimsy excuse to cut the visit short, said that he and David were leaving before noon. She cleared the table and laid the morning newspaper before him. The biggest headlines were of battles.

"Lucky for you you're not in the war," she said. "You're German, aren't you?"

"That's my ancestry. Otherwise, I'm an American."

"Yes, aren't we all."

Mr. Dodd was up before the bus was due. Wearing white duck pants and a cashmere pullover frazzled at the elbows, he had the air of landed gentry. His smile for Shell and David diminished when he realized they were leaving. He stuck a hand out to David.

"Haven't got to know each other, have we?"

Mrs. Dodd said, "Go eat your breakfast."

The bus stop was a short way down the road. Mrs. Dodd said her good-byes at the end of the brick walk, where she gave David a sudden and surprisingly affectionate chuck under the chin. "I see good things coming to you. You have a future." Turning to Shell, she lowered her voice. "You tell Helen I was asking for her."

On the bus David sat with his face to the window, a hand shading his eyes. When the bus started up, he said, "I don't want to see her again."

"I didn't think you would," Shell said. "She has nothing to do with us."

On the ferry David gave his father a stricken look. "I forgot the camera."

"Just as well. I'll get you another."

David thrilled to the swarm of Grand Central Station. Soldiers in tans and sailors in whites were everywhere. Here and there were marines in fancy dress. "I wish I was old enough."

"I'm glad you're not," Shell said.

It was late when they arrived back in Haverhill. It was the night of the Fourth, and someone was defying the ban on pyrotechnics. Behind Moody School shots were fired high into the sky, where they hissed and popped and flowered into a glitter the darkness swiftly wiped away, like an eraser sweeping a slate.

III ≡ III

Sitting in a lawn chair on the hospital grounds, Helen watched a beech leaf tumble from an upper branch and said, "Another summer down the drain." Then she dipped her head and said, "I'm sorry, I don't know you."

"Look at me close," the man said from an uncomfortable crouch. "Bill. Bill Weskett."

"Sorry. My mind wobbles."

"I was your insurance man. We were friends, more than friends."

His words were an intrusion. She would have preferred eavesdropping on the conversation of birds, but he pushed his voice closer.

"I've never gotten over you, Helen. Chances are, I never will." His hand touched her knee, only for an instant. "If I'd known you were here, I'd have come long ago."

All that was familiar about him was his suit, too thick for the glare of the day. She glimpsed sweat in his hairline. With a cool smile, the sort her mother might have given, she said, "Nice of you to come, Bill."

"Your husband cashed in one of the policies. The request came to my desk, and I called him. That's how I found out about you."

"How much money did he get?"

"Wasn't much. Under a thousand. He's sending the boy to private school. David. See, I remember your son's name."

An elderly man, spindly and sere in a superannuated coat sweater, gave them a toothless grin as he shuffled by, though his eyes seemed to register nothing. "Something rarefied about madness, don't you think, Bill?"

He stared intently at her. "Are you happy here?"

"Give me a moment. I'll try to be."

"You look wonderful. Still beautiful."

"Fair skin and straight noses were priorities in my family." She pointed to her left. "Look, there's a butterfly. Can you catch it?"

"I don't think so."

"You're not trying."

"I know I can't."

From one of the buildings came shrieks of hilarity, as if someone had whiffed laughing gas. From the beech tree came cries of jays. "Oh, dear," Helen said in sudden distress, and then, in discomfort, began tugging at her dress. "I've wet myself."

"What?"

"I've been holding it."

He was marvelous. After a quick look over his shoulder, he helped her skin off her underpants and provided a monogrammed handkerchief for her to dry herself. She tried hard to recollect him but couldn't.

"I'll keep the hankie," she said, "and wash it for you."

His face swam with sweat. "I'll take care of it," he said, and snatched it back as if it had become valuable.

"How long were we lovers?" she asked.

"Not long enough."

She couldn't imagine what she had seen in him. He had the rough big-nosed face of a peasant, the sort her mother surely would have mocked. "You may kiss me if you like," she said, and pushed her lips out.

The kiss could have gone on, but she curtailed it, leaving him with the taste of vermilion lipstick. Shell had brought her the lipstick on his last visit, though she had not asked for it. She bunched up her sodden underpants and stashed them under the bench.

"I'd have done everything for you, Helen."

"Everything can be too much," she said.

||| ≡ |||

They attended Sunday services at Trinity Episcopal, a small stone church snugged into cramped greenery on White Street, across from Hec and Joe's Diner. David was a choirboy in creamy ruffles worn over a black cassock, an alto dominated by sopranos.

The rector, Father Henry, was warm and gentle and known to drink. His sermon was on chaos and confusion, without which, he said, man would never learn how to put things in order. Without dreams, he intoned, man would never see the other side of himself.

After the service Shell waited near a stained window for David to change from cassock to street clothes. Father Henry, stationed at the high doors, bade farewell to the faithful readying to brave a stiff fall wind. When he closed the doors, Shell approached him.

"Your sermons are always interesting, Father."

"The greatest mystery, Shell, is the secret of ourselves. We're like books. Books can't read themselves." His smile was immediate and contagious. Fifty years were faintly scribbled on an uneven face made interesting by imprecisions. "How's David doing at Andover?"

"Academically he's fine. Otherwise, I'm not so sure."

"It's a fine school. It'll give him a key to open doors."

"I've tried to impress that on him."

David, in a herringbone jacket and flannel slacks, emerged from a narrow doorway near the altar. Father Henry, smiling, said, "You're an ambitious man, Shell."

"Yes, for him."

Shell and David exited the church. David, shod in cordovan loafers, shuffled through blown leaves. His hair flew up as they crossed the street. Shell picked up the Sunday paper in Aram's, a variety store with a soda fountain, where David had a quick Coca-Cola spiked with lime.

"Don't spoil your dinner," Shell said.

They sat in a booth in Hec and Joe's, where their roast-pork dinners were served by a heavyset waitress with a smile for everyone. Shell was separating the paper, the sports section for David, who was keen on the World Series. Baseball no longer interested Shell. No DiMaggio, Williams, Feller. The best were in the war. Rapidly he peeled pages for news of the Lindberghs and was relieved to find none. He knew that they had returned from England and that Colonel Lindbergh was flying combat missions in the Pacific. He also knew that Anne Lindbergh had given birth to more children, including a daughter.

"Aren't you going to eat, Dad?"

Shell tore a roll and buttered it. "Tell me about school."

"You want the truth? They're all rich kids. I don't fit."

"That's not the way to look at it." Shell narrowed his eyes. "Anyone giving you a hard time?"

"No, it's not like that. I'm a day student, an outsider, so I'm not included in extracurricular stuff. It's like I'm from another planet."

"How do the teachers treat you?"

"They're polite, but they know I'm different."

Shell was quiet for a moment. "Anything else?"

"A minor thing. Day students don't get lockers, so I have to carry everything around with me from class to class, no place to store anything."

Shell mentally tabulated his finances, which were tight. "What if I arranged to have you board there?"

"Too late for this year."

Shell wanted to do right by his son and feared he was doing wrong. In a sudden blaze of memory he saw himself shifting one baby for another, one warm and one cold.

"What's the matter, Dad?"

"Nothing." He composed himself quickly. He didn't want David to be second class but everything he was meant to be. "Will you try to stick it out?"

David mopped up gravy with a roll. "Will you hate me if I don't?"

"I'd never hate you."

"Then let me be like everyone else. Let me go to Haverhill High."

||| ≡ |||

At Haverhill High the American-history teacher, Mr. Pearson, threw chalk at the blackboard when faced with inconsistencies from the class. Confronting similar frustrations, Miss McCormick, the Latin teacher, took deep breaths. Mr. Munn, a pudgy and gentle homosexual who taught biology, showed a face naked with secret sorrows never voiced. Dr. Freeman, whose strength was Shakespeare, popularized bow ties by invariably wearing one.

In Latin class David ignored his book and studied the fall of Miss

McCormick's dense black hair, the cut of her tweed suit, and, when she turned to the blackboard with a stick, the curve of her calves. She had no tolerance for nonsense and unerringly called on him to conjugate verbs when he was least prepared.

"What's the matter, Shellenbach? Your head elsewhere?"

He blushed often. He was at once shy and assertive, withdrawn one moment and noisy the next. Among vital concerns were the razor crease in his gabardines, the fit of his corduroy sports jacket, and the knot of his knit tie. He never went anywhere without a comb in his back pocket. At times he was sure he'd been born special and at other times he feared he was no-account.

The student body was diverse. The Irish and the Italians were the athletes. A strikingly tall kid named Carrozzo, letters in three sports, had the eerie appearance of a gladiator. Greeks were the scholars, the most conspicuous a kid named Evangello who looked like a statue in a suit. No one would have been surprised had he appeared in class with scrolls instead of books.

Another Greek, Zeno, unscholarly, sat beside David in history class. He was languid and olive-skinned in colorful clothes acquired through the mail. Snakelike and perfumy, he slinked into class and slouched in his chair. Called upon, he never offered a thought, only a dream. Once Mr. Pearson fired a piece of chalk at him, missed, and hit David.

David had secret crushes on two Greek girls, Stella, whose eyes were like the darkest grapes in a vineyard, and Calliope, whose features were classic and whose parents were said to lock her up at night. Stella helped him with his Latin; Calliope he was too shy to approach. His dreams, however, were not of them but of Miss McCormick, unclothed, unfettered, except for a pencil clenched lengthwise between her teeth.

The next year he had crushes on two other girls, neither Greek. Barbara was Lithuanian, and Marie was French. Marie had a fragile beauty, as if illness were an essential part of it, and spoke in a voice meant to be half heard. Twice he ate lunch with her in the cafeteria and was devastated when she began eating with someone else. Barbara sat beside him in biology. Aggressively moody, absorbed in him one day and aloof the next, she always left him with the impression that somehow he had disappointed her.

In the middle of the year he was suspended from school for smoking in the boys' lavatory. Shell had to see Mr. Wallace, dean of boys, to get him reinstated. Driving him home, Shell said, "I didn't know you smoked."

David peered straight ahead. "Once in a while."

"Easy to get hooked. An old pal of mine from the Bronx was coughing blood and still smoking. He's dead now."

"I won't do it anymore. I promise."

"Don't promise," Shell said. "Just try not to."

The day Roosevelt died David was in Hale Hospital for an appendectomy. He learned about it from a nurse, who was crying. Her face splintered, she said, "Thank God we're winning the war." She was with him when they rolled him into the operating room and held his hand when someone placed a rubber mask over his face and put him under. When he awoke back in his room, it was as if no time had passed. Shell was at the bedside.

"Roosevelt's dead, Dad."

"I know," Shell said, tears in his eyes. "But you're alive."

||| ≡ |||

When Bill Heath, the crusty editor of the *Gazette*, summoned him into his office, Shell knew that a full-time-job offer was coming and that he'd have to decide on the spot, no hesitation. He also knew that the pay would be less than what he was making at Hersh Brothers.

"I like your work, Shellenbach. No fancy stuff, no bullshit. Just sensible English."

"Thank you, sir."

A Vermonter by birth and a zealous Republican, Heath had had no use for Roosevelt and now none for Truman. In an accusing tone he said, "You're from the Bronx."

"Yes, sir."

"This is not the Bronx."

"No, sir. I've been up here for some time."

"Long as I know you're not a socialist. You're not, are you?"

"I'm not. Never have been."

"And there's nothing criminal in your past."

"No, sir."

Heath stuck a pipe in his mouth, a corncob, part of the cracker-barrel image he'd brought from Vermont. "You know what I'm offering. You want to come on staff or not?"

"Yes, sir. I do."

Heath plucked the pipe from his mouth. "Why?"

"I want to make my son proud of me."

"Good a reason as any. Job's yours."

He gave his notice at Hersh Brothers the next day. Sarky the foreman said he was sorry to lose him but couldn't blame him for wanting to be a suit-and-tie kind of guy. "I guess you won't miss this place."

"You're wrong," Shell said, emotions suddenly tugging at him. "This is where I began a new life."

"This is none of my business, but can I ask you something? What brought you to Haverhill?"

"A Chevrolet," Shell said. "And I still have it."

||| ☰ |||

Gretchen Krause was spending a boozy evening in a bar with a soldier named Ned, who had puffs under his eyes, lacked a full head of hair, and looked too old for a private. He swallowed his fourth whiskey, downed it with beer, and explained he'd been busted down for decking an officer. Noting his hash marks, she asked how long he'd been in the army. He touched his sleeve and said, "Count 'em. All my fuckin' life." Noting his ribbons, she asked where he had seen action. "Everywhere," he said. In the Battle of the Bulge he got hit in the ass with shrapnel, but one of the army nurses was good to him and gave him hand jobs. "You didn't need to tell me that, Ned."

"No, I guess I didn't." He hung his head for a moment. "It's all over now but the shootin'. The Japs don't know that yet, but the Krauts do."

Gretchen toyed with the straw in her mixed drink. Her hair was longer than usual, and her lipstick was overly bright. Suddenly he was staring intently at her.

"You're no spring chicken, are you?"

She lacked energy to be annoyed. "No, Ned, and neither are you. You got a wife?"

"No more."

"Kids?"

"There's a question about that." His eye sought the waiter.

"Don't drink anymore," she said. "We can go to my place if you like."

They took a cab. At her place he had a momentary problem with the stairs. She unlocked the door and was met by stale air and a few telltale odors. While she opened windows he looked at snapshots of young soldiers and sailors pinned to a wall board.

"These all friends of yours?"

"Some of the boys I danced with at the USO. The one you're looking at, his name was Bud. He was killed. Normandy."

"Tough."

"His mother wrote to me. She thought I was his girlfriend."

"What were you?"

"Just a friend. Like I am to you."

He joined her in the bedroom when he heard her rustling off her dress. Her movements were quick. She drew back the spread and re-arranged pillows. He couldn't take his eyes off her. So much to drink in. Stepping close, he ran a hand over and under her bottom.

"You remind me of somebody."

"Don't tell me."

In bed, she did all she could, used tricks that had seldom failed, but nothing worked. He blamed it on her and said, "You ain't got your heart in it." His breathing mouth against her neck became an irritant. Finally he admitted, "It's me. I ain't myself."

"It happens."

He turned his head away and put a fist over his mouth. The belch was an organ note. "It's all comin' to an end, ain't it?"

"The war?"

"Everything."

She touched his receding hair, traced a finger down his brow, and brushed the bridge of his nose. "You going to be OK?"

"Yeah," he said, "I'm gonna grow old and die. So are you."

"You want to just cuddle?"

"No, I wanna sleep."

A while later, his breathing heavy, she left the bed, slipped on an old pajama top, and made up the sofa for herself.

She thought back to the only time Shell had slept on it and remembered holding a finger to her lips. She didn't want him to say a word, only to be good to her, a hug or two.

Her body was tired, but her head was wide awake. She picked up the phone, got the operator, and gave her Shell's number. When a young male voice answered, she said, "This must be David."

"Yes, ma'am."

"I'm Gretchen Krause. Has your father ever mentioned me?"

"Yes, ma'am. He said he grew up with you in the Bronx."

"That's right." She was pleased. "And you, David, you must be all grown up now. Do you have a girlfriend?"

He hesitated. "Sort of."

"Treat her nice. Is your father there?"

"He's gone to bed. He gets up early. Can I give him a message?"

She imagined Shell folded in sleep, a foot perhaps sticking out of the covers. "Tell him I don't like my life."

"Excuse me?"

"Tell him I'm getting married. The man's name is Ned."

There was a silence. "Do me a favor, David. Pretend I didn't call."

III ≡ III

The war was over. In downtown Haverhill the dance long dormant in everyone came out. Crowds thronged the sidewalks and swarmed the street. Motorists honked horns in the crawl of a parade. Children waved little flags. A woman selling long-stemmed roses gave them all away, her gift to the country. A police officer, for the sheer hell of it, fired his revolver three times into the air while men squeezed women they didn't know. In the doorway of Woolworth's David hugged a class-mate he was in love with, kissed her when she raised her mouth, and held on to her. "I don't want to let you go."

Her name was Johanna. She was quite tall, quite blond, and, wearing a cool aqua-blue dress, looked drinkable. She said, "You don't have to."

Shell, a feather in the band of his fedora, worked the street with pencil and pad for the *Gazette*, quick interviews with overexcited people who shouted in his face. Some were crying. A woman with reddish hair arched her bosom and said, "Put the fucking pencil away and kiss me!" He saw hazel eyes and freckled white skin in a face that looked painfully tight. With unexpected abandon he shared an open kiss with her, the first release of passion since the distant night on Gretchen Krause's sofa.

"Great, isn't it?" she said.

"What?"

"Being alive."

Together they pushed through the crowd and entered the swell of voices consuming Lenny's Tap Room. Everyone was standing, shouting, hoisting beer mugs and drink glasses. Shell and the woman got a booth for themselves. He lit her cigarette with the Ronson she had placed on the table.

"Did you lose anyone?" she asked.

"In the war?" He shook his head. "Did you?"

"My husband was a sailor in the Pacific. His ship went down."

"Then this is a bittersweet day for you."

"They're all that way. Do you plan to write about me?"

"Yes, I'd like to."

The waitresses were drinking. One was sitting on the bar. The bartender's laughter seemed to unhinge his jaw. Shell, rising, tried to catch his eye and couldn't.

"I don't live far from here," the woman said.

"I don't know your name."

"You don't need to."

She lived in a brick apartment house near the foot of one of the streets slanting into downtown. Swear words were chalked on the brick. She lived on the first floor, down a corridor, past empty milk bottles. The apartment was small and dark. She switched on lights.

"Excuse the mess."

On an end table was a framed photograph of a sailor, the smile on him gigantic. On the table's undershelf were magazines. Shell said, "Do you read much?"

"Only on the toilet. You married?"

"My wife's been hospitalized for some years."

"You mean, she's mental?"

"Yes."

"Good for her. She's out of it." She snatched up an empty Coca-Cola bottle from the floor, then a bowl from which popcorn had been eaten. "You go in the kitchen, there might be a beer in the fridge."

"No, thanks," he said.

"Look," she said, "I'm going to take a quick bath. Play the Vic if you like."

While sorting through records, he heard her run water. When he glanced up, the sailor in the picture smiled at him. He lifted the lid of the Victrola, activated the turntable, and played the Andrews Sisters' "Shoo-Shoo-Baby." A lover off to the seven seas. The record was scratchy. He played two by Dinah Shore. "Miss You" and "I'll Walk Alone." Something of a requiem in every love song. The sailor continued to smile at him. Putting on another record, he began to feel like unwanted company.

He tapped on the bathroom door and received no answer. The door was ajar. He gave it a push and looked in on her. Lying low and still in the half-filled tub, eyes unfocused, she gave off an exquisite air of unconcern. The water was red.

III ☰ III

His regular beat was police and fire, so he knew the faces. The ambulance attendants gave him queer looks as they hauled the body out. A uniformed cop started to say something to him and thought better of it. Detective-Sergeant O'Grady, whose large face threatened to eat up his eyeglasses, came out of the kitchen with an open bottle of beer from the fridge. He took a swig and said, "Wanna tell me what you were doing here?"

Trembling, Shell explained, or tried to.

Sergeant O'Grady frowned. His grubby brown suit gave him the look of an old cigar. "What are you scratching for?"

"Eczema."

"This is gonna be embarrassin' for you. Heath at the *Gazette* ain't gonna like it. Hanky-panky on the job. Maybe worse."

Shell scratched through his shirt and drew blood. "I'm worried more about my boy."

"Your kid? Should've thought of that before." O'Grady took another swig from the bottle. "I feel bad for you, Shell. I really do. But what can I do?"

Shell stared at the Victrola and at the records he had not returned to their envelopes. The Andrews Sisters were suddenly loud in his head. O'Grady handed him the bottle of beer.

"You didn't know she was gonna slice her wrists, right?"

"I swear I didn't."

"But no note. That's what don't make it look good. See my point?" O'Grady appeared thoughtful, as if he were trying to come up with ways to remove traces of a murder. "We both got careers, right? Tell you what, I can pretend you just got here, came for the story. Save you a lot of grief."

Shell was too stunned to speak.

"I treat you right, you treat me right. Enough said?"

Shell nodded.

O'Grady's smile was large, overpowering, like that of the sailor in the picture. "Get your pad out. You're a reporter, aintcha?"

||| ≡ |||

He phoned Gretchen Krause and in a nervous voice said, "Are you all right?"

"Why wouldn't I be, Shell? What's the matter?"

"Nothing. I was just worried about you." He was at his desk in the newsroom. He scribbled her name on a scratch pad in a hand that didn't look like his own. "You were on my mind."

"You're the one sounds funny," she said.

"It's a big day. Everybody's celebrating. Aren't you?"

"I guess I am. In a way."

"David told me you called."

"That was some time ago."

"He couldn't remember the message. You know how boys are." His eczema flared up, but he refrained from scratching. "I was going to get back to you and didn't. That won't happen again."

"Something's wrong," she said. "What is it, Shell?"

"I guess I'm in a funk." He underscored her name on the pad and then circled it. "I'd like to see you again. Maybe we could have a weekend together."

"Shell."

"What?"

"I'm married."

||| ☰ |||

On a drizzly evening in September Shell dined with Father Henry at Lomazzo's, a downtown restaurant across from Woolworth's. Father Henry, in the choke hold of a big bib, cracked a lobster claw. Shell picked at a piece of haddock he didn't want, no appetite.

"Spill it," Father Henry said. "What's bothering you?"

"Scared, I guess. I'm forty years old, and I don't know what I'm all about."

"We're our own mysteries, don't you know that? If we could see our secret selves, would we be happier or ten times sadder?"

Shell shrugged and momentarily turned his gaze to a young couple across the aisle, the fellow a talker, his red tie dangling dangerously over a plate of lasagna. Shell said, "I've been a good father but a moral failure. Can the two be reconciled?"

"I'd have to know the circumstances."

"I've done bad things in my life."

99

"None of us are saints."

"Sometimes I think I'm evil. I'm not sure I believe in God, but that doesn't stop me fearing hellfire."

Father Henry lifted his wineglass and swallowed heartily. "You're not evil, Shell. An evil man has no such fears. He believes that when his time comes he can sneak into heaven when the Almighty isn't looking."

"You don't know what I've done."

"Do you care to tell me?"

"The burden's mine alone."

Father Henry cracked the other claw, which had the look of a live ember squirting sparks. "Do you blame yourself for your wife's condition?"

"That's the one thing I don't blame myself for," Shell said, and for the third or fourth time noticed that the flimsiest waitress carried the heaviest tray.

"How is she?"

"This may sound strange, but I think she's where she wants to be. Away from the world. Away from me."

The couple across the aisle were preparing to leave. The fellow was using a wet napkin on the tail of his tie. The young woman was already on her feet. Her face, despite the provocative attitude of her body, bore the innocent grain of childhood and brought to Shell's mind an image of Gretchen Krause.

"As for me, Father, I feel abandoned, lonely. If it wasn't for David, I don't know what I'd do."

"You're not unique," Father Henry said. "A man sitting in the warmth of his family may still suffer loneliness, a condition built into him the moment he left the womb."

"I worry about David. He should've stayed at Andover. He deserves the polish of an Ivy League education."

"I wouldn't worry too much about David. Life leans us in the direction we're meant to go, either with the wind or against it."

Outside the wet wind had a sob to it. They hustled to Shell's old Chevrolet and heaved themselves in. Lately the motor had been kicking over only when of a mind. Shell gently pumped the pedal.

"The war's over, they're making cars again," Father Henry said. "When are you getting a new one?"

"David has asked me the same thing. He's learning to drive."

They drove the length of downtown and at the post office turned up Emerson Street, past the Boys Club, where Father Henry, though he had scant athletic skill, spent an evening a week coaching junior basketball. Shell speeded up to make the lights at the intersection of Winter and White. The rectory, a small stone house, was on a side street behind the church. A widower, Father Henry lived there alone. His only child, a daughter, lived out of state. The Chevrolet sputtered to a stop at the curb.

"It was a pleasant evening, Shell. Thanks for picking up the check."

"Thanks for listening to me."

Father Henry pushed his door open but remained seated. "I wasn't much help, was I?"

"I didn't give you much to work with."

"When my wife died I wanted to pack it in. Between you and me, I nearly did. Since then I've concentrated on the manageable chaos of daily life. It takes all my energy but keeps me afloat. Understand what I'm saying, Shell?"

He nodded. "One day at a time and keep busy."

||| ≡ |||

Shell won a regional prize from United Press, first place in the feature category, a story on the second anniversary of V-J Day about a sailor's widow who couldn't bear her loss and took her life in warm water. He enhanced a number of details and embellished her final moments, but the essence of the story rang true. The city editor ran his picture on page one, and Bill Heath gave him a ten-dollar raise. At the police station Detective-Sergeant O'Grady rattled the paper and said, "Nice picture. Looks like you owe me twice."

One day a week he filled in at the news desk and tried to do something about the usual design of butting heads and of photographs perched over unrelated stories, but the city editor told him to leave well enough alone. The rest of the staff was cool to him. Despite the prize, he was somebody out of a shoe factory and before that a refugee from the Bronx.

David said to him, "How come you get more bylines than the other reporters?"

"I work harder."

"One of my teachers, Miss McCormick, says you're a breath of fresh air."

"Nice of her to say that."

They were in a booth at Tuscarora's, a luncheonette up from city hall, in sight of the high school. David had finished off a cheeseburger and was munching on potato chips. "I have a girlfriend, Dad. We're going steady."

"I've seen the lipstick on your collars. I've been waiting for you to tell me about her."

"I've been sort of seeing her since we were sophomores, but now it's real. Her name's Johanna Medwick."

"Medwick. Any relation to the doctor?"

"Her father."

Shell was impressed. The Medwick name was prominent in Haverhill. "It's about time I met her."

"I want you to. We have lots in common. Her mother's dead."

"Yours isn't," Shell said sharply.

"I know, Dad, but you know what I mean. She's not with us."

Shell gentled his tone, smiled, and winked. "Now I have news for you. I finally got around to putting my name on the list for a new car."

"You're kidding! What kind?"

"What kind does Dr. Medwick drive?"

"An Oldsmobile."

"This one's only a Plymouth, but it's a convertible," Shell said with pride. "You'll have nothing to be ashamed of."

||| ≡ |||

Holding hands, they posed for a picture for the yearbook. They were a couple. They wore each other's identification bracelet, sipped soda from the same straw, and in slow kisses traded chewing gum. David relished the shape of her name on his tongue, Johanna in protracted moments, Jo in quick ones. Miss McCormick, a fading dream, had long ceased to occupy his fantasies. Johanna was reality.

They went parking in his father's still-new Plymouth convertible, which had a radio and a heater. Their favorite spot was at Kenoza Lake, the city's reservoir, girded by pinewood.

"This is our place," David said. "We own it."

Johanna's face projected light from the glare of the moon. David loved everything about her: the blue jots of her eyes, the plummy small of her back, the rush of feminine hair inside underpants of floral lace. The slick on his fingers was hers.

"We mustn't," she said, but inhibitions were slithering away, along with the floral lace, which burgeoned his sense of her. On the radio Perry Como followed Peggy Lee. David kissed nipples barely pink. Perry Como was a prisoner of love, David an explorer of the universe. Shadows nuanced Johanna's face into mystery. "Promise you'll be careful."

"I swear," he said as they began rearranging themselves. Her hair, lush when loose, grazed his cheek as she maneuvered a knee over his lap. Her chewing gum was in his mouth. Hands wedged under the warmth of her bottom, he murmured, "I'd go crazy if I lost you."

"You have me."

Later they half lay in each other's arms. Doris Day was bewitched. Dick Haymes was deep in a dream.

Dr. Medwick did not appreciate the late hour Johanna got home but waited until morning to speak to her, out of earshot of the live-in housekeeper. Sipping orange juice, Johanna accepted his reprimand with lowered eyes. Dr. Medwick stood with coffee cup in hand, his appearance solid and sober, from the stiffness of his short haircut to the unblemished shine on his stout shoes. His voice was deep.

"How much do you know about him?"

Johanna lifted her gaze. "What's there to know? Besides, I thought you liked him."

"For your sake I've tolerated him. In the meantime I've done some checking." He looked at her pointedly. "This is not a boy you want touching you."

"Daddy!"

"Has he told you where his mother is?"

"It's not anything he's tried to hide."

"Insanity tends to run in a family. Is that what you want, Johanna?"

"David's what I want," she said with a trace of insolence.

"Then you're a fool." He took a final sip of coffee and returned the cup to the saucer. "How about college?"

"I want that too."

"What's the sense if you get yourself pregnant?"

She verged on tears. "That won't happen."

"Let's hope not." Dr Medwick said, and turned sharply on leather heels.

In the spring, the evening of the senior prom, David brought her to River Street so that Shell, with a camera borrowed from the *Gazette*, could take pictures of them posed against the polished grill of the Plymouth. His eyes glazed at the wonder of them, David tall and handsome in a white dinner jacket and Johanna lushly faultless in chiffon. Lowering the camera, a Speed Graphic, he said to David, "Swear you won't drink. You have a precious passenger."

"I know that, Dad."

"He makes me feel precious," Johanna said.

David slipped into the Plymouth, behind the wheel. Shell, holding the door for Johanna, gave her a warm smile and a kiss on the cheek. "You remind me of someone," he said.

"Your wife, Mr. Shellenbach?"

"Yes, her too."

David drove with the top down, and Johanna didn't mind that her hair blew back. At the prom, the gymnasium festooned, they danced to "Star Dust" and "As Time Goes By." Johanna was a good dancer, David kept his eyes on his feet. Twice she danced with another boy, who had a longtime crush on her, while David pretended he didn't mind. Miss McCormick, one of the chaperones, embarrassed him by reading his face and eyeing him sympathetically as she angled by his table. Returning, Johanna also read his face.

"He doesn't mean anything to me, David. Only you do."

After the prom they didn't go to the Golden Anchor, a club-restaurant where many others were going. Instead, the roof raised, they drove to Kenoza Lake and parked under a pine, where Johanna loosened the tight top of her gown so that he could reach in if he cared to. He sat still, with little to say. They listened to the ring of peepers, the rustle of pines, and the random sounds from the night. Johanna removed her corsage.

"You don't have to be jealous. There's no reason."

"I don't mean to be."

"Oftentimes you are."

Without a word, he slipped out of the car and ambled toward the lake with a sensation that the night was measuring his steps and gauging his whereabouts. The fragment of moon was a talon. Johanna joined him at the water's edge.

"What is it?" she said. "Tell me."

"I've always been afraid of losing something. It began even before my mother went away. Now I'm afraid I'll lose you."

Her shoulders were bare, and she shivered. "Why do you keep saying that? It's silly."

He placed an arm around her. "I've never told this to anyone before, but I've never felt . . . safe. I guess that's the word."

"I don't understand."

"I don't either."

"You're safe with me, David. Am I with you?"

"I love you."

"Then don't let anything get in the way."

He kissed her. "What about your father?"

"He'll come around." She kissed him. "He doesn't have a choice."

Shell took more pictures of them at graduation, the ceremonies held on a perfect May day at the football stadium. Shell wanted Dr. Medwick in one of the pictures, but the doctor declined. His smile for David, rendered for Johanna's sake, seemed to cost him something. David glimpsed Miss McCormick and was struck with the realization that he would probably never see her again and she, perhaps as soon as tomorrow, would lose all memory of him.

Dr. Medwick's graduation gift to Johanna, along with a sizable check, was diamond earrings that had belonged to her mother. Shell gave David a Bulova watch and an emotional hug.

"I wish your mother was here."

"I do too, Dad."

Chums of Johanna were chatting about colleges to her. She had been accepted at Amherst, which pleased her father. David's grades were only fair. He was not Harvard material, nor Dartmouth. Suffolk University, a Boston school Shell had never heard of, had accepted him.

"Have I disappointed you, Dad?"

"You could never disappoint me."

Johanna reached for David's arm, and the two of them began pushing through the throng to turn in their caps and gowns. His eye trailing them, Shell turned to Dr. Medwick.

"Gorgeous-looking pair, aren't they, Doctor?"

"They're from different worlds, Mr. Shellenbach. David doesn't understand that, but I'm sure you do."

Shell was holding David's diploma, which was framed in Leatherette and garnished with a ribbon. "When I was their age," he said, "I understood everything. Now, nothing."

CHAPTER SIX

YOU GOT A CRIMINAL RECORD?"

"No, sir," David said.

"Wouldn't lie to me, would you?"

"No, sir."

The sergeant had fleshy pads under his eyes and ears pressed flat, like gills, against his head. He wore two rows of ribbons. "Anybody in your family ever been in a mental institution?"

"No, sir," David lied. "How about yourself? You ever been in one?"

"No." The sergeant was going through a checklist. The marks he made were in ink. "Have trouble sleeping at night?"

"No."

"Do you stutter?"

"Sometimes, I guess. When I get nervous."

"But you don't go bu-bu-bu-bu, do you?"

"No, sir."

The sergeant slid a sheet of paper across the desk and gave David the pen. "OK, you sign at the bottom. You won't have a problem with the physical. You look like a healthy kid to me, not like some that come in here."

When David left the post office, he was hot in the face and unsure he had done the right thing. The decision had been impulsive more than anything else. When he got home, he spooned Ovaltine into a glass of milk and said, "I joined the army."

Shell thought he was joking and then, with a jolt, realized he wasn't. "You didn't!"

"It's what I want, Dad."

Shell stepped to the table and sat down hard. A deep uneasiness instantly took hold. "I don't understand. You've been accepted at Suffolk."

"I'm not ready for college. I'm not ready for anything, Dad. I don't know what I want to do or be." He sipped his Ovaltine. "The physical's Friday."

"Maybe you'll flunk it."

"The sergeant says I've nothing to worry about."

Something tore at Shell's heart, he didn't know what. "What have I done wrong?"

"Nothing, Dad."

"What did Johanna say?"

"I haven't told her yet."

David told her that evening at Kenoza Lake. They were sitting in the open Plymouth in sight of the moon taking a picture of itself on the water. Insects racketed the pinewood. Johanna said, "Are you sure you know what you're doing?"

"I hope so."

She was wearing shorts. His hand was on her knee. She said, "Why didn't you talk it over with me first? It's like I don't count."

"You count for everything. You're my life."

"Doesn't sound it. Why did you do it, David?"

He didn't have a real answer and had to grope for one. It was something to do, a place to go, an urge had driven him. He said, "You'll be at Amherst. I'll hardly ever see you."

"I thought I knew you, but I'm nowhere near the mark," she said, and turned her head to look at the lake.

"Are you mad at me?"

"I want what you want, David, but I don't think you know what it is."

⫼ ☰ ⫼

The housekeeper said Father Henry was in the parlor having a little chat with God. "But go right in," she said. Shell found him sitting in an armchair. The glare of a lamp showed him smoking a cigarette. Also in the glare were the remains of a glass of port. Shell spoke softly.

"I don't mean to interrupt."

"Who says you are? Care for some port? No? Sit down then."

Seated, Shell said, "I didn't know you smoked."

"Only in certain situations."

"Anything wrong?"

"Nothing serious, just a crisis of faith. It happens every so often." Father Henry ground out his cigarette and smiled. "What can I do for you?"

"I hate to burden you with a problem of my own."

"Hit me with it."

"It's David," Shell said with a long face. "He's joined the army. It makes no sense."

"The world frequently makes no sense. It made no sense the day the Japanese bombed Pearl Harbor. It made no sense whatsoever the night my wife died. So there you have it. We live with it."

"You don't understand. He's making a mistake."

"It's his life, Shell. Not yours."

"He should have the best."

"Did you?"

Shell took a slow breath. "I wasn't supposed to."

Father Henry drained what little port remained in his glass, rose with effort, and moved with uncommon rigidity to a decanter. Slowly he refilled the glass.

"You're spilling it, Father."

"Am I? Yes, indeed I am." He returned at a slow pace to his chair as if letting his age catch up to him. Carefully he reseated himself. "You're a sad man, Shell, and I don't know why."

"Perhaps I will have some port," Shell said, and got to his feet.

"Did you hear what I said?"

"Yes."

"One of these days you're going to tell me something I don't want to hear."

"No," Shell said, "that will never happen."

III ≡ III

Evenings, when everyone else was asleep, Anne Lindbergh wrote in her journal. She transcribed her most intimate thoughts in a tight and nearly illegible hand. When she lost her train of thought she went into flights of fancy and filled pages with the hope of discovering herself. Afterward, favoring poetry, she read until her eyes gave out.

Her dreams were usually dramas of vague unrest and uncertainties. Occasionally invincible fears defined them. The latest one woke her with a start, and she reached for her husband with a hand that didn't wake him. His breathing was heavy, as if through willpower he could sleep the sleep of the dead, to be or not to be no longer a question. Her greatest fear was losing him.

They lived now in a private section of Darien, Connecticut, in a modest house almost too small for the family, which had grown to three sons and two daughters. Safety in numbers. She and Charles seldom mentioned their lost son, but one morning at the breakfast table, without meaning to, she said, "Do you realize how old he'd be now?"

"Yes." They were alone at the table, scrambled eggs on their plates. "He'd be in college."

"Princeton."

"Perhaps."

Her eyes were filling. "More coffee?"

"Please."

She was glad he was home. Often he was not. He was a member of a government committee on rocketry and an adviser to the Air Force, which was flying supplies to a blockaded West Berlin. A hidebound anti-Communist, he believed in aggression in the name of democracy

110

and was cold and absolute in his arguments. Opponents called him arrogant.

Anne feared for his safety. He was still an American hero but despised by those who had never forgiven his admiration and support of the Nazi regime before the war. Left-wing journalists were cruel, some vulgar. "His political opinions," one wrote, "have hardened into stools most people would find painful to pass." Anne destroyed the magazine before he could read it.

At noon she served him lunch in his office, which was a trailer installed behind the house. He was writing furiously, drafting a response to a congressman who wanted his views on military matters. Careful not to disturb him, she quietly set the tray on his desk and turned away. He reached out.

"Don't go."

Their fingers entwined. She knew what they meant to each other. Each was the other's rose on a gray day. He was a knight on a winged horse. She was the only one in the world he trusted. She felt safe only in his arms, though even there came moments of disquiet. In the worst of them she felt solitary, neglected, dominated. With the loss of her firstborn, she had surrendered much.

"What is it, Anne?"

Except in her journal, she could never hide anything from him. When he looked into her eyes she was sure he could see into her skull. Rising, he took her into his arms.

"Tell me."

"Life isn't what I thought it'd be."

"You've known that for a long time," he whispered. "But we go on because we're meant to. It's decreed."

Late that evening she was back at her journal, the pen pausing and then going on again. She listed the names of her live children. Jon, Land, Scott, Anne, Reeve. She feared loving any of them too much. Remembering Jon's childhood fantasy of living in a tree house hidden by foliage, she recorded it and added her own fantasy of paradise, which was an island, any island, where no human has set foot. Her dark eyes stared at the page when the pen again paused. Then it moved. *Charles leaves early tomorrow for Washington. I shall miss him.*

Charles was dead asleep when she crept into their bed. Soon she was asleep and dreaming of seawater, of waves carrying her out, no return, her cries for help unheard or, if heard, ignored. Then came a voice imploring her to hold on. Charles was swimming toward her.

||| ≡ |||

David spent eight days at the induction center at Fort Devens. He had a shorn head, wore shapeless fatigues, and looked like a refugee. He considered the shrill of a whistle at four-thirty in the morning an inhumane way of waking people up. Standing outside in formation with unbrushed teeth in the chill predawn was punishment for no crime committed and a bitch of a way to start the day. Many of the sergeants, some more than others, looked like maniacs. He felt he knew what a high-security prison must be like.

On the fourth day they added to his wardrobe a real uniform, but the pants didn't fit. Not his to reason why, he was told. A sergeant yelled, "Move on, Buster!"

So far, nothing made sense, and he suspected nothing would. A naked row of open toilets assaulted his sensibilities. Nobody should be made to move his bowels in glaring view of others performing the same function.

"What's the matter, Shellenbach?"

The speaker was Tony Tonetti from East Boston, with whom he shared a double bunk. Tonetti had the bottom because they had flipped a coin.

"I haven't had a dump since we got here," David said.

"Shit, man, neither have I."

"What should we do? Prunes?"

"Fucking pray," Tonetti said.

Everything was hurry up and wait. They stood in a formation for some officer to arrive. David whispered, "I hate it here. I wish I was home."

"We could hit our heads against a wall, make 'em think we're crazy," Tonetti said. "You do it first."

When the officer arrived a sergeant threw his shoulders up and yelled out. Everyone snapped to attention. Tonetti was short, but cockiness was a shim to his height, which didn't prevent him from whispering, "I don't like standing next to you. We're like Mutt and Jeff."

In the mess hall, eating off a metal tray, David said, "Why'd you enlist?"

"No fucking brains. What's your excuse?"

"That's the crazy thing. I haven't figured it out yet."

"You got three years to do it." Tonetti buttered his bread whole. "What's your father do?"

"He's a newspaper reporter."

"Then he can read and write. My old man can't."

On the weekend, after waiting in a long and boisterous line, David got to use a telephone and called Johanna. Clutching extra nickels, he said, "I miss you a hundred times more than I thought I would."

"I miss you just as much," she said. "I'm looking at pictures your father took of us at graduation. Do you know yet where you're going?"

"Nobody does."

"My father says there's stuff going in the world could lead to another war."

That was nothing he wanted to think about. His mind was only on her, on their separation. Would she wait? "I love you, Johanna."

She loved him too, she said, and told him that wherever he was sent she would write to him every day. Eventually people began pushing at him from behind and shouting at him. His extra nickels went for naught, for a three-minute call was all he was allowed.

On the eighth day many of the inductees learned they were being assigned for basic training at Fort Worden, which was clear across the country in the state of Washington. David figured that was where he was going too. Instead, he and Tonetti were sent to Camp Stewart in Georgia.

III ≡ III

The tingling sounds in Helen's head merged into a voice. Shell's. Shell, whom she remembered clearly, but who was this soldier son he was talking about? She could not remember having a child but for the sake of argument was willing to take his word for it. His hand wanted hers, and she let him take it and put it briefly to his mouth.

"How are you doing?"

She looked at him with annoyance. How could she explain a sourceless melancholy? How could he understand when she couldn't? With sudden anger, she said, "Who gave my hair permission to go gray?"

His eyes explored. "It's not all gray, but would you like to color it?"

An inane question. She wasn't going anywhere, though she did have visitors. "You're not the only one who comes to see me."

That caught him by surprise. "No? Who else?"

What was his name? Wessel, Weston? She couldn't remember. "Doesn't matter," she said. "He doesn't mean anything to me."

"Do you need anything?"

Cookies perhaps, the kind her grandmother had baked, icing on the edges. "What can you give me?"

He said something she didn't hear. His image dwindled. She could impose moods upon herself that distanced her not only from others but from herself. He spoke louder.

"I understand you're on a new medication."

A critical moment passed when she thought she might vanish. Her disappointment that she hadn't was immense. Shell's image returned in gray tones, which made him look old. Her lips gave out the illusion of a smile.

"Dear Shell," she said. "How is your cold?"

His eyes told her he didn't have one. Her mistake. When he rose to his feet he seemed to grow more monotone, as if his past were shrouding him.

"You look tired," he said. "I'll leave now."

"How long have you been here?" Now it was she asking an inane question. Time meant nothing to her.

"Maybe twenty minutes."

The kiss he gave her was dry. She felt like a child given a spoonful of pretend food. She watched him walk to the door and open it. She was not one of those who had to be locked in. When he looked back, she said, "Yes, I'd like to color my hair."

III ☰ III

Gretchen Krause's married name was Ryder, but the marriage didn't work. Ned had considered himself a career soldier, but after the war the army didn't want him any longer. For a while he lived off his mustering-out money and then off Gretchen, which she would have tolerated had he not been a drunk who went off on binges and returned brutal, never contrite. In bed, when able to perform, he thought he was still a soldier. Slam, bam. Thank you, ma'am. She'd have put up with that too had she been allowed to care for him, to nurse his hidden wounds, whatever they were.

"Marrying was your idea," he reminded her, "not mine."

Divorce was his idea, which came to him on a hot summer night when he was drinking whiskey as if fueling himself for winter. Wearing only army undershorts, he told her he wanted to go to Florida and marry some rich old bag. He was both drunk and serious, though his half-smile was open to interpretation. She chose to ignore it.

"I wish you luck," she said.

He looked at her hard, through a haze of his own making. "You'll be better off."

"We'll see," she said.

After the divorce she kept his name for reasons that made no sense only when she thought about them. After a week of gloom and biting back tears, she got herself a new job waitressing in a bar-restaurant. When business was slow she chatted with customers at the bar. Though no longer young, men still wanted her. One told her she was built for love. Blouse open, she was melons. On a bed she was a fruit basket for the needy.

With no word from Ned, she had no idea whether he had found what he was looking for in Florida. She sincerely hoped so because she didn't want to think of him dying in some fleabag motel. She had a dismal dream of him swallowing a jigger of whiskey that went down too hard and came back up. Then one day, picking up her mail, she stared at an envelope postmarked Miami but with no return address. Inside was a hundred-dollar bill and a slip of paper that read: *For the good times*.

She tucked the bill into her purse and saved the slip of paper. Had he bothered to sign it, she might have cried. One of her gentleman friends had given her a television set, but she still preferred the radio. Kate Smith singing "God Bless America" gave her a thrill. *Lux Radio Theatre* gave her drama, but after it was over she had none. The tick of the kitchen clock mocked her.

She hadn't been in touch with Shell in ages and, picking up the phone, hoped he was still at the same number. His voice warmed her. He said he'd been thinking of her, and she didn't doubt him. She remembered his boyhood smile and his habit of kissing half her face and saving the rest for Rudy.

"I'm divorced, Shell. I'm a two-time loser."

"I'm sorry."

"It was for the best." She twined the telephone cord around her wrist. "I'm more myself now."

"Then you're OK?"

"I'm coasting," she said. "I just don't know if there's anything ahead. You ever feel that way?"

"I've had my moments."

"I think I need a change, Shell. I mean, a big one." She freed her wrist. "What's Haverhill like?"

||| ≡ |||

At Camp Stewart they lived eight to a tent. The tents had concrete floors, wooden sides, and screen doors. David and Tony Tonetti had cots side by side. Tonetti said, "I feel like a fucking Boy Scout."

The Georgia sky had a pink glow, as if somewhere far off a great fire were burning. The texture of the air was different from that of New England air. Heat and something sumptuously sticky were built into it. The ground was red clay out of which grass merely pretended to grow. David heard horror stories about coral snakes but never saw any.

He trained with a carbine but was never really comfortable with it and barely managed to make marksman. He despised the look of a bayonet, too primitive a weapon, too simplistically lethal, and felt it belonged only in a John Wayne movie. A challenge was crawling on his belly while a machine gunner fired live rounds over his head. His only fear was that the gunner would riddle him for the sheer fun of it.

The most degrading duty, which Tonetti called slave labor, was pulling KP from sunup to sundown. The bosses were cooks in filthy whites who had evil eyes and unspeakable habits. When they weren't spitting on the floor they were spitting in the food, which made David question the necessity of eating.

He learned to block his fatigue cap with cardboard and blouse his boots with rubber bands so that he wouldn't look like a raw recruit. Real soldiers, he later learned, used condoms. The real *real* soldiers, he suspected, were the gung-ho types completing airborne training. They wore starched suntans and shiny paratrooper boots with distinctive laces.

"Fucking crazy," Tonetti said. "Imagine jumping out of an airplane."

"They must do it for the extra money," David said.

"Naw, they do it to prove something. Me, I got nothing to prove."

For David, the vital time of day was mail call. He lived for letters from Johanna, who, though busy with her studies at Amherst, wrote every day. He relished her long letters and brooded over her short ones. In his worst moments he imagined upperclassmen targeting her. Agonizing was when he received no letter from her, though he was sure to get two the next day.

Tonetti, who seldom heard from home, said, "You shouldn't let a cunt get to you like that."

David turned on him. "Don't call her that!"

"Jesus Christ, it's just an expression."

On a twelve-hour pass he and Tonetti went to a clapboard gambling casino on the outskirts of Hinesville. David found jerking the arm of a slot machine boring. Tonetti was a card-counter and felt he had an edge at the blackjack table, but the dealer had the odds and cleaned him out.

"Let's get the fuck out of here."

David had twenty dollars behind a secret flap in his wallet, emergency money his father had sent him. He lent half to Tonetti.

"I'll pay you back, I swear to God."

Downtown Hinesville was a gaudy strip crowded with soldiers and had slot machines in every little store. David bought picture postcards in a souvenir shop and settled at a window table in a hamburger joint to wait for Tonetti. Tonetti went to a cathouse on a side street, but the women were booked solid.

"This ain't my lucky day," he said upon returning, and sighed through his nose. "We should've gone to Savannah."

"We wouldn't have had time."

"I'd have made time. Fucking army owes me."

The bus back to camp was overloaded, and they had to stand in the aisle. A number of black soldiers, paratrooper braid on their caps, were talking loud and shouting to buddies deeper in the bus, which got on Tonetti's nerves.

"Fucking niggers," he whispered. "They must be from the North."

David glanced at him sharply. "How would you like it if I called you a wop?"

"I've been called a wop all my life. That's what I am."

They were among the first off the bus, a half-mile from the tent area. They walked in the wrong direction but soon reversed themselves. The night sky had a purple cast more mournful than rich. The moon, to David, was a skull without a brain. Tonetti broke a silence.

"You know the funny thing about you, Shellenbach? You never fucking swear."

David nodded. "I've been meaning to, but I forget."

His next letter from Johanna was postmarked Haverhill. She had gone home for the weekend, done a big laundry, bought a winter coat at Mitchell's, watched Milton Berle on television, and on Sunday dropped in to see his father. *Guess what*, she wrote. *I think he has a girlfriend.*

CHAPTER SEVEN

AT A TABLE IN HEC AND JOE'S, SHELL SAID, "HELEN'S gone. David's gone. She's a godsend, Father."

"Yes, I can imagine."

"It's not what you think. It's companionship. Being alone isn't easy."

"Tell me about it," Father Henry said with a dull edge, and stirred his coffee. A week ago he had glimpsed the two of them together and envisioned private scenes of great breasts blustering into Shell's arms, gifts from a good woman. "Actually," he said, "I'm happy for you."

"I've known her since she was a kid. She's had a tough time. Two bad marriages."

The only woman Father Henry had known in the round was his wife, and she was gone. To heaven, he hoped, though he had doubts about its existence. If heaven truly existed he did not imagine it crowded. "Companionship is important."

"Perhaps loving friendship is the truer description," Shell said.

"I think you're lucky to have her. What did you say her name is?"

"Gretchen Krause. Actually she goes by Ryder now. Gretchen Ryder."

Father Henry inclined his head. Names were important, and hers had a certain ring. His wife had been a Wetherbee and her mother a Martineau. His mind suddenly was full of names, like a phone book.

"I'm not sure David will understand," Shell said.

He remembered the name of the proprietor of the ski lodge where he and his wife had honeymooned, of the doctor who had delivered their daughter, of the nurse who had cared for her during her last year, though he had been the real nurse. Bathing her, dressing her, he had tried to preserve the waning curl in her hair. His daughter, living in Michigan, told him he couldn't do everything, and that was true. He couldn't keep her alive. He said, "What's there to understand? David's no longer a boy."

"That also weighs on me."

"You've done a good job raising him."

"Best I could, Father, that's the whole truth."

Father Henry restirred his coffee, which had cooled. The funeral had been a blur, his daughter in charge. Pills had provided him the smother of sleep, but eventually he'd had to get up. There had lain the challenge, each day a door to be forced open. "Gretchen Ryder, you say. I'd like to meet her."

"I want you to."

Father Henry thought of women as poetry waiting to be written. Men were prose awaiting editing. Occasionally such thoughts crept into his sermons, which bemused some of his fold. "Does she put night cream on her face?"

Confused for a second, Shell said, "I don't think so."

"My wife used to." Father Henry smiled through a mist of memory. "Not *every* night of course."

III ≡ III

Gretchen Ryder slept under model airplanes hanging from the ceiling in David's room. She used a single drawer in David's dresser and a corner of his closet and otherwise disturbed nothing except an old baseball glove that looked familiar.

Mornings she made breakfast for Shell and evenings had supper waiting for him. In between she looked for a job. She had her name in at the Belle Shoppe, Mitchell's Department Store, Mohegan's Market, and Karelis Jewelry. Shell suggested Western Electric. It was factory work, he said, but cleaner than shoe shops and better paying.

"I don't think I could be part of a herd," she said. "I have to stand out, at least a little. But I'll find something soon and get out of your hair, I promise."

"You're not in my hair," he protested. "It's like I'm living again."

She felt she was too, though in a curious floating way, her life in ambiguous transition. "Do you ever think of Rudy?"

"Now and then."

"Why didn't he take care of himself, Shell? He could've lived longer."

"It was borrowed time no matter how you cut it. Everything in my life is borrowed, even my son."

"That's a funny thing to say."

"I guess I'm being philosophical." He smiled. "It'll pass."

Within the week she was summoned to work at Mitchell's, in lingerie and hosiery, nine to five except on Fridays, which involved evening hours. When she brought back her first paycheck she said, "I'll start looking for a place of my own."

"I don't want you to," he said. "I want you to stay here."

"What'll you say to your son?"

"I've worried too much about that. I think he knows what it's like to need a woman's love."

"Is that what you need from me, Shell?"

He reached for her hand. "I need you here."

After supper they sat in the living room. He had bought a television set, but instead they listened to the radio. Gretchen seldom missed an episode of *I Love a Mystery*. Television forced her to keep her eyes open. She sat at the far end of the sofa with her legs curled under her. When the program ended Shell waited for her to open her eyes.

"You haven't told me much about your ex-husband."

"Ned?" She laughed unnaturally. "He wasn't much of a husband, more a boarder who came and went as he pleased. He used to scare me in bed. It was like he was still in the war and stabbing the enemy."

"I'm sorry."

"So am I."

"You've never told me anything about your first husband."

Again she laughed, though with less force and more reflection. "He was a hitter. Loved to bat me around. It made him bigger, me smaller."

"No children."

"I wasn't blessed. Maybe I wasn't meant to be."

Sitting with a stillness that seemed forever, Shell said, "Maybe I wasn't meant to be either."

"What are you talking about, you're a wonderful father. That's obvious to anyone."

They listened to another program, a variety show with guest comedians, whose jokes made them smile. Gretchen's eyes were closed, which allowed Shell to stare at length and measure the void between them. When the program ended, she fluttered her eyes open, uncoiled her legs, and stretched her arms.

"I'm going to hit the hay, Shell. D'you mind?"

He minded but said nothing. The kiss she gave him was on the cheek, not on the mouth. He watched her head toward David's room. The door was closed. Watching her open it, he said, "Do you have to sleep in there?"

She turned slowly. "It's unnatural, isn't it?"

In his bed their bodies treated each other as friends sharing old memories, none needing words. His cruising hand was pleasantly rough on her thigh. She remembered throwing a stone at an old man who tried to follow her home from school. She couldn't have been more than six. Shell remembered Rudy waiting his turn.

In the morning she breasted thick vapors and joined him in the shower. Naked, he was hard bones thrown together. Wet, her skin shined as if he were seeing her at her freshest moment. They had the look of secret lovers who wanted to be found out. He soaped her shoulders and her back.

"Am I what you remember?"

"You'll always be that," he said.

III ☰ III

Late in the day David stepped off the train in Boston's South Station and stood lean, smiling, and relevant in his uniform, his Ike jacket cinched tight at the waist. Shell embraced him. The concourse was dissonant rumbles of crowds pushing in different directions. David clutched a bulky overnight bag. Shell, leading the way, said, "Let me take that."

"I can manage, Dad."

The Plymouth was parked on South Street. Shell tossed him the keys. "Wanna drive?"

David tossed them back. "I don't know the way."

Traffic was dense, the streets narrow. On Washington Street came the blast of a policeman's whistle. In Filene's revolving doors were whirlpools of faces. Scollay Square was cobblestoned and glittery. Rose LaRose headlined the Old Howard's marquee. Not until they were out of the city and on Route 28 in Medford did Shell mention Gretchen Ryder.

"I've known for some time," David said, staring straight ahead. "I've been waiting for you to tell me."

"I wasn't absolutely sure how you'd take it."

"Is it that woman from New York?"

"Yes."

"I thought she got married."

"It didn't last." Shell was driving too fast. Up ahead boys on bicycles instinctively pulled over. "She's living at the flat. Do you mind?"

David looked at him. "Mom's not ever going to get well, I know that."

Shell's hands were rigid on the wheel, but the tension in his wrists was lessening. "Tell me about the army."

Basic training over, David was no longer at Camp Stewart in Georgia but at Fort Dix in New Jersey, things Shell already knew. Instead he spoke at length about his buddy Tony Tonetti. "He's not like anybody I've known before."

"Sounds a little like somebody I once knew," Shell said.

Thirty minutes later they were mounting the stairs to the flat. David smelled cooking. Inside the flat he saw a woman in an apron. She had blondish hair tied back, eyebrows in need of a pencil, and a smile that seemed embalmed in goodness.

His father introduced them.

"If I'm in the way," Gretchen said, "promise you'll tell me."

"You're not in the way," David said quickly, his smile polite.

"I hope you like beef stew."

"I can't stay." He looked fast at his father. "Can I borrow the car?"

Shell showed surprise. "You're not driving way out there tonight, are you?"

"I told her I was coming."

Shell tossed him the keys and then took a bill from his wallet. "You'll need gas money."

||| ≡ |||

He drove west, past Worcester and well beyond. He drove hard through the cold night and at times passed other cars where he shouldn't have. On a switchback curve the Plymouth nearly flew off the road. He was frightened a second time when a sixteen-wheeler bore down on him from behind, headlamps blasting, the driver playing games.

At the college, after consulting a hand-drawn map Johanna had enclosed in one of her letters, he easily found her dormitory. She was standing just inside the lit doorway and rushed out in a campus sweater inadequate for the weather. The sight of her rejoiced him. The feel of her propelled him to another plane.

"We can't stay here," she said.

With no known place for them to go, no Kenoza Lake, David drove around in search of privacy. The town looked idyllic in moonlight. Eventually he parked near the crumbling wall of an old graveyard, where headstones tilted randomly, as if the dead were restless.

"What's the matter with the heater?" Johanna asked.

"It conked out halfway up here."

Sex kept them warm, intervals of talking kept them close. Each had custody of the other's emotions. He wanted to know the books she was reading. He wanted to read them too.

"James Joyce," she said. "He's not easy."

"I'll remember the name. Who else?"

"Virginia Woolf. We have to write a paper on her."

"I'll remember her too."

A naked old tree in the graveyard kept a shadowy watch over them. In the moonlight the gravestones looked like crooked teeth that ought to come out. David said, "I think I'm going to be sent overseas."

"Where?"

"I don't know. I'm scared."

"Of what?"

"An ocean separating us. I won't know what you're thinking, what you're doing. I need to know you're mine."

"I *am* yours."

"I don't know what I'd do without you."

"You've *got* me."

In time their bladders forced them from the car. Not a sound came from the night. The moon, not quite whole but exceedingly bright, guided them through a gap in the graveyard wall. David turned his back and set himself. Johanna crouched. Each stared up at stars.

"I want to give you a ring," he said.

"Yes, I want one."

||| ≡ |||

He bought the ring at Karelis Jewelry. Gretchen Ryder helped him pick it out, and Shell provided the down payment and took charge of the payment book. "I didn't know diamonds were so expensive," David said.

"You wanted it to be nice, didn't you?" Shell said.

"Do you think she'll like it?"

"She'll love it," Gretchen said.

He gave it to Johanna for Christmas. He was on furlough and she home on holiday break. Her father wasn't pleased. At the dinner table, where David was an uncomfortable guest, Dr. Medwick said, "Neither of you is old enough to know what you're doing."

"We do, Daddy," Johanna said. "We really do."

"I trust you're not planning to get married right away."

"We haven't set a date."

"I would hope not," Dr. Medwick said, and looked at David. "Do you intend to make the army your life?"

"No, sir."

"It might be the only career you have."

"As you said, sir, I'm still young."

Johanna lifted a platter. "Another lamb chop, Daddy?"

Later she helped the housekeeper clear the table, and after that she and David went into the den to watch Milton Berle. A fire was going, and David stared at it as if the tongues of flame were trying to tell him his future. Seated beside him, Johanna clasped his hand.

"I want to meet your mother."

"She might not know me."

"Don't you want me to meet her?"

"Yes," he said. "I've been waiting for you to ask."

III ☰ III

The crude paw on Helen's knee was Bill Weskett's. Sitting near the window in her room, they gazed at the frost that flowered the lower panes. When he asked how she was feeling, she gave him a thoughtful look.

"I was myself yesterday. Today I'm someone else."

"And who's that?" he asked.

"I haven't been told yet."

His smile was sad and his hand an increasing weight on her knee. "I won't be coming back, Helen. I'm moving to Florida, the wife and I."

Though she didn't mind his hand, she no longer felt a man's touch gave meaning to her body or in any way spoke to what was inside her. "How nice for you," she said. "All that sunshine."

"I'll write to you."

"I like receiving letters if they're not too long."

He viewed her with a large trace of dolor, as if knowing he was already a broken strand in her memory. "Will you miss me?"

"I'll try."

"I suppose that's the most I can ask." He gazed hard into her face and then rose heavily and snatched up his overcoat. "You're the woman I love, God knows why."

"God knows everything," she said.

His wet kiss she could have done without. Alone, wiping her mouth with the back of her hand, she thought of herself as a window left open. Anyone could breeze in and sort through her secrets. She abandoned her chair and, drifting toward the bed, watched the door swing open. The nurse was a heavy bulk of white with a face that suggested she had seen everything.

"You have two more visitors. Are you up to it?"

"Who are they?"

"Your son and a young lady."

She did not remember having a son but did not deny the possibility, for she put stock in possibilities and none in certainties. The world could blow up tomorrow. Or God could alter the rules. "How is my hair?"

"I like the color," the nurse said.

She didn't have long to wait. Soon she saw a soldier and a striking young woman with a large lovely mouth in no need of paint. A pang of jealousy passed, the jealousy unfocused. Suddenly she was being kissed again.

"This is Johanna, Mom. We're engaged."

"So nice to meet you, Mrs. Shellenbach."

The young woman kept her nails nice, and Johanna was not a bad name, three syllables whereas her own only had two. The soldier, her son, vaguely reminded her of the first boy with whom she had touched tongues and allowed a quick feel below the waist.

"Johanna's at Amherst, Mom. Studying English literature."

"Your father and I went to City College." She remembered that quite well. She remembered a hot mind that sometimes wouldn't let her sleep and daylight hours that had the quality of dreams. "I chose your father because he had a safe face."

"I brought you something, Mom."

Chocolates in a ribboned box, which she put aside. Candy gave her toothaches. "Thank you."

David softened his voice. "I might not see you for a while. I'm going overseas soon."

"My grandmother always said one should travel. I never did." She felt they were waiting for her to add something, but she could think of nothing. She remembered long hours with her grandmother, their thoughts so much in common they'd often had only to smile.

"I love you, Mom."

They weren't going to stay, which was just as well. She was tired from keeping her face pleasant. The young woman embraced her and gave her a kiss on the cheek. At least it was dry. Then her soldier son kissed her. His hug was hard. It was the nearness of him that awoke something.

"How's your brother?"

He looked at her strangely. "I don't have one, Mom."

"Of course you do. He'd be big as you now."

Left alone, she returned to her chair near the window and sat with the box of chocolates in her lap. They were for her grandmother. Life, her grandmother had told her, was man and woman, Sluggo and Nancy, Tarzan and Jane, pestle and mortar, and in the end only yourself.

The chair was a rocker, and she rocked slowly, glad to be by herself, her secrets safe inside her skull where even she couldn't get at them. She heard the door open, felt a draft, and glimpsed a shadow. A woman in white nearly trampled her foot.

"What have we here?" the nurse said, gluttony in her voice.

"Step on my foot, I'll forgive you," Helen said. "Take one of my candies, I'll kill you."

||| ☰ |||

Anne Lindbergh dreamed of her firstborn. He was in her arms, and then mysteriously he wasn't. Where was he? She penetrated the dark of the nursery where a touch of moonlight revealed the eyes and nose of a man, who shrank back. She knew what was happening.

"May I at least kiss him good-bye?" she pleaded.

In a gentle voice the man told her not to make it harder on herself.

"He's all I have."

The man said, "No, you'll have others."

Her eyes couldn't pierce the dark, but she had the inner sight of the blind and knew the crib was empty. "What have you done with him?"

"He's safe."

"If he's not in his crib, where is he?"

"He's a man."

She woke with a start, reached for her husband, and roused him with a determined hand. Her head heated, she told him about the dream, word for word, nothing forgotten. "What if he's alive, Charles?"

"Don't torture yourself."

"There's something else." Her voice slipped away from her for a moment and then came back. "The man wasn't Hauptmann."

CHAPTER EIGHT

*T*ONY TONETTI SAID, "WE'RE LUCKY, HUH? MOST GUYS don't get to stay together."

They shipped out from Staten Island on a vintage troopship and spent much of their time in the depths, where hammocks were strung six high and meals served in rapid shifts were eaten standing up. They were at sea ten days. Neither got sick, but others around them did. Tonetti gambled in all-night poker games and did well enough to worry about his winnings, three hundred dollars of which he gave to David to hold.

Trains were waiting at the port of Bremerhaven, where David, duffel bag on his shoulder, suffered a moment of panic. Too many time zones separated him from Johanna, his hours alien to hers, her days his nights.

He and Tonetti were herded into a train that took them to Zweibrucken in the French zone. They settled temporarily in a replacement camp, took showers in fresh water instead of salt, and sat down when they ate.

"Fucking heaven," Tonetti said.

On the third day at the camp they received evening passes and took a taxi into town. The cobblestone streets were dimly lit and narrow, the low buildings huddled, and the air redolent of fossil fuel. Passing Germans, mostly elderly and bundled against the cold, ignored them. Tonetti buried his hands in his overcoat.

"Dreary, ain't it?"

The war had been over nearly four years, but rubble remained. A prostitute who looked battle-worn stepped from a doorway, scowled, and threw David a kiss. It could have been a dagger. Across the street near a fence of iron spears two men rubbed their hands over a barrel of fire.

"Fucking Hans and Fritz," Tonetti said. "Those are the guys burned Jews, kids and all."

"Watch it," David said. "We're supposed to be guests of the country."

"Fuck we are. We're the army of occupation."

A cold wind gusted. Someone clattering by on a bicycle could have been a man or a woman, or even a child.

"Hope our zone is better than this one," Tonetti said. "Otherwise I ain't gonna be happy here."

In a *Gasthaus* crowded with American military David tasted his first Wiener schnitzel. The waitress who served it had a face of sharp bones like pieces of a picture puzzle not all there. Eating knockwurst, Tonetti had mustard on his mouth and some on a thumb, which he licked.

"Still got my money?"

David nodded. "You want it?"

"Just wanna know it's safe."

The noise around them grew. At the next table a sergeant was entertaining corporals with war stories as if he were the voice of history. At another table was a scuffle of boots, and a sudden fight was quickly broken up. David, realizing he was eating veal, visualized the terror in a calf's eye before the blow is struck.

"You can keep a hundred of it," Tonetti said.

"Why?"

"We're buddies, ain't we?"

The beer they drank was dark. The waitress delivered another round, the mugs foaming over, and gave a fast wipe to the table with her bare hand. When she slipped on something, David caught her arm with a quiet strength that tended to surprise.

"*Danke,*" she said in a hollow voice, as if gutted of emotion.

131

Watching her edge away, David had a vivid memory of himself and his mother at Plug Pond, where he used to spit in the water to attract minnows. He remembered his mother removing her sneakers and wading in as if she might not come out. Once she had drenched her dress up to the waist.

The noise grew louder. Cupping a hand behind his ear, he said, "What?"

"I ain't ever had a real one."

"A real what?"

"A real buddy," Tonetti said.

III ☰ III

Late Sunday morning. Gretchen woke first and tried not to disturb Shell as she struggled out of bed. Standing on a braided rug, she lazily scratched her bottom while watching the sun announce itself in cold terms on the window. Eyes half open, Shell said, "You're beautiful."

"Long as you think so," she said, turning.

They gazed at each other as if each had something to explain but the time wasn't right and maybe never would be. He raised an arm to consult his watch.

"I've missed church."

"Father Henry will forgive you."

"Forgiveness is a big word."

"Not if the sin is little," she said.

He used the bathroom after she did, and needed to give the humid mirror several wipes. Shaving, he viewed his face as an old idea never adequately expressed. Nicking himself, he felt it was telling him something. The future was clear, it was his past that was uncertain. Gretchen called to him.

"Oatmeal OK?"

She served it with buttered toast on the side. The kitchen table was between two windows, where each could gaze out at the river, which had unfrozen and was running wild. Pouring coffee, she asked, "Are you visiting Helen this afternoon?"

Sundays he usually did. "I don't know. It doesn't seem to matter to her."

"Does she know about me?"

"There's no need."

Gretchen sprinkled sugar on her oatmeal and added milk. Shell ate his with butter. She said, "If you don't go will you take me to a matinee?" She was in love with Shell, and infatuated with screen stars. Clark Gable, Gary Cooper, Cary Grant. "There's something good playing at the Strand."

"How about this evening instead?"

"I don't want to miss my radio programs." Veiling an emotion with a smile, she poured coffee. "Ever miss the old days, Shell?"

"What old days?"

"You, me, Rudy. Remember when Rudy tried to carry me piggyback? He was scrawny, and I weighed too much."

He remembered instead an Irish tough slamming her against a wall as if to maim her. Was it he or Rudy who had first run to her rescue? Was it he or Rudy who'd had first dibs?

"He was never really a gangster, was he, Shell?"

How could he be sure of anything from a past that wavered and slanted? His parents had died so long ago he occasionally doubted they had existed. A few formal photographs were the only evidence. Even Mrs. Zuber's image was suspect, though somewhere among his possessions was a velvet pouch of baby teeth.

"Was he?"

"He was what he had to be," Shell said. "Same goes for all of us."

He spooned up the last of his oatmeal and helped her clear the table. At the sink she shook soap flakes into a dishpan. Her dress was an old one, not quite a fit.

"Yes, let's catch a matinee," he said.

She pivoted with a smile. "What made you decide?"

"You," he said.

||| ≡ |||

Privates Shellenbach and Tonetti were permanently assigned to Head-
quarters Company, Fourth Infantry Division, in Frankfurt on the
Main. The compound was a former Nazi command post unscathed by
allied bombings. They were billeted in the main building, in a third-
floor room with curtains on the window, single bunks, wall lockers,
and a writing table.

"This is better than I had at home," Tonetti said.

They were assigned to Supply, whose operations occupied the basement of the building. David was promoted to private first class, designated a requisition clerk, and given a desk near the coffee pot. Tonetti
was put in charge of laundry and soon learned that sheets and blankets
were valuable items on the black market.

"I hope you know what you're doing," David said.

Tonetti, stuffing a blanket into a carryall, said, "You gotta take
chances. Otherwise you're a nobody."

David engrossed himself in his job and drew compliments from the
supply officer. The supply sergeant, who had a face like heavy weather,
told him not to fuck up.

He wrote daily to Johanna. *Except for missing you, life is easy here. No
KP. German civilians do all the menial work, but it's sad to see them
rummaging through the trash.*

He told her he liked Frankfurt, busy like Boston, except GI's were
everywhere, jamming the trams, lining the streets, and crowding the
stores to buy Hummels and cameras. He did not mention the beer
halls in the Bahnhof district, in particular the Maier Gustl, where prostitutes lifted their dresses to cool their thighs and undid buttons to
breathe bigger.

Tonetti bragged he was getting more ass than a toilet seat. "It ain't
natural you ain't."

On David's bunk was a bunch of books Johanna had sent him. "I got
these."

"You can't fuck a book."

David opened Joyce and thumbed pages to Molly Bloom's soliloquy.
Molly was Miss McCormick with her hair down and her clothes off.

Tonetti said, "I'll give you a month at the most."

III ≡ III

Mrs. Dodd spent the weekend in Manhattan with an old school friend. When she returned late Sunday evening, her husband was in bed, his eyeglasses, his lower denture, and his good-bye note on the night table. Staring down at him, she expected him to smile or frown, but he did neither. She stood over him until she realized it was not possible to trick a dead man into living again.

The police were considerate. A neighbor called her family doctor, who came over immediately and prescribed a sedative. She didn't want one. "I'm fine, absolutely fine," she said, and watched when they took her husband's body away. "I feel I should wave."

"Are you sure you're all right?"

"Positive."

In the morning, however, she thought her mind was slipping. She stirred her coffee round and round and kept stirring until it slurped over. "I must get hold of myself," she said aloud.

She had phoned her son in California, but it was not until evening that she thought of Helen and called Shell. A woman's voice answered. When Shell came on the line, she said, "Who was that person?"

"A friend."

"Helen's father died in his sleep," she said abruptly, and almost as an afterthought mentioned the pills he had taken.

"Mrs. Dodd, I'm sorry."

"Darwin had it right. It's the strong who stay around." Suddenly her mind was at odds with her body, and she stiffened her stance as if to give an errant chemical in her brain time to correct itself. "There's no need for you to come down. I'm having him cremated."

"I don't know how to tell Helen."

"Is there improvement?"

"She's in and out of herself."

"There's your answer. Tell her nothing." Mrs. Dodd took a deep breath and then another. Through the window she saw neighbors coming up the walk with covered dishes. "You and I, Shell, we're survivors."

His response was slow. "Is that what we are?"

She decided on a small memorial service because she needed the at-

135

tention. The service was held at the Episcopal church where she was a member but not a supporter. She had little regard for Christianity and none for Christians, with the possible exception of Quakers, who, she'd heard, practiced what they preached.

After the service the rector approached her. She didn't like his face. It carried a chill, as if his real world were not skyward but underground. "With your loss," he said, "I hope we'll see more of you."

"My plans are indefinite."

Her son had flown in from Los Angeles. Together they walked to her car. The sky was darkening, which made her wonder whether her mood had caused clouds to come. "Is the soul imperishable, dear, or does it have only a shelf life?"

He didn't answer.

"Are you still Dane, or have you gone back to David?"

"I'm who I am, Mother."

"You know your sister named her son after you."

"In one of her ironic moments, I'm sure."

"Helen's quite unwell. Have pity on her, dear."

"You never did."

In the evening she made a light supper suitable for them. He had little appetite. An elbow on the table, she said, "You haven't done well, have you, dear?"

He shrugged. It was no secret his minor movie roles had shrunk to walk-ons.

"How do you make ends meet?" she asked.

"I manage."

"You're homosexual, aren't you?"

He sighed. "Dad knew. You could never admit it."

"You were my favorite, how could I?" She drove a fork into a lettuce heart. "Peter Pan lost his shadow. I suspect you've lost yours."

In the morning she drove him to the ferry, dark glasses shading eyes puffy from a poor night's sleep. She wished he wasn't leaving so soon. Another day or two would have been nice, time perhaps to straighten out a few things.

"I hate the word homosexual," she said. "Can't you people come up with a better one?"

"We're working on it."

She accompanied him to the gateway to the ferry, a slight hitch in her step. She felt as if she were seeing him off to war.

He said, "Will you be all right, Mother?"

"I might get a cat. Cats are clean."

"I had one that wasn't."

She removed her glasses. "It was good seeing you again, dear."

"Good seeing you too."

As he bent to kiss her cheek she said, "I think you should visit Helen sometime."

"No," he said. "*You* should."

III ≡ III

David wanted a woman from whom everything would be Yes, a great Molly Bloom *Yes!* loud enough to wake the world. Seated at a table in the crowded balcony of the Maier Gustl, he settled for the *Ja* of a prostitute whose expressive dark eyes told him time was money.

He didn't ask her name, nor did she ask his. Her place was too far away for them to walk. In a taxi she asked how old he was, and he added a few years to the truth, which didn't fool her. She pointed out Goethe's house, much of its war damage repaired. She lived one street beyond, in a building restored to half its original self.

They climbed stairs. She lived in a single room dominated by an iron bed. Her dress vanished as he was undoing his Ike jacket. The wedge of her underpants had the pattern of a fern. When her breasts fell loose, he saw Molly Bloom at her best and stood in a state of urgency.

"How long you been a soldier?"

He didn't answer because he was struggling with the knot of his tie.

"Come here. I help."

She stared directly into his face as she worked him out of his uniform with a skill that didn't fail to please. He stood expectant, of a boastful size that showed a sparkle of wet like a quivering light in the eye of a camera.

"Your friend says it's your birthday."

He nodded.

"Then come on."

He lay with his head in an enormous pillow. She sat cross-legged beside him, her hair tumbling, her eye scanning him.

"We play first, OK?" Her hand moved. The instant it touched him he surged, shot, and hit her hot in the eye. Her head bolted back. "*Esel!*"

He was an ass. He knew it. "I'm sorry."

She was on her knees. He sat up fast as she spun to grab a towel. A breast slugged him in the face. Suddenly she was laughing, and he began to. Wiping her eye to make it see again, she said, "Happy birthday."

He was twenty.

||| ☰ |||

Midafternoon Shell drove into Boston and was at South Station in time to greet Mrs. Dodd when she stepped off the train with a small suitcase and a pinched expression. Freeing her of the suitcase, he pecked her cheek.

"I'm glad you've come," he said.

"When do I see her? Not now, I hope."

"First thing tomorrow."

"That's better," Mrs. Dodd said, taking his arm. "I'm a little nervous, you understand."

The drive to Haverhill took less than an hour. He booked her into the Whittier, a small hotel near the post office and in sight of shoe shops. On the way to the elevator she gave him a look.

"Why am I not staying at your place?"

"I didn't think you'd be comfortable there. I have a friend living with me."

"Ah, yes, that voice on the phone. Are you hiding her?"

"Not at all. I was hoping we might have dinner here tonight, say six o'clock."

"Seven would be better."

"I could bring along another friend. He's an interesting man."

"Are you trying to fix me up, Shell?"

"I wouldn't dream of it."

At seven in the lobby Shell made the introductions. Gretchen Ryder, drawing a critical look from Mrs. Dodd, had done something to her hair that didn't suit her. And her dress was a shade too tight. Father Henry saw in Mrs. Dodd a beautiful woman of uncertain years. She extended a hand.

"Always nice to meet a fellow Episcopalian," she said.

In the dining room Father Henry held her chair. White linen on the table pleased her. A candle added luster to the silverware. Her glance told Shell she approved. During aperitifs she turned boldly to Father Henry.

"What has my son-in-law told you about me?"

"That you've lost your husband. Please accept my condolences."

"I didn't lose him, Father. It's true he died, but he departed on his own, a choice he made without consulting anyone. I bear a grudge."

Father Henry's knee inadvertently grazed hers. "I lost my wife some time ago."

Dubonnet gave Gretchen a voice. "I was married twice."

Mrs. Dodd broke a silence. "Wasn't once enough?"

Shell opened a menu. Staring at him, Mrs. Dodd decided he was losing his looks. Lines in his face, she noticed, ran deep. Slipping on reading glasses, he caught her gaze and smiled.

They ordered. Father Henry chose the wine. During dinner he asked Shell for a report on David and in the instant received a prideful grin.

"He's been promoted to corporal."

"A shame he's not an officer," Mrs. Dodd said. "A waste he's in the army at all." She slid a knife through a plump cut of filet mignon. "What's he going to make of himself?"

"He has it in him to be anything he wants," Shell said as Gretchen excused herself to use the ladies'. Her linen napkin fell to the floor, and Father Henry promptly retrieved it. Her exit was unwieldy. Mrs. Dodd shook her head. Shell said, "Please don't say anything against her."

"Don't be defensive, Shell. You have your needs, and I'm sure she's an armful. Wouldn't you say so, Father?"

"You're a rigid woman, Mrs. Dodd, and you don't have a warm voice. But I like you anyway."

"Are you flirting with me, Father?"

His smile increased. "Stranger things have happened."

"Then I should tell you something right away. I'm not a good Episcopalian, I'm not a good Christian, and often I'm not a good person. There you have it."

"So noted," Father Henry said, his spirits raised as if from a challenge.

At evening's end, in the lobby, he gripped Mrs. Dodd's hand and said, "A pleasure meeting you. I do hope we'll meet again."

"Stranger things have happened," she said.

Shell walked her to the elevator and told her the time he'd call for her in the morning. She fretted her brow.

"Will she know me?"

He pressed a button. "I'm sure she will."

The elevator wheezed open. Mrs. Dodd stepped in, turned around, and held the door. "Ever regret marrying my daughter?"

"No," Shell said. "Otherwise I wouldn't have my son."

||| ≡ |||

Helen's chill hand was pins and needles, and she shook it. Poor circulation, she explained. Her dress was gray and her hair uneven. She stood at the window and from time to time looked out. For a split second Mrs. Dodd wished she hadn't been left alone with her.

"Anything wrong, dear?"

Helen wanted to gaze out at flaming summer, not dead winter. "Nothing," she said.

"I was afraid you might have forgotten me."

"How could I do that, Mother?"

Stepping closer, Mrs. Dodd glimpsed a depth in her daughter's eyes she had never seen in her husband's or her son's, and for an odd moment her mind was a hall of mirrors, Helen in each of them. Helen as a newborn, Helen as a difficult child, Helen as a moody adolescent with a belief in past lives and a suspicion of having already lived some of her future ones.

"I've been sparing you, dear. But I suppose I must tell you. Your father's dead."

Helen edged along the window and sat sideways on the sill. "Did you kill him?"

"No, dear. He killed himself."

"Shell's father did too, threw himself into a river." She smiled. "Shell and I are two of a kind."

Slow to fade, the smile gave Mrs. Dodd the willies. Helen's left hand, lying limp, was bare. "Where's your wedding ring, dear?"

"I don't feel married anymore."

Mrs. Dodd could understand that and let it pass. "You must miss your son."

Helen turned her face to the window. One of the patients, an elderly man in a cloth cap, was shoveling snow with a child's shovel.

"David, dear. He's in Germany."

"He's in heaven."

"That's a strange thing to say."

The man was shoveling a path where none was needed. With her finger Helen wrote a word on the window and then rubbed it out. "I could tell you a secret, but I don't know if it's true."

"Tell me, dear. I'll decide if it's true or not."

Inclining her head, Helen absorbed her mother's stare without returning it. "I'll tell Nana, not you."

"I see. Still playing that game, are you?"

Helen saw the toy shovel flash red. The path was beginning to circle itself. "I've made a mess of my life, haven't I, Mother?"

"Perhaps it was fated," Mrs. Dodd said with a slight toss of her head. "Life isn't all that great anyway. You do your best only to end up starkers on a slab. No dignity in that."

Helen wrote the same word again on the window. This time she let it stand. The word was *GO*.

"Do you want me to leave?"

Helen nodded. "Please don't come back."

||| ☰ |||

Tony Tonetti picked up a Leica cheap from a peddler in the Bahnhof and took pictures in the Maier Gustl. David was with a woman who'd printed her mouth on a tissue and written her name around it. "Smile!" Tonetti commanded, and the click of the camera fixed a moment of them forever. Then he took one of David alone.

Later David mailed the one of him alone to Johanna. His letters to her had become sporadic and tinged with insinuations from a jealousy he knew was unreasonable. He asked if she were still wearing his ring. "Yes," she wrote back. "Do you have a guilty conscience?"

Tonetti, shining his shoes, looked up. "Troubles, Shellenbach?"

"I think I'm screwing up."

"You're having fun. That your problem?"

"I don't know who I am, don't know who I'll be. My father wants me to be somebody important, like it's my destiny. You believe in destiny, Tony?"

"Sure I do. Money buys it."

Each had excess furlough time and during their last year in Germany began using it. In Amsterdam they stayed at a turreted hotel, ate herring at street stalls, boated on the canals, and window-shopped whores who posed when Tonetti aimed his Leica. Some opened their robes and inhaled to force up their breasts.

In Copenhagen they watched the changing of the guard at Amalienborg Palace. Tonetti took a picture of the mermaid in the harbor and bought envelopes of pornographic postcards for resale in Frankfurt. In a bar on the left side of the Nyhavn canal he got into an argument with two Danes. One hit him on the head with a bottle, hard enough to stagger him, which left David fighting the both of them. A Danish doctor patched Tonetti's scalp and stitched David's split lip.

Back in Frankfurt, David read Johanna's latest latter. "My psych pro-

fessor," she wrote, "says there are two kinds of love. One comes from the heart, the other from every neurotic tendency we harbor. Which one is yours, David?"

He tore the letter up but later retrieved the pieces and saved them.

In the waning heat of September he and Tonetti went to Paris. Alone in the Latin Quarter he met a young woman from the Sorbonne, who wore a beret and charcoal eye shadow and wanted to experience an American. She told him that her pleasures were simple, falling asleep to rain was one. Her hero was Camus, and she likened David's face to his. He didn't meet up again with Tonetti until the last day of their leave.

Tonetti said, "Struck it rich, huh? Ask me what I've been doing? Taking pictures of the sights, three fucking rolls."

They were at a sidewalk café in Pigalle, cups of strong coffee between them. David was quiet. He felt a rush of street air against his face. A prostitute in a small dress arched her shoulders in a show of strength.

"What's the problem now, Shellenbach?"

"No problem. Just wondering what it'll be like when I get back to the States."

"You got plans?"

"Marry Johanna, that's a given, and probably go to college on the GI Bill. How about you, Tony?"

"Make money and be a big shot. The two go together."

"You could be dreaming," David said.

"I'm dreaming? Tell me who's bigger, you or me. You're taller and got an extra stripe, but I hold markers on you. How much you think you owe me now?"

"You're the one keeping track. You tell me."

"You don't owe me a fucking cent. We're friends, ain't we?" Tonetti made a fist and laid it on the table. "Over here it's fun and games, three squares a day and no worries. We get back to the States, it's the real world. Destiny don't come cheap, Shellenbach."

||| ≡ |||

Home in Staten Island Mrs. Dodd began suffering from a loneliness she hadn't thought possible. It angered her because it took away her strength. She phoned Shell and said, "I think I should be near her, whether she wants to see me or not."

Within the month she sold her house, furniture and all, and moved to Haverhill. With Shell's help, she settled into a furnished apartment in the Bodwell Manor, which was across the river in the city's desirable Bradford section. Father Henry gave her a tour of the city in his shiny black Ford. He showed her Plug Pond. Terrible name. It had another, but he couldn't remember it. He showed her Kenoza Lake, where Canada geese flapped their wings. She liked birds but was not particularly enamored of geese, whose droppings she was familiar with.

She supposed, she said, she'd need to go to the expense of buying an automobile of her own.

"I don't see why," Father Henry said. "Shell and I are both available to you. And, please, call me Prescott."

"Prescott Henry's your name? Not a transposition, is it?"

He smiled. "May I call you Dorothy?"

"As long as you never say Dot or Dotty."

He took her to the theater in Boston, a Tennessee Williams drama that repelled her. On the drive back she told him she had figured him for better taste.

"A slice of life, Dorothy."

"Not my life." Approaching Haverhill, he glanced at her with meaning and lowered his voice. "I really haven't been with a woman since my wife died."

"If you're talking sex," she said, "I'm not interested."

"It's a normal need, Dorothy."

"For a man, not always for a woman. Especially not one my age."

"You're not that old," he protested. "How old are you?"

"Like an old whore, Prescott, I don't give out my years."

On a chill but sunny day he drove her to Rye, New Hampshire, to a stretch of beach they had to themselves. The rushing tide rode roughshod over pebbles clattering as if in pain. A tidal pool smelled like a bait bucket. Mrs. Dodd breathed in deeply.

"I knew you'd like it here," he said.

"Of course I like it. I know the ocean."

The sand was granite. In their wake they left prints planted deep, as if for posterity. Mrs. Dodd hiked the collar of her cardigan.

"My wife and I came here often," Father Henry said.

"Let's not dwell on the past."

"The past is all we have."

They stopped and watched a wave swell. It rose, flared, and collapsed with the sound of crashing machinery. Father Henry drew back to avoid the spray, but Mrs. Dodd stood her ground.

"What are you afraid of, Prescott?"

"That the past *is* all we have."

"Don't you know how to live?"

"Few people do."

Farther along the beach they came upon a large round face someone had outlined in the sand. Pebbles were eyes, a knot of seaweed the nose, and a string of broken shells the teeth. They stared down at it.

"Could be you, could be me," Mrs. Dodd said. "What else are you afraid of, Prescott?"

"Dying empty."

They trekked back to the car. He switched on the heater because the hem of her skirt was wet and her sturdy shoes sodden. The drive back to Haverhill was slow because he was cautious at the wheel, as if she were valuable cargo. When they finally reached the Bodwell Manor, she asked whether he wanted to come in for coffee or cocoa, whichever he preferred.

"Either one," he said quickly.

"You just want to get in there, don't you?"

"It's been a lovely day, Dorothy. I don't want it to end quite yet."

Her apartment was warm from the late sun winging in through the windows. She shed her cardigan and removed a seashell from a pocket. Sitting, she untied the wet laces of her shoes. A moment later she was rubbing one foot and then the other. She glanced up.

"What's it like being an Episcopal priest?"

"Threatening," he said. "I'm beginning to question everything."

"Won't that endanger your immortal soul?"

"The question is whether man has one. There's no proof he deserves one."

"A bit more to you than I thought," she said, rising. "I suspect I'm older than you."

"Not by much."

She stepped to him and, staring him in the face, touched the beast in his pants. His breath caught. "How long has it been, Prescott?"

"Too God-damn long," he blurted out.

In the bedroom he lowered a shade without blocking all the light. She lay uncovered in the bed with her lower half at an angle, as if to make him look at her two ways at once. He crept onto the bed and crouched between her feet, which she had stretched to put at their best. With a wrench, she placed herself in his face to let him slum between her thighs.

Slumming, he was determined to miss nothing. Her cleft was endless. Her anus bore the aspect of a vaccination. When he finally came up for breath, she hurled up her arms, sequestered him, and told him to ram.

When it was over, she said, "I think you got what you wanted, not sure you deserved it."

"You're not sorry, are you?"

She let him linger on her. "Let's put it this way. Sunday you may see me in church."

||| ☰ |||

David came home with three years of army life stuffed in a duffel bag. His father embraced him. Gretchen Ryder kissed his cheek. In his bedroom he shed his uniform for a natty pullover and charcoal slacks, his weight unchanged from the last time he'd worn them. A Spitfire and a Messerschmitt hung over his head. Shell grinned from the doorway.

"You look like my kid again."

"I feel like your kid again."

Shell dangled car keys. "I guess you want these. Better wear a jacket."

The Plymouth remembered him, the motor purred, the heater

worked, but the drive was long and tormented him. November was a mean month, without color or feeling, the day dead before its time. Tension in his neck, the radio shouting in his face, he drove recklessly with a fear Johanna was a love affair that had transpired only in his head.

The Amherst campus was a cold oasis of lights. She lived in a sorority house now, which he easily found from a description in one of her letters. Shown into a sitting room, he waited while she was summoned. When minutes mounted he fidgeted. When he heard footsteps, he sprang from his chair and saw her as more beautiful than he remembered, longer of leg, Peggy Lee in her looks. She accepted his embrace but broke off the kiss.

"You should've told me you were coming."

"I didn't want to take the time," he said, feeling her slip from his grasp. Something was wrong. Everything was. He began to see her in fragments.

"We're not the same people anymore, are we?" she said.

"I am."

She repositioned herself near a narrow table that held a slender vase meant for a single flower. "All the time we were apart I had the awful feeling no matter how much I loved you it would never be enough."

He felt his temples bulge. He didn't want to hear any of that. "I don't know what you mean."

"What we had, David, simply didn't survive."

He seemed to detect an unfamiliar odor about himself, as if he were wearing someone else's clothes. He should've stayed in his uniform. "Are you seeing somebody?"

"That's not relevant."

"To me it is," he said, and realized her open hand held a ring, the small stone a sparkle bereft of meaning. When he wouldn't take it back, she slipped it into his jacket pocket.

"I'm sorry."

For moments his mind wouldn't move. Stepping forward, he touched her as if his hand had acted on its own. "When did you come to this decision?"

"You chose the moment, David. When you started accusing me of what you no doubt were doing."

He was a male. He hadn't known better. Couldn't she understand? "I can't let you go."

"You don't have a choice."

Reading, mostly books she had sent him, had led him to believe absolutely in a force running through nature, connecting man to other animals, animals to mountains, mountains to wind and rain. A force connecting him to her. "I'll never get over you."

"I'm positive you will."

"Then you don't know me."

"I agree," she replied.

He wanted anger in himself. Anger would have been a defense. Instead he felt a kind of terror that allowed her to lead him from the room and all the way to the outside door, which she opened quickly. The cold rushed in. Stepping aside, she wrapped her arms around herself for warmth as he hurled something into the night.

"That was foolish," she said.

"It's yours or no one's. So it's no one's."

Her face softened a bit as he zipped up her jacket and hiked the collar. "What are you going to do with yourself, David?"

"I don't know. I can't read the stars."

||| ≡ |||

Lowering her book, Anne Lindbergh gazed at her husband as he stood by the fire with an elbow on the mantel. The youth was gone from his face and the color from his hair, but his ability to sprout wings was intact. A consultant for Pan American, he traveled relentlessly, his energy in overdrive, as if he still had something to prove, not to the world, never to the world, but to himself and in some small measure to her. She spoke softly.

"You're my hero, Charles. You always will be."

He turned. "What brought that on?"

"You. Standing there."

His height gave him command. Implicit in his silence was the voice of authority. He could put his feelings on hold. The cry of a teething child had never bothered him but had torn at her. He took no pill to

148

fall asleep but lay awake for as long as it took. His strength was intended for the two of them. Sometimes, only for seconds, she resented him nearly as much as she loved him.

"Something's on your mind, Anne. What is it?"

"I don't know if I can find the right words." She silently closed her book. "After all these years I've adjusted to your absences, but I've never adjusted to myself. I'm at odds, Charles."

"I don't understand."

"I need to sort myself out, to weigh the parts of me that belong to you, to the children, and the part that belongs to me alone. It's not a crisis, but I need to get away for a while, all by myself. Do I sound selfish?"

His silence was heavy, her loyalty absolute. She was ready to recant. He said, "Where will you go?"

"I was thinking of the little island off Florida we once visited. Remember that remote cottage we walked by? I checked, it's available."

"The place is primitive. What will you do?"

"Collect seashells," she said.

Two weeks later she arrived on the island with the sun in her face and the barest of essentials. The cottage, shaded by a few pines, fronted the ocean's wavering colors. She cooked simple meals on a two-burner oil stove that emitted a tolerable stink. The small bed never would have fitted Charles, whose feet would have protruded well over the edge. Rudimentary plumbing pounded out only cold water, in which she showered with a Spartan fortitude that made her doubly aware of the miracle of the human body, her own in particular.

Wearing a loose shirt and roomy shorts, she roamed the beach. Sandpipers skittered from her path, gulls eyed her suspiciously, and pelicans lumbered over waves. Pirate treasure was prize shells she plucked from the sand and deposited in the hemp bag hanging from her shoulder. Other people were vacationing on the island, but she didn't run into them, though once from afar she heard a woman's voice and another time a child's. The child's voice haunted her for a day or two.

She reread Rebecca West and for the first time read Anaïs Nin, whose unorthodox experiences would never be hers, but she wanted to know about them, which Charles would find shocking should she tell him.

At night the ocean breathed into the cottage, murmured to her, and forced her into a sweater. Seated at an old desk, she wrote in a spiral-bound notebook. Writing about memories, she assigned bad ones the crouch and spring of cats. Tender ones were birdsong.

Another night she wrote: *The sinister thing about life is that the underlying chaos is not remote.* After a pause, she added: *Life clings not to us but to itself. We pass on, it goes on.*

Nine days passed. On the tenth, her last, she rose at dawn and went barefoot onto the beach with questions nagging her. Had she achieved insights toward personal harmony? Had she found strength in solitude, wisdom in weakness, purpose in loss? Waves thumped the beach.

With no one likely to intrude, she slipped off her shirt and shorts, lay back on her elbows, and let God gaze at her. God the Father, God the Mother. Eyes closed, she waited for waves to wash in answers. The first wave wet her heels. The second splashed her ankles. None brought answers.

At noon she closed up the cottage. Her lone trek to the pier was leisurely, the small suitcase of little weight. The greater weight was the hemp bag hanging from her shoulder. When she had collected the shells, they were silver and gold. Now they were keys to unknown locks.

Charles, who had just arrived, stood tall on the pier with their youngest son, the one who looked the most like him. They waved to her. After a glance back at the mystery she was leaving, she began running toward the known.

PART II

Another World

"GODS CONTRIVE TO DIE IN CLOUDS OF SNOW,

MORTALS SET ANCHOR SIX FEET BELOW."

— PRESCOTT HENRY

CHAPTER NINE

CHEMOTHERAPY HAD ROBBED SHELL OF HIS HAIR, BARED
his face, and brought out the bones. He was seated in a wheelchair outside Hanover House, where the care was private. A woman crossing the
sunstruck lawn as if on water made him wonder whether his death was
imminent. At first he thought the woman was Mrs. Zuber coming to
visit him from the unknown. Then he suspected it was Helen's ghost
and, giving out a little cry, felt a twinge that surged into pain. A nurse
rushed to him.

"Time I got you back inside, Mr. Shellenbach."

He pointed. "Who's that woman?"

The nurse shaded her eyes. "What woman?"

"Am I hallucinating?"

She was wheeling him toward a ramp. "Wouldn't be the first time,
would it?"

The pain lessened.

In his room he got out of the wheelchair on his own and lay on his
bed with an airy thought of death. But he didn't die. He napped a solid
hour and woke fresh, no pain.

Mr. Unger said, "You were talking in your sleep."

Mr. Unger was his roommate, his new pal. Each could have had a private room, but they preferred company. "What did I say?"

"Didn't make sense. Something about David."

"Which one?"

"How many you got?"

"I lost one. Destiny gave me another."

Mr. Unger was a retired stockbroker who once believed wholeheartedly in destiny and now believed in nothing except his own mortality. Standing in discomfort at the window, he feared breaking wind because of the near certainty he'd soil himself. He needed major surgery, but his doctor doubted his ticker would take it. Such was life. Such was destiny.

"How's the race going?" Mr. Unger asked. "How's he doing against Kenneally?"

Shell's mind slipped and groped. The race was political, he remembered that, but who was Kenneally? Did Unger mean Kennedy? Which Kennedy? So many had been snuffed. Shell had voted for John and would have voted for Bobby. That was long ago.

Mr. Unger moved slowly from the window, his heavy parts giving him trouble, and settled in an upholstered chair. "I've no use for Kenneally. Too Irish, too liberal, even for a Democrat. 'Course I'd never vote for any Democrat."

Shell said, "I'm a registered one."

"That's ironic."

Shell didn't see the irony and didn't bother to search for it. Then it came to him on its own. David was now a Republican. The whole family David had married into was. Good for him. He deserved the best.

"Times have changed, with Reagan in office," Mr. Unger said. "I think your son's got an outside chance."

His mind plunging deep into the past, Shell remembered that when John Kennedy ran for the Senate he came to Haverhill and strode into the newsroom like an overgrown kid, his birthright his credentials. Shell wrote a glowing story about him and caught hell from Bill Heath.

The *Gazette* endorsed Lodge, who lost. Later endorsed Nixon, who also lost. Terrible thing, victory.

"Ted Kennedy," Shell said suddenly. "Is that who you mean?"

Mr. Unger didn't answer. He was resting his eyes, his droopy face in collapse. He said, "Which of us do you think will go first?"

"Is it a race?"

"My whole life's been a race. Hasn't yours?"

"No," Shell said. "Mine's been a lie."

III ☰ III

Banners touting Shellenbach for governor festooned the banquet room of the Copley Plaza. Applause greeted David and Meredith Shellenbach, a handsome-looking pair, everyone said so. In bespoken pinstripes, hair touched with gray, David looked splendid and serious. Light winced off Meredith's jewelry. Her beauty, lyrically flowing in her youth, was frozen under a scarcely noticeable glaze of makeup.

Kipper Wainwright, her brother, immediately began working the crowd. Charm and eternal youthfulness made him notable. He was David's campaign manager in name only. Meredith called the shots. Polls gave David a large lead over his Republican opponents and enough of an outside chance against Governor Kenneally to raise money and hopes.

Smooth-shaven men pumped David's hand, and women in finery brushed his edges. Long ago Meredith had told him to make it look like play, not work. Politics, she preached, was half sexual, the most fun the foreplay. You flatter the men by exalting their wives. She gave him a greater chance than even the polls did.

Moving about gracefully, circling tables, Meredith distinguished men born to money from those who'd ripened pennies into dollars and blossomed bankrolls into fortunes. She approached men of honor one way and men with no notion of it another. Though her smile was the same, the timbre of her voice varied.

"Of course David will win," she said to a Saltonstall who'd been a friend of her father's. "Kenneally's fat, David's not. Kenneally's estranged from his wife, David adores me. Kenneally's a sordid story, my David's a sweetheart."

Seconds later a lobbyist with money to dispense led her into an al-

155

cove, where allusive promises were made, a bargain struck. A hand-shake formalized it, and a kiss on the cheek feminized it.

Soon she and David took a prominent place at the head table. During dinner the man on David's immediate left, a well-known building contractor who personified pure achievement, began airing his views on environmental regulations. David tipped his head back. Meredith leaned toward him.

"He's big bucks, darling, pay attention."

At dinner's end David rose to applause and delivered a speech reassuring to believers in fair skin, churches with steeples, and movies made in the Forties. He gave passing praise to the Reagan revolution and damned the excesses of liberalism. The speech could have gone on longer, but he elided several paragraphs. When he sat down, the applause rose into a standing ovation. Only Meredith was displeased.

On the chauffeured drive home to Andover, she sat between David and her brother. Kipper's head had fallen back, his eyes closed. In middle age Kipper had an unfinished look, an air of unaccomplishment clinging to him. David glanced over at him.

"All children are beautiful in sleep," Meredith said with an edge. "Why didn't you follow the script?"

David loosened his tie and undid the top two buttons of his shirt. "I did. I simply made a few cuts."

"A few too many. And your delivery was wooden, no highs and lows in your voice. You don't put your heart into it, darling."

"I think I'll write my own speeches."

"You do that, you won't even win the primary. For now, just tell people what they want to hear. You can be a maverick later."

The car was a leased Lincoln Continental. The driver, a trusted volunteer, maintained a cruising speed of fifty-five on the interstate and lowered it as they neared the Andover exit. David said, "What if I lose?"

Kipper, only half asleep, said, "You'll piss off my sister."

"I wouldn't want to do that, would I?"

"Not if you know what's good for you," Kipper said.

III ≡ III

In a dream Shell was late for an appointment but didn't know how late. His watch had no hands. His arms had no elbows. He woke stiff in the upholstered chair and found Mrs. Kaplan, his favorite nurse, standing over him.

"Am I dead?"

Mrs. Kaplan looked into his eyes and said, "No, you're not." She felt his face. "You're hunky-dory."

He was alert, but a sense of wholeness eluded him. Mrs. Kaplan gave him his medication, waited while he took it, and asked where Mr. Unger was. He guessed the common room in a voice that went vague.

"Anything wrong, Mr. Shellenbach?"

"Days we're not fully ourselves, who are we?"

"Sounds like a trick question. I'll pass." She went to the window on thin, harsh legs and let in some air, enough for him to taste the day. "Not too much of a breeze, is it?"

Her stance was slightly crooked, and in the flash of a second he saw not her but Mrs. Zuber, the image so sharp and exact that he glimpsed pins in her mouth and saw himself in his first suit. Tears started. He spoke in a full voice.

"Forgive me."

She passed by him. "Your age, Mr. Shellenbach, you should realize every sin is forgivable."

"Really?" He saw hope but not much. "Would you forgive Hitler?"

"Sure I would." She paused at the door. "If I could torture him first."

He was left alone but not for long. A heavy woman a bit out of breath was entering his room, and his face expanded as soon as he recognized her. Gretchen Ryder brought him fruit and candy and lessened his fear of irrelevancy. She also brought news clippings about David, some he might not have seen. With spectacles placed low on his nose, he sifted through them until drawn into thoughts of his biological son, the real David, dead before he'd had time to grow.

Gretchen touched the back of his head. "Have you been crying?"

"No."

"How are you feeling?"

"Better," he said, holding back tears, for she had gussied up for him. She always did.

"How's your eczema?"

"I think I've finally licked it." He put aside the clippings. "Have you seen anything of Father Henry?"

"He's in Florida."

"Yes. Yes, of course." He remembered now. "He has the old bat with him. She'll outlive us all."

"I've never heard you call her that before," Gretchen said.

He removed his spectacles, rubbed his eyes, and then stared up into hers, more familiar to him than his own. Was it too late to marry her? Would it be fair to make her a three-time loser? When she touched his arm and felt the bone, he said, "Not what I used to be, am I?"

She placed her bag on his bed. A small, tightly furled umbrella protruded from it. She never stayed home when it rained. She went out, did errands, read the paper in a coffee shop. Always ways to dent the gloom.

Shell looked toward the window. "Is it raining?"

"Not now. Sun's out, can't you see?"

"Yes. Take me outside."

He rose stiffly and slipped on a coat sweater she'd bought him years ago at Mitchell's.

She unfolded the wheelchair.

He could walk, but walking drained his strength. She wheeled him down the long corridor to exit doors that opened automatically. Mr. Unger stood just outside. Gretchen smiled and asked how he was feeling.

"A rich man, Mrs. Ryder, can buy time but only so much."

Gretchen wheeled Shell down the ramp, along the walk, and onto the damp lawn, where she came to a halt at a stone bench and a trellis of roses pretending to be fire. When she sat on the bench a calico cat that belonged to no one but was well fed brushed her shins. She petted it.

"I didn't need the sweater after all," Shell said.

"Best you wear it."

In the distance a bare oak, killed the previous summer by lightning, looked like a key to the sky. Eyes shaded to see, Shell imagined a giant hand turning it. He said, "What will you do?"

She knew what he meant. "I'll be fine."

He spoke with a different voice. "I'm not afraid."

"I know you're not. Rudy wasn't either."

Suddenly, startling her, the cat swept the air with an open paw and brought down a dragonfly. In a hollow voice Shell said, "I did that to an eagle."

"Really. What were you doing on a mountaintop?"

"Defying the gods," he said, and watched the cat eat its catch. "I haven't seen David lately."

"I'm sure he's busy, all that campaigning, fund-raising, and stuff."

"I need to talk to him."

Something in his voice alarmed her. "Is it urgent?"

A fast formation of Canada geese honked overhead as if narrating a saga. Looking up, Shell said, "No, it's simply the time."

||| ≡ |||

They spent the afternoon at a Worcester radio station, where David took questions from callers, his answers occasionally disturbing to Meredith, whose foot tapped his under the table. At one point she scribbled a note.

No need to take chances.

A male caller said, "I don't trust anybody in the state house. They're all puffing out their chests, covering their asses, and feathering their nests."

"That's why you need me there," David said.

Meredith whispered, "Nice."

They checked into the nearby Marriott, where later he was to address a Rotary gathering. In their room, over coffee and scones, they reviewed the speech, which varied little from the one he'd delivered at the Copley Plaza. Personal digs against Governor Kenneally, which he'd passed over, were now underscored. He sighed heavily, and Meredith stiffened.

"We've come a long way, darling. You're not going to spoil it, are you?"

"God forbid," he said.

Two garment bags, his and hers, hung in the open closet. Soon he would shed his solid suit for a pinstripe, his regimental tie for a faintly dotted one. He would arrange a smile and hold it for the evening, a small enough price for the prize they both wanted, each for a different reason. Hers was tied to her father. Her father was dead, but she was still Paul Wainwright's daughter first and Meredith Shellenbach second.

"I've an idea," she said and, rising, paused dramatically. The gods had given her looks and bearing and a long neck. Standing on attenuated legs in a narrow dress, her ears discreetly diamonded, she was the sort of female who belonged in a temple frieze, an observation David had made early in the marriage. "From now on," she said, "let's be wonderful to each other."

He suppressed an emotion and didn't respond. So much in the marriage had slid off course. "I think I'll take a quick shower," he said.

Her words stayed in his head as he stood with his eyes clenched shut and his face lifted to a fast lukewarm spray. Love was not the sine qua non of the marriage. For him it was identity, his status as a husband. With Meredith, it was another matter, which escaped him. She escaped him. She was one thing one day and something else the next. Sometimes he thought it was a device to keep him in line, though he knew it was deeper than that. He extinguished the spray and yanked open the curtain. She was there.

"I always did like seeing you naked."

He was not pleased. It reminded him of the morning his grandmother had withheld the towel and viewed him as if he were a specimen.

"You're still nice and lean, darling, but you're getting the hint of a belly. Must do something about it."

He dried his hair with one towel and began rubbing down with another. He was not sure whether she was viewing him with amusement or interest. Though he had no grounds, he suspected murmurs of other men in her head, phantoms from the past. She was smiling.

"Remember the night we made fools of ourselves?"

Of course he remembered. At the Touraine, the evening they met. "Aren't we too old for that?"

"Speak for yourself." She guided his hand to the start of her dress. All her dresses had chic labels, but not all were paid for. She made people wait. "Tear it off," she said.

"You have another?"

"Of course."

He tore off everything, and they did it where they were, he on the unlidded seat of the john and she astride him. At an intense moment his elbow struck the flushing lever, startling him to the degree that he nearly knocked her over. The ringing in his head was the telephone.

"Don't you dare!"

He didn't.

She shrieked. He hadn't heard that shriek in years and years, not since the first time, the pitch higher than all others. Artfully disengaging, shifting her bottom, she peed through his legs.

An hour later the phone shrilled again. This time he answered it. He was in pinstripes, she was in silk, diamonds still in her ears. The caller was Gretchen Ryder, who had tracked him down.

Meredith carried the copy of the speech to the door. When he stayed on the phone too long, she caught his eye and tapped the tiny face of her watch. Someone knocked on the door. It was her brother.

"Come on, you guys," Kipper Wainwright shouted.

When David got off the phone, she pointed the speech at him and said, "I expect another rousing performance."

III ≡ III

Gretchen Ryder sat in her favorite chair, where she could see the river. Full of tree images, it ran green in the dying day. An old floor-model radio posed as furniture in a corner of the room. A knob was missing. She imagined that if burnt-out tubes were replaced she could tune in programs from the past. In her head she listened to Jack Benny.

Your money or your life!

Benny hesitated.

161

She laughed.

A sound from the kitchen didn't disturb her reverie. The tenement, without Shell, was fraught with sighs and soughs, with murmurs that came and went. She was used to them. Her head lolled.

"I'm thinking!" Benny protested.

Again she laughed.

The sound was now definite. A real footstep. Retired Police Chief O'Grady had entered the tenement without knocking, as if he owned the place, owned her, owned Haverhill. His voice marched up to her.

"Christ, I thought somebody was with you."

"Next time knock."

"I did. You didn't hear."

He sat down where he also could see the river, which was losing light, sinking with the day. A full head of white hair, along with steel-rim glasses bolted into his face, kept him official-looking. Intimates called him Connie. She had never called him anything but O'Grady.

"How is he?" he asked.

"The same," she said, resenting his arrogant intrusion. His presence prevented her from keeping her thoughts random and unanchored.

"I'm gonna miss him."

She went rigid from a chill. "He's not dead yet."

"When you're sick as he is, you can time it. I know my wife did. I'm sitting at her bed at the Hale, and she says, 'Coupla minutes more, Connie, then I won't be a bother.' Her eyes rolled, and I went fucking nuts. But you know all that."

Gretchen wanted to laugh, not cry. She wanted Benny back. She wanted Shell home. She said, "Stop."

"It's life, Gretchen. It's what it all comes down to. All we got is what we can look back on. Can't hold on to nothin'."

Perhaps what had been was enough, she thought. Had she any right to want more? Did she even want to be young again? She remembered an Irishman who threw change at her and told her that was all she was worth.

"I saved his ass once," O'Grady said, "long time ago. I don't guess he ever told you about it. No reason he should've, between him and me."

"Keep it that way," she said quietly, her head held crooked. Shell was her prince and always would be.

"He never wrote a bad thing about me. Lotsa times he could've, maybe should've. Things I did . . ."

O'Grady's voice trailed off as he looked toward the river, the little that could still be seen. Gretchen secretly read her watch, which was never quite correct. The room was growing dim.

"You were saying," she prompted.

"Yeah, what was I saying?" He seemed to have forgotten. Much of him looked worn out. He said, "How come you and him didn't marry? Christ, I'd have married you."

What he didn't know was that in her heart she had married Shell when she was fourteen. Shell and Rudy. She had married the two of them, each quite what she wanted, good boys bulging with their urges and better to her than others.

"Tell you something, I would've proposed to you."

"I'd have been worth it," she said with no nostalgia, only a sense of what she'd had to offer, which only Shell had come close to appreciating, Rudy a distant second, though it was Rudy she'd thought she loved the most. Just goes to show.

The room had gone dark. With a reach she could have snapped on the table lamp, but a gap lay between thinking and doing, effort the factor. O'Grady's intake of breath was audible. His disembodied voice seemed stuck in time.

"I got nothing to go home to. Mind if I stay?"

"Yes, I mind."

Always she'd been too good to men of his sort. Takers, users, foot traffic on her emotions, which never failed to slop over. She thought of Ned Ryder and wondered whether he was still in Florida, buried there perhaps. She thought of Bud, one of the boys she'd brought home from the USO club, and wondered whether she was the only one left with a memory of him.

"I suppose we could watch TV," she said, tears in her eyes. Uncle Milty, Sid Caesar were long gone. What was there really to watch? She wiped her eyes. "Did you hear me?"

Maybe she hadn't expected an answer. Maybe she didn't want one. Effort spurred by will, she reached out and found the lamp switch. The light was bright and blinded her for the instant.

O'Grady was gone.

⫼ ☰ ⫼

"My doctor and I have agreed," Mr. Unger said. "I'm going to have the operation."

Shell nodded. "You'll be happier."

"Yes, if I live."

"Even if you don't."

Mr. Unger tipped his head. "You have a funny way of looking at things. You're not afraid of dying, is that it?"

"I'm very much afraid," Shell said. "I don't know what awaits me."

A nurse came in, not Mrs. Kaplan. She was much younger than Mrs. Kaplan and wore outsize tinted glasses that lessened her face. Shell, disappointed, stared at her from his bed. His mind was clear, but the rest of him was weak, no energy to keep his head erect.

"Where is she?" he asked.

"What?"

"He wants to know where Mrs. Kaplan is," Mr. Unger said.

"She has to have a day off sometime."

Shell missed Mrs. Kaplan's rough voice, her eagle-eye look, and her unbidden hand on his arm. The bones in her fingers were Mrs. Zuber's, and occasionally her voice was. The voice never blamed him but always professed to understand.

He took his medication, though not all. Some he slipped aside because he wanted to be alert. After administering Mr. Unger's dosages, the young nurse left.

"What time is it?" he asked.

Mr. Unger told him.

"When my son comes, would you mind leaving?"

"Why? You afraid I'll get careless and mess myself?"

"No," Shell said. "What I have to say is for his ears only."

III ≡ III

David looked down at his father, saw a face of hollows and sockets, and couldn't keep sadness out of his smile. He kissed him on the brow, which he'd expected to find feverish. It was cool.

Shell saw in the man the boy he had raised. From his pillow, with no need of his glasses, he detected the exact blue of David's eyes. On his lip was the scar David had brought home from the army. Staring harder, he saw dignity, intelligence, Lindbergh.

"How's your wife?" he asked.

"Fine, Dad, she sends her love."

For moments Shell slipped away. Rolling in his head and sounding in his ears were scenes from City College, snatches of Hamlet's soliloquy, the pupils of Helen's eyes. He saw Mrs. Zuber with needle and thread and that suit of his, the cigarette burn meticulously mended. Whatever happened to the suit? Had Helen thrown it out, or had he?

"How's Meredith?"

"I already told you, Dad. She sends her love."

He doubted that but said nothing. He hoped David was happy but doubted that too. But what is happiness? It's not a package that comes in the mail. He watched David draw a chair close to the bed.

"How are you doing, Dad?"

"Not well, as you can see. That's why I asked you to come. Your mother, David, you must remember her with love."

"I do."

"I'm another matter. I don't want you to hate me, but I'll understand."

David reached for his father's hand and gripped it. "How could I ever hate you?"

"After doing wrong, I've tried to do my best. My best for you. That's always been my priority."

"I know that."

Shell's smile was small and cryptic. He murmured something David didn't catch. Then he said clearly, "I always thought I did it for your mother, but I did it for me. I didn't want to lose her."

The smile disquieted David. His father's comments were like footnotes to a text he hadn't read, but he didn't interrupt.

"Now I might be doing wrong again."

David felt a chill, as if the weather were raw and a window had been raised. He felt like a child with no notion of what was going on.

Shell said, "I have to tell you who you are."

CHAPTER TEN

DAVID SHELLENBACH SPENT SIX YEARS AT SUFFOLK—
in the university and then in the law school. Lodged in the shadow of
the state house on Beacon Hill, Suffolk looked governmental, as if its
purpose were not to funnel knowledge but to store secrets. Students
lugging briefcases, a preponderance of them ex-GI's, had the look of
bureaucrats. In the army David had felt windblown. At Suffolk he was
anchored.

He roomed on nearby Myrtle Street, lived for stretches on beer,
bread, and sardines, and pored over his books at a table in the Beacon
Cafeteria, where Tony Tonetti, briefly a classmate, occasionally joined
him.

"I ain't so good with books," Tonetti confessed.

"I've never seen you open one."

"I'm still trying to figure out what kind of animal a bear wolf is. I'm
supposed to write a fucking paper on it."

"Beowulf," David said, and spelled it. "A Teutonic hero, existential.
Under the weight of fate man must be courageous, live life well, accept
destiny. If possible, die in glory so his name will live on. Put a trench
coat on Beowulf and you have Camus."

"Jesus, that's good. Write it down for me, will you?" Tonetti sugared his coffee and narrowed his eyes. "Who the fuck's CaMOO?" Then he whipped out a wallet branded with his initials, extracted a twenty, and pushed the bill across the table. "I got a better idea. Write the paper for me."

Obsessed with his education, David was seldom without a book in his hands. Reading rearranged him, placing him not so much in other worlds as deeper into himself, where he enjoyed comfort and safety. He admired Hardy's brooding novels and identified with Jude, and he liked Spinoza, who maintained that everything happens out of necessity, which was the only way he could rationalize his loss of Johanna.

Tonetti, though he received a high mark on the Beowulf paper, flunked out of Suffolk, which didn't bother him a bit. He was driving a florid secondhand Buick, dating a young woman from his Saratoga Street neighborhood in East Boston, and bragging of an iron in the fire. His godfather, who lived in the same neighborhood, was State Senator Sylvio DeFelice.

Parking was at a premium on Beacon Hill, but Tonetti's outsize Buick was never tagged. One of its windows flaunted a legislative sticker. Tonetti was a volunteer on DeFelice's reelection campaign.

At the Beacon Cafeteria he said to David, "Get on the bandwagon. Do some fucking work for us."

David stuffed envelopes for a while but then had no time, for he was working the summer as a sorter in the postal annex at South Station. With his earnings he bought a tweed jacket, button-down shirts, and chinos, and reentered Suffolk with renewed purpose. Tonetti gave him the once-over.

"You look like a fucking preppy. Remind me to bow."

In the November election David voted for Stevenson over Eisenhower and wrote off Eisenhower's victory to Cold War hysteria. Tonetti was interested in only one contest and was elated with the result. DeFelice easily kept his seat in the General Court of Massachusetts, where he had the ear of the speaker, who was Irish, and the friendship of the governor, who was Italian.

"I worked my ass off for him, he knows it. I'm in. You hear me, Shellenbach? I'm a fucking winner."

"What have you won?"

"I'm where the power is. Power attracts money."

Tonetti became one of DeFelice's aides and to look his best bought a powder-blue suit, the jacket a one-button roll, the pants pegged. De-Felice, whose clear-cut features made him noteworthy, told him to get rid of it and dress like a Yankee, not a Guinea. The Irish, he said, would pay him more mind. The Irish, who had the power to overrule, wore suits that needed letting out.

Tonetti was a swift learner. Like his boss, he wore leather heels to make himself heard on marble floors, for the first rule in the state house was to be noticed. The second was to respect the rigidity of the pecking order, sacrosanct in all cases. The third was never to forget a slight.

David had no wish for a tour of the state house, but Tonetti insisted. In an iconoclastic mood, David viewed the golden dome as a testament to dogma and politicians as platitudinous and posturing. Monitoring a session of the house, a bill to be voted on, he saw an arena where smarm was a tactic and sarcasm a knife.

Tonetti said, "You don't understand nothing. You got your nose in the air. This stage of the game you should have it up somebody's ass."

"I got it where it belongs," David said. "In a book."

||| ☰ |||

He made the dean's list. He collected Billie Holiday records, saw movies with subtitles, and haunted secondhand bookstores. He worked an-other summer at the postal annex and the next one as a night watch-man in a bank building, where he carried a toy gun and read Kant and Hegel on the job. Now and then he dated women from Suffolk and the state house, students and secretaries, nothing serious and only occa-sionally sexual. His life, he felt, was proceeding in a direction not yet revealed, unknown forces vectoring him.

Home for a holiday, dining at Lomazzo's with his father and Gretchen Ryder, he said, "I don't suppose you ever run into Johanna."

Shell shook his head.

Gretchen said, "Her picture was in the paper. She got married."

169

The color left David's face.

"I'm sorry," Gretchen said quickly. "Are you still in love with her?"

"That wouldn't make much sense, would it?"

Shell steered the conversation to baseball, to the Yankees, to the young Mickey Mantle, whose bat was a fatal argument to most pitches.

David's voice was shaky. "I'm a Red Sox fan, Dad."

"Right. As you should be." Shell was contemplative for a number of moments. Then he spoke quietly. "When's the last time you saw your mother?"

The last time he'd seen her she had on a heavy sweater and complained about her teeth. When he asked if she remembered Plug Pond, she said she remembered everything, even her first French kiss.

"I don't know, Dad."

When Shell left to use the men's, Gretchen put aside her coffee cup and said, "I didn't mean to upset you, David."

"You didn't."

"You need a woman," she said gently. "A woman holds a man together."

"Then Dad's lucky to have you."

"Yes, he is. But I'm luckier."

On his way back to the table, Shell stopped to talk to someone. Gretchen watched him with a protective eye and smiled faintly. "He loves you the most, David. He'd die for you."

"He needn't do that."

"No, but he would."

"What are you telling me, Gretchen?"

"I know my place," she said.

He was glad to get back to Boston, a check in his pocket from his father, the amount more than he'd wanted to accept, more than he felt entitled to. He paid his room rent in advance and his tuition for the next semester, bought a secondhand set of Dickens, and sprang for dinner at the Parker House with Tony Tonetti.

Tonetti, wearing pinstripes and sipping red wine, said, "What d'you think of Angie?"

Angie was his girlfriend. Angela Sciuto. David, whose mental image of her was always larger than scale, had met her several times and found her pleasant and quiet. "I think she's nice."

"She's built like a brick shithouse."

"You're complaining?"

"She's tall. She puts on heels, I'm eye-level with her nipples." Tonetti took another sip of wine. "But what the fuck. She loves me, I love her."

"Then nothing else matters."

Tonetti ran a thumb around the rim of his wineglass. "Anybody asks you, you're Catholic. Got me?"

"You want to explain?"

"You're gonna be my best man."

The wedding was in June, held in the Sons of Italy hall in East Boston. The bridesmaids were strapping young women, each a bale of chiffon. Tonetti danced with Angie to "Always" and was amazingly light on his feet. David, who wasn't, danced with her later. In his ear, she whispered, "Tony says you're like a brother."

David whispered back, "He's the closest I have to one."

A number of drinks loosened his legs by the time he danced with all of the bridesmaids, one of whom lay her cheek against his shoulder. His thoughts were of Johanna. He felt sure they were bound to meet again, as if all paths in life were switchback.

||| ☰ |||

He was in law school when the next presidential election came around. Again he voted for Stevenson over Eisenhower. Tonetti, though a Democrat, voted for Eisenhower because he said he didn't trust any rich egghead with a hole in his shoe.

"Stevenson don't do for himself, what's he gonna do for me?"

"It was a campaign ploy," David said. "A tactic."

"I know that, but the fucking shoe didn't get that way by itself."

Eisenhower was again an easy winner, and so was Senator DeFelice, whose victory celebration was in the ballroom of the Hotel Touraine, where the governor showed up to toast him and pump his hand in front of cameras. David stood in the crowd with Angela Tonetti, who was four months' pregnant and uneasy. Sipping ginger ale David had fetched for her, she said, "I wish he had lost."

David glanced at her with surprise. "Why do you say that?"

"Tony's at his beck and call. I never know when he'll be home or for how long. It's like he's married to Sylvio, not me."

"It'll slow down now."

"How can it? He's the only one Sylvio trusts."

She finished off her ginger ale. Tonetti had mounted the stage with DeFelice and was waving to her, trying to catch her eye. He wanted her up there for the cameras. She heaved a sigh and gave her hair a touch.

"Excuse me, David."

He repositioned himself and stood alone with a half-filled wine-glass. DeFelice, flanked onstage by his wife and two adolescent sons, was ready to deliver his victory speech. Twice, barely listening to it, David glimpsed a striking young woman aloofly reconnoitering the crowd's edges. She had the marvelous neck of a goose and the slimness of a dancer. Now, suddenly, he saw her again, angling toward him. Her smile preceded her.

"At last, someone who looks interesting." She stuck out a hand. "Meredith Wainwright."

She gave the greater grip as he mumbled his name, intrigued by hers. Wainwright was familiar in Massachusetts history and Republican politics. Her gaze went to the stage, to DeFelice, who was turning to another page of his speech.

"Not a bad-looking guy," she said, "but he doesn't know when to shut up."

"Politicians usually don't," David said, staring at her intently. Her hair, worn long, was chestnut brown. The bones in her face were superb, along with her coloring. She had the Wainwright chin. "You're beautiful."

"Yes, I know. Breeding. What's yours?"

"You wouldn't be impressed. What are you doing here?"

She lifted the wineglass from his hand and took a small sip. "Slumming."

III ☰ III

People were finally leaving. Thank God it was over. Angela Tonetti's back ached, and her feet hurt. Sylvio DeFelice kissed her cheek and said he appreciated everything she had done for him. During the campaign she had stuffed more envelopes than anyone else, made hundreds of phone calls on his behalf, and dished out lasagna at neighborhood fund-raisers.

"I had a vested interest," she said.

He glanced down at her waist. "Boy or girl?"

"Doesn't matter."

He returned somebody's departing wave. "I bet it does to Tony."

"All you guys want sons," she said.

Others were waving. "Tony doesn't treat you right, you let me know," he joked, and broke away to receive someone's parting hand-shake.

Waiting for her husband at the foot of the stage, she incarnated fidelity and patience, motherhood in her posture. After a while she shifted her weight from one leg to the other and thought of sitting down. Then she heard her husband's voice winging toward her.

"Where's Shellenbach? Where'd he go?"

"I don't know," she said. "Maybe he got bored."

"Damn! I thought the three of us could go someplace for a night-cap."

"I'm tired, Tony."

Reluctantly he piloted her to the door, through the lobby, and out into the night air tainted by exhaust fumes. She tried not to breathe deeply while he gave a dollar to a panhandler and another one to the youth who fetched their car. A shiny black Buick had replaced the gaudy old one and carried a thick payment book. With a hand on her knee, he sped through the tunnel into East Boston.

"This was a great night, Angie. Why ain't you happy like me?"

"I don't know, Tony. Why ain't I?"

He caressed her knee. "You don't feel so hot, huh?"

"I've felt better."

Their home was a large first-floor flat on Putnam Street between Bennington and Saratoga. The furnishings, except for the piano she'd practiced on as a child, were new. The pastel refrigerator and matching stove were gifts from her parents. The china closet and the crucifix on the bedroom wall were from her aunt. Everything else had been bought on time.

Tony ran an amorous hand across her back and said, "It won't hurt the baby. The doctor said so."

Two years older than he and wise in ways he didn't suspect, she knew how to manage situations. "Go to bed," she whispered. "I'll be there in a bit."

In the bathroom, her clothes at her feet, her pregnancy sprang out on her. Nude, she felt skinned and ugly and hurried into a cotton nightshirt. But then she took her time at the sink, loitered in the mirror, though the image was estranged from her, little chance of reconciliation. Tony's toothbrush was beside hers. Together, hers the pink one, the toothbrushes represented a moment's choice when she had been increasingly at odds with herself, with none of her other beaus ever likely to propose.

Tony was asleep. Knowing he would be, she slipped into the bedroom.

III ≡ III

David woke with a start in the half-light and felt the warmth beside him. She was asleep. Waking her, he said, "I thought I dreamed you."

"What time is it?"

Squinting, he read his watch. "Little after six."

"Go back to sleep."

He tried and couldn't. She already had. He gazed at the back of her head and the length of her naked neck in wonder. Until now other women in his life were abstractions of Johanna. Meredith Wainwright was solely herself.

It had been her idea to escape to the bar. In the bar, watching a spark fall from her cigarette, he had asked why she was booked into the Touraine. No mystery, she'd simply wanted a night out to herself and to let life take its course. Eating the olive from a martini, she'd told him her room was on the eighth floor. Riding the elevator with her, he'd felt privileged.

Careful not to disturb her, he eased over to the bed's edge. Rising, he stepped on her destroyed dress as he stood, dizzy until he got his bearings.

The small blemish on her throat was from birth, the dent in her knee from childhood. How, she had asked, did he get that scar on his upper lip? Grappling, they'd stumbled. Stumbling, they'd blundered onto the bed as if to mate as fortuitously as they had met.

He read his watch again. He had an early class he couldn't cut, constitutional cases, a quiz at the end. Stiff-legged, he stepped past the chair that held her unzipped overnight bag. It revealed only a change of underwear, robin's-egg blue. Draped over another chair was a London Fog. In the bathroom a towel she had used lay on the floor. Mirrors in the morning made him feel older than he was. He showered quickly.

Returning to the room with a towel tied to his waist, he parted the drapes to let in more light and viewed the surroundings as if memorizing evidence at a crime scene. His clothes were scattered. He searched for a shoe. One had crept away from the other. Meredith Wainwright's eyes were open.

"David, isn't it?"

Her voice straightened him. "Yes."

"You struck it rich, David."

He agreed. She had picked him out of a crowd. He wondered whether it was fated, whether he had lost Johanna in order to meet her.

"Our bodies definitely took a shine to each other," she said.

"That's one way of putting it."

She wanted a cigarette. He tapped a Pall Mall from her pack, lit it, and delivered it. She sat up, bringing the covers with her, and smiled. "Thank you."

"Have you done this often?" he asked.

"That's a brutish question." She drew on the cigarette. "I suspect we're the same age, but only in years."

175

Suddenly he was struck with the chilling possibility that he would not see her again. He suspected strongly that she was forgetful of faces and tried to impress his own on her. "Sorry," he said in a voice that signaled his feelings.

"I hope you're not going to tell me you love me."

"Not if you don't want me to."

He found his errant shoe and retrieved his clothes. His necktie had come off with the knot still in it. Two buttons were gone from his shirt.

"I don't sew," she said.

"I didn't think you did."

She snuffed out her cigarette and watched him dress. The missing shirt buttons were near the top. His necktie seemed to hide the damage. He buttoned his tweed jacket.

"I have to leave. I have an eight-o'clock class."

"Good," she said. "The morning after is seldom pleasant."

Standing with a certainty he was gazing at her for the last time, he strained for something fitting to say, something she would remember. From Tremont Street came the growing sound of traffic. "I'm glad I met you," he said.

She tossed aside the covers and rose naked from the bed. High-hipped, head erect, she sauntered past him to the bathroom. From the bathroom she said, "I think my father will like you."

CHAPTER ELEVEN

FROM HIS PILLOW, HIS VOICE STEADY, SHELL SAID, "I stole you."

David watched dust dance in sunlight from the open window and waited for breaks in his father's voice, something to suggest disconnection. The tale being told was too bizarre to be true and too monstrous to be a joke.

Words from the pillow continued in firm, simple shapes. "The ladder broke. I nearly dropped you."

This was not his father talking. This was not he listening, and for several seconds at a stretch, hearing the busy activity of birds, he was able to shut out the words. Dropping his voice, he interrupted with a trace of impatience. "What are you telling me, Dad?"

"Just listen, please. Hauptmann could've saved himself. He couldn't have given them me, but he could've given them Rudy."

David knew that Rudy Farber was a name from his father's boyhood. As was Gretchen Ryder. Gretchen Krause. Richard Hauptmann had been a kidnapper and a murderer, a man in the news.

"There was no murder. Hauptmann didn't know that. Lindbergh didn't either. Only Rudy and I knew . . . and your mother."

For an instant David felt an evil spirit was in the air. Lindbergh was a name in history, the first pilot to fly nonstop across the Atlantic.

"Colonel Lindbergh died in nineteen seventy-four," Shell said in a voice that had become strong though not louder. "Mrs. Lindbergh is still alive, living in Connecticut. After you, she had five more children. Three sons, two daughters."

David felt he was standing alone on the periphery of a smoky field, events taking place beyond his comprehension, the participants stick figures. His father's voice had taken possession.

"She wrote books. I read only one. *Gift from the Sea.* Delicate and beautiful. A seashell illustrated each chapter. I think she's found peace."

He knew of the book. Meredith had a copy. He remembered picking it up long ago and thumbing through it. Only the seashells had held his eye. He had meant to read it but never did. He had, however, read *The Spirit of St. Louis.*

"She's old now, David. Like me."

David's voice was cold. "Are you saying you're not my father?"

Shell raised his head. For the first time in months the skin of his face showed color and texture. "I'm every bit your father. But not your real one."

David's face contracted. He stood silent, a silence that sank into a deeper one. Passing a hand over his hair, he said, "Excuse me for a minute."

"Whatever you come to think of me, I'll understand."

Turning on a tap in the bathroom, he crouched at the sink and splashed cold water on his face. Two towels hung from a rack, one monogrammed, indicating it was Mr. Unger's. David used neither. Smoothing his hair with wet hands, he stared into the mirror and expected his face to shout. When it didn't he gave a tug to his tie, another to the jacket of his bespoken suit.

He resumed his place at the bedside, his expression set. "I don't believe you, Dad."

"There are times I don't believe it," Shell said.

III ≡ III

He left Hanover House and drove from the outskirts of Andover to the center, to the big house on School Street that his father-in-law had given them, in both their names. From a window seat in the study he glimpsed students from the academy crossing the street and a woman in sweats jogging up it, an Irish setter tagging along. He did not hear Meredith enter the room, though gradually he sensed her presence. Her voice was accusatory.

"How long have you been home?"

Home did not seem an appropriate word. Everything seemed illegal, fraudulent. Turning, shifting his weight on the window seat, he said, "What's my schedule for the rest of the week?"

"You're booked solid. Tonight you have that women's group in Belmont."

"Cancel it. And the rest."

"Are you crazy?" Her voice was sharp. "Why?"

"Things I need to do."

She stepped closer and gazed down at him as if through the chill of ice. "Don't blow it, David. Not when we're this close."

He thought he heard other voices beyond hers, but they were in his head. Actually, he decided, they were his own loud thoughts. Meredith touched his shoulder. From her, long ago, he had learned that love is a possibility, not a given.

"Something's wrong, David. What the hell is it?"

"It's personal."

"What do you mean, *personal*?" She withdrew her hand. "What's the matter with you?"

He was afraid. Afraid of his own voice. And of himself. The flow of his inner life and the privacy of his being were under attack. "It's my father."

"Oh, yes, your father." She stepped back. "We all know he's sick. Nothing we can do about it."

"He's dying."

"He's been dying for months, David. Are we supposed to stop living?"

Soon Joseph Shellenbach would be gone. The thought was striking him harder than ever before.

"You've got him in the best place imaginable. You're paying top dollar. What more can you do?"

Could he give in and take seriously the quiet ravings of a very sick man? Could he step back and discern truth in the wildness of the story?

"The dimensions of your problem are unclear, David. I don't even know what the fuck the problem is. Can you let me in on it?" Her face tried to absorb his. "Really, I want to know."

Her face nearly did absorb his. He remembered their honeymoon on the Greek isle, Meredith running from a breaker, her body a sweetness of logical simplicity, like the universe itself. All eyes on her. How could they not be?

Her voice softened. "At least tell me if there's anything I can do."

"It's not in your hands," he said. "Nor in mine."

||| ≡ |||

Nitroglycerine pills kept Father Henry alive. He'd once tried to stop taking them, but the pain was too great, so he decided to keep on living, though living did not seem the appropriate word. Besides heart trouble he had a hiatal hernia and a liver condition. His long-dead wife comforted him in the night, visiting him in one dream after another. Her nightly presence was so strong that during the day he often had the illusion she was still alive. During bouts of cold rationality he knew she was nowhere, but he thanked God for the dreams.

He also thanked God for the Florida sun, for the money that long ago had come to him out of the blue, and for Mrs. Dodd. He'd recently had a birthday, but Mrs. Dodd had let it pass without a cake and with scarcely a mention. She reminded him that in ninety years he'd doubtless blown out enough candles.

Mrs. Dodd, nearly a hundred but not ready to admit it, was a marvel. She still had a figure and most of her teeth and had broken no hips and suffered no surgeries except for cataract removals. Despite occasional shortness of breath, she was active. She chewed gum to exercise her face, squeezed a tennis ball to fight arthritis in her fingers, and ate food with fiber to guarantee good stools. When dining out, she wore high heels. Father Henry wore canvas shoes slit at the sides to relieve the discomfort of bunions.

They lived comfortably in a condo minutes from the beach and had no money problems because the year before Father Henry's retirement a member of his flock died and generously remembered him in her will. He called it pennies from heaven. Heaven, Mrs. Dodd said, was Florida.

Their bedrooms had a communicating door. One could see to the other. She would miss that if he died. They did not often talk of dying, though she figured death is tolerable. Surely you get used to it right away.

Her real fear was that Father Henry's condition would worsen and necessitate a nursing home, which would eat up his resources and leave her future in question. His death, though she cared not to ponder it, would be preferable. The bulk of his money would go to his daughter, but he'd assured her that she'd get enough to see her through.

Father Henry, who'd prided himself on good health, now believed that nothing, absolutely nothing, is certain, not even God, who one day may grow tired of himself and simply cease to be. Theology and mythology, he'd come to believe, are rather one and the same, the latter more trustworthy.

His greatest pleasure was sitting in the early-evening light on the balcony with Mrs. Dodd, who, if she ever felt sorry for herself, never said so. He admired that in her and wished he had a bit of it. He enjoyed her gossip about the widow in the condo below who argued with her cat, the two of them on equal footing, and he smiled at her quips about the current occupant of the White House, a Hollywood actor, whom she likened to Dopey of the seven dwarfs. After a while they simply sat in the silence of each other's company.

Each had concerns about Shell, whose health they knew was failing, the cancer not likely to go away. Gretchen Ryder, more than anyone else, kept them informed. Neither felt it fitting that Shell should predecease them. Mrs. Dodd considered the irony unnatural.

"I've outlived my husband and children. Now I'm going to out-live my son-in-law. Why am I sticking around, Prescott? Is there a reason?"

Father Henry had no answer, though he knew precisely why he read obituaries with a degree of smugness. Greater people than he were dying each day. He wanted his own death to be followed by the mournful melody of a bagpipe. "Amazing Grace." That was something he should write down rather than tell Dorothy. She might forget.

"No answer, Prescott?"

"You're like MacArthur, Dorothy. You'll simply fade away."

||| ≡ |||

The drive from Andover to Haverhill was twenty minutes at the most, but David, wearing dark glasses against the midmorning sun, took longer. He drove slow, one hand on the wheel, and sipped a take-out coffee, his head in the past. He remembered the day men took his mother away to Danvers, her gaze frozen like a dead person's. He re-membered the pressure of his father's arm and the first Christmas without her. Everything that had been on his list was under the tree. He remembered the hugs he gave his father.

Stepping out of his car, he smelled the river. The old tenement house looked no different. Pigeons shingled the roof's edge. He climbed stairs, knocked twice, heard a voice, and entered.

"I should've phoned first," he said.

Gretchen Ryder's face fell. She thought the worst.

"No," he said quickly. "Dad's OK."

She was wrapped in a rose robe that added to her weight. Her hair was not fully brushed. Yesterday's *Gazette* was on the kitchen table. "Coffee?"

Though he'd had enough, he nodded. They sat at the table, he at his father's place, and for several seconds he feared himself, the self he didn't know.

"But you've come to talk about him," Gretchen said.

He nodded. "How long do you think he has?"

"I don't know. I don't want to think about it."

"Nor do I." He gazed out at the river. The same gulls he'd seen as a boy were sweeping over it. "Do you think his mind is slipping?"

"I don't think so. We always have nice little talks, your father and me." She passed the milk. The skin of her cleavage was tarnished. "Why do you ask?"

He turned his full face to her. "Yesterday he told me something I can't believe."

She was quiet. Eyes lowered, she sipped her coffee.

"Do you know what I'm talking about, Gretchen?"

She shook her head slowly. "Whatever it is, David, it's between you and him. Father and son."

"I suspect you know."

Tears she couldn't explain were in her eyes. "I don't want to know," she said.

"But I have to."

In the pocket of her robe she sought a tissue that wasn't there. A twitch rode up her leg. "Have pity, David. Nobody's young anymore, not even you."

He again looked toward the river and imagined he could see paths in the air beaten by birds, not all of them gulls. His mother had fed sparrows on the sill. "Tell me if it's true."

"All I know is he told me he doesn't want to die a coward. He said it would diminish his death."

David took a final sip of coffee and got to his feet. "I'm beginning to believe I exist in other people's minds and nowhere else."

Gretchen remained seated as he turned away. When he reached the door and didn't look back, she said, "Don't stop loving him."

||| ≡ |||

At the Haverhill library he occupied himself with bound volumes of newspapers more than fifty years old. Photographs engrossed him. Charles Augustus Lindbergh Junior, twenty months old, ensconced in a child's chair, could have been him, but how could he be sure? He had no pictures of himself at that age, none till he was four or five, his hair closely cropped and his ears sticking out.

Photographs of Charles and Anne Lindbergh he'd seen many times before. Newsreels. *Life* and *Look*. A TV documentary. Now he looked closer. Colonel Lindbergh was a clenched mouth, a stoic, a stone. Yet he fancied a glimpse of himself in the stone, a likeness that brought to mind a color snap Tonetti had taken of him in Copenhagen, the mermaid in the background. He wondered whether Johanna still had the picture. No reason she should. And if she had tried to save it, one of her husbands surely would have thrown it out.

A photo of the young Anne Morrow Lindbergh haunted him. The camera had caught her unawares, a gaping moment exposing fragility, melancholy, fear. He plumbed her eyes. He contemplated the bridge of her nose and the tip of it, not unlike his own. Her lips seemed to speak, soft words he couldn't hear or even imagine.

He could be sure of nothing and rested his mind on advertisements, comic strips, movie announcements. A haircut cost a dime, a shave a nickel. The Katzenjammer Kids bopped unsuspecting heads with coconuts. *Tarzan the Ape Man* was at the Strand.

He went to another volume, peeled pages, scanned pertinent headlines, and read opening paragraphs. The baby's remains were found in tatters of flannel and wool. "Fractured skull, external violence." Colonel Schwarzkopf predicted swift justice. Anne Lindbergh was expecting her second child.

He closed the volume. He moved ahead. He knew the exact year and the approximate month to look for and took his time finding it. The capture. No mention of any Rudy Farber. No Joseph Shellenbach. Of course there wouldn't be. Not if he had it right. Or even if he had it wrong. What was there was a UPI photo of Richard Bruno Hauptmann, whom he knew would be executed the following year.

Hauptmann's eyes stayed in his mind as he returned all the volumes to the shelves. His own eyes were sore, and his head hurt. He brushed dust from his hands.

A while later the woman at the desk smiled at him. He was checking out *Gift from the Sea*.

III ≡ III

The flash of white in the room was Mrs. Kaplan. She said, "You look better."

"I feel better," Shell said. "I got something off my chest."

Mrs. Kaplan looked toward Mr. Unger's tightly made bed. "Are you praying for him?"

Shell stood neatly dressed, though his shirt was too big for him and his trousers sagged in the seat. "I don't think he'd want me to. It's against his principles."

Mrs. Kaplan winked. "Could even bring him bad luck."

It was the lunch hour. He ignored the wheelchair. He planned to walk to the dining room on his own. Mrs. Kaplan watched him take the first step.

"Need help?"

"Not if I go slow."

"Where's your cane?"

"I can do without it."

"As long as you don't overdo it," Mrs. Kaplan said.

A door stood open at a private room where an old man sat horribly naked. On purpose. He subscribed to girlie magazines for the center-folds, kept condoms for the possibility, and had his nieces and nephews buy him lottery tickets for the miracle.

"Don't mind if I close this, do you, Mr. Bainbridge?" Mrs. Kaplan said, and gently shut him in.

The dining room was in the west wing and gave a view of a garden and an old apple tree clumsy in shape and no longer fertile. Most tables were taken. Though Shell would have preferred sitting with a woman, he joined two men, whose names he tried hard to keep straight. The one who couldn't manage substantial food and ate pap was Water-house. The other, wearing a zippered sailcloth jacket and a yachting cap and had probably never worked a day in his life, was Ruggles.

"Where's Unger?" Ruggles asked.

"Boston," Shell said. "Surgery."

"Who's Unger?" Waterhouse asked.

Waterhouse's memory was diseased. A blessing, Shell thought, and smiled at the young Hispanic woman serving him salad.

"He'll die on the table," Ruggles said.

Since Helen's passing, Shell had put death into perspective, narrowing it to a bill to be paid. Nibbling the salad, he wondered about the first few seconds of death. Would he believe he was still alive? Deeper into it, would he come upon carcasses? The former he decided was likely, the latter irrational, which eased his mind and aided his appetite.

Waterhouse glanced over his shoulder. "I think I'm being watched."

"Who would bother?" Ruggles said.

A bubble appeared between Waterhouse's lips and popped. "My wife."

"She's dead, man. Get with it." Ruggles took a swallow of decaf. "How's your wife, Shellenbach?"

"I'm afraid she's dead too."

Ruggles angled his head. "Who's that woman comes to see you?"

Shell corrected himself. "You're right. She's like my wife."

He had finished the salad, his appetite waning, when the Hispanic woman brought him a plate of scallops, a roll on the side. She seemed to know he wouldn't eat any of it but left it anyway. Moments later she was back with dessert, which she knew he would eat. He smiled up at her. She was Hebe, goddess of youth and spring, Helen with a halo.

Ruggles pushed back his chair to leave. He had allergies. He was running at the nose. Shell looked around and saw others leaving. Then Waterhouse was ambling off, though in the wrong direction. Alone with a scoop of tapioca pudding, his hand trembling for no obvious reason, he felt anonymous.

In time Mrs. Kaplan appeared with his wheelchair and piloted him back to his room, where she felt his pulse and told him it was racing.

"Just jittery," he said, but knew anxiety was edging into anguish. Mrs. Kaplan knew it too. She left and returned with a pill to calm him down.

He lay on his bed, his eyes closed, and soon the pill gave him a sensation of floating high over all anxieties, all anguish, of gazing down at a world of people coming and going. Floating higher, he felt he was in uncharted space, Helen just around the corner.

An hour passed without his knowing it. It could have been an eon.

He couldn't remember seeing Helen but had a vague recollection of hearing her voice. And Mrs. Zuber's. Now he wondered whether they'd been one and the same.

He was about to drift off again when he became aware of tension in the air. Opening his eyes, he made out David staring down at him. David's voice was cold.

"I believe you."

CHAPTER TWELVE

DAVID SAW MEREDITH WAINWRIGHT NOW AND THEN, AT
her convenience, her schedule and perhaps her mood the determi-
nants. He waited for her on Park Street, outside the hallowed entrance
to Houghton Mifflin, where she was a glorified secretary to a senior editor, a job she'd gotten through her family name and Radcliffe credentials. She came out the door, took his arm, and whispered, "Have any
wet dreams about me?"

"No more than usual."

"You must tell me about them."

"Tonight?"

"Not tonight. I'm busy."

He walked with her up Park and down Beacon to the intersection at
Charles, where they waited for the lights to change. He looked straight
ahead, she looked at him.

"Don't you have another jacket?" she asked, scrutinizing the nubby
tweed of the one he always wore.

"Not at the moment."

"Do you own a suit?"

"Do I need one?"

"Not if you don't intend to be anyone."

They crossed the intersection and continued down Beacon to the brownstone where she had recently rented an apartment, her father's name on the lease. She ferreted for keys as she climbed the stoop to the vaulted doorway. He followed her, though he knew it was not one of the times she would invite him in.

"When will you not be busy?" he asked.

"Don't pin me down. I'll call you."

He tried not to think about the other men in her life but couldn't stop himself. Watching her fit a key into the door, he said, "Who else are you seeing?"

"Lots of people."

"I feel like your lapdog," he said.

She turned smoothly and kissed him on the lips. "I do like you, David. More than you know."

A month passed, during which he busied himself with his studies, participated in moot-court sessions, and saw several movies, all of them French. Then she called. Within the hour he appeared at her apartment in a suit he'd bought in the maelstrom of Filene's Basement, the sleeves a little short for his long arms.

"You're lucky," she said. "Most anything looks good on you."

He took her to a club off Arlington Street, where someone with a sax was playing "In a Sentimental Mood." He led her onto the dance floor. Flawless in a minimal black dress, she looked like a mannequin music was bringing to life. In his arms, she gave him the full fragrance of herself.

"How long have we known each other?" she asked, moving effortlessly to the music, leading him.

"I don't know. Six months, seven? Let me lead."

"Most of my friends are married. How about yours?"

"I don't have many."

"Your Italian friend is married."

"Yes."

They danced close to a piano rendition of "You Belong to Me." He was swollen.

"That night at the Touraine," he said. "What were you really doing there?"

"Meeting someone who didn't show. He wanted to put me in my place."

"Did he?"

"Hardly. He didn't know what he was losing." Her bold face smiled at him. "Are you jealous?"

"I don't have the right."

"Perhaps you do," she said, and purposely trod on his foot. "Let's sit down."

At the table, sitting close, they drank whiskey sours and listened to a beautiful black woman sing "Tenderly." At a nearby table were two women who looked unconvincing and may have been men. Meredith's gaze was aslant.

"You often mention your father, never your mother."

David lit cigarettes for the two of them. "Not much to say. She's been in a state hospital since I was a boy."

"Crazy, is she?" She placed a firm hand on his thigh. "As long as you're not. You're not, are you?"

"Who's normal? Are you?"

They had another round of whiskey sours and danced again. The black woman was back at the microphone. The song was "Don't Blame Me." Her voice had body, ache, edge. The two suspect women were dancing with men who looked legitimate. The small floor grew crowded.

Meredith said, "I wish you'd hurry up and become a lawyer."

"Why?"

"Why do you think?"

The voice of the singer engulfed the dancers, and the sound of the sax drew them closer and hemmed them in. Someone's rump brushed Meredith's and pushed her deeper into David. He kissed her hard and was kissed back harder. Her breast shaped his hand. Her hand spanned his crotch.

"I suppose you should meet my family," she said.

He had images of Main Street in Andover, of a town of Yankee sensibilities, of lives channeled into moneymaking during the week and serenaded on Sunday by Episcopal church bells.

"Can you afford a ring?"

"Not a big one," he said.

"We'll wait on that."

The song ended, the music died out. One of the funny women had split a seam. The sax player drained spit from his horn. The singer blew him a kiss.

"Let's get out of here, David. Let's fuck."

III ≡ III

Angela Tonetti's breasts were vessels of milk, her nipples sore, her baby burping in her ear. The decision to nurse, she said, was Tony's idea, not hers. Tony thought she was some kind of earth mother. "Here," she said, and deftly shifted the infant into David's arms. "I'll be back in a second."

He stared at the tender spot on the skull. The membrane was negligible, anything could go through it, his own thumb. Life was that fragile.

He waited. The table was set, but nothing was cooking on the stove. He'd been invited for six, already it was seven. Meredith was out with friends but was expecting him later.

Angela returned with a cradle, and together she and David fitted her daughter in. Straightening, she was a tired shape in a stained robe. She sniffed herself.

"I stink."

David looked at the wall clock. "Tony's late."

"Tony's always late. Why do you think I haven't started supper yet?" She too looked at the clock. "Mind if I take a quick bath?"

The baby began to fuss.

"Rock her," she said. "She'll fall asleep."

The bathroom was off the kitchen. She left the door ajar. Swaying the cradle, David listened to her run water full force. Pipes knocked when she turned it off. He heard her sinking into the tub. He said, "Tony's doing well?"

"Tony was born to do well. He's an operator."

The baby had quit fussing, and her eyes were closed. She had something of her father's face.

191

"But he could be headed to hell," Angela shouted.

David looked at his watch and fidgeted. He stepped softly to the bathroom door but didn't mean to get so close to the opening. She lay in bathwater as if Matisse had placed her there. Quickly he stepped back.

"I have to leave," he said.

"Hold on. I'll be out in a minute."

She was out in three, a humid presence wrapped in towels, one around her head, the other around her torso. She loosened the towel on her head and rubbed her hair, much of which fell in her face. She smiled.

"Meeting someone?"

He imagined that under the towel she was still wounded from motherhood, her body still in shock. "Yes."

"When do we get to meet her?"

"Soon."

"Tony's heard things about her."

"I don't want to hear them."

She tossed her hair back, dried her ears. "We don't want to see you hurt."

"I have to go," he said.

"Not yet. I have to ask you something."

Her damp feet, larger than most women's, led him into the living room. He remained standing. She sat on the piano bench, the towel tight around her.

"You're not a Catholic, are you?"

He hesitated. "No."

"The baptism is Sunday. I want you there, but you can't be the god-father."

"How do you know?"

"I'm not a fool." Her voice was hard. "It's not you I'm upset with, it's Tony."

"I'm sorry." He headed for the door.

"Words of advice, David. Be yourself."

III ≡ III

Gretchen Ryder went to the telephone, dialed. Without hesitation Father Henry agreed to see her. She was, he said, one of the few faces that brightened his day.

He was at the church, at the door when she arrived. He was in a mood, he said, for something sweet, so they crossed the street and sat at the fountain in Aram's. A chocolate walnut sundae was a gift from God, he said. Gretchen settled for a Coca-Cola.

"Day off?" he asked.

She had phoned in sick, something she rarely did. She hadn't been sleeping well. Dreams woke her. In some, men with dirty feet left footprints on her.

"What's wrong, Gretchen?"

She felt lost, like a child, without understanding. Without parents. Her earliest memories of them were slaps when she wouldn't sit still and worse ones when she wet her pants. When the epidemic took them she should've been sadder.

"Talk, I'll listen," Father Henry said.

She remembered throwing a stone at an old man who tried to follow her home. She remembered the gaping face of the first boy she let touch her. She said, "My favorite radio programs are off the air. I don't know what I'll do without them."

"You have television."

"It's not the same."

In the mirror behind the fountain she noted the soft decay in her looks. Father Henry saw her in tinted light. "What's really wrong?"

"I'm scared, Father, scared of everything." She stirred the Coca-Cola with the straw. "Shell and me, are we living in sin?"

He wiped a trace of chocolate from his upper lip. "You're two people who need each other. I wouldn't call that sin."

"I wake up in the night, I'm afraid one of us won't be there. I touch him, then myself."

Father Henry nodded. He'd had similar fears when his wife was ill. Now the fears were metaphysical, one being that the whole world might suddenly taper to a point, back to where it had begun, a gleam in God's eye, human existence a hoax, at most a daydream. Sometimes he thought only Mrs. Dodd had validity.

"Without Shell, I don't know what I'd do. I wouldn't be me."

He understood. Identity wasn't a given. Half of him had gone blank when his wife died, leaving him unable to separate reality from unreality, as if they coexisted in the spin of a coin. The question was which had the greater weight. He himself had been weightless.

"Shell carries secrets," Gretchen said. "I tell him everything."

"Some of us are that way."

She played with the straw. "I've had lots of romances, Father."

"People need to touch," he said.

"I've been good to men, but Shell's the only one who's been good to me."

Father Henry finished the sundae and drank water. Mrs. Dodd, in her own gruff way, was good to him. Mrs. Dodd sustained him. And there was the meaning of life in a nutshell. One human being giving another the will, if not always the strength, to go on. He said, "You must hold on to each other."

"I don't think he loves me, Father, but he cares about me."

"Caring is loving, don't you know that?"

"He worries about his wife. She's poorly. She talks about dying, like that's going to be her gift to him. It breaks his heart."

Father Henry was silent.

Gretchen twisted the straw, rendering it unusable. She remembered the boy who'd buried her only doll. He told her it was dead.

The eternal question of whether death is the dark or another dawn suddenly seemed irrelevant to Father Henry. For the sky has no ceiling, the ground no meaning. So where else can the dying go except inward, back into the kernel of energy that has done its job, a spent force, its miracle over?

Gretchen drank through ice and remembered Rudy Farber rubbing his penis for luck and getting none. "We live and then we die, is that it, Father?"

"No. We dream and then we die."

She patted her lips with a napkin and smiled. "I don't know why, but I feel better. Thank you."

Father Henry knew that occasionally his voice had healing power. The words didn't matter. The resonance of feeling did. He placed a fifty-cent piece on the counter. "We must do this more often," he said.

||| ≡ |||

"My grandson is seeing someone," Mrs. Dodd said. She was riding a stationary bicycle in the living room, her bare feet shod in red sneakers, her white hair topknotted. "A Wainwright, I'm told."

"Ah," said Father Henry from the best chair. He was watching *The Frank Sinatra Show*, Bing Crosby a guest. Often the lilt and lyric of a popular song enthralled him, as if he were sixteen again. Despite the terror, he'd have liked being sixteen again. "Who do you like better?" he asked.

"Bing," she said. "Did you hear me?"

"Yes. I'm impressed. Is it serious?"

"Serious enough. I wouldn't be surprised if he gave her a ring."

"Has Shell met her?"

"Not yet," Mrs. Dodd said over the handlebars. "But we expect to."

Father Henry turned his face to her. "What about us, Dorothy? Marriage, I mean."

She tossed him a droll look, which diminished meaning from the ballad Sinatra was singing. It even lessened something in his soul, which had always been more Greece than Jerusalem. A toga would have fitted him fine.

"It's not the first time I've asked," he said.

"We seem to be doing so well the way we are, Prescott. I don't know if I could take you twenty-four hours a day."

"I wouldn't be underfoot."

"I wouldn't want to live in that dreary rectory."

"I'm not that far from retirement."

"That's not a plus." Mrs. Dodd quit pedaling and sat erect. Father Henry easily imagined her astride a stallion, she and the animal equally magnificent. "Emotionally you're very vulnerable, Prescott."

"In some respects I suppose I am."

"My husband needed a lot of babying. You tend to be like him."

"I hadn't realized."

Mrs. Dodd dismounted, pressed a hand to the small of her back and stretched. "I like people with bright faces, their suffering on the sly."

Father Henry was not angry, not even hurt, and not in the least surprised. "That's what I love about you, Dorothy. You don't give an inch."

"No?" She plumped into the second-best chair. "I don't deprive you your pleasure, do I?"

"Once a week," he said with a gentle smile. "For which I'm grateful."

On the television was a toothpaste commercial. Mrs. Dodd dropped her head back and closed her eyes, effectively shutting him out. Her deeper thoughts she kept to herself. His she kept at bay. Love was a word they seldom mentioned, for she had assigned love to runaway reality in Hollywood movies.

"I'm tired," she said.

Father Henry nodded. "Tonight's not one of the nights."

"No, Prescott. Best you be going."

He was already on his feet. Her eyes were open. "Reality is what my mind tells me it is, Dorothy. My reality might not be yours."

"I've ruffled your feathers, haven't I?"

He kissed her. "Not in the least, but when will you realize we're two old birds who need each other?"

"I've known that all along, dear boy."

||| ≡ |||

"What do you think of the young man?" Priscilla Wainwright asked from a morning room full of afternoon sunshine. Windows looked out in three directions, one of which focused on a trellis of yellow roses.

"I rather like him," Paul Wainwright said with a wry smile. "What are your objections?"

"Only the obvious ones."

Standing in the doorway, Paul Wainwright kept the wryness in his smile, which in no way lessened his affection for her. Thirty years ago he'd thought of her as uncorked wine. One could only imagine the taste. Courting her had been an exercise in anticipation.

"Meredith said they met at a bar."

"She was pulling your leg, Pris. They met at a political event."

"Where did he say he was from?"

"Just down the road. Haverhill."

"Yes, Haverhill. Little shoe city. Lot of Greeks and Italians there."

"And Jews, Pris. Don't forget them."

"You're making fun of me."

He had married her for her polished nails, her feathery voice, and her beauty, not her magnanimity. Beauty, he'd never realized, could exhaust him, and he was relieved when hers faded. The loss made her more endearing and him more protective.

"Actually," she said, "he was born in the Bronx. That's what Meredith told me."

"Did she also tell you he was two when his parents moved to Massachusetts?"

"His poor mother, Paul. Isn't that a shame?" Turning, she inspected a lush pot of African violets, the proper care of which she had learned as a child. "Doesn't something like that run in the family?"

"Not necessarily," he said, watching her pluck a withered leaf. In nostalgic moments he thought of her as a throwback to the frills and furbelows of his grandmother's day, the ornate clutter of furniture dusted daily, the Victorian restraints on conversation.

"He is handsome, I'll say that for him."

Paul Wainwright agreed with a nod. "And he seems the serious sort."

"But unlikely to attract one of the big law firms. What school is he going to?"

"Harvard."

"You *know* he's not," she said with a grudging smile, and tested the soil in the pot for moisture. "All this is probably moot. I suspect she'll tire of him."

Meredith, their firstborn, was his favorite, and Kipper was hers. Kipper had her father's nose and not a few of his faults.

"Don't be so sure, Pris. She's past the debutante age."

Priscilla Wainwright, stepping toward the doorway, said nothing. Together they entered the elegance of a living room that resembled a stage set. Two oil portraits of past Wainwrights graced a wall and the portrait of a Taylor, Priscilla's side, another. Paul Wainwright's craggy features mimicked those of his grandfather, who had gallivanted with Teddy Roosevelt's Rough Riders.

Priscilla Wainwright paused near the massive fireplace, grasses and fronds etched into the marble. From a vase sprang extravagant pink-white peonies fresh from the garden. One had not yet blossomed and to the touch was a moist ball of fragrant soap not unlike the one she had bathed with that morning.

"I suppose," she said, "we should invite him and his father to dinner. But then there's the problem of the woman the father lives with. I don't think we should have her here, do you?"

"Maybe we should get Meredith's opinion on that."

Priscilla Wainwright sighed. "It's so confusing."

"I know," he said, and patted her arm.

A little later, alone in his study, he fed his fountain pen from an antique inkstand, three wells to choose from. Framed on a wall, some in parchment, were his accomplishments. Before the war he was a state senator, one of the youngest, and then a United States congressman, and during the war he served with the Office of Strategic Services, his exploits still classified. After the war he was chairman of the Republican State Committee. Now, his life more leisurely, he taught history at Phillips Academy, of which he was an alum.

Capping his pen, he heard his wife's approaching footsteps, which turned tentative. Turning, he saw tears in her eyes, a hand at her cheek.

"What's the matter, Pris?"

"I do hope she doesn't marry him."

He kissed her unlined brow and held her. "Prepare yourself," he said. "I rather think she will."

‖ ≡ ‖

The marriage ceremony was held in Cochran Chapel at the academy. Wainwrights and Taylors overcrowded the chapel, a sort of family reunion for them. Tony Tonetti was best man. As a favor to Tonetti, Senator Sylvio DeFelice was in attendance to add weight to the slim Shellenbach side. Father Henry, his voice in fine form, was allowed to officiate. The bride was beautiful.

The reception was next door at the Andover Inn. Priscilla Wainwright, crying openly during the ceremony, had since composed herself and actually smiled. She went out of her way to chat at length with David's father, whom she considered plain and uncomplicated, the sort who probably had never done anything extraordinary in his life. The grandmother she found a bit bizarre and insufferably haughty. Gretchen Ryder she ignored.

One of the Taylors, from New York, said to Father Henry, "My wife's side of the family is Church of England."

Father Henry, who'd been frequenting the open bar, had devilry in his eye. Actually, he said, he was a humanist at heart and, like Erasmus, wondered how a man could drive a dagger into his brother's guts and still live in the perfect charity that Christ claimed a Christian owed his neighbor.

David and Meredith danced to "Embraceable You." Meredith whispered, "This is forever, you know."

"Most things aren't," he said. "Let this be."

She danced with her father.

Later David led Gretchen Ryder onto the floor and danced with her to "Melancholy Baby," which happened to be her favorite. Afterward David danced with Angela Tonetti, who was pregnant with her second child, a son she hoped. Father Henry was a careless dancer, and Priscilla Wainwright's feet paid the price. Mrs. Dodd danced with Wainwrights and Taylors, young and old, her stamina amazing.

Nursing a glass of chablis, Shell watched from his table. In one way he was serenely happy and in another quite sad. Helen's absence lessened his triumph at seeing their son marry well. Eventually Gretchen coaxed him onto the dance floor.

"You look very handsome," she said.

He was trying to stay in step to "Whispering." "*Do* I now?"

"I'm not shaming you or David, am I?"

"Don't talk nonsense," he said.

Men with graying heads shook David's hand. A lawyer among them asked why he had chosen law. "To stretch out my education," he answered honestly. "And, of course, to make money."

A woman wearing pearls said that he reminded her of someone but for the life of her couldn't think who it might be. Did he have people in West Hartford? He shook his head. "Not that I know of."

She called her husband over, a Taylor. "Who does David remind you of, dear?"

He shrugged. "Jimmy Stewart?"

The Taylor who'd talked briefly with Father Henry mentioned him to Priscilla Wainwright. "Odd duck," he said. "I mean, for an Episcopal priest."

"I know," Priscilla Wainwright said, poised like a clock about to strike the hour. "The grandmother's no prize either."

Sitting down to rest, Mrs. Dodd felt she was in her element. The gracious decor of the Andover Inn, the glitter of the chandeliers, and the patrician looks of Paul Wainwright pleased her, though she saw nothing exceptional in his wife. In Meredith she detected strong hints of herself at that age. Kipper, whom she'd danced with, seemed no more than a glamour boy, the sort who expected the sun always to shine on him.

At some point the bride and groom vanished.

Only Gretchen Ryder immediately sensed their absence. In time they would go to bed, cuddle, and perhaps make a baby. It pleased her to think so.

Father Henry said to the bartender, "My God, to be young again."

A mirror in the powder room told Priscilla Wainwright she looked old and tired. Thirty years ago she was sitting in a bright classroom taking notes on Chaucer. Now her thoughts were on eternity. "Am I really almost fifty?" she asked. The mirror did not lie.

Shell, looking around for David, saw that he was gone.

"Six weeks," Gretchen said. "He'll be back."

"No," Shell said. "Not really."

||| ☰ |||

Shell brought Helen a basket of fruit. They sat close in facing chairs. Each was gray, each wore glasses. Hers had the thicker lenses. "Is that a new suit?" she asked.

"It's the one I wore to the wedding." He brushed a sleeve. "Mr. Wainwright is paying for the honeymoon," he said. "They're in Greece."

"I've never been to Greece."

"Nor I."

She stared at the fruit, which seemed to appeal to her sense of proportion, though not her appetite. "Socrates said know thyself. I'd rather not."

He began telling her about the Wainwrights.

She played with her hair. "If I had my life to live over, I wouldn't."

Mr. Wainwright, Shell said, had traced his ancestry to a street sweeper and a maid in colonial Boston. Subsequent Wainwrights became big in textiles, with mills in Lowell and Lawrence. One Wainwright served in the cabinet of Benjamin Harrison.

Helen picked up a peach, held it to the light, and decided against it. "You know my heart is bad."

For a moment his thoughts were crushed together. "Yes."

"I shouldn't be upset in any way. I should have absolute rest."

"Are you getting it?"

"You mustn't talk too loud."

"I don't believe I am."

She dug her nails into an orange, peeled a bit of it, and lost interest. "The insurance man hasn't been around. Not in years."

Shell scratched the back of his hand, his eczema kicking up. Conversing with her was like swimming against the muscle of a rip current. Sometimes he half let himself be dragged under.

"He may have gone to Florida," she said. "People want to die warm."

Bending in his chair, Shell retrieved an orange peel from the floor. He had to be careful what he said to her. Comments suitable one visit could be inappropriate the next.

"He asked me to keep a diary so he can read it," she said.

"The insurance man?"

"The new doctor. He wants to get in my head. Don't worry, I won't tell him." She sampled a plum and put it aside. "How long have I been here, Shell? No, don't tell me."

Shell felt his stomach churn. In his head was the image of a fish dangling from a line, waiting to be cut loose, to swim away with the hook still in its mouth.

"You're scratching."

"I know." He stopped. "I'm sorry."

"Don't let your lower lip droop like that. They'll think you're a moron and keep you here."

He could tell she wanted him to leave. He'd seen it coming. He rose with the fear his face would crack from holding the same expression so long. He leaned toward her.

"Please don't kiss me."

He pulled back. She was blaming him, blaming him for everything. He could read it in her eyes. She gripped the fruit basket and held it up at arm's length.

"And take this garbage with you."

III ☰ III

After a week of touring ruins, they boarded a boat to an isle in the Aegean, where the days were big, the sand blinding. Waves heavy in hulk labored in. Sitting on a towel, Meredith let wine dribble down her chin. She let the sun brown her breasts. When David stirred, she gazed at him through dark glasses and watched him stretch.

"You're lovely," she said.

"You're not so bad yourself."

A youth was running along the beach. They watched the flashes of his naked soles. The sails of several distant boats looked like feathers stuck in the sea. The sea was silver-threaded, the sun ferociously bright.

"Everything here is lazy, lazy." He sipped from her wineglass. "Hours pass, I don't know it."

"Sun and sex, David. That's what a honeymoon is." She lay back, open, fissured. "Accept the good life."

Near the surf two middle-aged women stopped to chat, one wearing something, the other not. The one without bore rather defiantly a battle scar of childbearing. David propped himself on his side. Someone was approaching.

"Better close up."

Meredith didn't move. "Here, who cares?"

In passing a bearded man smiled and a few steps later glanced back. David scowled.

"We haven't done it in the rain yet," Meredith said.

"That's because it hasn't rained."

Meredith sat up. In the next instant she was on her feet. "Let's get wet."

The sun beat on the sand. One by one heads turned as if somebody were pulling a string. Meredith flung her hair back. David walked as if on hurt legs but soon straightened his stride.

"All eyes are on you," he said.

"Good. Sometimes I need that."

"Even the women."

"I'm in my prime, David. I'm never going to be better."

The sand turned wet. Soon they were standing in a backwash, which thrilled their ankles and sloshed their calves. A fishing boat was plowing a path toward deep waters. David plucked up a glistening pebble gifted with an especially fine look, admired it, and tossed it aside for someone else to find.

"I see great things for us," she said, and placed a proprietary hand on his bottom. "I want you to be more than a lawyer."

"A lawyer is what I am."

"Not yet. You don't have a practice."

His skin accepted the blaze of the sun. Stretching his gaze to the horizon, he seemed to glimpse simultaneously the known and the unknown. "But I will."

"I want us to shine, David. I want you to be a prince."

"I believe I am one. I've married into royalty."

She took several steps into the sea and, turning, steeled herself against the concussion of a wave. "Don't disappoint me."

CHAPTER THIRTEEN

I'M NOT EMBARRASSED," MRS. KAPLAN SAID. "WHY should you be?"

His mind's ear heard another's voice and responded to it.

Mrs. Kaplan helped him off with his bathrobe and then into the shower stall, his bony buttocks like teeth bared from overbite. With a long reach, she adjusted the tap and achieved a lukewarm spray he could bear. His eyes apologized for his age and his illness. Stepping back, she partially closed the door of the stall and watched through frosted glass as he soaped himself with one hand while clutching the rail with another. When he faltered, she used her long reach to soap what he couldn't.

"How can a Jew wash a German?" he asked.

"You're not a German, Mr. Shellenbach. You're an American."

She began to dry him in a towel that bore the logo of Hanover House.

"I'm a lucky man."

"Yes, you are," she agreed.

"I know what love is. Thank you, Petra."

"Petra? Where did you get that?"

"I'm pretending, I guess. It's someone I knew long ago."

She dried him under the arms, between the legs. "All well and good, Mr. Shellenbach, but what about your friend?"

He saw Gretchen Ryder through a haze, as she used to be. Gretchen Krause. An afternoon when he had her to himself, Rudy not there. "Yes," he said, "she's held me together all these years."

"Are we dry?"

He looked down at himself. The head of his part looked like the rubber guard on the cane he sometimes used.

Mrs. Kaplan stepped back. "I'd say you've excited yourself. Best I get you dressed."

"That hasn't happened in years."

"Good for you, then."

She helped him dress. A check shirt. Poplin pants. She fitted his feet into white socks. He stepped into old comfortable loafers.

"It must be nice having Mr. Unger back," she said.

"I was afraid I might not see him again."

Mrs. Kaplan was overspending time with him. She knew that his insides were subject to tremors and quakes that had nothing to do with his cancer. "I haven't seen your son here lately," she said.

"He's very busy."

"If he beats Kenneally, he'll be sort of famous."

"He was famous the day he was born," Shell said.

After taking his pulse, Mrs. Kaplan left. He stood at the open window, conscious of the tranquillity of the day, of the scent of cut grass, of years he might have wanted to hold on to. Sudden sounds in the room alerted him, a breathiness, a weary tread. He heard a high female sigh and the plop of an obviously heavy woman dropping herself into the upholstered chair.

He turned around slowly, savoring the anticipation.

Gretchen Ryder smiled from the roundness of her face, her lipstick bright. Fanning herself, she said, "Hi."

Tears were in his eyes. "You're gorgeous," he said.

III ≡ III

Shell eschewed the wheelchair and used his cane. Gretchen walked with him, a hand ready to help, which he needed going down a step. He inhaled the scent of the lawn and viewed a friendly cloud in the vivid sky. Gretchen saw menace in the eye of a squirrel. They maneuvered toward lawn chairs, faces, voices.

Mr. Waterhouse had company, two gray daughters and a bald son, but they were leaving. Mr. Waterhouse's eyes were heartbreaking, like those of a pet dog being left behind, the family moving to another town.

"It's all right," Mr. Ruggles whispered to Gretchen. "In a minute he won't remember them."

Gretchen kept track of the squirrel, which scampered here, there. When living with her aunt in Queens, she'd been bitten by one.

Expressions on Mr. Unger's wrinkled face were hieroglyphs. "Guess what," he said, "I'm wearing a diaper."

"No shit," Mr. Ruggles said. "I mean, are you really?"

"It won't be for long. The surgery was a success."

"We didn't think you'd make it."

"Do you think I did?"

Shell's eyes roamed their sockets.

Mr. Ruggles said, "How you doing, Shellenbach?"

"He's doing fine," Mr. Unger said. "He's got his woman with him."

Gretchen smiled. She liked the identification. She gathered breath to speak and then didn't.

"So why are you wearing one?" Mr. Ruggles asked.

"It's a precaution, nothing more," Mr. Unger replied, his gaze on Gretchen. He had seen a snapshot of her at an earlier time. Too bad she'd let herself go. Now she was as fat as Shelly Winters, Rosemary Clooney, each of whom, at certain moments, she resembled.

Divining his thoughts, she said, "I used to be trimmer."

"I know," he said.

She breathed easier. The squirrel was gone. From briar came roses, a breeze lifting the scent. Shell smiled at her, which was what she'd come for. When they were apart her mind fed on the past, retasting pleasant moments, swallowing some whole and savoring others.

Mr. Unger knew all the words to "Hey There." It had been his second wife's favorite song, he said. Younger than he, she had died first. No children. Not by either, he said.

Mr. Waterhouse chose silence over talk. Gretchen watched him pick at his shirt cuff and wished there was something she could do for him.

After a look at his watch, the numerals writ large, Mr. Unger rose with utmost care from his chair. Mr. Ruggles also got to his feet, quickly, in a pretense of spryness. Each had medication to take. Mr. Unger said, "Toodle-oo."

Mr. Waterhouse remained.

"How are you doing for money?" Shell asked.

"No need for you to worry," Gretchen said.

She had saved whatever she could working at Mitchell's right up to the day the store closed its doors for good, downtown no longer a functioning enterprise. Then she had worked with children who had come up short genetically, their futures dependent on the moods of legislators and taxpayers. Now she collected checks.

"How's your blood pressure?"

"I take my pills," she said.

Shell removed his glasses, and his eyes shrank from the exposure. Mr. Waterhouse was smiling, as if from an interest in the conversation. Gretchen batted the air and drove away a wasp.

"I wrote to Ned Ryder," she said. "I wanted to know if he was still alive. Of course he wasn't."

"Why did you want to know?"

"Curiosity, that's all. If I'd stayed married to him, I'd have collected his veteran benefits."

Shell sleeked his hair back, hair that was no longer there and watched a number of women residents being wheeled into shade. All of them widows, he was sure. Women who'd once had lives. Gretchen was staring at him.

"What's the matter, Shell?"

"Just light-headed," he said. "I've no more lies to tell."

She made a warning face and whispered, "Should you be talking in front of him?"

"It's all right, he won't remember anything."

"Are you sure?"

"He's not real, Gretchen. Neither are we. We're figments of our imagination. Pretty scary, huh?"

She knew what was bothering him, what was always bothering him. "Hasn't David been back?" she asked.

"I don't think he will be."

"Let me call him."

"No. It's his choice. I can't influence it."

"Shell, don't torture yourself."

"You don't understand. I'm not his father anymore."

Gretchen fidgeted. They were talking as if Mr. Waterhouse were dead. He was sitting erect, listening, but, all the same, as if dead.

When it was time for her to go, Shell returned the glasses to his face. She needn't walk him back. Mrs. Kaplan should come for him.

On her feet, Gretchen said, "Your mother-in-law is worried about you."

"I doubt she's worrying very much. Tell her I'm at peace."

"You're lying."

"Yes."

She bent over him. Her lips, pursed for a kiss, made her mouth look like the work of a rubber stamp. The kiss vanished in the hollow of his cheek. "I love you, Shell."

"I love you too."

Before leaving she went over to Mr. Waterhouse and kissed his cheek. The sudden smile was what she wanted.

||| ≡ |||

David returned from a rambling walk and learned from Kipper that people with grave concerns were waiting in the study. Confronting him, Meredith said, "Before we go in there, I want to know what's going on with you. What's banging around in your head, David?"

"Nothing."

"You mean you're not telling me."

"Have it your way."

"Leave him alone, Sis."

Meredith glared. "Shut your mouth, Kipper."

She and David made their way to the study, from which Kipper was excluded. She entered with her head held high, David with a hand in his pocket.

"Gentlemen," she said. "Please, stay seated."

There were three of them, their bespoken suits nearly alike, but David knew only one would speak. Carver. Carver linked Saltonstall Republicans with Reaganites, spoke for the party, dispensed money, and represented quid pro quo.

"Let's not waste time," Carver said. "What's the problem, Shellenbach?"

Seated in a scroll-back chair, David shook his head. "I didn't know we had one."

"Polls say otherwise."

"When we were doing well you told me they meant nothing."

That was not the answer Carver wanted. He had a cleft chin and an air of holding playable cards that were not of the deck. The other two, with dry regular features David associated with members of Christian fellowships, could have been fraternal twins.

"We have the impression you're not trying," Carver said.

"He's been under the weather," Meredith interjected, and was ignored.

"It's late in the game to question whether you're serious. We need to know we're not flushing money down the toilet."

David glanced at the other two. A distinguishing difference was that one had flat hair and came close to being a child impersonating an adult. David said, "I'm doing my best."

"That's hard to believe," Carver said. "You're not following the script."

"It's not always to my liking. Nor are those negative television commercials."

"Your wife approved them. We presumed you did too."

He had no answer. His mind wasn't with it. Other things were, things that defied his understanding.

Carver spoke slowly. "Are you one of us . . . or someone we don't know?"

He found the question insidiously ironic. He had sort of an answer but didn't speak up, no spark to his tongue.

"David, are you listening?"

Meredith's voice. He nodded.

Carver's face was cold and closed. "Let me remind you there's a lot of money on you, a high percentage of it from out of state. Big donors. You mess with them, you're playing with fire."

David awoke. "Are you threatening me?"

"I suppose you could read it that way."

"Make it plainer," David said.

"People don't take kindly to being made fools of. That's as plain as I can be."

Carver got to his feet, a cue for the other two to do the same. The one with flat hair viewed David as if he were a fallen angel. Meredith walked them to the front door, which she opened wide. Carver, holding back, gestured the other two out into the brightness of the sun, where a limo stood waiting. He turned slowly.

"What the fuck's wrong with your husband?"

"He's going through something. I'll handle him, trust me."

"I wouldn't know how."

"Do you have a choice, Carver?"

"Yes, I do." His eyes were steel. "We could cut our losses now."

"That would leave you with your face hanging out."

"Better than my dick."

Meredith pushed the hair from her face. "You haven't changed, Carver."

"Did you expect me to?"

"I still haven't forgiven you."

"After all these years, what does it matter?"

"You have a point." She stood with her arms tightly crossed. "Stick with us, Carver. I'll get him back on track."

"How?"

"That's my job."

She walked with him over groomed grass, past the radiance of summer phlox, to the waiting limo. A door sprang open. Carver paused.

"Tell me something," he said. "Doesn't he know what it would mean to be governor? Doesn't he understand the power, the greater possibilities?"

Meredith smiled. "Not fully, but I do."

⫴ ≡ ⫴

He was watching the tail end of a black-and-white movie, one set in World War I, when airplanes were flimsy and propeller-driven, when pilots wore leather caps with goggles and dangling chin straps, when air battles were considered sport. Meredith entered the room in the midst of the final duel between a British ace and his German counterpart.

"Don't turn it off," he said.

She lowered the sound. "We have to talk."

He kept his eyes on the screen. His locked face was not enough to keep her out.

"I can't let you quit, David. I've worked too hard for this."

He watched the German plane go down in smoke, an eagle falling from the sky. "I'm not quitting. I simply need a break."

"This isn't the time."

"I'm tired, Meredith. Can't you understand?"

"Are you ill?"

He shook his head. The movie was ending, but another would soon be coming on. He had the schedule in his hand. *Casablanca.* Bogart and Bergman. Bogart brought to mind Camus. A physical likeness. And he found in Bogart's persona much of Camus's philosophy.

"Is it your father?"

He'd been watching many movies lately. He'd even gone to Cinema Showcase to see current ones. Of the present male actors his favorites were, in descending order, DeNiro, Christopher Walken, and Mickey Rourke. Rourke was John Garfield with an attitude. Walken was a thin slice of Richard Widmark. DeNiro was DeNiro.

"I don't want to think about my father," he said.

"Then for God's sake, David, what is it?"

What could he say? What did he know? He said, "I don't like your friend."

"Carver? I don't like him either, but we need him. When you're governor you can be your own man."

"I don't like his threatening me."

"Means nothing. That's just his way. He's in this to win. He thought you were too."

David's gaze stayed fixed on the muted screen. One commercial after another, a processed world, reality run through a strainer, reconstituted, granulated, packaged, Disney wrappings.

Meredith lit a cigarette. "That old chum of yours, does she have anything to do with this?"

He stiffened. "It has nothing to do with anybody but me."

"Do you still see her?"

"No."

"Why not?"

"There's no point."

The movie was coming on. Dooley Wilson at the piano. Bogart wore a fuming cigarette on his lower lip, like Camus.

"Please," David said. "Put the sound up."

III ☰ III

Mrs. Dodd turned a page of the Miami *Herald,* which she was reading with a magnifying glass. The obituary page held her interest, the ages, not the names. People popping off were well younger than she. Her least fear was of death, her worst that people would think her superannuated.

Father Henry, who'd gotten off the phone with Gretchen Ryder, was eating toast. Toast with peanut butter. That was his lunch.

"Shell's not going to be around much longer," he said. "I think we should see him before he goes."

She turned to international news. A picture of Libya's Qaddafi with a raised arm and pointed finger. A handsome man. She wondered if he had a harem. "What does Gretchen say?"

"She doesn't think he'll last the summer."

Mrs. Dodd rattled back pages and was momentarily enraged. All this religious shit going around, it was even on the entertainment page. A picture of a gallery painting of Jesus Christ toting an American flag through a battlefield. She said, "Gretchen overreacts."

"I don't think so. Not this time."

She swept back to the front page. Nancy Reagan's photograph offended her for a second time. The tinsel face, the fake air of aristocracy, a Hollywood Republican bearing no resemblance to Republicans of Mrs. Dodd's day. "What makes you think so?" she asked.

"The finality in her tone," Father Henry said.

The thought of flying from Florida to Boston began to excite her. She liked the bustle of airports, the bounce of faces, people on the go. "Are you fit for travel?"

"I don't know, but it's worth the try."

"I wouldn't want you croaking on the way."

"What about yourself?"

"I have better genes than you."

"I suspect you're right," Father Henry said. "Survival of the fittest. Darwin was thinking of you."

Casting aside the newspaper, Mrs. Dodd had memories of her girlhood, her maidenhood, everything about her smart and keen. She had thought life would be endless, and so it was, for her anyway. "I'd have to go first-class."

"I can afford it."

In girlhood she'd had specific goals, grand ones, but now she couldn't remember precisely what they were. She had no regrets, however, none at all. How many people could say that? Clearing her throat, she said, "Shell's the only family I have left. Shell and David."

"Then why don't we think about it?"

They went to their separate rooms and took naps. Hers was longer than his, full of dreams. She was a young woman again in a changing time. Art nouveau was a scandal, Beardsley was pornography. Men in boaters surrounded her like dogs awaiting scraps. She woke with the joy of having been young again. She had seen the turn of one century and wondered if it was at all possible for her to see the turn of another.

Father Henry was barefoot in the kitchen. He had sliced a lemon and was making ice tea. The plaid shorts he was wearing were new. She stared at his brittle legs, which were shaky.

"Maybe I should go alone."

"No," he said, turning. "You need me."

III ☰ III

David was sitting in the dark. Meredith turned on a light that shot straight into his eyes. She was in a nightgown, her body a vague shape. She said, "Maybe in time you'll tell me what it is you won't share with me."

"Yes," he said. "But not now. Not yet."

"When?"

"Soon."

The light was cruel. She switched it off and put on another, weaker, which placed them both in shadows. "I don't know what's burdening you, David, but you don't know tragedy. I haven't been myself since I lost my father."

His nod was sympathetic. Paul Wainwright had drowned in wide waters off Rye Beach when winds from a rainsquall maddened waves and capsized his sailboat. "I know," he said slowly. "I'm sorry."

"If you'd listened to him years ago, you'd already be a senator."

"Perhaps."

"You were as much a son to him as Kipper. More, if you want the truth."

"You were the son he wanted. He spoiled you rotten."

"Nothing wrong with that." She half smiled. "You did well by him yourself, didn't you?"

She moved into the light, her skin coloring the gown. She was deeply tanned all over. She could've been brass. In the soft light she was young again.

"I won't press you on this anymore, David."

"Thank you."

"Are you coming to bed?"

"Not right now."

She moved to the doorway and paused. "If we'd had a child, would it have made a difference?"

"I'm glad we didn't," he said.

||| ☰ |||

In the airport Mrs. Dodd bought a tabloid to read about the sex lives of celebrities. Father Henry had the sniffles from allergies. His nose was crimson-tipped from overblowing.

Boarding the jetliner, he said, "Scared?"

"Certainly not."

Father Henry wore his priestly suit and collar. That way he received added consideration. The flight attendant, as blond as any Norwegian or Finn, helped him down the aisle. Mrs. Dodd strode straight.

Seated she said, "If we crash, I wonder if we'll end up in the same place. Assuming there is another place."

The attendant had secured Father Henry's seat belt. "Death, Dorothy, comes down to a question of being elsewhere or nowhere. I figure there must be an elsewhere because if there's a *here* there has to be a *there*. Two sides to everything."

They held hands during the takeoff. Which was smooth.

Mrs. Dodd soon lost interest in the tabloid. The escapades of Burt Reynolds were stories retold, and the magnifying glass detracted from her facade.

"Celebrities," Father Henry said, "are the happiest people in the world except any hour they're alone."

They catnapped, Mrs. Dodd more deeply than he. She snored. Until old age, she had given no significance to dreams. They were waste, the brain emptying itself like a bowel. Now, except for the occasional unpleasant one, she looked forward to them and found meanings of her own choosing in them.

Waking from one, she said, "I wouldn't want to live forever, but possibly that might be my fate."

Twice the blond attendant helped Father Henry to and from the

216

lavatory. Mrs. Dodd went once, by herself, on high heels. Over New England, wearing her strongest glasses, she looked down at the crown cover of woodland and the crooked line of a river.

"Won't be long now," she said.

The landing was a lark. Father Henry tried to slip the blond attendant a gratuity, but she wouldn't take it.

Gretchen Ryder awaited them in the terminal. From a distance neither recognized her. Then they did.

"My God," Mrs. Dodd whispered, "she's a cow."

||| ☰ |||

Earlier Shell had had a bit of trouble breathing, but he was better now. Seated in the upholstered chair, he heard footsteps in the corridor and knew instantly whose they were. His heart gave a little jump.

A moment later, rising from a smaller chair, Mr. Unger said, "Would you like me to leave?"

"If you don't mind," David said.

"Surely not. Father and son need time together."

Mr. Unger closed the door behind him. David sat in the chair left vacant, at a distance from his father, not his father. He said, "It must have taken superhuman strength to sustain a lie of that magnitude."

Shell's expression was fixed. Only a hammer could have broken it. "It's all right to hate me."

"I don't hate you. I don't understand you. I guess I don't know you."

Each sat well out of the reach of the other. Their many years as father and son had come to a halt.

"All my life I've felt something was wrong," David said. "My mother, your wife. I never felt like her son."

"Did you feel like mine?"

David didn't answer. He didn't want to give him the truth. He said, "She couldn't take it, could she? That's why she went crazy."

Shell managed a voice, not much of one. "I tried to replace what she'd lost."

"Hardly a merit in view of your method," David said, his voice a lawyer's in a judge's chamber, the judge absent.

Shell remembered the scene in the bathroom, Helen's eyes, her mute scream to reverse the unspeakable. He relived a portion of the drive from Hopewell to Newark, the reborn David a sleeping bundle beside him.

David uncrossed his legs, as if from a need to relax, to retain his calm. "Why have you told me now, after all these years?"

Shell's mind moved in and out of the past. The present had no place for him, and his thoughts had long ceased conjuring a future.

"Maybe the real question is whether you should've told me at all."

The door opened for a moment. Mrs. Kaplan was an apparition who glanced in, smiled apologetically, and vanished. Petra, don't go, he nearly said.

"But you did," David murmured. "What am I to do with it?"

Shell thought of the dead man in Crotona Park, whose pockets he and Rudy Farber had ransacked. Rudy bought chocolates for his mother, and he bought a glove to field grounders and catch flies. The glove was gone, but the one Rudy got hold of, Mulheim's munificence, remained. Somewhere.

"Who have you told?" he asked.

David looked away. "No one."

"It's something you must think about."

"Don't give me advice. You no longer have the right." David rose, a lawyer without a case. "Too late to have you arrested. What good would it do?"

For a single second Shell saw Helen wholly alive in a slim red dress. She obliged him with a smile. Shakespeare's tragedies, she said, were exhausting. All this in a flash, and then she was gone.

"Have you no sin, David?"

David was at the door, opening it. "None that will ever match yours."

"Can't we say good-bye?"

"We already have."

III ≡ III

The room was dim. Meredith sat in a deep chair with her eyes closed. She was listening to television. The Boston Pops. John Williams saluting Jerome Kern. Footsteps on hardwood were an intrusion.

"I'm going to bed," Kipper informed her.

She kept her eyes closed, her ears open to the music. "You do that."

"I'm tired," he said.

His voice was a shallow sound that annoyed her as if it were a shout. "Aren't we all," she said.

He lingered, which annoyed her more. He was a wastrel. He'd gone through his inheritance and hadn't held a real job in years. Her charity gave him room and board and kept him afloat.

"What is it, Kipper?"

"What do you think is wrong with David?"

She sighed. "I'm not in the mood to discuss him."

"Maybe you're being hard on him. I mean, some people aren't cut out for politics."

She was trying to control her temper. Losing it would accomplish nothing. "Go to bed, Kipper."

Eyes still closed, she sat deeper in the chair and didn't hear him leave. She heard only the music. Music, someone once told her, possibly Carver, is a world without clocks. Carver at one time in her life could strike her like a match.

The Pops was still on when David came home. She wasn't interested in where he'd been and didn't ask. She merely opened her eyes to acknowledge him. Hovering, he seemed to be collecting himself.

"I'm listening to music, David. What is it?"

His gaze fixed on her. Something was wrong. She could tell he was weighing his words before opening his mouth. She raised the remote and muted the sound.

"Damn it, David, what is it?"

"I have something to tell you." He stepped to a chair, dropped into it, and smiled queerly. "It's possible you won't believe it."

CHAPTER FOURTEEN

PAUL WAINWRIGHT BOUGHT THEM A HOUSE ON SCHOOL Street. David, who hadn't planned on living in Andover, thought the house much too grand and was embarrassed.

Meredith said, "What would you prefer, a flat in Haverhill?"

His father-in-law could have gained him entry into an established law firm in Andover, but David wanted to go on his own—and not in Andover. Paul Wainwright respected his decision. Meredith did not understand it.

"You thinking of setting up shop in Haverhill?"

"Boston," he said.

"You'll have to commute."

"That's not a hardship."

Her sigh was deep. "Everybody needs help starting out. What makes you different?"

"I'm not," he said.

Tony Tonetti gave him a loan, cash in an envelope, which David stuffed into the inside pocket of his suit jacket. They were seated in the midst of Suffolk students in the Beacon Cafeteria. David said, "I don't know how to thank you."

"What the fuck are friends for?"

"I'll pay you back as soon as I can."

"You pay when you can, no sooner."

"You're doing well, huh, Tony?"

"I ain't doing bad." He grinned. "Politics is people. Me and Sylvio, we're Guineas, but he knows how to work the Irish. He's chairing the committee on counties now. That's where the candy is."

"Jesus, Tony, don't get yourself in trouble."

"It's legitimate graft, Counselor. No law against it."

David rented a street-level office on the shabby side of Beacon Hill and hired a secretary named Nancy Potts, who was a year out of high school and could type without looking. She was shy and plain, with a face rife with freckles and with no experience in a law office.

"Me neither," David said. "We'll wing it."

When she asked what she should call him, he said David was good enough.

His first clients came to him on Tonetti's recommendation. They were gaunt-eyed women hiding bruises and seeking divorces. All were from East Boston, most were Italian, and few could afford his low fee, which he halved in some cases and waived in others. His presentations in probate court were cogent, thorough, and from the heart. Judges tended to like him.

Tonetti said, "You're doing OK, Counselor. People trust you. I know the women do."

"But I'm not making any money."

"Look at it this way. You're gaining experience. Pretty soon you'll get a name."

His first full-paying clients were also from East Boston, young chain-smoking hoodlums whose families scraped up the fee. Aggravated assault was a frequent charge, breaking and entering in the nighttime another. A crowded docket made plea bargaining easy, probation the usual sentence.

Nancy Potts said, "Some of those fellas scare me."

Tonetti was in the office. "Ain't one of 'em gonna lay a hand on you. Most they're gonna do is count your freckles, like I do."

Nancy Potts smiled through a blush. "How many do I have?"

"Good kid like you, I don't expect to see 'em all."

He went into the inner office to see David and closed the door behind him. The single window looked out on an alleyway. The walls were pine paneling, bare except for the law degree from Suffolk.

"You oughta put pictures up," Tonetti said. "I'll get you one of Sylvio. And, hey, maybe we can get a picture of you and the governor together. Make you look important."

Smiling, David capped his fountain pen. "Still got your Leica, Tony? Maybe we can get Elvis Presley in it."

"Don't be fucking smart. You doing any work on the Kennedy campaign? The guy's gonna be our next president."

"What makes you think so?"

"Nixon's a shithead. Even Ike don't like him." Tonetti dropped into a wooden chair. His suit was three-piece, and his shirt bore French cuffs, the links large and gilt. "You're starting to make money now, huh?"

David nodded. "I've got you to thank."

"You do good for these people, they owe me a favor and Sylvio their vote. Cuts all kinds of ways, Counselor." Tonetti touched the knot of his necktie and then tightened it. "A widow lady from my neighborhood, Mrs. Cammarano, wants to set up a trust for her grandchildren. We're talking fifty thou. Can you handle it?"

"Sounds easy enough."

"The beauty of it is if you need a quick interest-free loan, you can dip into it. 'Course you gotta make sure you pay it back."

"Doesn't sound like a good idea, Tony."

"I'm just giving you options. What you do is your business."

A few minutes later David walked with him out of the office, past Nancy Potts, and out to the street, where Tonetti's car was illegally parked. He'd upgraded from a Buick to a Chrysler, black with gold trimmings and a low-numbered plate.

"Nice," David said.

"So's the new payment book. Angie ain't seen it yet."

"How is she?"

"Up to her ears in shitty diapers. Two tries, she ain't given me a son yet." Tonetti leaned a hip against the front fender. "Call Mrs. Cammarano and set up an appointment. Better you go see her instead of making her come here. OK?"

His brow furrowed, David watched an old man stoop to pet the apparent love of his life, a wirehaired terrier on a short leash. The dog looked better fed than the man. "What's the matter, Counselor?"

"Sometimes you scare me, Tony."

||| ≡ |||

Detective-Sergeant O'Grady had risen in rank to lieutenant and now to captain. Cronies staged a celebration for him in the rear of Lenny's Tap Room. The women present were not wives. Shell, a reluctant guest, whispered to Gretchen, "We don't have to stay long."

Men sizing her up as if all things were possible made her feel too big for her dress and too bare for the occasion. "Why'd we come, Shell?"

"He's hard to say no to."

"He always seems to scare you."

"Your imagination."

Voices grew loud, at times drowning out the three-piece band, which was playing gratis. A police lieutenant named Flanagan, dressed in a two-tone sports shirt and check pants, downed a shot of rye, smeared peanuts into his mouth, and asked Gretchen to dance.

"Shell asked first," she said swiftly.

"Shell don't mind. Right, Shell?"

"Yes, I do," Shell said quietly, and guided her onto the floor. In each other's arms, each was the other's security, particularly when other dancers jostled them. There were moments when the thought of losing Shell hammered her mind, her heart.

They'd have danced longer, but the band suddenly took a break. Speech time. Flanagan shouted for attention. A yellow-haired woman was laughing with her head flung back until someone told her to shut up. Flanagan told a couple of off-color jokes and then started a long round of applause for Captain O'Grady to give a speech. O'Grady rose with a drenched face and told everybody to go on having fun, he wasn't much for giving a fucking speech.

The band came back.

Shell left Gretchen alone at a table while he went to the men's. Munching peanuts, she began coughing. Out of nowhere Flanagan appeared with a drinking glass. What she thought was water was gin, and the swallow she took nearly stopped her heart. She couldn't see. Who was hoisting her to her feet? Not Flanagan. The face was wet. O'Grady dragged her onto the dance floor.

"Please," she protested.

People made room. She was stumbling, O'Grady was staggering. She was ill, O'Grady was sloshed. His round spectacles, steel rims housing safety glass, spun at her.

"I see why Shell keeps you hidden," he said into her face. "You're a lotta woman."

"Please, I have to sit down."

"Fuck you do, talk to me."

Shell came out of the men's and glimpsed what was happening. Flanagan, with the physique of an old prizefighter not altogether gone to pot, blocked his way.

O'Grady kept her moving but not at all to the music. "Something tells me you're a great hunk of ass. How come only he gets to enjoy you?"

She turned an ankle. She saw splashes. Men inflict pain, women endure it, but women are getting smarter. She had read that in a magazine.

"I ain't such a bad guy, once you get to know me."

Tears came. She wanted permanence, fixity. She wanted to be identified as Shell's woman and no one else's.

"What are you crying for?"

Crying put fractures in her face, and abruptly she was unwanted goods, passed-over merchandise left teetering. Shell, dodging Flanagan, finally got to her.

"I'm sorry," he said. "We never should've come."

"I can't walk."

"Try."

His hand under her arm, she hobbled with him toward a side door, a fire exit duly designated. Glimpsing herself in a panel mirror, she saw a shattered face and a pendulant lower lip, which made her want to scream.

The scream came from elsewhere.

O'Grady had caught hold of a waitress and thrust a hand under her brief cocktail skirt. She spat in his face. O'Grady never should have hit her. He broke her nose.

"We've got to get out of here," Shell said.

He yanked the door open, and together they squeezed through. In the alleyway they took deep breaths. They drove home, to River Street, in the old Plymouth that ran as if new. A nylon top had replaced the canvas one. The tires were whitewalls.

Stairs had to be climbed. Gretchen winced with each tortured step. Inside the apartment she pulled off the dress she'd never wear again. Her large body overwhelmed her underwear. Tears returned.

"What do they want with me, Shell? I'm not what I was."

She waited for the sound of his voice and the warmth of his smile. Each had a gripping power. But he wasn't listening, he wasn't looking at her. His blank gaze was directed at a bowl of fruit.

"What's the matter, Shell?"

"I'm in trouble."

"You didn't do anything."

"But I was there," he said.

||| ☰ |||

Three nights later, wearing a gray civilian suit, Captain O'Grady appeared at their door. "Please," he said, "let me come in for a minute."

Shell stepped aside. Gretchen, turning off the television in the middle of a drama, didn't want to look at him. She said, "I'll get coffee."

O'Grady trod a worn carpet and sat in a chair that had cushions and wooden arms. "Nothing in the paper. I'm grateful, Shell."

Shell remained standing. "I don't owe you anymore."

"I agree. Debt paid in full."

"Many times over," Shell said coldly.

"I also want to tell you I'm coming out of this OK. The waitress ain't filing a complaint." O'Grady shifted one way and then another in the chair. His large black shoes were the ones he wore with his uniform. "But it's costing me plenty. The cottage I got at the beach, it's gonna be hers."

"Something like that is hard to keep quiet."

"It's all perfectly legal. There's a selling price, but she don't have to pay it."

"That's not what I mean," Shell said.

"I know what you mean."

Two full cups rattled in their saucers on the shaky tray, which Gretchen managed to place on the coffee table. The creamer and sugar bowl were crystal. Using her employee discount, she had bought them at Mitchell's.

Shell said, "The captain isn't staying."

O'Grady rose with a grunt, buttoned his suit jacket, and stared at Gretchen. "I just wanted to tell you I'm sorry. I wasn't drunk, it wouldn't have happened."

She busied herself with the coffee, spooning sugar into a cup she hadn't intended for herself.

Shell said, "You have anything more to tell us?"

"Something crosses my mind I'll let you know."

Shell accompanied him to the door. O'Grady looked back at Gretchen. He tried to catch her eye and couldn't.

"You're a lucky man, Shell. I wish I had a woman like that."

"You have a wife."

"She ain't well." O'Grady lingered. "You're worried, ain't you?"

"Of course I'm worried. I'll probably lose my job."

"That happens I owe you."

||| ≡ |||

Within the week Shell knew it was over. The city editor, who had never liked him, was smugly polite until after press time. Then he came up behind him and, irony in his voice, said, "Mr. Heath wants to see you. Maybe you're getting a raise."

Shell cleared his desk of torn sheets of copy from the wire machines, screwed the cap onto a paste pot, and deposited proof pencils and a steno pad into a metal drawer. Rising, he hooded his bulky typewriter.

Mr. Heath didn't tell him to sit, so he stood and wondered how long it would take. Eczema gnawed his wrist, and he scratched it. Mr. Heath lit a corncob pipe.

"You and Captain O'Grady close friends?"

"No, sir. But he's been a good source of information through the years."

"Nothing you couldn't get off the blotter. His name's been in the paper more than any other cop. Would you say that's true?"

Shell quit scratching. "I'm not sure."

"I am. You were at that party for him and never turned in a story. Rumors are he hurt a woman, but no one's speaking up. Are the rumors true?"

"What rumors, sir?"

The pipe smoke was thick. "Are you playing games with me, Shell?"

He felt himself a fraud as a newspaperman, a fraud as a husband and father and maybe as a man. "I guess I am, sir."

"I accept your resignation."

He waited ten days to tell Gretchen. He anticipated her reaction. She thought it was her fault and couldn't be convinced otherwise. He woke in the night and found her staring down at him from a propped elbow.

"I'm bad luck," she said.

"You're my only luck."

"We're alike under the skin, aren't we, Shell?"

"No, you're better."

The next evening Captain O'Grady was back at the door, this time in full uniform, a car waiting for him. "I got something for you. A job in the mayor's office."

"I don't want it," Shell said.

"Same pay you were getting, I'm seeing to it. The mayor owes me."

"I want nothing from you, Captain. Nothing at all."

"You want to be a martyr?"

"No, simply a man."

III ≡ III

Sunday afternoon in autumn. David played golf with his father-in-law, a sport that didn't especially interest either. David had a strong drive but was an impatient putter. Paul Wainwright was meticulous but mediocre. Each enjoyed the conversation. Politics, in which Paul Wainwright had a deep interest and David an abstract one, was a frequent subject.

"I don't believe anything coming out of Washington," David said.

"You must read between the lines."

"I see only corruption."

"Corruption is intrinsic," Paul Wainwright replied, watching David's putt roll wide of the hole. "Greeks and Romans bribed their gods. Popes sold indulgences. But usually the good balances the bad and sometimes even tips the scale."

"You've raised a lot of money for Nixon."

"Not a man I like, but I'm loyal to the party."

David finally tapped the ball in. "I'm voting for Kennedy."

"Doesn't surprise me. He may win, but I doubt it."

"Bet?"

"Make it easy on yourself."

"Five dollars."

The Sunday after the election they strolled the academy grounds. The afternoon was gray and chill. Wearing a rugged sweater that gave him shoulders he didn't have, Paul Wainwright fished a bill from a pocket of his corduroys and paid off the bet.

"His father bought it for him, and Daley gave it to him on a platter."

"Are you being a poor sport?" David said.

"Not at all. Politics is politics."

Students sauntered by, boys in tweed jackets and chinos. Paul Wainwright knew them all and greeted each. Some had famous fathers.

"I went here," David said. "For a semester."

"I didn't know that. What happened?"

"I didn't fit in."

"It's not for everybody, but it should've been for you."

"Why do you say that?"

"I don't know. It's just something about you, David. Don't ask me what."

They neared one of the dormitories. Ivy that had scaled the brick was cut back. Privet hedges were groomed. Paul Wainwright walked with the posture of an army officer.

"How's it feel being a lawyer?"

David ran a smoothing hand over his hair. "It's an education."

They crossed a stretch of lawn where an almond tree had been cut down. Three tender ones had been planted to replace it. A squirrel that appeared lost scampered one way and then another.

"The law's a good stepping stone."

"To what, sir?"

Paul Wainwright winked. "Politics."

They parted at the chapel. David walked down School Street to the house that was too big for him. Cars lined the drive. He knew what was going on, a committee meeting, League of Women Voters, Meredith one of the youngest members and among the most active.

Entering by a side door, he heard the voices. He walked over terra-cotta and then through a carpeted passage. Pausing at a glass door, he gazed in at a private world from which emanated the fullness of women. They sat with teacups, their legs demurely crossed, knees straining nylon, as the photographer from the local paper took pictures. None, David noted, quite had Meredith's bearing. Watching her brought to mind the way a flower spends the vital part of its energy being beautiful.

She caught sight of him and gestured him in.

"David, you know everybody."

More or less he knew them. He'd been to some of their houses for dinner, met their husbands, and in some cases their children, but he couldn't remember their names. He tried to sweep everyone in with a smile.

"I've been trying to get David to grow a beard, but he won't," Meredith said.

He knew she liked showing him off. She liked the looks he received, along with the mildly flirtatious smiles.

229

"I like him the way he is," one of the women said.

As soon as she spoke he remembered her name. Bellwood. Her husband was a senior executive at a diversified holding company. He remembered being at their home at a pool party, and he remembered Meredith coming out of the pool in a white bathing suit and, looking for her towel, dripping from man to man.

"Keep a firm hold on him," Mrs. Bellwood added.

"Indeed," Meredith replied with a laugh. "He's the cream in my coffee, the bounce in my step."

"As long as I'm not the fly in your ointment," David said, and, drawing laughs, retreated.

In the study he sank into a club chair with a newspaper, turned a page, and remembered a condom floating in the Bellwoods' pool. A tasteless joke. He remembered the face of the man who owned up to it but couldn't remember his name.

||| ☰ |||

The first week of December was freezing rain. Ice armored trees. David left his car home and commuted by train into Boston. Nancy Potts, who lived in Dorchester, took the subway. Whoever arrived at the office first made the coffee. He was now getting a few clients on his own, mostly accident cases.

For Christmas there was much snow on the ground. Christmas dinner was at the Wainwrights'. He left early and drove to Haverhill so that he could visit his father and then the two of them could visit his mother. His father looked thinner, grayer, and Gretchen Ryder looked herself, though a little larger. They exchanged gifts. He'd brought one for his grandmother, who wasn't expected until later, with Father Henry.

Gretchen took him aside. "Maybe next Christmas," she whispered, "you and your wife could have dinner here."

"Yes, that's a good idea," he said.

During the drive to Danvers, his father didn't have much to say, as if the trip were depressing him. Much of the time, his hands folded together in his lap, he stared out the window.

Breaking a silence, David said, "I still don't understand why you left the *Gazette.*"

"It was time. I was slowing down."

"What you're doing now can't be easy."

"You're wrong. I like pumping gas."

"In the winter?"

"It takes me back. I almost feel young again."

The hospital loomed. It looked military but from another age. They stepped out of the car into blustery and frigid air. The milk-blue skin of the sky veiled a shapeless blob of sun, brilliant but heatless. A scattering of evergreens stood stuck in deep snow like Napoleon's soldiers.

"Need help?" David asked. They were crunching over tufts of ice on the walkway.

"I'm fine."

They entered the hospital, each with a brightly wrapped gift in hand. A nurse informed them that Mrs. Shellenbach was having one of her bad days.

They found her sitting in a chair. Her shapeless blouse was a fruit bowl of colors. She was without her glasses, which she had broken. Indeed, the nurse said, she had stamped on them. The nurse stayed within calling distance in the event of trouble.

Helen knew neither of them or pretended she didn't. She occupied herself with the gifts. Fleece-lined slippers from Shell, which she tried on and kept on. Chocolates from David, which she sampled and put aside. She looked at David as if he were there to taunt her and at Shell as if he were there to let him.

"Not wanted, are we?" David whispered.

"Not this time," Shell conceded.

She averted her cheek. She wanted no good-bye kisses. Before leaving, Shell spoke privately with the nurse and stepped away with his face rigid.

Back in the car, the sun slipping away, David said, "She doesn't look well."

"I don't think we'll have her much longer."

"I never did have her, Dad." It was the truth, but he wished he hadn't said it. Reaching over, he gripped his father's arm. "But I've always had you."

During January he saw little of Meredith. His caseload increasing, he was seldom home before ten o'clock. Meredith spent the weekends skiing in Vermont with former Radcliffe classmates. He'd never been on skis and didn't care to learn, not even when she coaxed him. He said he couldn't take the time. She told him he was too tightly wrapped around his work.

"What are you trying to prove, David?"

He supposed he was trying to live up to something, either his father's expectations or his own. He'd grown more at ease in a business suit, as if his body had been tailored for one.

"Maybe you're trying to show up Kipper," she said.

Kipper, two years out of college, was between jobs. Kipper felt only a high-paying one would authenticate him. An allowance kept him afloat, women kept him busy.

"I'm trying to build a practice," David said. "I'm trying to establish who I am."

"Don't you know who you are?"

"Do any of us?"

In February trucks spewed sand over icy School Street. The cold was punishing. Meredith and her mother spent much of the month in Florida. David missed her but, paradoxically, felt more married to her when they were apart than when they were together.

In March he manipulated a large out-of-court settlement for a woman who had been struck by a speeding taxi, her injuries multiple and serious. His take was nearly six figures. He paid off Tony Tonetti, raised Nancy Potts's salary, and hired a law student from Suffolk to help out part-time. He also took Meredith to dinner at the Ritz.

"Pretty proud of yourself, aren't you?"

"I did good," he said. "For my client and myself."

They had her car, a silver Thunderbird. They drove home at a fast clip, her hand on the wheel, his on her thigh, each with the same thing in mind.

She took the lead up the stairs. He left a light burning. Her bra fastened in front. She undid it and let her breasts fall into his hands. On the bed she lay bright-legged, her personal hair dense enough to braid, her body so quiet and clean he hesitated touching it.

She motioned.

He knew when her shudders would come and his own would take over. He stayed in. His spurts were prodigal.

"I love you," he said.

They lay apart. She stretched a leg and grazed his foot with her toes.

"When are we going to have a child?" he asked.

"Something I should have told you long ago, David. I can't have one."

||| ☰ |||

A maiden woman named Mary Gosselin, a lifetime member of Trinity Episcopal, died in her sleep at age eighty-eight. Father Henry officiated at the funeral. Two weeks later he learned he was a beneficiary in her will, the money amount substantial enough to guarantee comfort should he choose to retire, which he'd been considering.

Outside the lawyer's office he raised his eyes and said, "Dear sweet Mary Gosselin." The irony was that she had been among those critical of his relationship with Mrs. Dodd.

At the package store he bought an expensive bottle of French wine sheathed in wicker and drove to Mrs. Dodd's. She took one look at him and, with unwonted vulgarity, said, "Take the shit-eating grin off your face."

His news silenced her for several moments. He uncorked the wine.

"So what are you going to do?" she asked. "Retire?"

"Why not?"

She supplied glasses. He decanted.

"But would you be happy?" she asked.

It was a question he'd been pondering. As a very young man he'd entered the church for the make-believe, for the shelter of stained glass, for the glory of the good. He could flit like a child between the real and the unreal. Now he was tired of flitting, tired of spinning sacred yarns.

"I believe so."

They clinked glasses. She sipped. He gulped. She said, "Are you sure you'd be comfortable? You've been in the fold so long with all those beliefs and things."

"I'm a good Christian, Dorothy, but I'm not an idiot. I don't believe in Adam and Eve."

"I just mean it'll be different. What will you do?"

"I can read all the books I've meant to and haven't. I can visit my daughter and grandchildren now and then. I can . . . I can do a hundred things."

Mrs. Dodd's face tightened, went a little sour. "You haven't asked what I'd like to do."

"For God's sake, girl, tell me."

"The two of us, we could move to Florida."

He laughed. "No more winters. Wouldn't that be something?"

"And maybe," she added, "we could marry."

Suddenly, with a surge of satisfaction, he realized he had, for a while at least, the upper hand in the relationship. He poured more wine. "It's something to think about, isn't it?"

III ≡ III

Gretchen Ryder was watching television. Presently Shell joined her. On the screen was the heavy face of a woman he did not recognize, though something was oddly familiar about her. Then he felt an emerging chill from a memory of long-ago newspaper photographs. The woman was Anna Hauptmann. Edward R. Murrow, a cigarette burning between two fingers, was interviewing her. Her voice was stronger than her looks. After all these years she was still proclaiming her husband's innocence.

Shell got up and changed the channel.

"Why'd you do that?" Gretchen protested. "It was interesting."

He switched the dial back, avoiding Anna Hauptmann's face but not her voice. Turning, he said, "You watch it. I'm going to lie down for a while."

"Don't you feel well?"

He didn't answer. His voice would have been a giveaway, a naked assault on himself.

In the dim bedroom he shucked off his shoes and lay down. He curved an elbow over his face. Never, he brooded, can the mind rest, not even in sleep. Active, it darts from one thing to another. Passive, it defies sleep and dredges the depths. God help me.

Some minutes later, maybe ten, Gretchen looked in on him. "Sometimes," she said, "I feel I'm doing wrong and don't know what."

"You're doing nothing wrong."

"Was it something to do with Anna Hauptmann? Did you know her?"

"No."

"Did Rudy?"

"No, why do you ask?"

"I don't know."

She faded away, back to the television. He almost called her back to him. She was a generous answer to his loneliness. He closed his eyes. Sleep was his armor against the world but not himself.

She woke him.

He hadn't really been asleep, only half. Half in this world, half in another. His mother was working in the button factory. His father was floating in the river.

"It's over," Gretchen said.

Mrs. Zuber had pins in her mouth. Rudy Farber had a wild scheme. "What's over?"

"The program," Gretchen said. "The program's over."

He patted the bed. He wanted her near. "A bit at a time, it's catching up to me," he said.

She lay beside him. "What is?"

"My real life."

||| ≡ |||

She had lingered, but now she was going. Shell received the call at the gasoline station while he was filling the tank of a brand-new Chevrolet

Impala, whose owner told him not to leave any finger smudges on the paint. His boss took over for him.

"I'll be there right away," he said into the phone.

He tried calling David and then Mrs. Dodd but reached neither. Perhaps it was just as well.

He wiped his trembling hands in a greasy rag and drove to Danvers in what he was wearing. *Ted's Texaco* was stitched on the front of his shirt, over the pocket.

At the hospital someone directed him to the infirmary. In the infirmary a nurse said, "There's nothing that can be done."

"Yes, I know. Could we be alone?"

He drew the curtain around the bed. He wanted to be utterly alone with her. He leaned over her. Her eyes were closed.

"Helen," he whispered.

"I hear you," she said.

Though she had difficulty breathing, she was lucid. She looked almost herself. Someone had put a bow in her hair. He remembered her wearing one in a sepia photo. She couldn't have been more than six or seven.

"Shell?"

"Yes."

"You smell like I remember. Gasoline."

Her eyes open, she tried to lift a hand. He lowered his face. The ends of her fingers brushed his cheek.

"How much of you is true, Shell?"

"Not much," he said. "How about yourself?"

She attempted a smile. "I'm a story you've heard before."

"Then it doesn't bear repeating."

He was holding both her hands now, gently, waiting for her to regain her breath. The wait frightened him.

"Where is he?" she asked. "Is he here?"

"David? No, I couldn't reach him."

"Will you ever tell him?"

He hesitated. "I don't know. Do you want me to?"

"It's your decision now."

The wait this time was longer. Her hands were weightless inside his. Her hair was thin. He could see her scalp.

"I'm locked inside myself, Shell, but soon I'll let myself out."

He imagined her floating away, waving to him from afar, vanishing. He felt heat behind his eyes. His hands were trembling over hers.

She spoke in a low voice. He missed the first sentence and caught the second. "What will I say to him, Shell?"

"Who?"

"God."

His eyes were full. "Tell him the truth. I did it, not you."

Moments passed. Her face showed subtle traces of sweat. He composed his own face but not his emotions. When he sensed she was going, he fell forward to kiss her.

"Don't leave me," he whispered. "Please don't."

III ≡ III

The nurse said there were personal belongings he might want. They went to Helen's room. The bed was stripped, the mattress folded back. In the closet were a few cotton dresses, a coat. A dresser drawer revealed underwear and the like. He saw nothing he wanted.

The nurse pointed. "Those fleece-lined slippers are practically new. She didn't wear them more than once."

His eyes, which had been so wet, were dry. "Give them to another patient," he said.

"How about these?" the nurse asked.

Old picture postcards from Florida. From somebody named Weskett. Who was Weskett? It didn't matter.

"Did she keep a diary?" he asked.

"Not that I know of. If she did, she must've destroyed it."

He was relieved and yet not. He gazed out the window. He was alive. Helen was dead. It seemed extraordinarily one-sided.

"I almost forgot," the nurse said, reaching into her uniform pocket. "Sometimes this turns up missing. I made sure hers didn't."

A wedding ring fell into his open hand, as if from another time, another dimension. Its weight exaggerated itself, and he pocketed it. Helen was gone. The world would go on. One day he wouldn't.

"Where are you having the funeral?" the nurse asked. "I'd like to go."

He told her. Linnehan in Haverhill. He'd heard that Linnehan did good work. His eyes dampened.

"You loved her very much, didn't you, Mr. Shellenbach?"

"She was the grand moment of my life."

||| ☰ |||

Another winter approached. David and Meredith argued about the holidays. She said she had always spent them with her family, and that was not something she could change, not for him, not for anybody.

David said, "You look down on my father, don't you?"

"Don't be silly," she retorted. "Though I'll admit I'm no fan of the simple soul he lives with." She lit a cigarette. "There's a solution of course."

"Of course."

He had Thanksgiving dinner at the Wainwrights', but he spent Christmas day at his father's. Gretchen Ryder set a fine table, more food than the three could eat. His father ate slowly and not much. Gretchen told stories about some of the more demanding customers at Mitchell's.

After dinner Shell got on the phone to Florida. David spoke briefly with his grandmother and then handed the phone back. While his father talked at length with Father Henry, he helped Gretchen out in the kitchen.

"He doesn't look all that good, does he?" Gretchen said.

"He could use a little weight."

"He hasn't been the same since your mother died."

David dried a plate. "I don't understand that. They were apart all those years."

"I understand completely," Gretchen said, her hands deep in dishwater. "Do you still think of Johanna?"

He picked up another plate and dried it. "Every damn day," he said.

He was glad when the holidays were over, glad to be back in his law offices, which he had expanded. He had hired another law student. The original one had graduated, passed the bar, and was working for him full-time. Nancy Potts, who had proved herself indispensable, had a part-time assistant. His accountant advised him to increase his estimated tax payments.

Occasionally he lunched with Tony Tonetti at the Parker House. Once, briefly, on his way to another table, Senator DeFelice joined them. DeFelice resembled a tall George Raft. He had dark, compelling eyes and a significant voice, and never gave out a full smile except to constituents. The only words he said to David were: "So you've married into the Wainwrights. That means you've got the world by the balls."

Then he was gone, seating himself at a window table of ranking Irish politicos, Knocko McCormack and Onions Burke among them. Tonetti said, "The guy's fabulous, fits in with everybody, plays 'em like a piano."

David said, "How's Angela?"

"Bitchin' to me about how she's got no time for herself. Who the hell has? I know I don't. Do you?"

"Maybe we don't want time for ourselves, Tony. If we did, what would we do with it?"

"You got no imagination, Counselor."

"No? What would you do, Tony?"

"I'd fly to Scandinavia and fuck three Swedes and a Norwegian."

"Then what?"

Tonetti speared a broccoli head. "I see your point."

Later David stepped into the Parker House barber shop, first time he'd been there. The floor was black-and-white checkerboard. He saw ten chairs that looked fit for royalty and mirrors that might have been framed in pure gold. He sat in the chair of the owner, Al Moscardelli, whose customers, according to Tonetti, included the rich and famous. Moscardelli threw a cloak over him, cinched it under his neck, and appraised the shape of his head.

"Just a trim," David said.

"A trim is all I do. You walk out of here looking like you just got a haircut, it means you got a bad one."

David closed his eyes, felt a comb in his hair, and soon heard the swift snipping of scissors. "A friend of mine says you've cut the hair of a lot of celebrities."

"A few. James Michael Curley was a regular."

"What sort of fellow was he?"

"He was an Irishman. What can I say?" The snipping paused for a moment, then resumed. "When Babe Ruth came to town, I cut his."

"That must've been something."

"The Babe had a bad case of dandruff. I cured it for him."

"How's mine?"

"You don't have any."

David tilted his head forward and enjoyed the sensation of an electric shaver on the back of his neck.

"Charles Lindbergh was in town a couple of weeks ago. I did him." Moscardelli turned off the shaver and resumed snipping. "Know what?"

"What?"

"You got a head shaped like his."

III ≡ III

John F. Kennedy was dead. Killed in Dallas. Impossible to believe, but there it was on the TV screen. Walter Cronkite wouldn't lie. Kennedy was dead.

The set was a Motorola plugged in behind David's desk. Perry, the young lawyer working for him, had tears in his eyes. Nancy Potts was trembling, and Perry curled an arm around her. Footage of the motorcade was rerun.

"This is not something that should happen in modern-day America," Perry said.

David said, "He was someone people loved to hate."

"But why?" Nancy Potts asked. "Why?"

"He had more than others. More of everything."

The footage of the motorcade was run again and again.

David phoned Meredith. She wasn't home. He really hadn't expected her to be. With a glance at Nancy Potts, he said, "I'm done for the day."

Traffic out of Boston was light. A green-eyed signal told him to go. The radio was on, but he soon turned it off. There was nothing more he wanted to hear. Had he stayed on Route 28 he'd have gone straight into downtown Andover. Instead, reaching the outskirts, he veered onto Route 125. Which took him to Haverhill.

The shoe factories, their numbers drastically diminished since his father had worked in one, were oddly quiet, little work being done. At the post office the flag had already been lowered to half mast. Downtown was strangely deserted except for a crowd gathered in front of the *Gazette* office. A man in the window was chalking bulletins.

When he was younger, more of a believer, he thought of God with arms permanently open, ready to receive. He wished he could still think that way.

He made a turn and, circling, passed Ted's Texaco, where he saw his father pumping gas. He slowed but didn't stop. Perhaps later. Later perhaps he and his father could have dinner at Lomazzo's, just the two of them. Then he remembered that Lomazzo's had closed.

Again he passed the *Gazette* office, the crowd growing. Women were weeping. He parked a short distance away and began walking toward Whelan's Drug Store for a quiet cup of coffee. Then his heart jumped. Walking toward him was a handsome woman he recognized instantly. It was Miss McCormick, dressed in tweeds, in grays, as if her body were utterly confidential. She had changed hardly at all.

He slowed his step. He wished he remembered enough Latin to address her in it. As they drew near he smiled.

"Miss McCormick."

He wanted to throw his arms around her. He wanted the two of them to hug.

Politely she returned his smile and passed by. She did not remember him.

III ≡ III

The phone call was from Florida. Shell took it. Father Henry wanted him and Gretchen to come down for the holidays. A perfect time, Father Henry said. Catch the rays, miss all that cold. His daughter and grandchild were visiting, but they'd be leaving soon.

Shell crimped his brow, pondered the possibility, then said, "I'd like to, but I can't. Thank you for asking, Father."

"Are you sure? If it's money, I can help out."

"It's not money, I'm doing all right. It's just that I'm stuck in my ways now." Emotion took over for a moment. "But I do miss you. I even miss her."

"Dorothy?" Father Henry laughed. "I guess that's saying something. She's a bitch, but what would I do without her? She loves it down here. The old bucks think she's special and treat her like a queen. The women don't like her."

"I take it she can't hear you."

"She's napping. She naps a lot. Fifteen, twenty minutes at a time. She says it keeps her young."

"And how are you doing, Father?"

"I'm half in the bag, hope you can't tell. Did you get the oranges I sent?"

"Yes. Thank you."

"The coconut?"

"That too."

There was a silence. Then: "Damn it, Shell, I miss you, too. You and Gretchen. Let me speak to her."

Shell called to her, gave her the phone, and dropped into a chair. He believed in intuition, and intuition told him that Florida was a bad move. He might die down there and nothing in his life and David's would ever be settled.

He heard Gretchen say, "I don't go anywhere without Shell."

She chatted a number of minutes more and then extended the receiver. "Say good-bye to Father Henry."

For supper she made liver and onions. Calf's liver, she told him, was the best. They ate quietly. She looked at him with concern because his appetite was off. He looked at her with gratitude. She was the stabilizing force in his life.

"I'm glad you took the day off," she said. "You need the rest."

He smiled at her. Sometimes he felt useless. He was not up to bedtime love anymore. She had told him not to worry about it. Sex gave her a backache.

"The liver's delicious," he said.

"I knew you'd like it." She used the salt, not too much, doctor's orders. "Maybe you should reconsider Father Henry's invitation."

He didn't respond, and she didn't press.

They did the dishes together, always a pleasant time. He brushed against her. Closeness was safety. Safety was each other. They could let down their guard.

After watching an hour of television they went to bed. A window let in cold air and sounds from the river. Stretching his legs under the covers felt wonderful. Gretchen's warmth reassured him.

"We could try," he whispered.

Her arm fell over him. "No, let's just hold each other."

||| ≡ |||

David was working on a brief when his associate, Perry, rapped lightly on the half-open door, entered apologetically, and said, "Can I bother you for a minute?"

"Sit down."

Perry did. His face, too bland for secrets, was prone to confession. His expression was diffident except during litigation, when it required purpose and character. "It's about Nancy Potts."

David wasn't surprised. He knew that after the Kennedy assassination they'd been seeing each other socially. "What about her?"

"We have something going."

"Really."

"I'm in love with her."

"Nothing wrong with that. Is she in love with you?"

"Not yet. The problem is I think she has a crush on you."

243

That was a surprise. "I think you're misreading something, but if it's true I'm sure she'll get over it." David paused. "Anything else?"

"I just thought you ought to know how I feel about her. I'm really serious about her. I know she's kinda plain, but I'm no Paul Newman."

"Thank you for confiding in me, Perry. I don't anticipate any problems in the office, do you?"

"No, none at all. You have my word."

David resumed working on the brief, the client a recidivous criminal with a murderous past. He wished he had not taken him on. The relative of a friend of Tony Tonetti's. Tonetti seemed as much a part of his life as Meredith.

He rose from his desk, stepped out of his office, and stretched his arms. Nancy Potts was at a file cabinet, the top drawer pulled open. Turning, she smiled. His wife, she said, had left a message, a reminder to be home on time. A party at the Bellwoods'.

He stared at her fully and for the first time noticed the cut of her reddish hair. He took in her freckles, her figure. From the corner of his eye he glimpsed Perry in his office. He hoped they'd be happy. He wished he were.

||| ≡ |||

The Bellwoods had a grand house off South Main, a quarter-mile from the academy, with a cavernous drawing room perfect for parties. It was crowded by the time they arrived. Voices drowned out the harpist. David plucked drinks from a tray and gave one to Meredith. She was wearing black. Many of the women were.

"Cheers," he said, forcing a smile.

"Circulate, darling. And be charming."

Mrs. Bellwood—Sarah—kissed him on the mouth. "We were afraid you weren't coming. You work too hard."

He cruised a long buffet table, everything to choose from, except he wasn't especially hungry. He tried an hors d'oeuvre and wished he hadn't. Too tart.

He moved from one knot of males to another. The talk was college football, the exchange rate of the dollar, politics. LBJ was deemed little improvement over JFK. Drawn into the conversation, David confessed to being a Democrat, which raised eyebrows.

"What does your father-in-law think of that?"

Nursing his second drink, he moved on. Women seemed the forces, their presence emphatic, their husbands amiable and governable. A young woman greeted him with a smooch on the cheek. She wore a dress with a low tight top, her breasts jammed together, as if daring a man to divide them.

"You're not very good on names, are you?" she said.

He had called her Janet. Her name was Joyce.

She called to her husband, who glanced over his shoulder. He was husky, with a solid all-American face, the sort Tab Hunter had, a smile to match.

"What's up, dear?"

"Mr. Shellenbach has insulted me. He forgot my name."

"You're kidding me. Should I punch him out?"

Smiling, David almost wished he'd try and immediately felt juvenile.

Drifting, he drew close enough to the harpist to hear what she was playing. Gowned in white, blond hair flowing to her spine, she looked ethereal. He tried to catch her eye to signal his appreciation but she was rapt.

He came upon Meredith near the grand stairway. She was talking with a man named Shaw or Shey, who stood stalwart in charcoal-gray. He was a leading player in a securities firm. Horn-rims gave him a quiz-kid look.

David said, "Hi."

Turning, Meredith looked angry. "I've lost a fucking earring," she said.

David was taken aback and viewed her boldly. "The loss of an eye or a leg is serious. An earring isn't."

A third drink was out of the question. He went outside and stood in the cold of a moonless and starless night, which gave the dark too heavy a weave. It was easy to imagine murder and equally easy to imagine himself the victim. After several deep breaths, he went back inside.

He wanted to leave and looked for Meredith. She was no longer at the foot of the stairway. Sarah Bellwood caught hold of his wrist. Her lips were newly painted, the bow somewhat exaggerated.

"You're too stiff, David. You must learn to loosen up." Her hand ran up his arm. "Is that not possible?"

Diverse couples were scattered in deep conversation up the stairway. He began the climb, for the most part unseen or, if seen, ignored. At the top of the stairs, well to the right, he saw Meredith under the staid portrait of a Bellwood forebear, and he saw Shaw or Shey with a hand halfway up her dress.

His sudden presence seemed to surprise the portrait more than them. They separated. Meredith patted her hair.

"David, please. Don't say anything."

"Sorry, but I have to hit him."

The horn-rims flew off. The back of Shaw or Shey's head struck the wall, jarring the portrait. He clutched his mouth and fell to one knee. Knuckles bleeding, David shook his injured hand and grabbed Meredith with the other.

"Come on! We're getting out of here."

They had arrived in her car. She had a Corvette now. He took the wheel, lowered a window for air, and drove without hurry.

"My hero," Meredith said. "I think you broke his teeth. Probably crowns."

He said nothing.

"David, I'm sorry. I was tipsy."

The air was too cold for her. He raised the window a bit.

"It was stupid," she said. "I apologize."

They were silent the rest of the way home. She went into the house. He put the car away. For a number of moments he considered climbing into his own car and driving away. Where? To his father? To Nancy Potts?

Meredith was in the bedroom, her jewelry removed, her pumps off. She said, "Nothing really happened. People flirt at parties and then go home with their mates."

"He had his hand up your leg."

"Not all the way, I assure you." She undid the back of her dress. "That was an inane thing for me to say, wasn't it?"

He was not amused. "Is this marriage working?"

"I think it can. I think it will." She worked off her dress. "I love you, and my father thinks the world of you. I'd call that double barrel, wouldn't you?"

He sat fully dressed on the bed's edge, not sure he was staying, not sure of anything, his mind and body in tumult. She dropped her bra, her breasts meant to dazzle him. For a second they did.

"When we make love," he asked, "what are we exchanging? Anything?"

"What do you want from me, David?"

Her voice was sharp. She was naked now and stood with her hands on her hips. His jacket was off. His tie and shirt were next. Rising, he would soon be Adam. She was already Eve.

"An apple without a worm would be more than enough," he said.

CHAPTER FIFTEEN

GRETCHEN RYDER PUT THEM UP. THEY NEEDED SEP-
arate beds, so she put Mrs. Dodd in David's old room and Father
Henry in hers. Hers and Shell's, though she knew Shell would never return to it. Father Henry's appearance had shocked her. He looked so
old, so frail. Mrs. Dodd, on the other hand, was amazing. How could a
woman nearly a hundred years old stand so erect, with so much bearing? It seemed a trick of nature.

Unpacking, Mrs. Dodd said, "Why are those airplanes hanging from
the ceiling? They look decrepit."

"They were David's," Gretchen said. "Shell never wanted them taken
down."

"Where are you sleeping?"

"The sofa's fine."

Mrs. Dodd placed lingerie in a drawer. Turning slowly, she said, "You
and I got off on the wrong foot. It's nice we've both lived long enough
to make amends."

A warmth rushed through Gretchen, and a deep emotion gave her
color. She was too filled to speak.

She made coffee. She set a dish of frosted cupcakes on the table.
Father Henry, who had shed his collar for a blazing Florida shirt and

white shoes, ate two and would have taken a third had Mrs. Dodd not frowned.

"I never realized what a beautiful view you have of the river," he said.

"It is beautiful, isn't it? Sometimes I just sit here and gaze out."

Mrs. Dodd said, "Tell us about Shell."

"He's improved a little and is holding his own. I don't know for how long."

"We're not up here on a false alarm, are we?"

"I don't believe so," Gretchen said quietly.

Mrs. Dodd tried one of the cupcakes. "This Hanover House, I've heard of it. It must be very expensive."

"Insurance takes care of a little. David does the rest."

"How nice to have a rich son. Mine died without a penny in his pocket. He wasted away, terrible blemishes on his face. I never realized it was from that dirty disease."

Gretchen wasn't sure what Mrs. Dodd meant.

"AIDS, that's what they call it," Father Henry explained, his eye on his watch. "Is it possible to see Shell now?"

"What's the rush?" Mrs. Dodd asked. "He's holding his own. Besides, you're not going dressed like that."

"I'd like to see him alone."

"I'll drive you," Gretchen said.

Mrs. Dodd said, "I'll rest."

III ≡ III

Each was shocked at the deterioration of the other. Gripping hands, each did not want to let go. Finally Father Henry did and withdrew to a chair, which he inched closer to Shell's. Shell's voice didn't carry well.

"Your mother-in-law came up with me," Father Henry said. "She's planning on visiting tomorrow."

"No rush."

Father Henry smiled. "That's what she said."

"How is she?"

"She's already outlived herself. I'm next."

Shell readjusted his eyeglasses. "We had a death here last night. A man named Mr. Waterhouse, a victim of Alzheimer's. He died a stranger to himself."

"I'm sure during the final moments he came together," Father Henry said. "I'd be supremely surprised if he didn't."

"I don't have a season ticket, Father."

"I know. That's why I'm here."

"Do you remember my mentioning a sin, one I never confessed to you?"

"I'll hear it now."

"It's already been told. It's off my shoulders."

"Good," Father Henry said with a sigh. "Now you're free of whatever it is."

"Not really, Father. I'm afraid of what awaits me." Shell's hands were trembling, his face so pale he looked spectral. "I wake in the night terrified."

Father Henry leaned forward, ignoring a pain in his back, another in his neck. "Nothing awaits you. The mind dies with the body. Nothing's left."

"My soul," Shell said.

"Soul is mind. Mind is essence. Without substance, there's no essence. You've nothing to fear."

Shell took a breath, "Thank you."

"Don't thank me," Father Henry said. "It's the way the world is."

||| ≡ |||

David was right, she didn't believe it. Ravings of a dying man, she said. He said his father had been perfectly lucid. She laughed. "And you believed him." Not at first. It was too bizarre. She agreed. "I'm going to bed."

In the morning she went to the Andover library and scanned the same ancient headlines and examined the same pictures he had in the Haverhill library. Surreptitiously she tore some of the pictures out and slipped them into her bag.

When she returned, he was in the study, a closed magazine in his lap. When she laid out the pictures, he flinched. Suddenly the subject was

250

too sensitive for him. When she spoke, she felt she was touching the tender spot on a newborn's scalp.

"I'm sorry I told you," he said.

She stared at him with fascination, as if seeing him for the first time. "I'm not saying I believe you," she said, "but there's a resemblance. The more I look at you, quite a resemblance. You have Anne Lindbergh's eyes, the same expression, but the rest of the face could be his, Charles Lindbergh's."

His eyes sought a safe place to rest, away from hers. She thought she heard a slopping sound from his stomach.

"Don't you want to know for sure?"

"I am sure," he said.

"There's a test you could take."

"I don't intend to do that."

She continued to stare. He stirred her imagination. "Don't you want to know who you are?"

"Who I am," he said, "is what I've become."

At lunchtime she glanced out a window and saw Kipper tossing a golf bag into the trunk of his car. Good. One man sitting around the house doing nothing was enough. David wasn't hungry, she was. She had a pizza delivered, anchovies, mushrooms, peppers, the works, and pigged out. An excitement was growing in her.

David was roaming in the garden, the sun cooking his face. Flaming hybrid lilies lit the air. The sky was aggressively blue. He gave a start as she came upon him.

"David, can he prove it? I mean, he could be crazy."

"He's not crazy. For a while I thought he was, only because I didn't want to believe him. He never should've told me. Never."

"But he did." She sought his hand. He avoided the touch. She said, "If it's true, he's a monster."

He couldn't respond to that. It touched something he didn't want to consider.

She lit a cigarette. "Looking at the positive side, David, it's the break we've been waiting for. It's a gift from heaven. Don't you see the potential?"

He was looking at colors in the garden. Oranges and yellows. The shaky beauty of foxglove. The purity of the Madonna lily. Meredith trailed after him.

"Don't you understand, David? You're the Lindbergh baby! It'll be a media circus. The country will be at your feet. You'll beat Kenneally in a walk."

The soaring ambitions of the daylilies seemed to amaze him. He stood with a cluster of them reaching his shoulders. He looked back at her.

"No, Meredith. I'm out of the race."

"Don't talk stupid."

He moved past her, glad to be out of the sun.

||| ≡ |||

Bound in a bright one-piece bathing suit, she spent the rest of the day by the pool while trying to contain an anger that wouldn't stop growing. Long tired of Andover, which had become atrociously dull and pretentiously Yuppie, she wanted Beacon Hill, all of the whirl, and every God-damn perk that goes with it as a governor's wife. And not just any governor but the firstborn son of Charles Lindbergh. David on the covers of *Time* and *Newsweek,* she beside him. Four years as governor, then Washington. Why not?

She showered. She dressed as if to go out to dinner, though no plans had been made. She looked for Kipper. He had not come home yet. Undoubtedly he'd met a woman at the country club, married of course. Kipper was futureless. She had been their father's favorite. She should've been the son.

And she should've had a child. Whose fault was that?

Christ, she was almost crying. Composing herself, she did her face.

David was back in his study. Sunk in a big club chair, he looked as if he'd been napping. Still a handsome man. Graying hair gave him distinction. But where were his guts?

"Have you changed your mind?"

His face gave her the answer.

"Do you know what you're throwing away?"

If he spoke, she didn't hear. She sat on the wide arm of the club chair near his, crossed her legs, and lit a cigarette. Inhaling forced her breasts up.

"I could easily leak this to the media."

He glanced up. "Who'd believe you?"

"I'd tell them everything you told me. And I'd lay out the pictures."

"They'd accuse you of a publicity stunt. And they'd think you're a wacko because I'd deny everything."

His attitude infuriated her. He appeared quite prepared to drift back and forth from a life in reality to one wholly in his mind. Rising, she let an ash fall on the carpet. "What's left of us, David? Anything?"

"You be the judge of that," he said.

||| ☰ |||

"I remember when you wore your shirt collar spread over the outside of your jacket," Mrs. Dodd said. "Thank God you stopped doing that."

Shell hadn't looked forward to her visit. Now he was glad she had come. The permanent edge of her voice made time stand still.

Mrs. Dodd, on the other hand, had second thoughts for she realized that this shrunken man, nearly swallowed up by an upholstered chair, no longer touched her life. In her extraordinarily long existence he was a memory better kept in its place.

She said, "I thought I might run into my grandson here."

"No." Shell spoke in the phlegmy aftermath of a cough. "I don't expect to see him again."

She thought she had misheard. "Too busy running for public office, is he? Too busy being important."

"It's between him and me."

"Secrets, huh? One's never too old for them."

Shell no longer had secrets, so no answer was necessary.

"Or does it have something to do with that wife of his? I always felt she was too much woman for him." Mrs. Dodd crossed her nylon legs, shooting pain in one of them because of the pumps. "I thought the same about Helen and you. Do you miss her?"

253

"I miss everybody," he said. "I miss my parents. I wish I could remember what they looked like."

She feared he might turn mawkish. That would defeat everything, eat away at her own foundations. Uncrossing her legs, she felt a pain in the other one. She rose.

"I can't stay, Shell. I'm tired. I tire easily."

"I understand."

She was glad to get out of there, glad to see the sun, taste the air. Gretchen Ryder was in the distance, roaming the grounds like someone with nothing to do, nowhere to go. A terrible state to be in. Father Henry, wearing a decent shirt, was seated in a nearby lawn chair. With twinges in each leg, Mrs. Dodd strode to him.

"He could linger for weeks," she said. "We can't hang around up here forever."

His expression was abstract. She was an interruption, a voice of the real. He had been lolling with great freedom in spiritual thoughts and long flights of fancy, like a deviant submitting to his vice.

"Did you hear me, Prescott? Or have you gone deaf?"

"I'm not sure I want to go back, Dorothy."

||| ≡ |||

Within twenty minutes of leaving Andover, Meredith was approaching Boston. Under the warm overcast sky, the city looked like a rubbing from a gravestone. Her father had loved Boston, its streets mercilessly incoherent, its architecture an alliance between history and glitz, its Irish pols passionately primitive and knavishly entertaining. She had no such amorous feelings. The Hancock was blue ice. Red signals flew off the top of the Pru as if from a head wound.

She relinquished the BMW to an attendant and strolled into the Copley, toward the more intimate of the bar-lounges. She knew he would be late. That was his style, his arrogance, his way of treating her from the long-ago beginning. A man in braided maroon seated her at a small table well away from the bar. The afternoon crowd was sparse. The piano player, too young to have grown up with the music he was playing, smiled at her. The suave waiter, leaning low to take her order,

254

gave the impression of knowing and appreciating the intimate smell of women.

She had her drink and was jostling the ice when Carver joined her, his knee grazing both of hers as he pulled in his chair.

"Been here long?"

"Long enough." She broke open her purse and took out a cigarette.

"Why do you still smoke?"

That didn't warrant an answer. She eluded the return of his knee. Her thigh remembered the spread of his hand but wanted no part of it. She lit her cigarette from matches on the table.

"Too bad the Touraine's gone," he said. "We could've met there."

That was unnecessarily cruel. Certainly she had never expected him to change. They'd met while she was at Radcliffe and he was working his way through Boston University, a poor boy with aspirations and a chip on his shoulder. The cleft in his chin had fascinated her. Her love for him had been real, his a ruse, as if to make her pay for the chasm in their social standing.

The martini he'd ordered arrived. Sampling it, he approved. "So," he said, "what's the story?"

She realized that what she'd come to tell him was double-edged, a kind of revenge. The memory of the quack he'd sent her to had never softened, never would.

"Are you going to make me hold my breath?"

She remembered thinking she could forgive him, but on the evening they were to get together again, after a painful absence, he never showed up.

"David's taking himself out of the race," she said. "I'm making the announcement tomorrow."

Carver's face, cold and composed, stood bare during a silence. "That would be the worst mistake you and he could make."

She crushed out her cigarette and lit another. A spark fell. The smoke was a boundary between them but not much of one. She could see him obliterating it with a wave of the hand.

"Even if he did stay in, Carver, and got the governor's chair, you and your people would not be able to control him. He'd be his own man."

"Nobody in politics is his own man. Give it to me straight, Meredith. What's the matter with him?"

"He's not himself. Let's leave it at that."

"You can, I can't." He scraped his chair back and got up. "I gotta take a piss. Don't go away."

When the waiter stopped by to check on her drink, her perfume reached out. He breathed deep. The piano player was lost in the oblivion of the music. Always in moody places like this the music was Gershwin or Porter. She and Carver had danced to both.

Carver returned. He said, "I thought you pulled his strings."

"I never said that. If I did, I lied."

"The two of you played me for a patsy. No question about it, I gotta hurt him."

"No, you won't, Carver." She felt herself trembling. "You won't go near him."

"Really? When you get knifed, you feel no immediate pain. But what comes later is excruciating."

She went white. "Good God, is that what you've become?"

"I'm speaking metaphorically."

"No, you're not. I think you're capable of anything."

He smiled. "I got an idea. Let's check into a room, for old times. Maybe you can convince me to go easy on him."

"Fuck old times," she said. "And fuck you."

He was on his feet, staring down at her. Then he was gone. She needed a number of moments to collect herself. She reopened her purse. Old times was her taking care of the check. The tip would be generous.

Women customers pleased the waiter. He liked the fall of their hair, the swish of their dresses, the gusts of their scent, and their little dramas. He liked them best when they looked directly into his eyes.

"Thank you, madam," he said.

||| ≡ |||

Kipper was home. In a chair in his room. He was eating a sandwich, drinking imported beer, and watching an unsavory video. She said, "Turn it off."

His brows shot up. "I didn't hear you."

He couldn't find the remote. She stepped over his outstretched foot and did it manually. For a second she felt dizzy but stayed on her feet. Everything passes. Catastrophes subside. Cemeteries open and close every day.

She said, "Did David tell you?"

"Yes, he said he's dropping out. What's the matter with him, Sis?"

"He's fucked up. Thinks he's someone else."

"Really? Who?"

"You wouldn't believe it, though I did for a while, when it meant something. Where is he, Kipper?"

"I don't know. He went out, didn't say."

She stepped past him and sat on the end of the bed. Watching him chew on his sandwich and swig beer scraped a nerve. Kipper was a freeloader. He was a taker, a user. In a superficial way he was Carver without the cunning and little of the cruelty. But a parasite all the same.

"Is he having a breakdown, Sis?"

"You could call it that."

Watching him put aside the beer bottle she wondered why she had taken on the responsibility of supporting him. Was it because he was family, her flesh and blood, or because he was one of her toys from childhood?

"I feel bad for him," Kipper said. "He's always been good to me."

"Too good. Same as I am."

Kipper let that slide. He brushed crumbs from his lap. "Are you going to stick with him?"

"That's something I have to think about. Good men are an endangered species." She stared at him. "We're not young anymore, are we, Kipper?"

"I don't feel old."

"No, you wouldn't, but possibilities aren't what they used to be." Suddenly she was no longer sitting on the bed but standing at the door. "Kipper."

"What?"

"I want you out of the house."

"What?"

"Bag and baggage," she said.

||| ≡ |||

Shell stood with a cane that twitched under his frail weight. He was about to fall when Mrs. Kaplan rushed to him. "Let's get you in bed," she said, and had no trouble lifting him off his feet.

Mr. Unger, who was already bedded down, turned his face to the wall.

"The pain is back," Shell murmured.

"We'll see what we can do," Mrs. Kaplan said, tucking him in.

She phoned the doctor from her station. The doctor listened. "I think he's also had a mild stroke," she said. "Should we get him to the hospital?" The doctor didn't see the use of it.

"Do you?" he asked.

Sadly she didn't.

"Give him all the morphine he needs," the doctor said.

Shell took to the hypo the way a baby takes to the bottle. He still had his glasses on. Mrs. Kaplan removed them and placed them on the night table.

"Petra," he said.

She smiled. "There you go again." She patted the covers. "I'll look in on you shortly. Ring if you need me."

After she left, Mr. Unger turned his face around, spoke from his pillow. "Are you going to beat me to it?"

"Is there a bet on?"

"Probably."

Shell's voice thickened. "I simply want to float away, but gravity won't let me."

"Give it time."

Behind his closed lids, Shell was confronted with a frozen mosaic of compressed memories that represented his past. His eyes opening, the image vanished. Closing them again, it returned.

"Shell . . . I have a Bible."

258

He didn't want one. For him, the Bible was Abraham's willingness to sacrifice his firstborn. And for what? The whim of his Maker. Divinity making sport of human life.

"Shell . . . shouldn't your son be here?"

His eyes lidded, he said, "I don't have one."

III ☰ III

Standing at a front window with a cordless phone to her ear, Meredith saw David's car bulge out of the night fog and drift up the drive. She didn't know where he'd been. She suspected the library, those old newspapers.

"He's just arriving now," she said. "Thank you for calling."

Had she not intercepted him in the entrance hall he would have gone directly up the stairs. His face was drawn, his tie was loose. She still had the phone in her hand. She gestured with it.

"That was Hanover House. About your father."

His expression altered, as if his life had narrowed, squeezing him.

"Do you want me to go with you?"

"No," he said.

CHAPTER SIXTEEN

DAVID WAITED WHILE HIS FATHER-IN-LAW FILLED A
feeder for winter birds. Chickadees and titmice waited in the spruce.
Snow that had fallen three days before remained clean except for hints
of wood ash blown from the chimney.

Minutes later they walked up Bartlet Street and began their stroll
along cleared pathways through the campus. Each had on a down
jacket. Paul Wainwright wore a flat cap. A crow meandering over the
sunstruck snow looked like a priest in heaven.

With a smile, Paul Wainwright said, "I saw your damn picture in the
Globe again."

"Not a good one," David said.

"I didn't read the piece. What case are you on now?"

"One of the usual ones."

David had gained a questionable reputation as a defender of political protesters, draft resisters, and flag burners. A TV camera was frequently on him when he stepped out of a courthouse. Journalists
sought him out for interviews, newscasters wanted him for sound
bites. Paul Wainwright, with many good-natured reservations, was
proud of him.

Often they differed on issues but always while standing on common ground. David sympathized with the civil-rights movement, his father-in-law to a lesser degree. Paul Wainwright thought it was spinning too fast and for the life of him couldn't understand blacks burning and looting their own neighborhoods. Out of frustration, David had suggested.

Paul Wainwright skidded on a plate of ice, and David caught him under the elbow.

The assassinations of Martin Luther King and Robert Kennedy had shaken their faith. Charles Manson was an aberration, no other answer. Neil Armstrong walking on the moon was America at its technological best, William Calley at My Lai its moral worst. Paul Wainwright saw validity in the Vietnam war, the need to contain Communism. David maintained America was there to kill Vietnamese for their own good. An ad hominem argument, Paul Wainwright said.

They crossed Salem Street and stood by the low fence surrounding the bell tower. Near the tower students had made a snowman and used a carrot to simulate a pecker. Paul Wainwright purposely looked away.

"Meredith tells me you've taken in another lawyer. That makes three now, doesn't it?"

"Yes," David said. "One's a partner."

"You're doing well, David. I wish Kipper were."

Kipper was an overage hippie. The last time David had seen him, perhaps three years ago, was at the Wainwrights'. Kipper had brought home a young woman who wore a black turtleneck and no makeup and used the F word in casual conversation, which upset Paul Wainwright more than his wife. Priscilla Wainwright refused to be shocked until she discovered that the young woman, sitting negligently in a rocker, wore no underpants.

"Have you heard from him?"

"Not lately," Paul Wainwright said. "Apparently he doesn't need money at the moment."

David knew from Meredith that Kipper was living in a commune in southern California, where he functioned barefoot in a Socratic robe. Into mind-bending drugs and Eastern thought, he was trying to establish a cult of his own but, lacking charisma, succeeded only in impregnating two women, the abortions paid for by his mother, which Paul Wainwright was never to know.

Paul Wainwright said, "How are you and Meredith doing?"

The tone of voice put David on the alert. He had left Meredith sitting by the fire, reading *Portnoy's Complaint,* a book about a guy, she said, who jerks off.

"Sometimes we wonder," Paul Wainwright said.

"No need."

"Honest?"

"Honest."

"I'm relieved. It's not my place to say, but I wish you two had had children, at least one."

"Some things aren't meant to be."

"Yes, that's the way to look at it. All in all, David, I'd say you've made a damn good life for yourself."

David didn't mention that he felt too American, too well-off, too well-fed. He said, "Not without a little help from you."

"What are fathers for?"

They turned back. It had turned cold, a wind kicking up. Paul Wainwright shoved his ungloved hands into the big pockets of his jacket.

"Glad you still have time for these Sunday walks, David."

David said, "I'm glad you make time."

III ☰ III

She was still by the fire, stretched out on the sheepskin rug with her head in a pillow, asleep. He thought of her as Paul Wainwright's daughter and incidentally as his wife. They had never settled anything. They had simply stayed together. She opened her eyes. He placed another log on the fire.

"Finish it?"

She raised a knee. "It was a fast read."

She broke the spines of books she didn't like. Philip Roth lay intact.

"I meant to tell you, the Bellwoods are separating."

He wasn't surprised. A spur-of-the-moment strip-poker party, which he and Meredith had watched from the sidelines, had led to wife-swapping. A couple of divorces had already taken place. He watched the log catch hold and flare.

"Sarah's a silly creature," Meredith said. "She went to Bradford Junior College. That's where dumb rich girls went at that time. They graduated in two years with the misconception they were educated."

David thought of Sarah Bellwood in terms of frozen-white thighs, men jockeying for uninterrupted looks at her as she shed the last of her lingerie.

"Who's her lover?" he asked. "Shaw?"

"Shey, David. You never did get his name right."

"First party we went to at the Bellwoods', he was the one tossed a condom in the water."

"Good God, how did you remember that?"

He gazed at the fire as if it were a story being told. "It was my initiation into Andover. All those fucking Unitarians and Trinitarians."

"Don't be cynical, darling." Meredith sat up on propped arms. "Sarah wants to know if you'll handle her side of the divorce."

"Absolutely not."

"That's what I told her."

He stood watching the flames, drama unfolding. The new log was snapping. He wondered what his father was doing and tried to remember the last time he'd seen him.

"David, I have a question for you. It's something I've given a lot of thought."

He waited. "What is it, Meredith?"

"Would you like to adopt?"

"No," he said.

||| ☰ |||

Police Chief O'Grady pulled up at the pumps at Ted's Texaco in a black Buick, property of the city of Haverhill. "Fill it up, high test," he said. Then he got out of the car, full uniform, red face. The wind was sharp. Shell, wearing a cap with earflaps, worked the pumps. O'Grady said, "When you gonna let me do something for you?"

"Why do you have to?" Shell said without looking at him. "Can't you see I'm doing fine?"

"I could get you a sweet desk job, nothing to do but keep your eye on the clock. You'd be a sorta timekeeper."

"I'm OK. How many times I have to tell you?"

"Stubborn old bastard. I feel responsible for you."

"You don't have to. I'm responsible for my own actions."

Shell pulled out the nozzle, screwed the tank cap tight, and hooked up the hose. "City paying for this?"

"Yeah, mark the tab." O'Grady lingered. "Don't know if you know it, Shell, but my wife's in the Hale. She's dying."

Shell had thought she was already dead. "I'm truly sorry to hear that."

"I know you are." O'Grady pulled at an ear, then rubbed it. "Right now you got more than I got. A woman that's gonna be there when you get home."

"I didn't check the oil," Shell said. "You want me to?"

"No, it's OK."

The sound of the wind, deadening his words, was a requiem. He clamped a hand over his gold-braided cap to keep it from flying off, which it almost did. With a shuffle, he climbed back into the black Buick and held the door open.

"Looks like I'm driving a fucking hearse, don't it?"

Shell leaned forward. "Funny thing, Chief, you had me worried. I thought you'd come to arrest me."

"Why would I wanna do that?"

"I always thought that one day you would."

||| ≡ |||

Charles Lindbergh was not well. A doctor in Darien gave him an antibiotic for a fever attributed to fatigue, reminded him that he wasn't getting any younger, and advised him to cut back on activities. The doctor diagnosed a persistent rash as shingles.

Anne Lindbergh fretted when he began losing weight. At a private consultation she said, "What's really wrong with him, Doctor?"

"I don't know, Mrs. Lindbergh. It has me baffled."

"What do you suggest?"

The doctor, who had Scottish forebears and traces of their burr, recommended tests at Columbia Presbyterian in New York.

"He's stubborn, Doctor. He doesn't want to admit he could be sick."

"I know."

Lindbergh spent much time in his favorite chair watching the Watergate hearings. He despised John Dean. He admired H. R. Haldeman and John Ehrlichman. He was beginning to pity Nixon. Little pleased him, much annoyed him. He pointed at the screen.

"What do you think of *her*?"

The image was of John Dean's wife, her blond hair yanked back to display a doll's face. The camera sought excuses to return to her.

"Is she real or only a damn mannequin?" he asked. Then he coughed. He put a hand to his mouth.

Anne knelt by his chair. "Please, Charles, you're not getting better."

"It's a bother," he conceded. "A real bother."

"Will you let me make the appointment?"

"Yes," he said.

The test results were known three weeks later. Colonel Lindbergh was in the advanced stages of lymphatic cancer, with little time left to live. The doctor at Columbia Presbyterian, who had made many such prognoses, was not hardened. His heart went out to both, in particular to Mrs. Lindbergh, whose quiet beauty had vanished but whose grace and charm were imperishable. The tender look she gave her husband touched him deeply. The stoicism of each astounded him.

"I've reserved a room here for you, Colonel."

Lindbergh shook his head. "I don't intend to die in a hospital bed."

Home in Darien he told Anne he had much to do. Reviewing a will was one thing, sorting out his writings was another. And good-byes needed to be made to a select few. First, of course, would be the children. Grown, scattered, with children of their own.

Anne didn't think he'd have the strength to do much of anything, but, in short bursts of energy, he prevailed. One evening he talked for more than an hour on the phone with his eldest son, Jon. He told Anne he'd been dreaming vividly of all his children.

"*All* of them?" she asked.

He didn't reply.

The television stayed silent. He couldn't bear the noise. Anne, sitting beside him, read aloud from the *Times*. On the day Nixon resigned, he quipped, "We're both leaving office."

At times Anne had to bathe him, shave him, comb his hair, but that was only when he was at his worst. His determination to maintain his dignity surmounted most obstacles.

Then, quietly, secretly, the middle of the month, they left Connecticut. They flew across the country and then on to Hawaii, where a few years earlier they had bought a vacation hideaway, a small rustic house perched on a cliff on the island of Maui. It was where he wanted to be, the two of them together, apart from the world. Anne, though frightened, viewed the journey as spiritual.

She knew he wouldn't last much longer, days at the most. Windows stayed wide open so that he could hear the crash of the Pacific. Bird sounds startled him. At times his eyes lost their human quality.

One evening, his head moving on the pillow, he reached for her hand, to reassure her. In half a voice, he said, "I want you to know I'm not afraid. Death is flight, freedom."

"But I'm afraid," she said. "So afraid, Charles, of being alone."

He slept. When he woke, she was still at the bedside, still holding his hand. Smiling, he said, "I did dream about him."

She faintly heard him. She said, "Charles, are we finally going to talk about him?"

"We've never had to," he whispered. "We've known each other's thoughts."

"No, Charles. You don't know mine. And how could I ever know yours?"

"They're of you," he said.

She sensed when he was slipping away. She could feel his death in her own flesh. It tightened her face. Pressing his hand, she murmured, "Good-bye, my darling."

III ≡ III

David was at his desk, and Angela Tonetti was seated in front of it. She was dressed up, her crossed legs coiled in speckled hosiery. In an hour she was meeting Tony for lunch at the Parker House.

"Who's looking after the kids?" David asked.

"One of my aunts." Angela was the mother of five now, all girls, the youngest a toddler, the eldest in high school.

"Still trying for a son?" he asked.

"I've had enough childbearing. A woman knows when enough is enough. Besides, I've other things on my mind." She turned slightly in the chair. "Tony's being investigated."

David had heard the rumors while hoping they weren't true. "Are you sure?"

She nodded ruefully. "Usually he tells me nothing. This time he did because it'll be public pretty soon. I'm scared, David."

"Is Tony?"

"He says he can handle it, like it's all a game."

That was what had always fascinated David: Tonetti's view of reality. Nothing was straight. Everything was angles. He said, "How about De-Felice, is he also being investigated?"

"Yes, but Tony's the one up front. It's about that county jail built last year. Kickbacks. Doesn't look good, David." She took a handkerchief from her bag and twisted it. "Don't worry, I'm not going to cry."

"What can I do?"

"Be around if he needs you. If I need you."

He accompanied her out of the office, out of the building, a solicitous arm around her. The sun was brilliant. A U-Haul van was having trouble maneuvering a corner. A policeman lifted a white-gloved hand and halted traffic. Angela donned dark glasses.

"He doesn't deserve me, David, but what can I do? Five kids."

"How are the girls doing?"

"The youngest is starting piano lessons. It's the sheet music that puzzles her. She can't understand how a tune can be played from a spotty page."

"Nor can I," David said, and kissed her. She kissed back.

267

"I wish something of you had rubbed off on Tony."

He returned to the building. Nancy Potts motioned to him. She was married to Perry now but had kept her maiden name. Perry had become his partner.

"Mr. Tonetti called," she said. "He wants to know if you can have coffee with him late in the afternoon."

"Where?"

"Beacon Cafeteria."

"Like old times. Call him back, tell him yes."

‖ ≡ ‖

David was there on time. Tony Tonetti arrived ten minutes later and wriggled into the booth. He'd gained weight and lost some hair since the last time they'd met. David said, "Don't you want coffee?"

"I had enough. Drink yours." Tonetti scrutinized him. "You know, don't you? Angie tell you?"

"How serious is it, Tony?"

"Feds are involved. Federal money went into the jail. What I wanna explain is that I can't use you on this. I need a lawyer who knows how to play with the U.S. attorney's office. What I mean is, somebody who's been there before and knows what strings to pluck. Radical lawyer like you, feds would turn their noses up. You understand, don't you?"

"Perfectly."

"If it works out like I think it will, I'll get the extortion charges dropped in return for pleading guilty to accepting gratuities and a few other minor things. What'll I get? Five to seven? I'll be out in eighteen months."

"How about DeFelice?"

"I'm taking the fall. But I'll be taken care of. Better than you know. Better than you wanna know. And Angie's gonna be OK, she just don't know it yet."

"And you trust DeFelice to follow through? He's a snake, Tony, stunning to watch."

"But I ain't no fucking toad. He knows he misses one payment I'll fry him."

David lifted his coffee cup and took a slow sip. "So you have it all figured out."

"Best thing about working inside the system, Counselor, is you know how it works. I probably know more about it than your father-in-law. That's because in this state you gotta be a Democrat."

David consulted his watch. "I have to get back to the office."

"Yeah, I know. One thing, when I go away on my vacation I don't want you coming to see me. I don't want Angie and the girls coming either. Phone calls are good enough."

"If that's the way you want it."

"I do. And another thing, you still handling Mrs. Cammarano's trust?"

"I am. I'm paying out on it to the grandchildren."

"Bet you never borrowed from it. Honest as the fucking day is long, ain't you?"

"Not really."

"Yes, you are. That's why I trust you. I want you to look after Angie for me."

III ≡ III

The state bar association honored David for his extraordinary number of *pro bono* cases, the bulk involving women suing for nonpayment of child support. The *Globe*, Sunday edition, published a lengthy story about him. A large flattering photograph of him in shirtsleeves and striped suspenders accompanied the story, along with a smaller picture of him standing with his partner, Perry, with Nancy Potts in the background. David had wanted her in the forefront, but the photographer had his own ideas.

"It's where I belong but not for long," Nancy Potts had whispered. She was a student at Suffolk Law, evening division.

Though a registered Democrat, David attended a Republican black-tie banquet with the Wainwrights and was asked to rise to be recognized, his so-called radical past forgiven though certainly not forgotten. His last notorious case involved a fringe member of the Weather Underground, whose mission was to humiliate the Establishment and piss on the flag.

Guilty over not seeing more of his father, he tried to visit him at least once a month but often lessened it to a phone call. Greater guilt came from an image of his father in the coveralls of a mechanic. He tried to give him money, but Shell would take nothing. Nor would Shell consider the suggestion that he and Gretchen Ryder move to an apartment in Andover.

"I'm fine where I am, David, and you're where you belong."

Once a month, without fail, David phoned Tony Tonetti, who was serving a sentence at a prison camp in Allenwood, Pennsylvania.

Quoting from the *Globe*, David read him Senator DeFelice's latest denial: *If money was passed, I never saw a dime.*

Tonetti laughed. "He's covering his ass, Counselor. I'd do the same, wouldn't you?"

"How are you doing, Tony?"

"I'm doing swell. I was with one of the fucking Watergate guys for a while, same room, but he got transferred. He wanted to be closer to California." There was a pause. "When's the last time you seen Angie?"

"Two, three weeks ago. I took her and the younger kids to McDonald's."

"Big fucking spender."

"It's where they wanted to go. Don't you talk to her?"

"It's worse when I do. She says my grammar's gettin' worse. Hell, I talk better than my father. He's been here sixty years and still speaks broken. I ever tell you what he did for a living?"

David sensed a strain in Tonetti's voice. "No."

"He hung around South Station because of the crowds. He was a pickpocket until arthritis twisted his fingers out of shape. I was a kid I wanted to learn the trade, but he said he couldn't teach me. It's a natural gift, he said."

"Tony, is there anything I can do?"

"Nothing you can do. I made my bed, here I am. But I'm worried about Angie."

"She's fine."

"She's still a real woman. A real woman gets horny, I understand that. If it had to be, I wouldn't mind if you . . . what I mean is, I wouldn't want no one else."

David was acutely embarrassed. He said, "For Christ's sake, Tony!"

"I don't know what she's doing. I don't know anything. You don't know what it's like."

"Yes, I do," David said. "When I was in the army."

III ≡ III

He had not seen her in years, not since that evening at Amherst, but he seldom failed to look for her face in a crowd. He never thought he'd glimpse it. And then he did. A terminal at Logan. He'd gotten off a shuttle from New York, and she must have been on the same one. He reached out.

"Johanna."

She turned. Time seemed not to have touched her, merely brushed her with a breeze that had kept her fresh. It took him a moment to realize her hair was attractively gray, not blond. She said lightly, "Are you someone I know?"

"Not in a long time."

"How are you, David?"

"Fine. Can we talk for a bit? Have coffee?"

Her hesitation was the tick of a second. "Why not?"

They found a cleared table in a cafeteria. He fetched the coffees and laid down two packets of sugar beside hers. "See, I remembered," he said.

"Those were the old days. Sweet 'N Low now."

"I'll get some." He started to rise.

"Don't bother. I have some in my bag."

He couldn't help staring. "How did I miss you on the plane?"

"You had your nose in a magazine."

"You've hardly changed at all, Johanna."

"Either you need glasses, or you're lying through your teeth. Are they your own?"

"More or less."

271

Now it was she who was staring. They embodied each other's youth.

"You really haven't changed much, David, though I knew that. I've seen your picture in the paper often enough. As you said you would, you've made something of yourself."

"Tell me about you."

She was a marketing consultant, her own business, and before that she was in public relations. She'd been married and divorced twice, she said, with a son and daughter from the first marriage, none from the second. She produced snapshots. Her children looked stunningly like her, as if she'd seeded herself. Her son, she said, was in his first year at Columbia. That's what she was doing in New York.

He passed the pictures back.

"None to show me?"

He shook his head. "How's your father?" he asked, with a memory of Dr. Medwick's disapproving eyes.

"Wonderful. I never thought he'd marry again, but he did. He's retired, they're living in Fort Lauderdale."

"Where are you living?"

"Here in Boston, Back Bay." She lowered her coffee cup and looked at her watch. "I can't stay any longer. David, it was truly nice running into you."

"Wait." He didn't want her walking out of his life again so fast, with no chance to look at her at length, to talk, to share a few memories. "Could we have lunch sometime?"

"Lunches are impossible for me. I'm up to my ears in work."

"Then a drink somewhere, at the end of the day."

"For what purpose, David?"

"Does there have to be one?"

"I'm living with someone."

"Does that preclude a drink?"

She sighed. She smiled. "I'm in the book. Medwick Associates."

||| ≡ |||

He told Meredith he'd bumped into an old friend from high school and was going to have a drink with her sometime. Would she mind? he asked. Meredith raised her dress to adjust her panty hose. She was on her way out to a selectmen's meeting, at which she would present the League's point of view on a wetlands issue.

"Mind, why would I mind?" she said. "Everybody should have a friend. Someday you must let me be yours."

He phoned Johanna three times before she could spare time to see him again. They met on Boylston Street and went to a nearby lounge with low tables, tepid lighting, and an aged piano player. He had chosen the place.

"Cheers," he said.

Her wine was indifferent, his beer could have been colder, but the pretzels were tasty. Things he'd planned to say to her stayed in his head. The dance floor was small.

"Let's," he said.

"No, my feet are tired."

"Please."

He danced with her as if they were young again, eighteen years old, the dark of the night awaiting them. His father's Plymouth. The pines at Kenoza Lake hallowed by love memories. He danced too close.

"Don't, David."

"Can't help it."

"Yes, you can."

One dance was enough. They returned to the table. She still smoked. He lit her cigarette and took one for himself from her pack.

"Who are you living with?"

"He's a nice fellow. Let's leave it at that."

"I'd like to see you once in a while."

"Why would you want to do that, David?"

"Once you were a big part of my life. You *were* my life."

She looked away. She blew smoke. "Briefly."

"But at a vital time," he said. "The most vital."

She crushed out her cigarette. "Is this doing us any good, David?"

"Is it doing us any harm?"

"What do you want from me?"

He watched her put her cigarettes back into her bag, along with the complimentary matches that had come with the table. "Dancing, having you in my arms again, brought it all back. I do want to see you again."

Her face went hard. "I've had a mastectomy."

"I'm sorry," he said. "But what difference does that make?"

"How's a hysterectomy grab you?"

"Johanna, please."

"It's all true, David. And what we had was all wasted. I remember burning stacks of your letters. Well-written letters. I always thought you'd be a writer. Never thought of you as a lawyer." She snapped her bag shut, slung the leather strap around her shoulder, and rose. "Thanks for the wine."

"That's it? We don't see each other again?"

"You have my number. If you want to make it harder for me, do indeed ring me up."

Watching her leave, he knew he wouldn't.

||| ≡ |||

Tony Tonetti served eighteen months almost to the day. Angela arranged a homecoming party at the house. Senator DeFelice was not there, nor anyone else from the state house. Mostly the celebrants were relatives and neighborhood people. David recognized many. He had represented them at various times.

Tonetti mingled in the crowd with a cigar fuming in one hand and a champagne glass spilling in the other. People slapped his back, hugged him, kissed both cheeks. One of his weightier aunts enveloped him. Angela's assignment was to take candids with his old Leica. He hollered to David.

"Remember ones I took of you, Counselor? A few you couldn't send home."

Angela needed help reloading the camera. Breaking away, pinching the expansive bottom of one of his female cousins, Tonetti went to her aid.

"Gimme that, I'll do it." Then he whispered, "You and me, we're gonna fuck all night, ain't we?"

Angela pushed long strands of hair from her face. "Whatever you say, Tony."

He nuzzled up. "Were you true to me?"

"I couldn't be otherwise. You had the whole neighborhood watching me."

She snapped a picture of him and David toasting each other; then another of each with an arm slung around the other, buddies lacking only their army caps.

Tonetti said to David, "Who's this peanut farmer thinks he can be president? You seen him on TV, all those teeth? Fucking smile on him could blind you."

"He was up here last month, money-raising party in Cambridge. DeFelice was there."

"Sylvio must smell a winner."

"I don't see him here," David said.

"He'd be dumb to come. There are ways to keep in touch, this ain't one of 'em."

"What are you going to do for work?"

An ash tumbled from Tonetti's cigar. With a smile he said, "I'll think of something."

Within months David heard rumors from other lawyers that Tonetti was the conduit between Boston's mafia family and the state house. He was someone to whom others still slipped money.

Within the year David attended the wedding of Tonetti's eldest daughter, who'd inherited her mother's looks and was her father's favorite. The reception was held at the Copley. David couldn't begin to estimate the cost of it, particularly with the presence of Woody Herman's orchestra.

Dancing with Angela, he said, "Looks like Tony's bounced back."

She sighed in his face. "It's like he never left."

III ≡ III

Priscilla Wainwright went to bed with a headache and woke with it. Midmorning it worsened. The cleaning woman asked if there was anything she could do. "Call my husband," Priscilla Wainwright said. Paul

Wainwright, still someone whom party doyens called upon for advice, was in Washington. The cleaning woman, watching Priscilla Wainwright clutch her head, called for an ambulance.

Paul Wainwright took his wife's death hard. He saw only injustice. She'd been perfectly healthy when he left for Washington. Who could've known she had a brain tumor?

Kipper Wainwright, brown from the California sun, flew home for the funeral. At the casket he touched his mother's embalmed face—cold, hard, and solid—and went to pieces. Paul Wainwright couldn't deal with him, and Meredith wouldn't. They signed him into Baldpate, a small and discreet psychiatric facility in a neighboring town, where he spent nearly a month. Upon his release, he moved back into his old room at the family house and, with his father's help, got a job with a local real-estate broker, a job that didn't last.

Paul Wainwright retreated into himself, worrying Meredith, who said to David, "You must spend more time with him."

"Of course, but shouldn't it be you?"

"I am, but it's your company that seems to pick him up."

Paul Wainwright made it through the winter and into the summer, when he began spending much time alone at a rented cottage at New Hampshire's Rye Beach. He bought a sailboat. In his younger days he had frequently sailed.

The last time David saw him alive was at the cottage, the weekend before Labor Day. They were sitting outside, looking out at the ocean from lawn chairs, while Meredith prepared lunch. Paul Wainwright tugged at the visor of his yachting cap.

"Depressing times, David. Politically, I mean."

David agreed silently. A warm wind made the ocean creamy blue. The sun gave it dazzle.

"My party's changing, David. Swollen with Reaganites, disaffected Democrats, Christian fundamentalists, Joe Six-Packs. They're setting the agenda, but not altogether in Massachusetts, not yet at least."

David removed his sunglasses and rubbed his eyes. "It's an uncomfortable time, sir."

"Yes. That's why you should get into politics. You could make a difference."

"I doubt it," David said, "but I'm flattered you think so."

Paul Wainwright breathed in deeply. The brackish smell of a salt marsh was evident from a mile away. Waves rousting pebbles gave out a language.

"How's your father, David?"

"He suffers from eczema, one of his body's small failings. Other than that, he's fine."

"You see more of me than him."

"Right now you're a priority, sir. Meredith is worried about you."

"Tell her not to be. I know what I'm doing."

||| ≡ |||

Dignitaries from across the state and many from out of state, both parties, attended Paul Wainwright's funeral. President Carter sent a letter of condolence. At the wake Meredith and Kipper greeted each one. Meredith was dry-eyed, holding her emotions in. David delivered one of the eulogies at Cochran Chapel. He feared his words were wooden until he saw tears running down Meredith's cheeks.

At the grave site she faltered for a moment. David gripped one of her arms, Kipper the other. Shrugging them off, she said, "I'm fine. I'm his daughter."

Kipper said, "I always knew that."

The graveside service was brief. In the walk to their waiting limo, Meredith held her head high. In the limo, Kipper lit a joint.

"Throw it out the window," Meredith said. "Do it now."

Kipper did. Then he settled back in the plush upholstery as the limo started forward. "I don't understand."

"What don't you understand?"

"What was he doing out in deep water?"

David looked away.

Meredith said, "Think about it, Kipper. It'll come to you."

||| ≡ |||

Father Henry and Mrs. Dodd regularly attended services at the local Episcopal church. The rector, a native Floridian, sibilated through his teeth when he spoke. Mrs. Dodd called him whistling Jesus.

"I bet he was born a Baptist," she said.

Occasionally Father Henry filled in for him, a grand opportunity to wax poetic. Lightning, he said, is all elbows. Ocean waves suffer from monotony. The wind howls even when it's not hurt, and the moon has seen it all. The moon, he said, is God's face when God chooses.

"Was that a sermon or a performance?" Mrs. Dodd asked.

"Comes to the same thing, Dorothy. Theater."

"So long as you don't make it comedy."

"That was always my criticism of Jesus. He didn't know how to laugh."

Once he officiated at the wedding of a young couple at the peak of ripeness. In their looks were children waiting to be conceived. The bride's bodice swelled her breasts, their fullness celebrating life. And her own youth.

Dancing with him, Mrs. Dodd said, "Good God, Prescott, you're horny."

"No," he said, "I'm alive."

The music was from their past, somewhat more his than hers. He gazed at her with sentimental eyes. She said, "You're either a satyr or the most religious man I know. I suspect you could be both."

"I love you, Dorothy."

"I'm beginning to suspect that too."

Some weeks later Mrs. Dodd heard from her son, a phone call that woke her, for he was calling from California time. He sounded different. In fact, she didn't immediately recognize his voice. He wanted to visit her, actually to stay for a while if that was all right. She said she'd get back to him.

She talked it over with Father Henry in the morning. Adding celery salt to his tomato juice, Father Henry said, "I don't see the problem."

"I don't know how long a visit he's talking about. No doubt he's broke."

"You can't deny him."

She pondered the possibility. "He's homosexual."

"What am I to say to that?"

"Do we have room?"

"We'll make room," Father Henry said.

Dane Dodd arrived the following week, and Mrs. Dodd saw at once that he was ill, shockingly so, almost too weak to handle his luggage at the airport. Father Henry came to the rescue. Mrs. Dodd helped.

Father Henry's car was a roomy Oldsmobile. Dane Dodd had the backseat to himself. During the drive out of Miami, he said, "I played in community theater here once. A long time ago."

"You must've been very young," Mrs. Dodd said. "I don't remember."

"I sent you a playbill."

"You sent me many."

She was glad to get home, glad to be out of the car, where his presence had pressed upon her. Father Henry dumped his luggage in the room where he was to sleep. The room was perfect, he said. Mrs. Dodd watched him unpack medication from a carryall. "What's wrong with you, David?"

"That's the problem. The doctors don't know."

"Maybe we can find one around here for you. Father Henry goes to a good one." She started to leave.

"Mom."

She pivoted. "Yes?"

"I won't be a bother."

The flight had tired him. He slept through the supper she had prepared for the three of them. Father Henry told her not to worry, it wouldn't go to waste.

"Shh," she said. She could hear him talking in his sleep. "What do you think is the matter with him, Prescott?"

Father Henry speared a chip of fried potato, for which he had a weakness. "He's come home to die."

"This isn't his home."

"It is now."

Dane Dodd died six days later. Father Henry's doctor listed the cause of death as a pulmonary infection, the best he could come up with. Mrs. Dodd stood by a window.

"They're gone, Prescott. Both my children."

⚏ ☰ ⚏

Paul Wainwright's will provided for several generous scholarships, some in memory of his wife, for deserving and needy students. Equally generous were bequests to Phillips Academy and Harvard, and more than generous was one to Wheaton, Priscilla Wainwright's alma mater. David understood, and certainly Meredith did.

"His way of keeping his world going," she said.

She and Kipper were provided for, though not as substantially as expected. Only Kipper was disappointed and more so when he learned that the family house, built in the late eighteenth century, had been deeded over to the Andover Historical Society.

"Why the hell did he give it to those prissy people?" Kipper said. "It should be mine."

"I think he knew what he was doing," Meredith replied.

"It's OK for you. He gave you a house."

"Go away, Kipper. Before I say something I'll regret."

"Sis, I'm sorry."

Sweeping a sudden arm around him, she spoke in cold and precise terms. "We're the last of the line, Kip. Let's live up to it."

In the following weeks she busied herself in a distant downstairs room she'd converted into an office for herself. Her voice melodious, she was making telephone calls throughout the state, mostly people her father had known. David didn't pry. He figured it was her way of dealing with grief. And he was busy himself, wrapping up a large class-action suit against a chemical company. Then one evening, returning late from Boston, he found her sitting in the front room, the lights dim, a drink in her hand.

"Come in," she said, "I want to talk to you."

He dropped his briefcase in one chair and himself in another and stretched his long legs. After yawning, he gave her singular attention.

"This life is all we have, David. Are we going to waste it?"

"I hope not."

She sloshed sherry around in a brandy balloon. He remembered breaking one, the set a gift from one of her great-aunts. She said, "You know what my father wanted you to do."

"Politics is out of my league. Besides, I'm too old."

"You're the same age as Governor Kenneally, except you look ten years younger."

David refused to take her seriously. "This is absurd. I could never beat Kenneally."

"That's right. As a Democrat you wouldn't even make it to the primary. As a Republican you stand a chance, trust me."

"Meredith, be reasonable. I've never held public office."

"That's to your advantage. You're clean, and as a lawyer you've fought the good fight." She crossed her legs. After all these years her legs were still innuendos. "I've been talking to people. Top Republicans. They're receptive. Your face is fresh, your name's not unknown, and you're Paul Wainwright's son-in-law. That alone gives you credentials."

He loosened his tie. He was interested only in the abstract.

She said, "Women of both parties will vote for you. They know you're on their side. And Republican men would come around. That's how I read it."

"You're forgetting Kenneally. He's popular."

"But his administration isn't. It's had its share of scandals, and that big jolly smile of his goes only so far. Think about it, David. The man's vulnerable."

He raised his wrist, read his watch, and pulled himself to his feet. He had to be in court in the morning, early. "It's not realistic, Meredith. And I'm tired."

"David!" She tipped her head back and finished off her sherry. "I know someone who can make it happen."

"Really? What is he, a miracle man?"

"He's worked on many campaigns behind the scenes. He's a strategist, a money-raiser, and an operative all in one. Will you at least talk with him?"

David heaved a sigh. He felt he was creeping beyond the margin of authenticity into the weightless world of caprice, where he could easily imagine himself floating.

"I can arrange a meeting this weekend," she said.

"Who is this guy? Have I heard of him?"

"Probably not. His name is Carver."

‖ ≡ ‖

He was still awake, his eyes open in the dark, when she slipped into bed. He waited until she settled deep under the covers. "Why did you marry me, Meredith?"

"One reason was your future value," she said. "I knew it would be high."

"What's another reason?"

"I knew my father would like you."

"That's it? Didn't love enter into it?"

"It must have." She inched closer to him, sherry on her breath. "Of course it did. Why did you marry me, David?"

"You were a fantasy, quite unreal."

"That's it?"

"I had this fear that when my eyes weren't on you I'd never see you again. That something unforeseen would take you from me. Marriage was an answer."

She was silent for several moments. "I have a request, David."

He waited.

"Let me be that fantasy again."

‖ ≡ ‖

Meredith opened the door to him, and for a single instant his smile made her feel vulgar. Showing him into the study, she said, "David will be down in a minute."

They chatted. In the privacy of the wait, her manner told him that anything beyond pleasantries and business was off limits. He mentioned financing. One of her many memories of him was that of his face turning stark and primitive in discussions of money.

282

"Is it a problem?" she asked.

"Money is always available when a candidate is salable."

"How many strings would be attached?"

"Strings can be broken later." Again that smile. "Not all of course."

David appeared.

"David, this is Carver."

They shook hands. They sat in opposing chairs, with Meredith seated slightly to one side. David's gaze rose from the small neat knot in Carver's regimental tie to the cleft in his chin.

His voice flat with dispassion, Carver said, "We think you have a chance."

"I'd need more than a chance," David said. "I don't want to make a fool of myself."

"If you make a fool of yourself, you make one of me. I wouldn't let that happen. Like your wife, I think the time is right. Kenneally can be beaten. Worked right, you could do it."

"I'm not a Republican."

The smile again. "So you see the light and become one. The party of Cabot, Lodge, and Saltonstall. What's the problem?"

Meredith said, "There is none. The party needs moderates."

Carver kept his eyes on David. "You interested, or am I wasting my time?"

"He's not wasting your time," Meredith said. "He's interested."

"I need to hear him say it."

"You're putting a lot on my plate," David said.

"That's right," Carver said. "It's big league. It's pure hardball. Once you're in, it's a commitment, no backing out."

"Give me a month to think about it."

Carver rose. "I'll give you a week."

III ≡ III

Shell's body, obedient for years, began to let him down, roughly about the same time Ted's Texaco went self-serve. Home, nothing to do, he missed the regular customers and the give-and-take of those who'd joked with him. Stiff, his back bothering him, he said to

Gretchen Ryder, "Old people look for handrails. That's what I do now."

She set down plates of franks and beans, their Saturday supper. "Didn't you know you were old, you old coot?"

"How come you're still young? You haven't got a wrinkle in your face."

"That's because I'm fat." Sunday they took a slow stroll along River Street, past tenement buildings identical to their own, past Delbeni's used-car lot, all the way up to the Lithuanian social club and beyond to Moody School.

"David went there."

"I know," Gretchen said. "You've told me a hundred times."

They watched boys playing baseball on the grassless ground beside the school. The boys were using a taped-up ball that resembled a glob of iron; lucky they didn't break the bat hitting it or their hands catching it.

"Rudy and I used a ball like that."

"I remember," Gretchen said. "Behind Mulheim's. Rudy's sister was smart in marrying Mulheim."

"He's dead."

"I bet she isn't."

On the walk back Shell needed to pause several times for want of breath, which worried Gretchen. She was more worried when he had trouble climbing the stairs to their tenement. Closing the door behind him, she guided him to the sofa and made him lie down.

"You should see a doctor," she said.

"What's he going to tell me? I'm an old man?"

"Have you ever had a medical checkup in your whole life?"

"Must have," he said. "Just can't remember."

She made a chocolate milkshake in the blender, an egg in it, and served it to him. He sat up to drink it.

"This will do the trick," he said, but took only a sip.

She took the glass from his hand and placed it within reach. "You're not well. I'm going to tell David."

"No," he said. He was adamant.

"Then we bargain. You go see a doctor."

III ≡ III

David looked for Perry. Perry wasn't in the office. He found Nancy Potts in hers. She was sitting on the edge of her desk, talking on the phone, waggling a foot. Smiling, she gestured for him to stay.

He sat, waited. He'd thought freckles faded with time. Hers hadn't. She now wore contacts instead of glasses. Her lipstick was a bold shade. His gaze dropped to her waggling foot: the navy pump, the trim ankle, the strong calf. Marriage, a law degree, and several successful cases had transformed her.

Suddenly she was off the phone.

"Were you ogling me, David?" She winked and returned to the chair behind her desk. "No such luck, right?"

"I've something to tell you."

"Sounds serious."

"It's confidential. You can tell Perry of course, but no one else. I've been approached to run for governor."

She gave him an incredulous look, and for a second he saw not the stylish lawyer but the scraggly secretary who had helped him set up shop.

"I'd be running as a Republican."

"I can't picture that."

"I wouldn't be the usual sort," he said.

"This is too much too fast." She plucked up a pencil and poised it as she once had when preparing to take dictation. "It's a while off yet, isn't it? I mean, when Kenneally's term is up."

"I'm told time is of the essence."

She put aside the pencil. "You'll make a fine governor."

"I haven't made an absolute decision yet."

She was quiet for several seconds. "Do you know what I miss?" she said slowly. "Those beginning days when it was just you and me here, and neither of us knew what we were doing. But we did it."

"Yes, we did."

She was looking at him as if she wanted to confess something. He hoped she wouldn't. She didn't. She said, "You've already made up your mind, haven't you?"

"I guess I have."

||| ≡ |||

It was May in Connecticut. Anne Lindbergh's eyesight was not what it had been, but she continued to write daily in her journal. She wrote: *The magnolia is in bloom and seems to give out the message that one should be in church or ringing a bell or reading a poem. Some sort of quiet celebration.*

She loved her garden.

She toiled in it through May and June and into July. Lilies flourished in July. They cartwheeled their colors, flaunted their height, kissed the breezes, and taunted her eye. Crouching, removing one of her gloves, she touched the soil and gave thanks not to God but to Nature. Nature had never let her down.

She tried not to pity herself. A source of strength were her five aging children, six really, for she saw two beings in Jon. His birth had followed Charles Junior's, which symbolized a rebirth.

None of her children was happy over her living alone, but she preferred it. Her housekeeper arrived daily, and a nurse kept weekly tabs on her. That was enough company. Her daily walks were treats, though less so when she ran into people.

An adventure of sorts was a trip to the dentist's office, where she bared a bad tooth she expected to lose. The dentist saved it by crowning it. The young woman working for him asked for her autograph, a request that usually would have secretly annoyed her. This time, for some reason, she was pleased.

"I loved your book," the young woman said.

"Which one?"

"*Gift from the Sea.*"

"My favorite," she said.

The sun was still strong when she returned home. Her journal under her arm, she went out to the garden and sat in her chair. The housekeeper brought her ice tea with a lemon wedge. She remembered another housekeeper bringing hot lemonade to her bedroom. Sometimes it seemed the taste had never left her mouth. That was nearly fifty years ago, moments before the world went wrong.

Phlox, hot and scented, bloomed high off the ground. A large blueberry bush quivered. Jays were in it. Uncapping her fountain pen, she watched a tanager zip by as if on a wire. She opened her journal.

At the moment of death, she wrote, *do we get answers?*

CHAPTER SEVENTEEN

MR. UNGER'S SNORES DIDN'T BOTHER SHELL. NOTHING did. Lying in his bed, his arms outside the covers, he knew what it was to live in that slender world between consciousness and oblivion, living and dying, in the transcendent state in which one is neither real nor unreal but suspended in an aura of undiscovered geometry.

He rode a wave. He soared. Water and air were one. He glimpsed Mrs. Zuber in the distance, a beckoning hand aloft, and he swam toward her but not near enough. A couple of times she dissolved, and each time he waited for her to reappear. The second time she didn't. Though only a bit of his speech was intact, he managed to call out.

"Where are you?"

"Here," she said.

He had spoken to the ether. Here was nowhere.

Drifting back to his bed, he discerned a ghostly figure in the half-dark of the room. The figure hovered the way a spiderweb stands on air. Then it swayed close, lifted his wrist, and felt for a pulse.

"Am I alive?"

His voice didn't reach.

Out in the corridor Mrs. Kaplan held an arm aloft at the sound of rapid footsteps and beckoned when she saw David. His face was stark, his necktie yanked loose.

She said, "You'd better hurry."

Briefly he gripped her wrist. "Call Mrs. Ryder. She should be here."

Shell didn't hear the footfalls into the room, but he sensed a presence by the change in the air, as if a bird had flown in. In as much breath as he could muster, more than he could spare, he said, "Who's there?"

David leaned over him, peered into the hollows of the face, and whispered, "Your son."

Moments later Mrs. Kaplan came in. David stepped aside and watched her feel for a pulse, her hand remaining well beyond the time that determined there was none.

"I don't think he heard me," David said. "It was important, very important."

Mrs. Kaplan straightened. "Whatever it was, I bet he did."

Mr. Unger, awake and sitting up, said, "He beat me to it."

III ≡ III

On the obituary page Shell was listed as a former *Gazette* reporter and Saturday editor. Unmentioned was his employment at Hersh Brothers and Ted's Texaco. Gretchen Ryder was not mentioned among the survivors, *Gazette* policy. David, as a well-known lawyer and former gubernatorial candidate, was mentioned high up in the obit, as if the father's real status stemmed from the son.

Father Henry and Mrs. Dodd waited in the kitchen to take Gretchen to the wake. Gretchen was not herself. In shock, she went from one thing to another without knowing what she was doing. She'd run a bath but had forgotten to take it. The dress she'd laid out was the wrong one. Then she discovered there was no right one. She stripped off her underwear because it was frayed. Naked, she thought of her body as one thing piled atop another. She would have sunk to the floor but there was no time. She threw an inadequate towel around her and traipsed into the kitchen, forgetting she wasn't alone. She scampered back.

"Oh, dear, how much of my ass did you see?"

Father Henry looked at Mrs. Dodd. "Why don't you help her?"

"I'd just be in the way," Mrs. Dodd replied.

In the end Father Henry went to her aid. "Forget the bath," he said, and, eyes averted as much as possible, helped her dress, though the dress he chose wasn't one she thought was right. He assured her she looked wonderful in it. He applied her lipstick because her hand was too trembly to do so.

They went in her car, with Father Henry behind the wheel and Mrs. Dodd beside him. Sitting in back, she leaned forward and tapped Mrs. Dodd's shoulder.

"I want to look good for him. Do I?"

"Under the circumstances," Mrs. Dodd said.

Linnehan's Funeral Home was a grand white house on Kenoza Avenue, though it didn't impress Mrs. Dodd, who regarded all funeral homes as extravagant way stations to the cemetery. Father Henry tottered around the car and opened doors for both women. Gretchen barreled out like a girl on a date. Mrs. Dodd theatrically protruded a leg. Patterned hose made it look leprous.

David was waiting for them in the viewing room. He kissed his grandmother's cheek and shook Father Henry's hand. Embracing Gretchen, holding her close for several seconds, he asked if she was up to it. She nodded at once. He told her to take as much time as she wanted and then watched her move tentatively toward the casket, almost on tiptoes.

Mrs. Dodd said, "Somebody better keep an eye on her."

"She's fine," Father Henry said.

And she was. She stood over the casket with held breath, which she released slowly. Shell looked better now than he had during the final weeks of his illness. His sparse hair, however, was parted on the wrong side. With loving fingers, Gretchen began putting it right.

Mrs. Dodd said, "What the hell is she doing?"

"What I hope you'll do when I'm lying there," Father Henry said.

When Gretchen stepped away from the casket, her skein of grief was woven too tight to show. David steered her to a chair, and Mrs. Dodd, kneeling, took her place.

At seven o'clock others began to arrive, people from Ted's Texaco and a few former colleagues of Shell's from the *Gazette.*

Father Henry found himself chatting with some of them and soon saw that he and they had differing ideas about death. Theirs went directly to mystery, his to putrefaction.

Retired Police Chief O'Grady spoke briefly to the funeral director, whom he knew well, and then hobbled directly to the casket, where he spent several moments on his knees. Blessing himself, he rose with effort. David and Mrs. Dodd stood together to receive condolences. O'Grady glared.

"Shouldn't Gretchen be standing with you?"

"We asked her to," David said.

"She's happy where she is," Mrs. Dodd added, and watched him lumber away. "Who in the world is that?"

"I've forgotten," David murmured. "Maybe I never knew."

O'Grady sat himself beside Gretchen. For moments he didn't speak, not until she looked at him and said, "Thank you for coming."

"Did you think I wouldn't?" He stared at her. Her mouth was bright red and very intense. "Are you all right?"

"As long as I know he is," she said.

When it became apparent that no more visitors were coming, David spent several minutes at the casket, his head bowed, his eyes full. He didn't know where his father was. The body in the box had become something left behind.

"We're both going to miss him," Father Henry said.

David's jaw was set hard. "But I have a guilty conscience. Something I couldn't comprehend and still can't."

"Nietzsche said that conscience is the pain we inflict upon ourselves."

"You like Nietzsche, Father? I'd have thought Kierkegaard would appeal to you more."

"I've read him several times," Father Henry said, "and have decided neither the Either nor the Or is the answer. There is no answer. Your father may have believed the same, though I don't know that for a fact."

O'Grady was gone. Gretchen was sitting alone. David said, "Excuse me," and went to her. Mrs. Dodd sidled up to Father Henry and spoke close to his ear.

"My feet are killing me. Let's get out of here."

||| ≡ |||

Mr. Linnehan had locked the doors of the funeral home more than an hour ago but was still in his office when the front bell rang. He made his way to the door with an intuitive knowledge of what to expect. Through the years he'd seen the many faces of grief and learned to deal with each. He opened the door slowly.

"Mrs. Ryder," he said.

"Please, may I see him again?"

He read the anguish and didn't hesitate. "Of course."

He turned on half the lights in the viewing room. Any more would have exaggerated the emptiness of the chairs. He reopened the casket while she waited just outside. Then he motioned to her. He knew what she would do. From her knees, peering into the face of Joseph Shellenbach, she would try to will him back into existence.

"Call when you need me," he said.

Discreetly, at five-minute intervals, he checked back on her. After more than a half-hour had passed, he closed the office door behind him and picked up the phone. Chief O'Grady, whose wife he had buried, lived a few streets away.

"I thought I'd call you first," Mr. Linnehan said before explaining the situation. "I don't think she intends to leave."

"No sense bothering the family," O'Grady said. "I'll be right there."

||| ≡ |||

Shell was buried in Linwood Cemetery, beside Helen. Father Henry said the final words and tossed the handful of earth. David stood with bowed head, his grandmother beside him. Chief O'Grady was there, but Gretchen Ryder no longer needed his arm. She stood alone.

Three days later David opened his father's safe-deposit box at the Haverhill National Bank. It was jammed with newspaper clippings, which he transferred to a briefcase. He read and reread them all over a period of three days, from the very oldest to the few that were recent. Many, mostly the early ones, he'd read before, at the Haverhill library. From a recent clip he learned that Anne Lindbergh still lived in Darien, Connecticut.

He spent an afternoon with Gretchen. Standing in his old room, he said, "Do you want me to take those model airplanes down?"

"No," she said, and brought out a cardboard box of things she said he might want to sort through. "He saved everything of yours."

David lifted out a stack of report cards, from Moody School through Haverhill High. Then letters and postcards he'd written while in the army. Newspaper clippings about him. Then he pulled up an old base-ball glove, small and funny-looking.

"I remember when he gave it to me. I didn't want it, but I didn't want to hurt his feelings. I may not have ever used it."

Gretchen said, "I remember it well."

David held the glove up. "There was a name on it. I can't read it any-more."

"Honus Wagner."

He dropped the glove back in the box, felt around, and came up with a velvet drawstring pouch that looked quite old, as if it held something precious. A jewel or two. He opened it. Baby teeth.

"Mine?" he asked.

"He never said, but I don't think so."

David rose. "I don't want to take anything. Could you put the box out with the rubbish?"

"You know I could never do that. I'll keep it here. Maybe someday you'll want it." She teared up. "I don't guess you'll ever know how much he loved you."

"I loved him too," David said softly. "But I wasn't his son."

Gretchen took his arm and walked him out of the room. "You'll al-ways be his son."

That day's *Gazette* lay on the kitchen table. He idly turned pages and paused on page seven. Miss McCormick had been given a retirement party by colleagues and many past students. He wished he'd been there.

"I wonder what we would have become," he said.

Gretchen didn't understand.

"The real David and the real me."

||| ≡ |||

He was having a drink at the bar in the Andover Inn when a woman hiked herself up and sat beside him. What was her name? Joyce or Janet. It was Joyce. "What are you drinking?" she asked. Then, quickly, to the bartender, "I'll have the same, whatever it is."

The bartender, acquainted with her tastes, said, "You won't like it."

"Try me." Her eyes darted back to David. "I heard about your father. I'm sorry."

"Thank you."

The bartender served up schnapps. She took a taste and smiled. "I like it."

David stared straight ahead. He was looking at bottles, scanning labels, testing how good his vision was. Joyce asked after Meredith. "She's fine," he said.

"I heard you two were separating."

He jerked his head at her. "Who told you that?"

"Can't remember. It's not true?"

"Not that I know of." He turned his face away. "Unless gossipers can see into the future. I can't even see into the past."

Joyce pushed her hair back, a different color from what he remembered. "Our circle is shrinking, David. So damn many divorces. They started at the Bellwoods' strip-poker party. Remember? You and Meredith wisely held back. I did too. Nothing to do with modesty. Only on whether I wanted to expose my belly bulge and the puckers on my thighs."

"How's your husband?"

"I bet you don't even remember him."

"Yes, I do. Tab Hunter."

She laughed. "You haven't seen him lately. He's ballooned. You wouldn't know him."

"That's all right. Sometimes I don't know myself."

Her hand slid smoothly over his thigh. "That seems a solvable problem. Maybe we can do something about it."

"I doubt it." He tossed his head back and finished off his schnapps. "But I thank you for the offer."

"Playing hard to get gets you nowhere."

He dropped money on the bar to cover his check and hers. "My loss."

"I thought you were going to be the next governor."

"It wasn't meant to be."

Her penciled brows came together. "None of us really know you, David. You're a loner. So tell us, please, who the fuck are you?"

He was on his feet. "Lindbergh."

Eavesdropping, the bartender smiled.

Joyce laughed. "Sure, but can you fly?"

||| ≡ |||

Father Henry rented a unit with kitchen facilities for him and Mrs. Dodd at a motor inn near Haverhill's Westgate shopping plaza. Gretchen Ryder's mannerisms had gotten on Mrs. Dodd's nerves. She would have preferred returning to Florida without delay, but Father Henry procrastinated.

"You're not really serious about staying up here, are you?"

"I've been giving it thought," he said.

"Well, don't. You'd never make it through the winter."

"I'd rather die here than down there."

She bristled. "What about me? Have you given that any thought?"

"You can go back if you wish. I can manage your expenses."

She pondered it for a moment. "Am I in your will, Prescott?"

"You're mentioned."

"Mentioned. How much am I mentioned?"

Father Henry sighed heavily. "What is it you want, Dorothy?"

She knew what she wanted more than anything else. She wanted immortality. "Answer the question, Prescott."

"Let it be a surprise."

Gretchen Ryder arrived a few minutes later and drove them to the supermarket at Westgate. Mrs. Dodd loved supermarkets, the glory of abundance. Moving down an aisle, she stumbled and caught herself on Gretchen's ample shoulder.

"Why are you wearing heels?" Father Henry asked. He was wheeling the carriage.

Coffee was on sale. It usually was. She picked up a brand not on sale and dumped it into the carriage. With Father Henry's money she was a careless shopper. In the fruit and produce section she plucked up a peach, wiped it on her sleeve, and bit into it.

"Are you going to pay for that?" Father Henry asked.

"Certainly not." She turned to Gretchen, who was tagging along. "Aren't you shopping, dear?"

"I didn't bring my coupons."

"I never use them, too much bother." Mrs. Dodd ran a hand over oranges from Florida and glanced over her shoulder at Father Henry. "This is where we should be." Then she angled away and cruised past chicken parts packaged in clear, tight plastic to fish lying headless on ice and clams heaped on a tray like old money. "Prescott, come here."

Reluctantly he broke away from a conversation with Gretchen. "What is it, Dorothy?"

"Does any of this interest you?"

He let out a slow breath. "There was a time, Dorothy, everything interested me. Now I can't concentrate long enough to be either interested or bored, though I lean toward the latter."

"Very amusing."

Gretchen drove them back to the motor inn and carried in one of the grocery bags. Father Henry asked her to stay for a soft drink, Diet Coke, which he served with ice. In the bathroom Mrs. Dodd rid herself of pumps and panty hose. Father Henry, settled into a deep but uncomfortable chair, asked Gretchen how she was faring. Before she could reply, he dozed off.

"Mustn't mind him," Mrs. Dodd said. "He often does that. He can't keep up."

Gretchen tried not to stare at Mrs. Dodd's legs. Without hose, they were old knives stabbing tennis shoes. Gretchen sat with her dress too high over her large knees. She pulled it down.

"Mind if I ask you something?" Mrs. Dodd said. "Why didn't Shell marry you? He should have, you know."

"We didn't need a piece of paper. We were more than married."

"That's all well and good, but how has he left you?"

"He didn't have much," Gretchen said, "but what he did have is mine. David has seen to that." She held a sliver of ice in her mouth and let it melt. "Why didn't you and Father Henry marry?"

Mrs. Dodd snorted. "First it was me didn't want to. Then it was him. He didn't want to antagonize his daughter because of the money. She was afraid I'd get it all."

"You're like Shell and me. More than married."

"That's one way to look at it." Mrs. Dodd yawned. "I'm rather tired too, dear. Do you mind?"

Father Henry woke some ten minutes later and found Mrs. Dodd staring at him in a manner that startled him. He gripped the arms of the chair.

"Where's Gretchen?"

"Gone, thank God."

"Something's on your mind," he said. "What is it?"

"I hope you have the courage to go on."

"Why wouldn't I, Dorothy? I have you."

Mrs. Dodd broiled two pieces of sole. Father Henry uncorked a bottle of Chablis. His little nap had done him good. His spirits were up. Mrs. Dodd's were down.

"If Shell had stayed himself," she said, "we'd still be in Florida."

"Death is a terrible disturbance. Life wants to run right over it."

Mrs. Dodd toyed with her portion of sole. The wine didn't agree with her. Father Henry poured himself a second glass.

"What's the matter, Dorothy?"

"I have no clean underwear."

"I'll wash some out for you." He scrutinized her face. "How are you feeling?"

"At my age, how should I feel? I'm alive, but my generation is extinct. And leave my underwear alone."

They retired early and watched television from their separate beds. A Lee Marvin movie. Lee Marvin was punching someone out. When Father Henry dropped off, Mrs. Dodd killed the picture with the clicker, though it took her time to find the right button to press. Her head in the pillow, she hoped she wouldn't have to get up in the night. Half asleep, she remembered the porcelain pot kept under her bed when she was a child.

In the middle of the night Father Henry sat up straight and in an eerily loud voice talked to his wife in the dark. Rousted, Mrs. Dodd slung her pillow at him.

"This has got to stop."

"I'm sorry," he said. "It was so real."

"You don't hear me talking to my husband, do you? Give me my pillow back."

Twenty minutes later she was still awake and knew he was too. She had too many thoughts in her head, too much aboil.

"You know I can't go back to Florida alone," she said.

"Neither of us were meant to go back, Dorothy. You know that."

||| ≡ |||

Standing silently in the doorway, Meredith waited to be noticed. David was sitting at the desk, concentrating on a road map. Finally he lifted his head, his face in slow recovery from an intent frown. He rubbed an eye.

"What is it, Meredith?"

"Have you heard from Carver?"

The question obviously annoyed him. "No, Meredith. Why should I?"

"Because you haven't heard the last of him."

"You make him sound sinister."

"Damn it, David, he is. I know him better than you do."

"I'm sure you do. Should I worry about my safety?" When she didn't respond, he said, "I'll keep an eye over my shoulder."

Meredith took tentative steps into the room and dropped a hand on the back of a club chair. An emotion seemed to hold her there. Her voice was troubled as it stretched toward him. "There are rumors about us. Have you heard?"

"Yes."

"Did you start them?"

"No," he said. "I thought you did."

She tried to see into him, but his face was shut tight. "Why didn't you want me at your father's funeral?"

"We never once had him at our house. You always found excuses, some very imaginative."

"I was wrong."

"No, I was. You wanted your father to be mine."

"David, that's absurd. I swear."

"Perhaps. But while we're on the subject, where's Kipper? I haven't seen him in days."

"He's gone. I kicked him out. Do you mind?"

"He's your brother, not mine. Or am I your brother?"

She strode closer to the desk. "Don't talk that way."

"Why not?" he said. "Are we ever what we claim to be?"

She made her way around the desk. She reached out to touch his shoulder but stopped herself. The road map was of New England, folded back to Connecticut. "Are you going on a trip?"

"A short one."

"Would you care to tell me about it?"

"No."

"When are you leaving?"

"I haven't decided."

Again she reached out, this time without pause. Her hand lay firmly on his shoulder. "Are you going to see your mother?"

"It's a possibility."

"If she is your mother."

299

He shifted his shoulder away from her hand. "Nothing's ever certain," he said, and slipped the map into a bottom drawer.

III ≡ III

He rose late. No decisions made. No goals for the day. Meredith had left fresh coffee for him and a note written in her elegant hand on toned paper. *Am at the Historical Society if you need me.*

Why would he need her? He crumpled the note, went to the front door, and looked for his morning papers. A limo was parked in the drive. A rear door swung open.

They met in the drive. David stood in sweatshirt and jeans, Carver stood tailored. Carver's smile preceded his words. "I went out on a limb for you, Shellenbach. You cost me."

"Unforeseeable events," David said.

"That doesn't cut any ice. You left me with shit on my face."

David patted a back pocket of his jeans. "Sorry, I don't have a handkerchief."

"Fucking blasé about it, aren't you?"

"Sorry. I was answering in kind."

"I can't just let it ride, you know," Carver said, and made a sucking sound with his teeth. "I had a few drastic things in mind, wouldn't leave you looking too good, but then I came up with something better. How well do you know your wife, Shellenbach?"

"Probably no better than you."

"I know every pore of her."

David stepped to one side to get the sun out of his eyes. "I've suspected that. Are you the one who stood her up at the Touraine?"

"You got it, Buster. I knew her way back. The only thing that got on my nerves was she shrieked when we fucked. Gave me an earache, know what I mean?"

David tensed himself.

"Are you going to take a swing at me, Shellenbach? You think you're that good with your fists?"

David relaxed. "Why should I do that? You're not worth it."

"There's more," Carver said, enjoying himself. "She ever tell you why you two never had kids? She was carrying mine when she had the abortion. The quack I sent her to botched it up."

"I've changed my mind," David said quietly.

A single blow knocked Carver to the ground. The driver of the limo leaped out and started forward. Rising, Carver held him back with a gesture. Checking his teeth, Carver spat blood. His mouth was swelling from a split lip. He whipped out a handkerchief of his own and applied it. His smile was back, though grotesque.

"You fucked up, Shellenbach. You were getting off easy and didn't know it." A pale sporty car was ghosting into the drive. Turning, Carver said, "Here's your wife. Give her a kiss for me."

Meredith ran toward David as the limo backed away. David was nursing his knuckles. Meredith shuddered.

"What the hell did you do, David?"

"Take a guess."

"He could have you killed, don't you know that?"

"Is that where he's coming from?" David said, and dropped his hurt hand.

Meredith took his arm to steer him back to the house. "What did he tell you?"

"What you should've told me a long time ago."

III ☰ III

Father Henry died first. Mrs. Dodd knew he would. "The bastard!" The manager of the motor inn tried to take her arm. She flailed. "Don't touch me!" The body still lay in the bed, for the ambulance hadn't arrived yet. "Cover his face," she said. "I don't want to look at it."

Gretchen Ryder arrived the same time as the ambulance and guided Mrs. Dodd outside, past a trash receptacle, to a wooden bench. At first Mrs. Dodd wouldn't sit down. She was in heels and wobbling. A brooch of scabby glitter hung off her blouse. Only when Gretchen grabbed her arm to keep her from falling did she agree to sit on the bench.

"She's hysterical," Gretchen explained to a young police officer who came upon them. Attendants were placing Father Henry's body into the ambulance.

"I'll need some particulars," the officer said. "You can give them to me later."

"I can't handle the arrangements," Mrs. Dodd said. "Someone else will have to."

"He has a daughter," Gretchen said. "She will."

"He has money, you know. He can have the grandest funeral in the world."

The ambulance was leaving. The officer was talking with the manager. Each was lighting a cigarette. Mrs. Dodd swayed from side to side.

"I thought he was sleeping. How was I to know he'd croaked?"

"No way to tell," Gretchen said. "He looked so peaceful."

Mrs. Dodd patted her hair down. "I had to dress fast. I didn't want anybody seeing me looking like an old hag."

"You look fine."

"I had the man call you. I didn't know who else." She stopped swaying. "Alone at my age. What will I do?"

"You can stay with me," Gretchen said.

"That dump! What do I want to do that for?"

Gretchen looked away. "I'll call David."

"My son? He's dead, my daughter too."

"Your grandson."

"What's he good for? Nothing. What's he ever done for me?" The officer and the manager had tossed away their cigarettes. The officer had a small notebook in his hand and was approaching them. "I know what he wants. His fucking particulars."

"Please, Mrs. Dodd," Gretchen said.

"Tell him the priest and I were shacking up."

||| ≡ |||

David phoned Tony Tonetti, not at his home in East Boston but at a club in the North End, where he knew he could be reached. To the voice on the other end he said, "Tell him it's an army buddy."

Within moments Tonetti was on the line. "What can I do for you, Counselor?"

"Been a while, hasn't it?" David said. "How many grandchildren you got now?"

"I quit keepin' count, but I've been keepin' track of you. You were smart to pull out. You couldn't've beat Kenneally, don't know why you thought you could. What's that Greek word?"

"Hubris."

"That's it. Fucking hubris. Wasn't like you. Running like a ritzy Republican. I couldn't've voted for you, you know."

"I couldn't have voted for myself, Tony."

"So why you callin'? You got a problem?"

"I've screwed up, Tony. I'm in trouble."

"Money?"

"No. His name is Carver."

Tonetti knew the name.

"I thought you might."

"Him and me ain't that far from being in the same business, different levels is all. Tell me about it."

‖ ≡ ‖

He slept, but not well, in Kipper's room. In a dream he danced with Johanna and magically stayed off her feet. Other dreams came and went, breaking his sleep while leaving no traces. He was up at the approach of dawn, at the window, the night a great ship sailing out of sight. Meredith stepped into the room.

"Are you sleeping here now?"

She stood in one of her less attractive robes, no makeup. He saw her as she was. "I haven't been sleeping well," he said. "I didn't want to disturb you."

"I'll buy that if you want me to."

He moved from the window. "It's up to you."

"Are you staying up?"

"Yes."

"I'll make breakfast."

"Coffee's enough."

303

He shaved, showered, and dressed carefully in a dark gray suit, blue cotton shirt, maroon tie. Then he went downstairs to the breakfast nook. Meredith, hair half combed, negligent in her stance, poured coffee. He remembered a time when she dressed to make every inch of herself tempting while carrying herself imposingly. They sat across from each other.

"I have a confession," she said. "I listened in yesterday. You did the right thing. Fight fire with fire."

His expression hardened. "You shouldn't have done that."

"You have to protect yourself. I got you into this."

"I got myself into it."

Her face flushed, Meredith sipped her coffee. She was working on a reserve of heat and energy. "You look very nice," she said.

"Thank you."

"Why do I feel your mind is elsewhere?" When he didn't answer, she lit a cigarette. "David. Is today the day?"

"Today is the day," he said.

III ☰ III

Anne Lindbergh sat in her favorite chair in a garden that had lost its summery splendor, only a few mums and asters in bloom. A coat sweater tended to overwhelm her. Her glasses were thicker, for her eyesight had worsened. Petite in the thick sweater, fragile, she seemed more spirit than body. Lifting her eyes, she discerned a figure near the gate, none of its details, nothing to proclaim a man or a woman, a friend or a stranger. Her mind mocking her, she sensed someone both known and unknown.

"Is there something you want?"

The voice, a man's, was hesitant. "I don't want to disturb you."

Strangers put her on guard. Why didn't this one? She wished her vision was better. It was as if she were gazing through the wrong end of a telescope, each lens in need of a wipe.

"Come closer."

He came through the gate and stood several feet away. Light netted his face. Always she was on the alert against people enthralled with celebrities, though God knows she was no longer one, just an old woman living out her life.

"What is it you want?"

David said he was in the area looking for property, a small house where he and his wife might live within the smell of the ocean. He despised himself for the lie.

"This isn't for sale," she said.

"I know. I was simply admiring it."

Something about his voice snagged inside her inner ear, causing her heart to race. The voice reminded her of Charles's, but softer, the edges smoothed. Occasionally she was not certain what was true, what was real, and this seemed one of those times.

"I don't believe there's anything for sale around here," she said.

David was trembling, she seemed to be too. Impressions soaked into him, heatedly. In his head: *This is my mother. This is Anne Lindbergh as she is now.*

A figure emerged from the side door of the house. Anne Lindbergh, who knew the footsteps, said, "This is Emma, my housekeeper."

Emma, a full-sized woman with gashes of gray in her hair, was usually even more suspicious of strangers than her mistress, but this man impressed her. The dignity in his bearing, and so neatly dressed.

"The gentleman is looking for a small house for him and his wife," Anne Lindbergh said. "You don't know of anything, do you, Emma?"

"No, ma'am."

"Is your wife with you, Mr.—"

"Dodd," David said. Shellenbach was too German. He was afraid that, after all these years, it would upset her. "No," he said. "She's up in Massachusetts. She sent me here on a scouting trip, to see if there was something we might like."

Half-lies came so easily. Was it because he was a lawyer or because misrepresentation was a product of his cloudy beginnings?

Emma said, "Would you like some apple cider, ma'am? Perhaps the gentleman—"

"No," David said softly. "I won't intrude any longer."

Anne Lindbergh fidgeted. Why did she not want to see him leave?

305

Sitting erect, she extended a hand and said, "It was nice meeting you, Mr. Dodd."

He came forward.

The quality of his face, which she glimpsed through a haze, brought to mind the chill of dawn. When his hand encompassed hers, hers trembled as if it remembered something.

"I hope your trip won't be a waste," she said.

He stepped back. "Sometimes everything wrong comes out right."

She watched him leave, her hand still trembling. What made her certain he had wanted to kiss her cheek?

The housekeeper's sigh was drawn out. "Such a nice gentleman."

||| ☰ |||

Sudden rain on the window was like the tapping of a blind man's cane. A brief shower prematurely darkened the daylight. The housekeeper had a small fire going in the sitting room, enough to take the chill away, though Anne Lindbergh, immobile in a rocker, was still in her coat sweater. A Tiffany clock, a long-ago wedding gift, chimed the hour.

"Why do I feel so strange, Emma?"

"You haven't eaten. You sure you don't want me to make you something before I leave?"

What was skulking on the periphery of her thoughts? What was forcing her inward? "That man's voice, Emma, it echoed my husband's. It was as though Charles had come back for a few moments."

"It was a nice voice," Emma said, "the kind that's comfortable."

"What did you think of him?"

"He had that look."

"What look is that, Emma?"

"Breeding."

Staring at the fire without seeing it, Anne Lindbergh said, "Why do I feel I know him from somewhere? Dodd. Dodd. I don't know any Dodds."

"I know what you mean," Emma said. "A total stranger gives you the creepy feeling you've seen him before. Happens to me all the time."

306

"Not to me. Never to me before."

Emma glanced at her watch. "Unless you need me for anything more, I'll be leaving now."

Anne Lindbergh half heard her. "No. Thank you."

Emma vanished and returned with her coat on. Suddenly she rushed forward. "Mrs. Lindbergh, why are you crying?"

"I don't know, Emma. You tell me."

||| ≡ |||

Meredith held her questions. She lit a fire in the study, the flames providing the only light. She brought in sandwiches and bottles of dark beer on a tray. She was wearing old lounging pajamas, and David was out of his suit, back in sweatshirt and jeans. Sitting on sheepskin, their shoes off, they ate near the fire.

"You look tired," she said.

The sandwiches were corned beef. She'd made two apiece. Each ate only one. They finished the beer. She ran a napkin across her mouth, put aside the tray, and sat cross-legged. She was wearing no makeup, only faint lipstick. Her hair was brushed loose.

"Can we talk about it now?"

He nodded. "I merely wanted to see her, look at her, but I don't think she saw me clearly. Her eyesight is bad."

"Then you didn't say anything. You didn't—"

"No."

"Good," Meredith said. "She wouldn't have believed you. Or if she had, the shock might have destroyed her."

He spoke from weariness. "Both scenarios passed through my mind."

Uncrossing her legs, Meredith shifted closer to him and softened her voice. "What do you think? Is she your mother?"

"There's always room for doubt, isn't there? Room for doubt in any relationship."

"Seeing her, David, has it done you any good?"

"I'll know later."

Her hand moved up his arm. "Are you in shock?"

"I was," he said. "Not anymore. Put a label on me, Meredith. Tell me who I am."

"My husband," she whispered.

"Your husband. But not the governor."

She placed her arms around him. "I don't want to lose you, David."

"No?" His smile was uneven. "Why not?"

"I'm afraid."

"Of what?"

"When I take off my makeup, I'm no longer me."

He kissed her. His hands ran over her. One found its way to the plummy small of her back. A thumb tugged at the elastic top of her pajama bottoms.

"Yes," she said. "Please."

Amid dark duckling fuzz, the dent of her navel was the tender spot on an infant's skull.

"David, do you love me?"

He was kissing her underbelly. The dint he glimpsed through the whorls of hair turned into a slash when she opened her legs. He didn't know what he was doing, but she did. He was returning to the womb.

CHAPTER EIGHTEEN

THE LIMO DROPPED CARVER OFF AT THE TURN IN THE
drive. He lived in a brick house in Brookline. Lots of high shrubs cast
wide shadows in the moonlight. Walking toward the front door, he saw
a row of blank faces, zeros in a data sequence, and stopped short. He
should've run.

One of the men got him in a choke hold, and another pressed a
small pistol against his stomach. A third stood with a length of lead
pipe. White gauze masked their features. The one gripping the pipe
said, "You gotcha mother livin' here, huh? Just the two of you. What are
you, a fuckin' mommy's boy?"

Carver made a gagging sound.

"Nice old bag. We saw her through a window. She's watchin' television and smilin'. Must be a sitcom."

The choke hold loosened slightly so he could breathe, though only
in gasps.

"You threatened a friend of a friend of ours. You know who we're
talkin' about?"

Carver couldn't speak. He answered with his eyes.

"You picked the wrong cookie to threaten. We don't ever wanna hear you doin' that again. We know you, you don't know us. That gives us the fuckin' edge, don't it?"

He was gagging again.

"You love your mother? Nod, you fucker!"

The hold loosened so he could. Then reclaimed him.

"OK, I take it we got ourselves an understanding. But we gotta do something to you so you know we're serious. Do your best not to scream. You don't wanna scare the old bag."

The one with the pistol stepped aside. The length of pipe shattered Carver's left knee, the deed done in the wink of an eye. Carver didn't scream. He couldn't. The man holding him lowered him carefully to the ground, where he passed out.

The man putting away his pistol said, "She wasn't watchin' a sitcom. *Miami Vice* is what she was watchin'."

||| ☰ |||

Chief O'Grady drove Gretchen Ryder to the cemetery, where she placed flowers on Shell's grave and then on Helen's. O'Grady said, "Did you know her?"

"I never met her."

There was a wind. The wind was ruining her hair. She didn't care.

"First year my wife died," O'Grady said, "I didn't dream about her at all. Now I dream about her lots. I ain't proud of my life."

She had yet to dream of Shell, but she'd had other dreams, several of Rudy Farber coughing the cough of the consumptive, spitting up blood, some on her. In a nightmare she'd seen her head on a store shelf and her body elsewhere, thrown aside like unwanted goods. The dilemma was how to buy herself back.

O'Grady said, "That time at Lenny's Tap Room, I did wrong. I was out of line. I wanna apologize."

The wind rocked them. She remembered that when she was a child she'd expected the wind to pick her up and throw her away.

"Do you forgive me?"

"Nothing to forgive," she said.

A stone nearly as new as Shell's announced itself in block letters.

DOROTHY DODD. The dates indicated an unusually long life. Mrs. Dodd had died ten days after Father Henry was put under. Gretchen had flowers for her too, and some remaining.

O'Grady said, "Story is she treated you like shit."

"That was her way."

"Ain't my way. I'd be good to you."

The wind swept away his words and kept them in the air. She remembered gazing out at laundry on the line when she was staying with her aunt in Queens. Her uncle's shirts grappled with the wind, his work pants kicked at it. Undershirts waved for help.

"I ain't a good catch," O'Grady said in a louder voice. "Angina. Can't go anywhere without my pills. But I got a house, a real house you could live in."

She'd had enough men in her life, and Shell had been more than enough. Now it was as if Shell had been the only one, except for Rudy. She remained loyal to each.

"Christ, Gretchen, I'd marry you."

She pushed the hair from her eyes. "I've always taken care of a man. Now I'm tired."

"Maybe I understand, maybe I don't," he said. "I guess it's up to you."

Clutching the remaining flowers, she said, "Time to visit Father Henry."

||| ≡ |||

David visited his law offices, first time in months, which gave him an inexplicable shiver, almost as if he didn't belong there anymore, his presence unneeded. Perry was out. Nancy Potts was too, but soon she was back, bursting into his private office. He rose and kissed her cheek. She kissed his.

"We've missed you," she said.

"You've done terrific without me."

"You may have noticed we've added two more lawyers. We wanted to confer with you first, but we couldn't reach you."

"You and Perry are in charge, you know that."

"We need more space, David. Perry's been looking at suites on State

Street, around there. High-rent district, I know, but I think we can swing it. A total move, what do you think?"

He smiled. "Sounds heavy. Big time."

"We need your input. Are you back?"

"Not yet," he said, dropping into his high-back leather chair. "Not really ready."

She sat on the edge of his desk, near him. "Why did you drop out of the race, David? Papers said it was because your father was dying."

"Politics is a dangerous game," he said. "I never realized how dangerous."

She reached for his hand and held it. "Do you have plans? Do you have something in mind?"

"Toying with the idea of writing a novel. Based on something my father told me."

"Sounds exciting, whatever it is. Will it be under a pseudonym or your own name?"

"You're jumping the gun. I don't know if I have the talent. Probably not."

The door, ajar, swung open wide, and Perry poked his head in. "Are you back?"

"Not quite," David said.

Perry smiled at his wife. "Hey, you still got a crush on him?"

Still holding David's hand, she said, "I'll always have that."

The telephone rang, David's private line, startling him.

His hand freed, he picked up the receiver, listened, and then clamped the other hand over the mouthpiece. "Private call," he said, and was left alone.

"I'll lay odds he won't bother you again," Tony Tonetti said.

The tone alarmed him. "What did you do?"

"Don't ask questions."

"Christ, Tony, he's alive, isn't he?"

"What d'you think I am, a fucking hoodlum? 'Course he's alive. He's just a guy needed a little sense talked into him."

"Tony, thank you."

"What the fuck are friends for, Counselor?"

After putting the phone down, David stayed at his desk for another thirty minutes or so, during which one of the new secretaries came in and introduced herself. Then the two new lawyers did. After they left he placed a few items in his briefcase. Into the wastebasket he dropped an old slip of paper on which he'd scribbled Johanna Medwick's telephone number.

On his way out, briefcase in hand, Nancy Potts caught up with him. Heads turned. Secretaries were interested.

Nancy Potts said, "David. Are you ever coming back?"

III ☰ III

Late in the afternoon Meredith was skimming a copy of *Vogue,* her left hand restlessly flipping pages, when the telephone rang. Her right hand stretched for it. The voice was strange. A crank call?

"Who is this?"

"Carver. Do you hate me that much, Meredith?"

"What's the matter with your voice?"

"Like you don't know. I'm on fucking crutches, like you don't know that either. Why didn't you tell me your husband has friends in low places?"

"I have no idea what you're talking about. Make sense."

"You bitch. You got your revenge, didn't you?"

"I can't hear you very well, Carver. You're hard to understand. Can you speak up?"

"Tell him to keep those fucking goons away from my house. Away from my mother. Tell him he's a winner."

"I'll tell him, but I don't think he'll know what you're talking about. I certainly don't." She started to put down the receiver, then drew it back. "One thing from you, Carver. Don't ever call here again."

David came home a little later, and she was there to greet him. She took his briefcase, which seemed to have little in it, and placed it on the hall table. His London Fog she hung in the closet. She went up on tiptoes and kissed him.

"Thank you," she said.

"For what?"

"For lots of things. You look better."

"And you look refreshed."

"I'm not sure that's the word," she said, "but it's close enough. How about an aperitif? You game?"

In the study she poured Dubonnet. They clinked glasses.

"To us," she said.

"To us," he repeated.

"It is us, isn't it, David?"

"Don't keep asking, Meredith. You don't have to."

She tried to turn it into a joke. "A gal likes to be reassured. Wants to know her man can't do without her. Are you in a bad mood, David?"

"It's nothing," he said, planting himself in a club chair near the window, where he could glance out at what was left of the day, at what remained of the leaves. "I saw a car accident on 93. Wasn't a bad one. I don't know why it got to me."

Actually he did know. He had seen the accident through layers of light and dark, life and death, and wondered whether the driver, out of harmony with himself, had withdrawn from the world by falling asleep.

Meredith sat on the arm of his chair. "You let too much get to you," she said.

He remembered when he'd had his appendix out at Hale Hospital. Coming out of ether had given him a hint of what eternity must be. No time at all. He took a large sip of Dubonnet and sought Meredith's hand.

"There must be another reality besides this one," he said. "This one has too many flaws."

"Let's not be perfect, David. Together, let's be ourselves."

III ≡ III

Anne Lindbergh didn't sleep well and rose at the first flicker of dawn, the miracle of light, no bird blind to it. *Darkness has no doors,* she once wrote in the journal she now kept only in her head. *You can enter at any point, but only light can lead you out.*

She showered. Baths took too long. Her years had preserved her thoughtful impatience to make the most of a moment. She'd once told Charles that the present is all a person knows. The past is suspect, and the future belongs to others.

She plugged in the coffee maker, made toast, and soft-boiled an egg. Protruding from a row of cookbooks was a Gideon Bible, the property of the housekeeper, who tried to read a passage a day, though mercifully not aloud. Anne pushed it back into place, out of sight. W.C. Fields, aware of his sins, was said to peruse the Bible daily for a loophole into heaven.

Emma arrived at nine. She poured herself coffee from the Silex, adding cream but no sugar. She could not understand how Mrs. Lindbergh could take hers black. She sensed Mrs. Lindbergh smiling.

"Aren't our bodies strange, Emma? Sometimes they tell us something our minds don't. Through sensations, I mean."

"What's yours telling you, ma'am?"

"Occasionally the body doesn't need the mind and is better off without it. Today my body doesn't feel brittle at all. If I fell, I wouldn't break."

"Thank God for big favors," Emma said, and finished her coffee, which she always drank fast when work was waiting.

Anne watched her climb the stairs to air out rooms and change bedding. Emma was needed. Emma was the only one with whom she'd ever spoken at length of her firstborn, of her nightmares of the empty crib, even of her irrational fantasies that he'd defected on his own, a toddler able to brave the elements and survive. Fantasies about the weathered body in the woods, *not his.* Charles had seen what he'd expected to see.

Emma had listened without comment, knowing none was wanted, and she had gone on to tell Emma how each morning Charles faced the ordeal of surmounting the sorrow in his soul and getting on with the day without ever showing his agony and his rage. Everything shut up, bolted in.

"No one penetrated his armor, Emma. Not even I."

Emma came down the stairs with laundry in hand and took it down to the basement. Returning, she said, "I was thinking of a nice Caesar salad for your lunch."

"That sounds good, Emma. For the two of us."

"Your color is better today, Mrs. Lindbergh."

"Is it? Maybe I'm getting younger."

They ate at a quarter after noon. Surprising was that her appetite matched Emma's. More surprising was the small bottle of wine she broke out, rather expensive, a gift, though she couldn't recall the bearer.

"Are we celebrating something?" Emma asked.

"Only my high spirits. I want to keep them up."

She poured the wine, German, not a gift. She remembered now that Charles had bought it. No wonder the bottle was dusty. No wonder she had saved it so long.

"Is it too cold for me to sit out in the garden, Emma?"

" 'Fraid so, ma'am. You'd freeze your tush."

"Pity."

"Besides, there's not much garden left."

"More of a pity."

Midafternoon she sat in a wing chair in the front room and listened to Mendelssohn on public radio. Eyes closed, she fully expected to doze off and a half-hour later was surprised she hadn't. Opening her eyes, she saw Emma peering out the bow window.

"What is it, Emma?"

"That nice gentleman we liked so much. He's coming up the walk."

The face she had seen through a mist wavered in memory, but the touch of the hand had left a mark on hers.

"Mr. Dodd, ma'am. He's come back."

Anne Lindbergh's inner ear heard the footsteps, her inner eye gazed seaward, through a filigree of reawakening years. Why was she not surprised?

The bell rang.

COBURN   Coburn, Andrew.
           Birthright.

$23.00

DATE			